Sch
Schmidt, Heidi Jon.
The bride of catastrophe

$24.00
ocm52312831

1st ed.

The *Bride* *of* *Catastrophe*

Also by Heidi Jon Schmidt

Darling?

The Rose Thieves

The *Bride* of *Catastrophe*

Heidi Jon Schmidt

Picador   New York

www.picadorusa.com

Picador® is a U.S. registered trademark and is used by St. Martin's Press under license from Pan Books Limited.

Library of Congress Cataloging-in-Publication Data

Schmidt, Heidi Jon.
    The bride of catastrophe / Heidi Jon Schmidt.— 1st Picador ed.
        p. cm.
    ISBN 0-312-28177-3
        1. Eccentrics and eccentricities—Fiction.   2. Man-woman relationships—Fiction.   3. Women college students—Fiction.   4. Recovering addicts—Fiction.   5. Problem families—Fiction.   6. Lesbians—Fiction.   I. Title.

PS3569.C51554B75 2003
813'.54—dc21
                                                        2003049897

First Edition: October 2003

10 9 8 7 6 5 4 3 2 1

For Roger and Marisa

The belief that a person has a share in an unknown life to which his or her love may win us admission, is, of all the perquisites of love, the one which it values most highly.

—Marcel Proust, *Swann's Way*

Part One

One

"I GREW up on a farm."

I had said this so often in my life, trying to explain myself, that I barely heard it anymore. The images that came with it—the hydrangea tree in our front yard with its loose, faded blossoms; my sister Sylvie feeding a new lamb from a bottle; the brilliant maple leaves swirling down out of the October sky—meant everything to me; that I came from a beautiful, fertile place; that I was innocent rather than ignorant; ardent, not reckless . . . that I, like all things stamped "natural," must be, essentially, good.

I was explaining myself right then to Philippa Sayres, my professor of Comparative Literature at Sweetriver College, bastion of cultural and political enlightenment. The year was 1974. Philippa (Sweetriver was antihierarchical; faculty members were to be treated as senior colleagues and addressed as peers) had yanked me into her office after class to explain the mistake I'd made in calling Causabon (the aged pedant to whom Dorothea Brooke, the heroine of *Middlemarch*, is so grindingly yoked in marriage) dull.

"No, *no*," she said. Being so small physically and so quick mentally, she had the aspect of a hummingbird—one sensed that she kept still only by dint of great effort; in her case an effort of mind instead of wings. "He is not at all dull! He is, *in fact*, on a magnificent quest! 'A Key to all Mythologies' [the manuscript onto which Causabon's head drops when he finally, mercifully, dies] would be invaluable if carried through. Here, let me show you a couple of essays."

I sat before her, nodding *so* seriously. My life had moved by means of study. If I hadn't been a good student, I'd never have escaped from home. But here I was at Sweetriver, safely taking a note: Causabon—scholar/hero. When I looked up, I saw Philippa squinting at me, trying to puzzle me out. Where had I come from, where was I going?

And I had that feeling she was seeing all that was wretched in me, so made the standard farm answer. And saw her blink in surprise.

"On a farm? In, like, Iowa?"

"No, Connecticut."

"The wilds of Connecticut?" she asked, looking intently, for some reason, at my hands. I was proud of my hands—they were slender and pale and seemed to speak of virtue. Someone had once told me they were perfect piano-playing hands, so they stood in my mind for all my undeveloped aptitudes, the possibilities latent in me. At home I'd sit under the mulberry tree, drawing on the back of my father's old stationery just to watch those hands at work. And to know my mother would look out the upper window and see me—diligent girl in beautiful landscape—and feel, for a minute, calm.

"You'd be surprised how wild it can get in Connecticut," I told her, with some hint of insinuation which she caught with a raised eyebrow.

"What kind of a farm, though? Dairy?"

No one had ever asked me this question, and I barely had an answer. "A . . . sheep farm," I said, "sort of. I mean, we have chickens too. And, a pony. And, you know . . ."

"I do? I know?" she asked, blinking rapidly, considering. "No, I don't think I do," she decided, and fixed me with a piercing look. "Sheep, for mutton? Does one *say* mutton anymore?"

"Mutton," we both tried at once, and looked at each other amazed. Was it true there were two people on earth who would repeat the word "mutton" to catch its musty sound?

"One thinks of Hardy," she said to herself. Then to me: "Or, sheep for wool? What breed of sheep, for instance?"

"I . . . I don't know." Of course, there were different breeds, the kind with black faces, and others I'd seen at the county fair. Ours were all white, with wool so thick and oily you couldn't push your hands deep enough into it to touch their skin. They grazed and gamboled, the bells around their necks tinkling in a very authentic alpine way. One of my deepest satisfactions was to pretend I was herding them back from a high field after a long day . . . to imagine how gratifying such work must feel. We had them sheared every spring, but I had no idea what breed they were, or what we had done with the wool. I didn't seem to have solid answers for any of Philippa's questions.

Curiosity was unheard of at Sweetriver. The students were from Westchester or Malibu, they summered in Cannes and the Hamptons, they knew *everyone*, and if they were ignorant of something that was only because it wasn't worth the bother.

Philippa found this amazing—she was fascinated by whatever her eye lit on. The students laughed at her fast talk, her unseemly enthusiasm, but she was our teacher (though she was barely older than we were) and—she was a lesbian. This gave her a mystique her more prosaic qualities couldn't dull; it made her seem dangerous and exotic even as she amassed notecards in the back corner of the library. Rumors swirled: Philippa had put a curse on a student who refused her advances and the girl developed a nervous condition, left school, and either committed suicide or became a Hare Krishna, no one was sure. Or: Philippa went to the East Village and bought "forty minutes for forty dollars."

"Forty minutes of what?" I'd asked, but the question was unanswerable somehow, though its dark suggestions were clear. And seductive. It was impossible not to keep an eye on Philippa, because you knew she was going to surprise you. Though you'd never expect her to do anything as jaw-dropping as taking an interest in me.

I was there on a scholarship. My cheeks were still pink, I was still young and hopeful, and the dean felt Sweetriver students needed exposure to such a person. They managed to overlook me, though—it was pretty clear that I was not going to become a useful contact. Catching my reflection in a dorm window, I'd see myself burrowing along, face screwed up tight like a mole in fear of weasels. Dressed up for a dance, I looked like a braless Little Bo-peep.

Philippa saw me as raw material. And (this, it would take me years to understand) as a kindred spirit, one of those few others on earth who would repeat the word "mutton" until she'd heard every one of its implications. I wracked my brain, knowing she was truly interested in what kind of sheep we'd been raising, that she would attach as much meaning to my answer as she did to Causabon's dry pamphlets, so I couldn't get away with being vague.

"I mean, it's not just farming, we have a little ping-pong ball factory too," I said, trying to prove my legitimacy, but her eyes widened hugely.

"My."

So there. I'd surprised her; I'd had an effect. Somewhere my mother must be feeling a little spring of happiness: her dreams for me were coming true.

———

AND SHE—my mother—had not only given me my life, but had saved it, saved me from a heinous crime even before I was born! I'd heard the story a thousand times: my father had wanted to kill me, to kill all three of us in fact. How else could it be, that when he was driving her to the obstetrician (on a wide, newly paved road, on a dry, sunny afternoon), he swerved "to avoid a rabbit" and ran utterly off the road?

"There *was no rabbit*," she'd tell me, and Sylvie and Dolly and Ted, her poor little children . . . children conceived, alas, with a man she despised, children sitting quietly, waiting for their dinner while this man washed his (very nearly bloodstained) hands at the kitchen sink . . .

I glanced at Philippa, to see if she liked the story, and saw her face was full of suppressed laughter. My mother played even her own misery for laughs, though one had to give just the right laugh—one that denigrated my father and pitied her, while admiring the joke too. A single false note and one would be banished to her internal Siberia, to break rocks in the frigid dark. So I was glad I'd found a good tone for Philippa: it was becoming imperative to me to entertain her.

"Okay, homicidal father, got it. Pray continue."

She leaned back. I was the perfect butterfly for her pin—a representative of that rare, unlovely species, the American. She had been lectured on such creatures from birth, by her father the bricklayer and her mother the file clerk, who had come together from Naples, anglicized *Sarafoglio* to *Sayres*, and undertaken to immerse themselves in their new culture, as soon as they could find it. They never did. To become ordinary Americans would have been to achieve grace, but everywhere they looked they saw only other immigrants searching for ordinary Americans to emulate. So they went on in perplexity, keeping their bushes trimmed neater every year, trying to live within an outline whose contours they couldn't see, bent on one thing: that their daughters (they had no sons) should have a full, "American" education. So here Philippa was with her Ph.D., still getting it all figured out, and she had stumbled into me—my family that wasn't striving for anything. She'd never seen such a spectacle. She wanted to hear it all.

And there is no flattery to compete with true listening. My mother used to listen so closely; I'd run down the dirt road from the school bus, full of stories, each a bright gift for her. She rarely set foot off our land by then, and I realized she was seeing the world through my eyes . . . that I could shape it to please or comfort her, to keep her from crumbling. She was so fragile, but listening to me she'd seem to grow stronger: How intelligent the art teacher was, after all, to have noticed my pig! Yes, I *had* got the exact shade, not pink, not tan, but a perfect pale pig color. And could it be that Chip Murray had really brought a live mouse to school in his lunchbox? She laughed, she who was usually so sad.

Recalling her for Philippa, I kept to the laughter. I'd have gone on about the beauties of farm life too (I was as grateful to recall it now as I'd been to escape it the year before), but Philippa would cry "Wordsworth, too Wordsworth!" to pull me back from the pastoral abyss.

"*Mordant*, not *verdant!*" she'd remind me when I started looking homesick, and I'd snap back and go on with my story. Philippa had considered a career in archaeology, and wanted every detail.

"What were you having for dinner, I mean, a typical menu?"

I saw Ma at the stove, frying, yes, a sliced puffball. She'd picked it in the woods, where one didn't see other humans or undertake conversations. Velveeta has more taste and texture than fried puffball, but puffball: (*a*) defies convention (*b*) demonstrates privation and so (*c*) sets those who dine on it above the commonplace others one might meet in the grocery store. The dinner table was small and low: they'd gotten it for ten dollars at a garage sale, and every time they drew their chairs up and bumped their knees, they could be reminded that they cared not for the things of the material world, that their lives were centered on love. We had five chairs for six people, so the last to come to dinner would find himself standing, until Ma learned to dramatize her sense of isolation by eating her meals seated on the washing machine, feet swinging, plate on her lap. She needed to dramatize her every thought and feeling, for fear no one would notice her and she'd just disappear. And as her heart and mind were fixed completely on my father, the washing machine was the perfect spot—it was right behind his place at the table so she could make satirical faces over his head at us while he spoke.

Because after all, what was he saying? "Everything in moderation"; "Still waters run deep"; "What cannot be cured must be endured." Murderous platitudes, meant to kill ambition, silence debate, keep Ma from doing whatever it was she was bent on, her eyes blazing, foot pressing some cosmic accelerator, hands gripping her dinner plate tight because any minute she would, *finally*, take off.

Out of the corner of her eye, she'd see something—a spilt juice cup, a gobbled dessert—and flash over into rage. These were not, to her, merely childish lapses of manners, but proof we were shameful creatures, manifesting all the greed and sloth she'd worked so hard to conquer—or at least, to hide, in herself. Was she going to have to despise us, her own children? But then, suppose she managed to perfect us? Then—of course!—*we* would despise *her*! She was waiting for that sign that would prove what she knew at the bottom of herself, that we didn't really love her. A wrong look, a wrong word, a wrong bite and *ba-boom*, in a blinding flash, the mother we knew would be gone.

She loved fire. What else destroys with such majesty? In winter she stared into the hearth for hours, in summer went tree to tree with her torch, lighting the gauzy gypsy moth nests with a grave, ceremonial air. The caterpillars inside popped like corn.

When the clouds towered up, late on a summer afternoon, she felt the torch was coming for her.

"Thunderheads," she'd say, portentous. "Inside, now, all of you." She herself towered on the doorstep, calm in the face of danger, calling her chicks in under her wing. For once her purpose was clear: it was to close all windows, unplug all appliances, and hurry us into the closet under the stairs, where we'd wait out the summer shower as if it were the tempest itself.

"Okay," Philippa said. "She heroically shelters her children from a peril she has, essentially, invented. I *love* mothers."

"Well, I never thought of it quite that way," I said, but I could see Ma standing in the closet doorway, murmuring *"thar she blows,"* with a drama no less heady than the fragrant summer air. She was about to shut us in the stifling dark, where we would huddle close for an hour or more, hot, sticky, and feeling the thrill of being safe together amidst danger.

"It's just like London," she told us, "during the blitz."

She had grown up in New York, had never been to London, so if she was going to discuss the blitz, this—a closet with four small children in it—was the proper forum. And she needed to talk about the blitz: the tension of her own life found a mirror there. She smouldered, yes, but no one knew when she'd blow, and this was such a source of suspense that we hated to leave the house for fear of missing that moment. It was the focus of our lives.

So I did have to laugh, hearing Philippa's view, though this felt vaguely sacrilegious toward my mother. "Lightning *is* very dangerous," I said, in the tone of a model third-grader. "Have you ever seen ball lightning? When my mother was little, one came in through the window and scared her to death."

"I have little doubt that balls of lightning turn up around your mother," Philippa said. "But 'scared to death'? No. I'd say she awaits them with breathless anticipation."

"Well, there is that," I admitted. We were laughing, and the little office with its posters of Philippa's idols—Napoleon and Catherine Deneuve—felt as cozy as that linen closet all of a sudden.

Which pricked my heart, since it seemed to betray my mother.

"I know, it was peculiar, but it was nice," I said. "All of us together there in the country like that. The place had its own magic, it was so beautiful there. It attracted people, it made things happen . . . kind of like *Howards End*." (We'd been studying E. M. Forster and there was a whiff of oxygen in making a literary reference to Philippa, as if I was up on Mount Olympus chatting with Athena.)

The corner of her mouth turned and a sharp dimple appeared in her left cheek. "Really," she said.

"They—Ma's generation—suffered from the Second World War, somehow," I went on. "I mean, they weren't anywhere near it, but they were children then and—I think the idea of hiding in a closet from an evil force, that it sank in deep, with her."

"Why?"

"I don't know, because she's crazy! To hear them at dinner, night after night, reliving that damn war, the chance escapes and chance murders . . ."

I shook my head, which was full of those stories: Nadia for instance, age five, who threw a tantrum at the border so the harried guards waved the family through—she was screaming for the nursemaid they'd had to leave behind, as if she guessed the woman's fate. Cautionary tales, but what was the moral? That ordinary people can do unspeakable things; that Chance can destroy anything, so all effort is futile—all will be tears in the end. That you may not recognize the face of evil, even if it belongs to your neighbor, even if you see it in the mirror every day.

"What if you were wading in the brook and the water got hotter and hotter until it was boiling?" my father asked me one night.

"I'd jump out on the bank!" I was eight years old, first in my class, and I assumed he was testing me, that I'd give the right answer and win his love like a spelling bee prize.

"And if the bank was hot? Hot as an iron skillet?"

"I'd climb up a tree!" My eagerness only baited him. Did I really imagine I could outrun life's terrors? Outsmart him? His eyes gleamed; he'd show me . . .

"What if the tree turned out to be nothing more than a red-hot wire, like the element on the stove? And the skin on your hands melted against it and pulled off like gloves?"

"I guess I'd burn up and die," I'd answered . . . the answer he'd wanted, that showed I understood how he felt about everything.

"*Howards End?*" Philippa shrieked suddenly, laughing like Grace Poole, "If that isn't the summit of Wolfean rose-colored thinking: You feel you grew up at Howards End? The *House of Usher*, you mean. Oh, really, *Howards End!*"

Had I learned nothing from her classes? My father was clearly Dickensian, and he married a woman who'd stepped directly out of Poe! "You *must* learn to read more closely!" she said.

Two

IF ONLY my father could have managed our deaths better than he had our lives. If he'd driven faster, turned sharper, but no, he had swerved without true conviction and instead of smashing into the light pole, the car had skidded over a shallow embankment into a little grove. My mother climbed out, dusting herself and preparing to sail proudly onward, but felt something at the back of her knee, brushed it, and found blood on her fingers.

A hemorrhage, and the doctors urged an abortion: the child would be retarded, they said. Heroic, she insisted on carrying the creature to term, and so five long months had passed, with this rabbit question looming. It was a figment of his imagination, didn't he see? He hadn't wanted a *rabbit to die*, because he didn't want the baby, didn't really love her, would have done anything to escape.

She sailed proudly on, with never a reproach (if there was something of the martyr in her movements, well, who could blame her, expecting this poor damaged child who would need constant care). And he, the gentle boy she'd married, became unaccountably sullen, withdrawn. He had *seen* a rabbit, he *had*— he had swerved to spare it. He was young and tender-hearted, it was his worst fear that something should suffer because of him. In fact, that was part of the reason why—why he had married her.

She'd been the girl from the valley whose divorced mother took in washing. Every week he brought the laundry down, to peer down the dim hallway with its smells of liver boiling and cheap perfume, the apartment doors left open for air in summer so he'd see old women groaning in their beds, children peeping back at him. He had the loose, quick gait, the lifted chin of a frat boy: an exotic in their world. Behind the next door: Claire Ledoux, eyes narrow, cheeks wide, carriage . . . majestic, despite the mountain of wrinkled shirts in her basket. She would escape this place; she would iron her way to the stars.

The girls he knew could afford to be gentle. The doors of the future were wide open to them. Claire had only her presence, and her iron. When he asked her to the movies, her eyes blazed and something flashed open in him; a carnal premonition. What might it be like to lift her out of this place—wouldn't her gratitude make for a fiercer love?

She knew him, from the labels on his father's shirts. She knew what he represented. She spent the whole day preparing, was still ironing her sweater when the doorbell rang. Yanking it over her head she was seized with a qualm—was there a wrinkle? She must be perfect; this might be her only chance. She picked up the iron without thinking and pressed it to her heart.

Waiting at the doorway, he heard her scream. A minute later though, she opened the door and smiled with perfect, if seething, composure, grimacing only when she'd straddled the motorcycle behind him and he couldn't see her face anymore. She wrapped her arms around his waist: the girls from the Academy wouldn't have done this; they'd been sheltered unto inanity. Claire was free of their scruples, better than they. She *had* to get somewhere; he was going to give her a ride.

They went to see *A Streetcar Named Desire*. How is it we remember the fifties as a neat, false decade, when they knew everything about sex back then? To take a man into your body is to possess him entirely: from then on his raw voice will call only your name. Of course this knowledge must be kept quiet, as it could drive whole societies mad. But they were reminded that they knew this secret, and each felt the other's awareness. Riding home she held him closer than before, arms across his chest, thighs against his, cheek pressed to his shoulder . . . all delicacy, she saw now, was a sham.

Kissing her, he pulled her in tight with a motion he'd just learned from Marlon Brando. In fact she reminded him of Stella—made for love, for childbirth—a real woman. He'd always suspected that real life took place along the dim corridors where stains were scrubbed from the collars of the upper class. His parents were away for the weekend—he'd take her home. He wanted her to see what he had to offer her. A Tudor cottage, with a steep roof of slate scallops, herringboned brick, and holly trees in dark masses beside the door. And Claire, burning with defiance—and confidence: men, even strangers on the street, seemed to recognize something powerful in her that she could only believe when she saw it reflected in their eyes—followed him in through the rounded oak door with its four leaded panes inset, into the hallway with the brass salver and the woodwork rubbed with oil. The grandfather had been an ironmonger, come over from Germany or somewhere, "done gates and fences for all the best people in Manhattan. J. P. Morgan, for one," said her mother, who took her own status from that of the people she washed for.

Claire went to the window—the harbor glittered there, and Brooklyn beyond. To have grown up looking out over these places—to know things from above that way—it was nearly as if he owned them. The windows were clever: one pane in each belled out to accommodate a small trapdoor. She lifted one and found a screened panel—for fresh air, in wintertime.

"God forbid you should suffer a draft," she said, thinking of the matchbook under the sash at home.

"It saves oil," he explained, stung.

So, then, what she thought mattered to him. "It just . . . shows such care." She smiled so warmly, to salve the little wound. Impossible not to touch her, and when he did, her smile only became more tender. The wondering, grateful smile that broke from him at this was the most beautiful thing she'd ever seen.

There was a wistfulness in it, poignant to her because she'd have been wistful herself if life had allowed her such liberty. In her face he saw a fierce aspiration, which would have counted as crass at the Academy. What if it were possible to become like her—unrestrained?

"We come from different worlds," she said, sounding so hopeless and picturesque, as if they were in a movie together. The harbor lights, the plush carpet, the leaded windows that reflected, yes, her own beauty. Her burn was stinging.

"We'll make our own world," he thought, feeling he'd fallen into this movie too. He kept from speaking it, though, thinking that he'd just met her, how could his feelings run this high? Her breasts moved him to tenderness as much as lust. That she was willing to let him touch her: she was so terribly kind. He would return the favor, would rescue her. He recast her mother's flat in his mind, from shabby to truly squalid, so the deliverance would mean more. In bed beside her, in the incredible luxury of it, he tried to confide the deepest things in himself, how his father died just after the first pictures came back from Auschwitz—as if his ancestral people had turned to monsters, his pride turned to shame, and it killed him.

"Cancer, cancer," she said, holding him tight, keeping her own horrors swallowed. "Not divine retribution."

"I know," he said, squeezing her breast to remind himself, love and warmth were right there.

And she, arching up to say, "Take, take of my love and warmth"—she had infinite warmth to give, to him who would otherwise have so little. The sterility of that house, these people embalmed in their own wealth. They wanted fresh air, did they? Well, here she was. (Coming to "Tyger, tyger, burning bright" in her anthology of English poems, she'd felt a thrill of recognition. She would burn bright too.) She'd save him from his own stolidity. Behind him, on his mother's piano, stood a globe, colored the hallowed gold of old documents, that showed the earth as men had once imagined it. It was encircled in a double ring of iron, as in the hands of a benevolent god—it must have belonged to his grandfather. The ambition that showed there, the intention to possess! Yes, she would take her part in this tradition, beside this boy; she could see how soft he was, how he needed her. She leaned in toward him . . .

He was beyond speaking. After all, they had things in common: the same loneliness, the same longing. Now it would be fulfilled. And they slipped together into the forest of the night and lost the sense of the outer world.

TWO YEARS later he was drafted and woke out of the ether of that love.

It was 1955; he was stationed in Verona, which was more than she could bear. Her father had been there in the war; she could still see the red pushpin on the world map that she used to fix her eyes on to keep her balance, as she practiced her pirouettes. Eyes on that pushpin, she kept steady for three years, until the day his ship returned to New York. She was eleven years old: her dress had a red bow at the collar; her gloves buttoned at the wrist. A thousand soldiers streamed past her—all of them in the arms of their families by the time her father came sheepishly down the gangway. He had a new baby daughter, in Europe; he was going to return there. All the time he was away and she was tending his image in her heart, keeping him alive there with memories and prayers—he had simply allowed himself to forget her.

If my father had been sent to Berlin, or the Philippines—who can say? But this struck too deep a nerve. Every day she wrote to him, and every night took the day's letter, ripped out the abject parts, and worked the rest until it showed her with castanets flashing. This was how it worked: you created a magnificent self so a man could fall in love with you, then you'd have to keep that self up, so as not to lose the man. And that way you'd never disintegrate.

But when he didn't write back, she found herself begging. "You're all that matters to me," she wrote.

It was the abjection that moved him—she needed him so badly her life depended on him, so he could dare to count on her. And she'd given herself so easily, so fully, she deserved something in return. He went home on leave, half thinking to reassure her and escape, but just being near her he felt the old drowsy warmth overwhelm him. When he left she was pregnant. They were married; then came the rabbit in the road.

And the sense they were damned to each other, and to this child, the indelible proof of their shame. He hadn't really loved her, had married out of duty. She knew this by the instinct that taught her everything. He'd rather she were dead, rather he *himself* were dead, than yoked to her. He denied this, of course, but without real feeling. And there *had been no* rabbit! What more was there to say?

By the time I was born, they were living with his parents and he'd started his own business, raising praying mantises in his mother's greenhouse.

"HIS FIRST venture," I told Philippa, shaking my head with a rue I barely noticed, so completely was *venture* linked with *failure* in my mind.

"You feel sorry for him!" Philippa said. "It has never occurred to me to feel sorry for either of my parents." She squinted into the distance, trying to imagine it. "They'd be mortified," she said, with a shudder.

"Aphid control," I said, feeling sorrier, wishing I could go back there to that first failure and flip the switch to set my father on the right track. He'd put an ad in the Sunday *Times*, which should have left him two weeks of incubation to take orders and make deliveries, but Saturday morning they started hatching and by afternoon there were thousands of them, advancing in phalanxes across the glass, cocking their eerie little heads.

I had the story, like all stories, from Ma. And her stories existed to illustrate why she didn't, and why I shouldn't, love him. "The praying mantises were infinitely more important to him than *you* were," she'd explained, telling how, when her waters broke (how *like* her, to go into labor like that right when he was in the midst of a disaster), he'd insisted she hold on until he herded the mantises to safety.

But, here came the great moment of her life—the advent of motherhood, with its absolute authority.

"You have to take me to the hospital right now," she'd said, amazed at the quiet certainty of her voice, and anger had flashed over him. Who was she, to tell him what to do? Then he remembered: she was the mother of his child. He'd wrought this change, he would have to live with it. The deep, lush world she'd taken him into that first night, that he'd dreamed of swimming off into forever—where had it gone? He'd meant to rescue her from her fears and rages; instead, he'd found her mad stare fixed on him.

"It's the whole investment, gone," he said, and she, incensed, lifted the perfectly wrought latch and smacked the greenhouse door open with her flat hand. She was sorry it didn't shatter, the fine old thing with its row of wrought-iron fleur-de-lys along the ridgepole to keep the pigeons away. The emblem of wealth, comfort, and enervation. People would ask: "What does your husband do?" "Why, he raises praying mantises," she'd have to say. The creatures marched out, turning their cold, curious faces toward their liberator, and streamed away. They'd have baked to death before the Sunday *Times* ad came out in any case.

So, his project sputtered as hers was born. With each contraction, she loathed him more violently, until he seemed to be the force that convulsed her, the author of all her pain. And then the storm was past, the room was quiet, there were a few soft clouds in the sky, and in her arms, the baby. Seeing it, red and wrinkled, eyes screwed tight, fist up in futile defense against the light—she was overwhelmed with tenderness, for everyone, even for him. She remembered how badly they'd wanted each other, how their first touches seemed to be sacred. Here I was, whole, like the love that produced me: their new life, their real life, could begin. There *had* been a rabbit; from now on they would believe in this rabbit together. Exhausted, proud, filled with feeling, she smiled up at her husband, she forgave.

"Retarded, indeed," she said. "Look at her. She's brilliant!"

He recoiled. Yesterday she'd known the baby would be an idiot; now it was brilliant before it opened its eyes. For months she had despised him, and he'd believed she was right: never mind his intent, he *had* nearly killed them, and this child would shamble beside him for life as the visible proof of his guilt. Now she'd changed her mind, and he was to forget his anguish, dance and sing? To agree would be to consign himself to the fire of her madness.

"Don't be ridiculous, Claire," he said, and she, her bubble of hope burst, turned away.

"Brilliant," she repeated, though what her imagination conjured in my scrunched little face was more than brilliance: some kind of supernatural talent that would prove her own hidden genius and so resolve all her torments, sing her demons to sleep finally, make her whole. She held me closer, she kissed my forehead with that smile of infinite warmth that must certainly have reminded him of the way she had loved him once, showed what he'd be missing from now on.

"A HUSK," Philippa cried, "the inseminator cast aside! A mother is red in tooth and claw. Praying mantises indeed."

I couldn't help laughing. It was so good to see them as pawns of nature—if this were true, I wouldn't have to go back and back over their story in my mind, trying to understand what poisoned their love, so I could look for the antidote.

THEY BROUGHT me home, stood over me terrified, working up their courage to change the diaper. How did you avoid hurting such a tiny, fragile thing? It needed them every second; Claire would barely fall asleep after a feeding before it woke crying again. Its diaper was dry, it wouldn't take her nipple, what was wrong? Claire held it—her daughter—tight, rocking her, saying, "It's all right, it's all right, your mama's here," waiting for maternal grace to take effect, for the baby to relax and sleep. But fretting turned to screaming, until Claire was sobbing too in the fear that she couldn't give what the child needed, that she was not a natural mother.

Ted slept through untroubled; she'd have liked to smash his skull. He'd rather have killed her than marry her, now her daughter had been born under an evil star. The baby whirled its arms like propellers, and Claire cried so deeply, she sounded to herself like an animal baying, low and angry and hopeless, in pain.

"Wake up, wake up, can you be so deaf?" she asked her husband, shaking his shoulder.

He sat up, bleary and irritated. Wasn't this supposed to be *her* job?

"I can't, I don't know how to do it, I don't know what to do!"

"Well, what do you expect *me* to do?" he asked. Why had she *had* to have this baby, if she couldn't take care of it?

But just then, Claire rested her head on his chest, and her crying calmed; she seemed to be consolable suddenly. Knowing how she'd have felt if she could have comforted the baby, she'd thought to give *him* this satisfaction. This was her instinctive intelligence, and she used it in this secret way.

Ted had never seen himself have such an effect. He took the baby to his chest and made a low, manly sound, like an engine. And the baby was quiet, his little Beatrice, and Claire kissed him right over his heart. They were a family, it was like a miracle.

They were alone together in the desolate dark . . . they held each other, and each promised, silently, to do better, to make it all work. Warm and drowsy under the feather quilt with him, she remembered a library book she'd loved as a child, about an orphaned girl raised on a farm, where privation and satisfaction went somehow hand in hand. The farm family awoke before dawn, stoked the fire, fed and milked the cows, cut the hay or tapped the trees, ate heartily and simply, and in the evening, settled back at the hearth while grandfather read aloud. Their floor was always swept, herbs dried in the rafters, days of work led to evenings of satisfaction, their children grew healthy and strong.

The next weekend they took the Saw Mill River Parkway north into Connecticut, and when they arrived at the old house at the end of the long dirt road, she knew they belonged there. It had been somebody's folly—built of fieldstone and heavy timber so the walls were two feet thick, surrounded by a "formal garden" utterly overgrown, and fifty acres of marsh and bracken, two wide meadows full of brambles, a brook running along at the base of the hill, an old root cellar with potatoes and squash still piled. They could see the sky through the barn roof, and it smelled sweetly of hay, of the farm in the library book where wishes came true. They crossed the brook on a log bridge and walked up the hillside. Claire bent down to touch the flowering blueberries, lifting the wax bells with her fingertips so he could see how many berries they'd have.

Ted looked out over the fields, thinking of the work it would have taken to build the stone walls between them. Work makes the man. To go forward, in work, in marriage, one needed to be able to forget the past. He would begin by forgetting that day when he'd seen life coming at him with all its terrible decisions and had driven off the road. He'd been afraid of having a child who needed his guidance. If he had no answers to give, if he failed at fatherhood—that would be more than he could bear. But here was his wife beside him, and his little daughter, and it gave him courage: yes, he'd like more children, more soft little things like milkweed fluff, who flew to their parents for love. He'd borrowed against his inheritance and bought the place that day.

THESE WERE the people I was doomed to love! She, seething with an ardor entirely unfocused, smoking, smoking, her eyes narrow, her silence terrible: my first glimpse of beauty. And he, in one of those bursts of optimism that punctuated his despairs, was fitting the coop with chicken wire—his old T-shirt, faded red, my favorite color then and now. I squeezed into their embraces, to feel them wanting each other. Or, at least, how desperately they wanted what they couldn't get from each other. Their passion swam along underneath us, we felt it move there, we never knew when it would rise up and flick our little boat over with its tail. He went to Agway for chickenfeed. She rocked back and forth on a kitchen chair, biting her knuckle to keep herself from sobbing.

She was pregnant again and again, and so came Sylvie, Dolly, and finally Ted, our parents' *folie à deux* becoming *folie à trois, quatre, cinque, six* . . . Pop faded, grew dim, and Ma intensified, like a storm. She was always pregnant—there was the one too vigorous who tore the placenta away and starved, the one born months early. We could have named her Sadness, this fragile sister; she was the incarnation of our wistful parents' wishes, curled translucent under the incubator lamp, sucking the bud of her thumb through her few hours of life.

Ma's head ached and ached; we tiptoed around, hoping to avoid the invisible tripwires that seemed to set those headaches off. I'd drawn with crayon in my copy of *Goodnight Moon*: how could it be, that a child of *hers* could do such a thing? She gathered the books in her arms, took them out to the trash barrel behind the barn and set them on fire. Books were sacred, sacred: Did I understand? Her grandmother's poems, bound in cloth printed with violets, were kept face out on the shelf, a reminder of the high place from which her family had fallen. They'd been literary, way back, far above my father's common moneymaking sort of people. When Ma was twelve, she won a medal for reciting more Shakespeare from memory than any other twelve-year-old on

Staten Island—it was made of real gold. Did I understand? In her high school yearbook, her quotation was: "Nobody understands me." And looking into the eyes of that smouldering girl, it was hard to tell whether this was a lament or a boast.

He, our father, was away, on some kind of business (we didn't ask what kind; it was frightening to see him search for the answer as if he himself didn't exactly know), and she didn't trust the car, was sure it would burst into flames when she was driving. She would only use it in an emergency, so we were always at home, becoming strange together, contorting ourselves to fit each other and keep the rest of the world at bay. We were not suited to the work of farming—it meant doing the same thing day after day, with no immediate result, and thus it could not pull our attention away from our own drama. We took naps, we wandered up and down the stairs looking for a lost pencil, we sat at the window and stared. When the phone rang a terror gripped us and we cried, "Answer it, answer it!" as if it had come alive suddenly and would have to be slain.

Some days, though, we managed to seem like the characters in her childhood book, the book that had gotten us into this trouble. Braving the musky darkness of the coop, I'd go along hen by hen, thrusting a hand in beneath each one to bring out a warm, shit-spattered egg, carrying them down the hill in a tin pail, knowing that my reward would be the feeling that I was a farm girl, part of the beautiful scene in my parents' imagination, which was the one thing they really shared. I'd climb into the willow tree to sit all afternoon, reading, watching the brook swirl over the stones beneath. Did I love to read? To hear the water? God knows. I loved knowing that Ma would look out the bedroom window when the headache let up, and see me. And soon she'd be leaning in the front door, all gentleness and hope, so beautiful you couldn't take your eyes off her, her soft smile showing mostly amazement, that her life had come out like this, her land stretching in front of her, her children reading in the trees..

RECALLING IT for Philippa, I remembered only that—how beautiful it was. The place, the people, were far away, unable to barge into my vision with all their ungainly wants and rages. Oh, I missed them, I missed the immense love I'd borne them as I sat on the hillside in the evenings, having edged away from the table and its enduring argument, turning the screen-door catch with my hand to silence it so I could escape unnoticed, to look down at the warm light beaming from the windows, all of it more dear to me the more I was estranged.

"Untouched by the outside world," I said, tears of nostalgia stinging.

"Well, they had to send you to school," Philippa said, with swift professorial authority, through which, suddenly, shot a spark of doubt. "Right?"

"On and off," I answered. "You know, when the mood struck." I laughed, with a little edge of danger—which she caught and reflected in her own laugh, making me tipsy. No one had ever seen danger in me before.

"The school question had to run the rapids between Ma's contradictions, like everything else," I said, with a little swagger, having transformed my poor mother to granite with the turn of a phrase. Her ambitions for me had been boundless, but she hardly expected any mortal teacher could help me fulfill them. Teachers were small and ordinary people like my father, who would only want to shrink me, to show me limits instead of possibilities. And there must be no limits, because I was going to grow immense and all-seeing, become a sorceress and save her soul. After three days of kindergarten, she'd had enough of public school and blazed into the headmistress's office at Northwest Country Day to declare my genius. I hung behind her, avoiding the woman's eyes while greedily taking in the details of her presence—tweed suit, gray pincurls, a perfume whose fragrance would come to represent constancy to me, so that each afternoon, as I shook her hand before running out into whatever maelstrom my family was suffering that day, I'd breath deep, hoping to carry a whiff of her away with me. My mother's pride—which had to be immense so as to wrestle down her shame—made her seem at least twice the headmistress's size. I edged a little further behind her, wanting more than anything to just go home.

Or not quite "more than anything." More than anything, I wanted to be good, which meant only that I must make amazing accomplishments and love my mother best. I had to see that smile in which all her furies were resolved, everything calmed and completed by . . . me. The school terrified me—my classmates were Miles Armbruster III, Eliza Anne Cornwell, etc., children who spoke with the commanding voices they learned from their riding teachers, and whose chauffeurs delivered them to school because their parents were occupied in the manner of normal people, whatever that was. I barely dared move for fear the secret stigma of our lives would somehow be revealed to these people; I couldn't possibly raise my hand and ask to use the girls' room. Which left me hearing the unfortunate—"Miss McGinty? Beatrice wet herself again," from Eliza Anne, and receiving the kind loan of a pair of Miles Armbruster's mittens to replace my drenched socks.

Years later: Ma and I were watching Reagan's Inaugural Ball on TV and Miles Armbruster danced by. "Do you remember when he lent you his mittens for socks?" she asked. "*That's* what you call a connection, Bea." Another of the gifts Ma had given me. But every school morning, she had stood bereft in the kitchen doorway as if I betrayed her by leaving, and looking back at her I would feel something blur in my heart. She loved me so, loved to take me up into the woods to read stories in a glade we'd found where bright green grass grew under a canopy of laurel, loved to sing to me while she hung up the laundry and I ran back and forth under the blowing sheet. She loved me and I abandoned her, that was just the way her life always went.

Sylvie would try to catch my eye, to keep me there, but I wouldn't, I couldn't stay home. I was on an errand whose great if unnameable purpose I felt every minute, and I had no idea how to go about this except to go—fervently—to school. And Miss McGinty had noticed my nearsightedness; I had glasses now and knew that trees were made up of individual leaves.

Sylvie understood (this was her genius). "I have a little cough," she said, and Ma's hand went to her forehead and finding no fever, smoothed her fine hair back and kissed her brow.

"*We'll* bake bread," she said, closing me, the faithless, out of the family circle. "Cinnamon swirl."

Let them stay then, I thought, hating them, wondering why I was so mean. By the time I was in fourth grade and some financial misfortune had dashed me down from Olympus back to public school, we were used to the idea that I was bent on fulfilling my own ambition, while Sylvie was so kind and gentle that she wanted to stay home and help. They stood at the end of the driveway to watch me off to the bus, Sylvie holding Dolly by the hand—it was September, the chicory and goldenrod bloomed on the roadside and I startled redwings out of the marsh grass as I ran, heart tearing, up the dirt road. Our life was so beautiful, it *must* be as Ma said, that it was more authentic, more fine and true than other lives.

The bus was full of kids from real farms, who reeked of manure from their morning chores. In the valley, where the blacktop *crossed the line* (into the state of New York, also the state of sinful fantasy for me), it stopped in front of the autobody shop to pick up Butchy and Donna Savione; then we got back into Connecticut and girls named Debby and Lisa would get on with their stables of plastic horses, and the bus picked up speed as we passed the Armbrusters' and the other great houses along Main Street, heading toward the state of perfect receptivity, not to a subject, but a teacher, whoever he or she was that year—the live being whose magnetism would pull all my loose, mad atoms into alliance and lift me away from my family into the world I was going to conquer for them.

Vietnam was on the news every night, but it had no more to do with us than the antacid commercials that interrupted it. Our reality was there in that house. The essential news we took from the tension in Ma's voice each morning. Waking up, I listened to hear her in the next room, to guess whether she would adore or despise me that day.

This depended, mysteriously, on my father. He was away on his vague businesses and when he was coming home, she'd clean the house with a blind fervor and prepare herself as carefully as for that first date. Clouds of scented steam billowed from the shower stall where a few hours earlier mushrooms had been sprouting— now it was spotless and she stood with bowed head against the water, swaying like a woman at prayer. She emerged healed some-how, shining with physical pride, her ironing scar an angry Gothic arch over her left breast. All her doubts were behind her and she strode in magnificent nakedness downstairs to get a pair of her wretched panties (she *would* not spend money on panties, she'd have counted it impure).

She unnerved him—she was so hungry, she might eat him alive. Her breasts were beautiful, but he couldn't help remembering that heart beneath. Hearts must be compared to fists for a reason, and hers was fearfully strong. So he kept his distance, kissing her in a way she said was typical of the passionlessness of the upper classes. He felt he'd married beneath himself, did he? She was quite sure he did, though as always he was wrong.

"Pearls before swine," she said, when I wrote a little poem for him. Well, she was going to drag me and my poems up from the pig wallow, or die trying. After all, he was a Nazi (yes, she had filed away those early confessions, so she'd know where to attack). This, obviously, was why she had dreamt the SS were chasing her up the back hill. And she, though apparently a Catholic, was truly at heart a Jew. Was she not extremely intelligent? And persecuted everywhere she turned? *Sephardic*, she told me—spritzing herself with a little Mediterranean glamour, just in case. *His* was the face of evil in the mirror! Why couldn't anyone see?

He went upstairs to change (into a T-shirt, not Stanley Kowalski) and she, lonely in the world she'd banished him from, noticed that Sylvie had failed to mop the kitchen; she dissolved in a tearful rage. See? He'd come home and found us wanting, and now he would go away, and leave us alone to starve in the woods, like the Jews in Germany. She was leafing through *Treblinka* for the appropriate passage, and he was steeled against her, did we see how he steeled himself against her, his own wife, whom he had promised to love and honor, in sickness and in health? But no, she could *not* turn to him, he did not listen and did not care, she had nowhere to turn because nobody understood her and she had married a murderer, there had *been no rabbit* (and, aside to me, who, being the oldest, seemed always on the verge of driving somehow, so that little tips ought to be welcome: "You must never, *never* swerve to avoid an animal in the road. Human life comes first." Raging glance shot at my father). I was eleven, and seeing the phrase "lost control of the car" in a newspaper accident report had naturally assumed a car could develop a mind of its own and slam itself and its driver into, say, a bridge abutment, out of . . . spite . . . or whatever.

But, was that a rumble of thunder? Distant, but lightning travels at the speed of . . . (behind her my father was wearily shaking his head; this drove her to greater urgency). "Sylvie, unplug the television, Dolly, *now*, come with me, please; no, Teddy, don't cry, everything's going to be fine, honey." She held his head tight to her shoulder, reveling in his fear, his need for her, her voice taking a new, thrilling turn as she pointed west: "Look at the sky," where the clouds were boiling, gray and green. "Up, up, come on," and then a sharp crack, to which she responded with an immense shudder as if it had split her in two, my father with eyes cast heavenward at the performance as she pushed my head down through the low door, and turned to say, "Any phone calls to make, dear?" We all knew that the most indoor lightning strikes come over the phone wires.

It was close in that cupboard, all of us cramped together in the dark. Dolly was protesting, as always, her little fists clenched, little arms crossed, little mouth pursed with disapproval. Of what did she disapprove? Of Ma, for hysteria. Of Pop, for condescension. Of me, for acting above it all. Of Teddy, for being overwhelmed. She huddled closer to Sylvie, then pulled back. "You smell like hot dogs. Gross."

"We had hot dogs for dinner. You smell like hot dogs too."

"No I don't," Dolly said, insulted, pulling further into the corner in case this was true. Ma sang to Teddy, rocking him on her lap, twirling his curls around her finger, comforting him as someone ought once to have comforted her. She told us about the ball of lightning that had come in through her window, right after her father left for the war: a brilliant, sizzling pompon that zipped across the room, lighting on the lamp, the radio, the metal doorknob, all the while she, a little girl with no father to help her, sat mesmerized, sheet up to the chin, waiting for it to hurt her, until it was sucked into an electrical outlet and disappeared.

"No one believed me," she said. "They never believed me." So she had given up truth. She made facts of her feelings; menaces grew to fit the terrors they aroused in her, wounds deepened to prove the extent of her pain. She flinched mightily, at a thunderclap, murmuring "It's okay, it's okay," into Teddy's hair as if the fear was his.

There was pleasure in the linen closet, a deep calm. Finally, we'd worked it so the danger was outside ourselves, and we were banded together against it, safe. When we emerged, into a freshly washed landscape, the last violet clouds ragged over Skiff Mountain, the charge in the air was dispelled, and there was some sense of forgiveness, and we heard the parents giggling together in the middle of the night. In the morning, for no discernible reason, they'd become the kindly, striving people they'd always wanted to be, Pop swinging the little ones up for a hug as we came down the stairs.

Once I asked him how it happened—what made the grim détente between them dissolve all of a sudden. He thought a long time, and finally said, "Well, I guess we made love, honey."

Sex did it. I did not, of course, know what sex was. On my seventh birthday, he'd taken me aside and, saying solemnly, "I wish you didn't have to know . . ." looked deep, deep into my eyes and explained the physical act with no context, so it sounded repulsive and bizarre and I pictured them managing it in the bathroom. I doubted I could ever love any man enough to bear such a thing, and so had given the thought up, but here it was again. Any earlier murder attempts seemed to have been forgotten and there was even a suggestion of some future in which we would all live happily together, and all because of sex.

After breakfast that day Pop left and returned with a newborn lamb. Its mother had rejected it, so the farmer had given it to us. Sylvie took it into her arms as if she finally had a baby of her own, naming it Forsythia, feeding it from a bottle. We were going to become sheep farmers—we'd build up a flock, sell the wool, learn to spin it, to make cheese from the milk. Why had we never thought of it till now? Lambs in the fields, three sisters spinning in the firelight—all this, while, not far from us, in the suburbs to the south, wives were being swapped, Valium swallowed, malls built, gas guzzled, life and love wasted day by day.

SO HOW was it *we* were the crazy ones? The house was giving way to nature—vines grew in through chinks in the walls, opening them wide enough for snakes, then mice, then squirrels. The chickens had gone from fluffy Easter gifts to flea-ridden nuisances—they stepped delicately into the kitchen through the tear in the screen, to peck at the bugs in the corners. The cats were afraid of them and moved up to live on the roof, forgotten and starving. One summer night, we were managing to act like a regular family—having a barbecue—when they came swooping down from the eaves over the grill, snatching chops out of the flames and hunkering under the porch to eat, and lick their singed paws.

"It's a madhouse!" Ma said, arms out, ready to leap into the fountain of wrongness that watered everything we grew.

Not the first time desperation has been mistaken for ecstasy. That night the sheep found a gap in the fence and, panicked by freedom, ran around and around the house all night, hooves clicking on the stone path. Ma dreamed the Brownshirts had her surrounded; they were about to break down the door.

The next morning, her headache was back. "I wish you could just stick a screwdriver right here, in the corner of my eye," she said, jamming the heels of her hands against her eyes. I looked out the window: the sheep were trying to push back into their field, all at once, so they were bunched in a woolly knot at the fence, their bottoms wiggling urgently.

Pop had business in the city. "You'd rather I was dead," Ma wept, hoping this was terrible enough that he'd *have* to contradict her, but he told her to stop exaggerating.

I wrung out the hot washcloth while Sylvie went up to deal with the sheep. I walked Ma to the brook so she could lie on the bank and dip her head into the icy water, put her back to bed, and went up the willow tree with my book, trying to read, waiting to hear her call from the window. She looked out and saw I didn't care what she endured, how overwhelmed she was, by all these little children who needed her until there was none of her left, by this pain slamming in her skull. I thrived while she suffered, and why? Because I had a *mother who loved me!*

"You might have thought to pull my curtain," she said when I went in, her eyebrow quivering over a cold stare.

"I'm sorry."

"You don't *sound* sorry."

I kept still for a minute so as not to say, "I'm sorry I don't sound sorry," and asked if I could get her a cup of tea. Which amounted to the same thing—I *knew* she didn't like people who drank tea. Had I joined the other side? And the dog was baying; the collie up on the mountain was in heat. I dragged ours to the barn by the collar, shut him in, and turned on the fan in Ma's room, but all night we could hear him whining and suffering. Next morning, I went up to find his nose poked out under the barn door; he'd clawed it to splinters and his paws were bleeding. I got his collar with both hands, but as I bent down to hook the chain on he looked up at me with such pleading anguish that I felt it was hateful to hold him against such a power, whose enormity I only realized that day.

Ma's headache had become nearly constant. We tried mor-
phine: "Look, Beatrice, look at all the butterflies!" she said, joy-
stricken, like a child. My mind raced: How to fill the room with
butterflies before the drug wore off? I couldn't bear to see her disappointed. But already something was twisting and she looked at
me suddenly with strange cold eyes and said, "I can see right
through your face."

Her blinding headache had given her new sight, and she
noticed I was becoming a woman—her natural enemy. She herself had armed me, filling me with strength and confidence; now
I'd use these powers to strike her down.

I felt the slap of this, the injustice, and I knew she must be
right. There was something in me that didn't give a damn if her
head ached, that would have trampled my sisters and even little
Teddy, just to get my own way. If she'd been right to have me,
against the advice of the doctors, if she was right about my brilliance (I rolled my eyes at this only because I cherished it too
deeply and secretly to let it ever be known), if those intuitions
were true, then this despicable thread she'd found must be just as
real.

The headache over, the butterflies were forgotten and she
became defiant—she did not miss my father and when she met a
man on the street her posture changed, her laugh deepened, her
smile hinted at great adventures in store.

"I've discovered the secret of sex appeal," she confided. "You
just have to be thinking about it all the time. It shows, it comes
through in your eyes."

One day she said: "I'm writing a novel." I must have looked
skeptical, because she added, defying me instead of Pop for a
change, "It's about sex. *You* wouldn't understand."

She adored me, would support me in anything, told me fifty
times a day how beautiful and brilliant I was, how much beloved,

bought me dresses covered in ruffles and lace while she herself wore an old silk bathrobe cinched with a necktie for special occasions. If only *her* mother had loved her this way. She made sure I had all the advantages, like the girls she'd envied and despised, and *no*, of course she didn't envy and despise me, I was her daughter, her own creation.

Besides, she had something I didn't: sex, the golden key to the door of adulthood, which she intended to lock behind her now.

LATE ON a March night; the windows so thickly feathered with frost we couldn't see through, I thought I heard something crying, up the hill. We'd been "snowbound"—held in the house by Ma's fear of icy roads—for days. Ma had gone to bed with her ache, and Sylvie and I had been playing cribbage on the floor in front of the woodstove before facing the cold upstairs.

Sylvie put her hand to the window and melted a palm's worth of space to look out. "A light," she said, with Ma's portentousness. "What could it be?"

We went to the back door, praying she was right, that a strange light—a mystery—was visiting us; that Danger and Excitement, seeing we could not get out to meet them, had come to our back door. I put my head out into air too sharply cold to breathe.

"Nothing," I said, but then I heard some kind of grunt and of course whispered breathlessly, "You're right! There's someone up there. Put on your boots." We scrambled into our things and up the hill, to meet our intruder, but coming around the sheep shed, heard a commotion and went in to find Forsythia lying in the straw, in labor a month before her time. She kicked and groaned, surprised by each pain, then forgetting it completely, looking on mildly as the contraction rolled through her wool in a deep wave.

"What should we do?" I asked Sylvie, whose empathy had

grown so strong by then it had become a sixth sense, a great competence. That she had "seen a light" just at this moment didn't surprise me; she was rooted in nature like a woman ought to be, so of course she was drawn to this birthing. It wasn't fair, that all my schooling, all my ambition had cut me apart from this. And I hated deferring to her, when I had studied everything so carefully.

A shadow crossed Sylvie's face when she saw me in doubt. "The cats just do it by themselves," she said.

Something appeared then—the lamb's folded knees. Sylvie knelt to touch them, looking up at me with awe. Here it was, and fate had chosen us to see! Only fitting—*we'd* done the work, borne the responsibility day by day, now nature would reward us with a marvel. We glanced at each other in bold complicity: after all, we'd been told not to disturb Ma for anything less than a catastrophe. We'd keep this for ourselves. There was another contraction, and another, but still only the knees were visible, and Forsythia looked bewildered and bleated as if she was asking us something.

"Do you think I should pull?" Sylvie asked.

I knelt in the straw beside her.

"I think . . ." I said, stalling, and heard the lamb's neck snap as a final contraction forced it out through the ewe's torn vagina. Then came Forsythia's uterus, tangled in the lamb's back legs. She gazed at us, over the bloody inert mass of her body, with immense liquid eyes.

Sylvie screamed—as if she could scream loud enough to put things back the right way. The vet said there was no point in his coming, Forsythia would be dead by morning.

He was wrong, though. She survived another day, struggling back and forth across the barnyard in search of her baby, her bloated womb dragging behind her through the snow.

"What were you thinking?" Ma asked, with her persecuted

glare, the headache warping her eyes out of alignment. "Taking things into your own hands like that, when a life is at stake?"

We'd sold all the living room furniture by that time and the huge empty space felt more like a stage, with her as a Greek apparition.

"When will you understand that your actions have consequences? Life isn't a game for little girls to play." She turned from us in revulsion. The veil between us and all that was dreadful was no more than gauze; it would tear at a touch. Why couldn't I, who was alive only by the most incredible stroke of good fortune, see that? *Now* had I finally learned?

Sylvie stayed in her room all day. In the evening I went up to the barn and found Forsythia dead at last, curled against her trough.

In her grief Sylvie looked suddenly like an old woman. She blamed herself; Pop knew the fault was mine. Wasn't I supposed to be the smart one? "You're always so *sure* of yourself," he said, between his teeth. "You may not care, but what about your sister? Look what this has done to her." He looked at me with bewildered disappointment, as he had looked at me so often. Where was all the kindness, the natural softness one seeks in a woman? At least Sylvie was crying—as if she'd lost her own child, and he comforted her while I stood there numb.

"I—" I said, but guilt swallowed my voice. Why indeed was Sylvie unable to look at the things I was so curious to see? What was the coldness in my nature, this selfish stubbornness that made me refuse to look at life through his eyes?

SPRING CAME; its beauty would keep us safe in our trance a little longer. Ma took her coffee out to the back steps in the morning, picked a tiny child's bouquet of white violets and set it tenderly in a vase, as if it represented the gentlest part of herself, the part she had to guard with bared teeth, the part that was like Sylvie.

I at least had learned not to attach myself to soft and fragile things. I would be straighter, prouder than the rest of them—I'd bear what they could not. I walked down the dirt road, crouched beside the spring from the hillside and pulled up a flower that seemed to bleed in my hand, opened its curled leaf and with it a cocoon: a transparent unborn spider unfolded its long legs and clambered desperately away. Now that no one could see me, I cried and cried. Downstream there was an island, maybe ten feet long, moist and dank and overgrown with skunk cabbage and ferns. I read *The Yearling* there in one long day, listening to the brook split and rejoin itself around me. It was the first time I'd ever read a book without meaning to please my mother—it felt like the first time I'd ever really been alone. I smoothed each page open with the feeling I could dip my hand into the text as easily as I could trail my fingers in the current beside me.

Three

A N AUTODIDACT," Philippa said sharply. "Everyone is, really."
Sadness, lostness, were not qualities favored by the Italians, and trailing one's fingers in a current . . . well, it was *not* the act of a conqueror. She did me the kindness of ignoring my pathos so I could step out of it and push it aside. In my pale face with its eager, uncertain expression, she saw something she'd long been waiting for—a tabula rasa, on which the volumes of Sayresian discovery ought to be inscribed.

"Excellent, though," she said, "excellent that you cast a cold eye already at such a young age."

"Excuse me?" Casting a cold eye did not come under "excellent" at home.

"That you can look closely, you're not blinded by feeling."

I glanced across the desk at her, furtively—I wanted to see the face that valued my estranged curiosity.

She saw I was moved, and waved it away. "Pray continue, Beatrice," she said. "I mean, we have Clytemnaestra with her axe, we have—"

"It *was*," I said happily, "it was Greek! Straight out of Aeschylus!"

"Euripides," she corrected me. "Bloodier." She blinked. "Beatrice, why didn't you have any furniture?"

"Oh, you know . . ."

"No," she said. "I don't."

"Me neither, really," I said. "I mean, we had to sell it."

The people who bought it had come from the continent of reality: they'd sold their dairy farm to be developed as a golf resort, and now they were buying things—our furniture, and a small plane. They were young and vital and their six kids went to school with me. The father talked about his pilot lessons while his wife smiled a beautiful red-lipsticked smile and shook her head over men and their toys. I stared at them with what I knew was naked hunger. I'd have liked to hypnotize them, so I could examine them and find out what made them the way they were. They laughed very heartily with my father and then they got up from the couch and their men came in and took it away.

A few months later, the man took his wife up on his solo flight, and descending for a better look at their old place, he lost control, crashed the plane, and they were both killed. It seemed as if they'd died of their prosperity. My parents couldn't get over the magnitude of this folly—they gathered us and held us all tight there in the empty living room, their heads bowed over us as if we'd narrowly escaped such a crash ourselves.

Success wasn't going to get its hooks into us. Pop's last venture, a radio station whose signal barely reached as far as the Poconos, had gone belly-up, but he had a new idea: he was going into ping-pong ball manufacturing. The sport was wildly popular, after Nixon's opening to China, and the balls could be bought ready-made—in huge, featherlight boxes, from Japan. We poured them into big machines like concrete mixers, tumbled them in pumice until the seams were smoothed, then dried and sorted them, and

shrink-wrapped them on cards printed THEODORE WOLFE SPORT-
ING GOODS, INC. ValuSpot was going to carry them in all of its 235
East Coast stores. At dinner Pop would take out the Sotheby
Parke Bernet catalog of Distinctive Homes and tell each of us to
choose our favorite estate.

"Sweetie, I can't afford that kind of thing!" he exclaimed, peering at me as if in fear for my sanity, when he caught me assuming
I'd go off to college.

He'd said it would only be another year before we had to
choose between the saltwater farm in Maine, and the miniature
castle in Bermuda. I had to go away from there, I had to. I'd die if
I had to live in a miniature castle with him.

"I don't suppose you remember," Ma said, "that your father
and I lost substantial income when we had to give up the farm."
She was constitutionally unable to love me and my father at
once—now *I* was the murderer and the whole story of the car
crash had fallen out of her mind. I tried to remind her, but she
said not to be ridiculous, it happened years ago, for heaven's sake,
everyone makes a mistake now and then. And rabbits were an
awful hazard: she'd seen three dead in the road while driving
home from work that day.

That's right, work: Had I thought she wasn't up to it? Well,
she'd show me, and anyone else who dared to question her. Her
zeal had trumped her timidity, and all the fears I'd lived to protect
her from had evaporated one day. She was teaching remedial English at my high school suddenly, but I pretended not to notice.

After all, *I* was in advanced placement. From the moment my
freshman English teacher had explained to us that the reason we
were reading "irrelevant" books (the Bible; *The Odyssey*) was that
all people need to have some common ground, I'd read anything
that might count as a classic. I was going to exorcise the family
metaphors (rabbits, Nazis, and all), and learn the language of the

civilized world. Nothing pleased me so much as lifting some huge famous book down from a high shelf, thinking how I was going to absorb it and become like its characters. I was too young to understand Anna Karenina's plight, or Russia's, but I pushed on chapter by chapter, thinking "So, *that's* how love progresses," and stumbled out of my room in the evenings vaguely expecting to see the peasants coming up the dirt road with the hay. I was diligently preparing myself, for life in the nineteenth century.

One morning I came downstairs in my nightgown, beat an egg, put a match to the front burner, and a flame as if from a blowtorch whooshed up into my face.

"I don't know why," I sobbed to Sylvie, "but whenever something bursts into flames I just go crazy!"

She commiserated so sweetly, holding an icepack where my eyebrow had been. I'd always been anxious, for some reason— some people are just born that way. Sylvie lifted the stove hood to reveal a mouse nest thick as a pillow; building it, they'd run back and forth over the gas line, leaving tiny tracks that finally wore it through.

Oh, to live beyond reach of spontaneous combustion! My mother was pulling fistfuls of mouse-nest fluff out of the stove, hips moving to "Stoned Soul Picnic" on the radio, when I decided to get away for a few days, take the train to New York to visit the Poet-in-the-Schools who had turned me on to Coleridge that winter. "Red, yellow, honey, sassafras, and moonshine," Ma sang, with all the promise of the times in her voice: yes, the age of Aquarius was come, it was a paradise like childhood was meant to be, with bright colors and sweet smells and something warm in the oven—only this time, the grownups got to play. She bid me a distracted farewell.

I was fourteen—Charles (my poet) called it the Age of Consciousness. He'd talked about poetry as if it were a religion, but a plain, hardworking religion in which transcendence would be attained through the daily effort at seeing deeply and transmuting that vision into words. His hair was thick and unwashed; his face pale and puffy, with dark circles under the eyes. Every one of my hungers was engaged: he'd show me the marvels he had discovered in sorrow; he'd let me bathe him. He recognized my avidity (my eyes were like an infant's hands—sticky from grasping at things to suck). "You with the red sweater and the . . . cheeks, can you give me an example?"

The other teachers were too polite to mention my blushing, or the inner state it revealed, so I assumed that Charles, as a poet, was more deeply perceptive than they were, and I blushed worse, watched closer, listened more carefully . . .

"EDUCATION IS naturally an erotic process," Philippa said.

"It is?" I blinked and looked across the desk at her. In my trance, I'd almost forgotten who I was talking to.

"Of course!" she said, eyebrows slashed in amazement at my ignorance. Everything about her face—thin straight nose, high cheekbones, lips set in amusement or disapproval, and especially those sharp eyebrows—was definite, and her expressions always seemed to telegraph her thoughts precisely.

"What about schoolmarms, and glasses, and everything?"

"Have you ever seen *Mäedchen in Uniform*? The movie about a girl's school?"

I shook my head.

"I think you'd like it." She laughed a little, rueful and tender, as if she knew all too well what I'd like. "They're all locked up in this school together, smouldering . . ."

I took a quick look at her and rushed back to the subject of Charles's place on East Third Street. It was nearly without furniture, just like home. There was a waterbed, a park bench to be used as a sofa, an immense red and purple painting that seemed to pulse when we were high, and the mimeograph machine on which Charles printed *Walleye*, his journal. The apartment was infested with rats and cockroaches instead of mice and chickens, and its oracle was not a woman but a three-dimensional astrological calendar on which the ephemera were meticulously charted in relation to Charles's own personal cosmology. His boyfriend, Barry, a set designer for an avant-garde theater company, was in and out, carrying the necessary objects for the current production, which centered on a few moments in the life of a geisha, during which she was masturbating in a rain barrel.

It was not, in short, "a farm." But, a cocoon—we drifted home from the theater in the middle of the night, amid the stragglers hanging around the Fillmore in hopes of a last glimpse of Janis or Jimi, got high and fell asleep curled together on the waterbed, in our clothes, with the record player set to repeat so Van Morrison was still singing "Caravan" when we stretched in the morning light (the apartment had once been someone's wide-windowed parlor), and tumbled out onto Second Avenue for a hot bialy from Ratner's. I have never lived anyplace more benign. I knew I ought to go home, but days passed and I felt too cozy. Then somehow I'd spent my return money on a Burmese llama coat, and safe in the llama's stench, my own hair as wild and matted as its fur, my glasses looking Ono-ish rather than owlish, settled in for another happy East Village evening.

"You're further gone than I am!" Charles had just said, with a mad laugh that had engendered a madder one in me (despite the fact that he'd had five mushrooms and I'd only nibbled the edge of one), when the phone rang. Charles's face went white as if slapped when he answered it, and he handed it to me.

"What the hell do you think you're doing?" my mother asked

me, in a voice straight out of a Bosch painting (Charles liked to dazzle me, and the day before, we'd gotten high in the women's room at the Met so as to try a new perspective).

"Ma," I said. "I—"

"You what? You couldn't care less about me? There's no need to explain that, it's perfectly obvious. Do you know how hard it was to get this number?"

How had she managed? I tried to remember if I'd told her Charles's name.

"How dare you just walk out like that? What were you thinking?"

"I . . . I told you I was going," I protested, feebly.

"You did not tell me you weren't coming back!"

"I was coming back . . . just . . ."

Didn't want to. But Charles gave me the money for the ticket, and in the station he kissed my forehead and said, "Stay well, my conscious one."

A true compliment, and from a Poet-in-the-Schools. When I looked out to wave to him from the train, I saw he was panhandling. He flashed a bill to show me the train fare was no problem, and I fell into a sleep full of magical dreams, as if I'd just left an enchanted forest such as childhood is said to be.

THE COAT frightened people; seeing me in it, they knew I didn't mind being stared at, so they couldn't guess what I might do. I was of course the same good girl I'd always been, just trying to be what my mother wanted—flamboyant, beyond the pale. A layered look—hairy coat, timid girl, and then, so deep only a Poet-in-the-Schools could see it: a dragon of ambition, who would singe whatever she breathed on! No wonder my cheeks were blazing. I walked the halls of Wononscopomuc Regional High dogged by the vice principal, who had sniffed out the secret drug references in popular music—the scent of llama meant danger to him.

These were the times into which I, strange fiddlehead, unfurled: I wore the coat to the weekly peace vigil on our village green. Ma didn't like it: true, a nation was burning, but then she herself was liable to burst into flame any minute and would I have kept vigil for her? Stricken, frozen, she gave me that mad look and I kept a light, friendly tone and got the hell out, into a cold, clear spring day, the kind that brings everyone out for a demonstration. The flower children arrived in their VWs, the democratic ladies came down the hill in their Volvos, we were all together, we had a clear purpose for once. One of my friends from school brought a thermos of milk and a hash brownie in tin foil, and there we stood on the threshold of life, giggling ever louder. "Please, this is a *silent* vigil," the minister's wife kept saying.

"Have you ever heard the word *love*?" I asked, with a delicious combination of insolence and sanctimony, "because that's what this is *supposed to be* about."

If there was one thing more fun than baiting the vice principal, it was making a liberal chase its righteous little tail!

Repeating this story for Philippa, I looked up, expecting to see her stern finger pointing toward the door, but she was smiling, with something like glee.

"There *is* that," she said, catching my eye, and there was an air of conspiracy between us suddenly—we'd have liked to build a little cherry bomb together and set it off under some pious ideal. Amazing, to have a meeting of mischief like this, with a teacher.

After all, education *is* naturally an erotic process—from the time of Miss McGinty, I had studied in order to bring myself close enough to the teacher that I could catch a hint of her perfume. My high school English teacher, a nice man in Sansabelt slacks, had read Faulkner's Nobel speech to our class with great feeling, so that I credited him with those sonorous ideals and had set out to consume him. He wanted to go over my midterm paper and help me refine my understanding of verisimilitude, but I rejected the chair he offered me and knelt on the floor at his feet. I could barely keep myself from running my hands up his thighs. He'd inch his chair back, then I'd shuffle, on my knees, a little closer, then the chair would do its little hop, until he was up against the bookcase and decided to lose the verisimilitude and let my peculiar notion of reality stand.

I did not think of this as a sexual passion—more religious. Education *was* equivalent to seduction for me; Philippa had, as usual, been right. As soon as I fell in love with the teacher, the book of the subject would fly open and I'd begin to understand. After all, it was the thing this teacher most loved, and you are what you love. My boyfriend would have read Faulkner aloud to me every night if he'd understood this, but for some reason he saw sex as a physical thing. I was reading modern novels in the hope of learning to fit in with him, with my times. I had no better grasp of *Goodbye, Columbus* than *Madame Bovary*, but I could *feel* it, and it felt *so* good. The New Jersey heat, the blazing blue suburban swimming pools, the cherries spilling out of the refrigerator . . . it was all about longing, just like everything else.

I'd just gotten to the place where Brenda says: "Make love to me on this cruddy, cruddy sofa . . ." when my mother came into my room with *Time* magazine rolled up in her hand and said, "If you want to have sex, go to the doctor and get something, but I don't want to hear anything more about it, do you understand?"

I did not. I was the age she'd been when she met my father; I hardly understood anything at all. But I nodded vigorously and called the gynecologist first thing in the morning, just as, if she'd offered me a plane ticket, I'd have called TWA. It seemed that the great true danger facing me was my longing for safety and comfort, for the peculiar stillness of home. If I gave in to it, I'd be lost, like my parents. I had to meet the world and let it change me, no matter how much it might hurt.

"I want to have sex," I explained to the doctor. He was slightly hard of hearing. His eyes widened and he asked me to repeat myself. I looked past him to the huge needlepoint picture hanging on the wall: a storm at sea. He was working on a new one, of a night-blooming garden. It was folded on his desk.

I felt embarrassed, but considered this was because of my age and tried to speak up like an adult. *"I want to have sex,"* I proclaimed, loudly enough now I remembered how my mother had wanted to keep it all for herself.

He looked weary, as if there were no end to the demands people made on a country doctor.

"Actually, my boyfriend wants to," I admitted.

Relieved, he peered inside me, wrote a prescription, and said in a courtly manner: "Your boyfriend is in luck."

Hello, love! I liked sex, it made me feel grown up. I knew, from the movies, that the condition of true adulthood was cold desolation (being accustomed to molten desolation, I mistook the icy sort for maturity and poise), and my boyfriend knew an abandoned house with an unlocked window. I'd stand (gingerly; it was easy to put a foot through the floor) beside the torn curtain in the streetlight, to see how I moved him, before we sank into the old striped mattress together. We were both in love with my body, its happy buoyancy and smoothness, the way you could probe into it for secrets—but I loved it more than he did. Anatomy is destiny; I couldn't wait to see where mine would take me.

The silence of sex unnerved me, though, and I was always asking him what he was thinking, while he was sucking my nipple, or when he was just about to come.

"I'm *not* thinking," he'd say, for the fiftieth time. I could not understand this. I'd be thinking of *Goodbye, Columbus*, their last embrace with the bulk of their winter coats between them, or of Levin in *Anna Karenina*, beating out the cadence of *will you marry me?* hoping Kitty would guess the words as they were too precious to be spoken aloud. There I lay, pondering, with a mildewed pillow under my ass to promote deeper penetration. Soon, he'd drive me home and go back to his own house, a neat colonial whose walls his mother had stenciled with grape and wisteria vines: a display of bourgeois enterprise that my mother viewed with absolute scorn.

Which just made me love him worse: I wanted to climb into his life, share his dinner—Hamburger Helper. I envied his mother's ironing board.

At our house, we'd forgotten we'd ever had furniture—we believed we didn't need any, because we lived in a world of pure feeling and spirit, not crowded with material goods. How cashiers must sneer as they rang up their sales—another poor fool with her hopes pinned on an ironing board. *We* ironed on a towel spread out on the floor, and tore up old clothing for menstrual rags. We were above *things*.

For Ma's thirty-fifth birthday, Pop bought her a gift, a big, store-wrapped gift such as we had rarely seen. She took it with a wondering smile, praising the paper and ribbon, exclaiming at its weight—it was one of those times when her rages abated and she seemed like a little girl. Opening it, she looked surprised at first—it was a cut crystal punch bowl—but she blinked back her skepticism and smiled up at him, too grateful, her eyes welling. She understood, he was trying to show her that he did love her, that he had all along. She was ready to take him back into her heart, to pour her hopes and griefs out to him finally, to do anything, anything at all for his love's sake . . . but that was how it always went:

one drop started a flood with her, one spark and the world exploded.

Pop froze, as one endangered, and became warily casual. When she said, "Why this one? Why a punch bowl?" he shrugged and said the salesman had told him punch bowls were all the rage. He must have been as stupid as she said. Or maybe he really was an emotional Nazi, because he could hardly have found a more effective way to remind her what heights he'd fallen from in marrying her.

"Yes, the Academy girls all drink their *punch* this way, don't they?" she said, "punch" coming out as an epithet somehow. "Tell me, how do they pop their pills? I wish to God you'd married an Academy girl, so you could have lived the empty life you were *destined* for, and left me alone!"

And out she went through the kitchen door, where, as we gathered at the window, she lifted the bowl over her head and dashed it on the stone path with all her considerable strength.

It almost seemed to bounce, and Sylvie and I looked at each other with horror, because we barely remembered which were our feelings and which hers . . . and we knew nothing infuriated her more than things that refused to shatter. On the third try it cracked down the middle and she gave up, looking at it with absolute disgust. Had he deprived her even of this, a full annihilation?

"Lead crystal is certainly durable," he remarked, heading upstairs. As if he'd given up on her, on us. Who'd have blamed him? Or her?

"BUT THEY were stuck with each other less out of love than suspense," I told Philippa. "They wanted to know what would happen." It was sacrilege to talk about them this way, but Philippa made me bold, and every time she laughed, she reduced their power a little.

She was shaking her head—"God, these people who want to make sex nice and tidy," she said. "As if it wasn't pure unconscious mayhem, just barely under control!"

"It's not sex," I said.

She darted me an amused look and asked: "No?"

"No," I persisted, without certainty. Philippa was always sure of things; she was standing on her father's solid brick foundation.

The 1972 election—Pop stuck with Nixon, Ma was a Democrat in a micromini. As it was ten miles to the polls, they agreed not to vote; they'd only cancel each other out. At a quarter to eight, when he went up the back path to shut the chickens in for the night, I saw the old Jeep fishtail out of the front driveway and peel out down the dirt road. Pop just sat at the kitchen table and laughed. . . . It was November, of course, but Ma's defiance felt like spring in the air. She was going to chop a hole in the wall around our family and let us out, blinking, into the light.

And then it was 1973 and I was standing, in my llama skin coat, at the edge of an abyss. Watergate was seeping out into view, and, Pop having meant to vote for Nixon, Ma was now able to trace a direct line from Hitler to the White House, and now she who had disdained the television realized it was our civic responsibility to learn from it every nuance of Republican depravity.

"Never forget," she intoned. They decided, finally, to divorce, put the house up for sale, go forward in some new way. But at the first breezy phone call, announcing a prospective buyer, Ma's face went white, and the next thing I knew, she was backing down the hill with a handful of cracked corn, to lure the chickens into the house. She would keep her family sheltered and whole, until such time as she cared to destroy it.

My father showed me the doomsday clock on the cover of *Harper's*. Four minutes to nuclear destruction, did I understand? We live to no purpose. Even the dearest hope, realized, would be dust soon enough, so why bother? Have another! Live to enjoy! The ping-pong ball orders piled up but he wasn't in the mood to fill them. He was in the mood to plan a family trip to the Seychelles. He believed in existential hedonism, not existential despair.

"We'll be together, we'll really have gotten away from it all," he said, leaning back in his low chair, pushing his dinner plate away. He didn't look at us; he wanted to imagine us rapt at his idea, though it seemed to me he was inviting us into his grave. He didn't see that we were growing up, we were going to go away and start our own lives. Or maybe he saw it quite clearly. "Curieuse, for instance, was a leper colony until the middle of the century," he said. "Now the population is—well—it's mostly sea turtles. We'd have the place completely to ourselves, wouldn't have to see another soul except when we went into Mahé for provisions once a month."

His fingers were laced behind his head, and he was smiling with perfect satisfaction and closed eyes. Sylvie and Dolly were pretending to wash their hair under a waterfall. My heart beat like it was about to be caged. Any day now I was going to be a woman, one of those utterly alluring creatures you saw in the movies, so soft and beautiful that love protected them everywhere they went. But he wanted to take me where there would be no one to love me, and if I said I didn't want to go, he'd count it as a betrayal, a new reason to despise me.

"And the world could do what it wanted," he finished. "As long as we had a source of fresh water, we could live for months there, for years."

I dreamed that night of a strange, ragged boy from school, a boy who, being an outcast, struck me somehow as kin. He just barely touched his mouth to mine, and at this shock I woke with the ancient cry in my throat and a great electrical tree branching along my nerves, and I understood finally about sexual desire, and what my boyfriend had been "thinking" all that time. A door sprang open, into a magical world, the world of dreams that had always been there, in those summer evenings thick with fireflies, in the cold swirl of the rain-swollen brook over the stones. . . . It had been there, but I'd known it only as a picture, not a dimension. One entered it (of course!) through touch.

The cats were on the roof outside the window, tearing apart a chicken carcass, and a june bug banged against the screen. I lay there expecting a dark angel to fly in and possess me. Instead, something—a mouse probably—dashed across my bed and down the hall. For the first time, I was sure I'd be leaving that house, and the minute I realized this, I was swept by a fierce wave of love for it. The neglect that let us grow wild there, the drama that whisked every thunderstorm into a tempest and had made an operatic cycle out of the rabbit question, the utter brokenhearted wrongness we lived in: against these things, every beauty blazed more vivid, and this seemed to me a blessing for which it was worth suffering the rest.

Four

"Y ES, BILL Canterbridge *is* my father, but that does *not* make me a modernist."

It was our first day at Sweetriver. We were sitting in a circle in Dove House living room, introducing ourselves. Olney Canterbridge, having made the effort to speak, balled his white linen jacket into a pillow, rested his head against it, and closed his eyes. He was so widely experienced as to be bored already, on the first day of school.

I was in awe. Who could guess, who could believe that I was at college, and not just any college, but Sweetriver. "The *right* place for *my* Beatrice," Ma had said, in her Voice of Great Importance, which was usually used for describing men other than my father. After all, look at the people who had taught at Sweetriver, when they were still alive. Here they were in the catalogue, the poets, painters, composers, dancers, whose ferocious originality had fueled a century of art—the Leninites and the Trotskyites, the beats, the bohemians—anyone who had raged against convention. The name Sweetriver had been synonymous with sex, whiskey, and irony, in an age when these were magnificently daring things. Just walking into a dorm room, you could feel the ghost of someone like Mary McCarthy sitting at the end of the bed, legs crossed, spitting an occasional nail.

God knows what she'd have spat if she'd seen the place when I got there. By the seventies, Sweetriver's ideals had been taken up by the very bourgeoisie they'd been developed to *épater*: you could grow marijuana in your windowbox at Wellesley; you could live in the gay dorm at Smith. Sweetriver went coed to avoid going under and still they had to accept almost everyone who applied. Which was good because, for some reason my mother could *not* figure out, I'd been rejected from Wellesley and Smith and all the other places whose names would have served Ma and wounded Pop (Not Yale, there I'd simply said to the interviewer: "I won't get in here, will I?" and had felt, as he mournfully shook his head, a rare happiness: the knowledge that I, unlike my parents, had some sense of reality).

Still, we walked to class across wide lawns that looked down over the Sweet River Valley, beneath elms as graceful in death as they'd been in life, along hallways that smelled of dry volumes and pipe smoke. Sweetriver seemed like a temple of reason and light to me.

"It's just like Oxford!" I kept exclaiming, to various uncomprehending stares. But if I was a farmgirl, then Sweetriver might as well be Oxford. If you closed your eyes and smelled the leaves as you scuffed along, you could certainly summon that Oxford feeling, and it seemed that the clear light of scholarship was falling over my shoulder as my roommate, Dotsy Maven, introduced herself. She was a "legacy" who told us she'd spent the summer "playing along the East Coast." Forever after, I thought of her wearing a striped romper, bouncing a huge beach ball. Dotsy told me later that I struck her as the exemplary college girl—my hair in a thick braid, my thrift-shop shirt printed with roses, my jeans frayed just so. I smiled—I'd spent days on this outfit. It was my forged passport and if the details were right, I'd be crossing the border, leaving the old country behind. I had real Tampax, too, and Clairol shampoo instead of the stuff Ma mixed at home out of dish detergent and raw egg.

It was almost my turn to speak. Horrors—were my parents modernists or not? Should I try to sketch the farm story? But no, they'd guess that I came from people who couldn't manage their own lives. My heart slammed and my mind raced ahead, deciding what to say so as to appear able and authentic. I imagined that when I opened my mouth some shameful broken language would come out and they'd all know how pathetic I was.

I was saved, though, when the guy sitting beside me refused to speak at all.

He sat silent, with enormous watching eyes, as if he'd been sent from another planet to observe us and record on an inner video-tape examples of the earthling notion that one might sketch one-self out in a few sentences—that one had some idea who one was. Now, even Olney opened an eye. The refuser's eyes, set in a long, skeptical face, became ever more comically baleful as we tried to prod him into speaking, or at least to guess his name. I looked at him in amazement, feeling he must be my kin. Finally Dotsy asked him if he would let us see his driver's license. Still silent, he produced it: his name was Sidney Brown, he was from Chicago, his height was six foot one, his eyes (which looked more like discs) were blue.

The first full sentence he spoke to me came months later, quite uninflected.

"Beatrice, I've been thinking that I'd like to make love to you."

We were sitting in a bar, among a hundred other students, and I turned to him with awed tenderness, his face suddenly so clear in my sight while all the others blurred. Me? He wanted *me*, this strange, strange man? But of course—he recognized our common peculiarity! I felt tears stinging—I had dreamed this would happen.

I reached out and touched his cheek. I knew I couldn't hesitate, that even a split second of reluctance might make the difference between catching the great outwardly bound train I'd been waiting for, and being left on the platform alone. On the drive up to Sweetriver my mother (after caustically warning my father not to mistake a paper bag on the roadside for a rabbit) had undertaken, for the first time ever, to advise me: "Don't dream yourself in love," she said, "with a man you don't know. Don't confuse sex with love; men don't think that way." My father, who was negotiating a hairpin turn, did not show that he'd heard this. There was real fear in her voice—she couldn't let my life go down like hers, but this flash of maternal protectiveness threw the rest of our relationship into relief: my God, if I went around taking her advice, it would be the end of me. What could she—who desperately craved the love of a man she utterly despised—possibly know?

Desire is a pure honest feeling and deserves to be acted on, no less than tenderness or sympathy or fear, I thought, lofty as a Salvation Army volunteer.

I'd long since learned to live by my own instinct, and when Sid made that stark proposition, I knew I should go with him. He too lived outside the ordinary bounds, so we could skip the formalities and plunge straight into deepest communion. We ran back to the dorm, along the dark streets of the town, past porches whose dry leaves still clung on their vines, rustling in the November wind. Yes, the time of warmth was coming, we would pull up the covers and whisper in the dark. Up the stairs to his room, where we faced each other and something lurched in me: *finally*, I was going to be transformed. I'd yearned for this, worked toward it, studying that I might give myself to it more fully—*it* being the joyful, shocking envelopment in love. I unbuttoned his shirt, feeling I was unveiling a great painting, except that you never get to touch a painting, and if you did, the painting wouldn't give up all its deepest secrets in one soft sound of longing and satisfaction, you wouldn't want to fall to your knees with gratitude for being allowed the enormous power of touch.

"I love you," I said. I couldn't help this, it just broke out of my throat. I wondered if he'd think I was crazy, seeing as I barely knew him. But the way he'd looked at me—our understanding was so deep, he'd know just what I meant by this declaration. No, I thought, still addressing my mother, I *did* know Sid, had always known him.

HE HAD a scalp problem; the smell of coal-tar shampoo became my favorite scent. He was studying classical guitar—his fingers moved with spidery precision as he worked the same piece, Bach's Chaconne, again and again, playing till he hit a wrong note, starting over. Because he said so little, the music seemed to speak of all the things he wanted, even his love for me. I knew, from knowing my mother, that love doesn't necessarily accomplish anything. And I prided myself on understanding that a man can hardly bear to feel tenderness, that he has to turn it to aggression. . . . and so, comes sex. With every thrust, I felt it, his wonder in me, and when he came it was his soul spilling into mine. Then I'd fall asleep while he practiced the Chaconne. In my dreams I could exert a force to guide him through the difficult passages, so he'd come out the other side of the music into my arms.

His dreams were specters: small, sticky creatures spoke to him in tongues, he broke into a cold sweat and woke up screaming. Soon I'd absorbed these fears and would wake just before he did, screaming so loudly myself that I'd short-circuit his dream. A few months after we started sleeping together, we'd forgotten which of us first suffered from night terrors.

One night I went back to sleep in my own bed, and was awakened by the Chaconne, echoing down the hallway, note-perfect, flowing all the way through, just the way I'd always dreamed it. It was Segovia, on tape, blasting so loud it seemed Sid must be calling for me. I got up, went toward the music, found Sid wasn't in his room. Then the piece ended and I heard, from the bathroom, a light laugh and a little splash like a fish jumping.

There he was, in the bathtub, with Cindy Crowe, the girl across the hall. It was ghastly, beyond imagining, and I stared the way I suppose a soldier would, when his own bone is suddenly laid bare. Sid had flinched back from her breast when he saw me, but kept his hand poised above it now, defiant. Their bodies had a greenish cast underwater, Cindy turned away, Sid looking me hard in the eye—had I really been so arrogant as to assume he loved me?

He was right of course—I'd never asked him for constancy. I'd thought that touch confirmed a pact between us. At home we'd kept ourselves a family by dreaming the same dream together, and I'd worked to bring myself into such accordance with Sid, to convince myself my dreams had come true with him. Now I felt a fool. I tried to speak but no—luckily, because it would have been that incomprehensible language I'd feared the day Sid saved me from speaking—grief and rage and shame. So I stood staring until Cindy pulled herself up out of the water, and, refusing to cover herself, strode away, wet and regal, down the hall. Sid's face showed real feeling then—contempt. He pulled the plug and left me alone in the glare of the bathroom, staring into the drain.

I TRIED to bear this bravely (not the betrayal, but the shame of having been so hurt by it; everyone wondered what was wrong with me, that I was so dependent, so possessive), but as the weeks passed and Sid's lectures ("I don't believe you can own another person's love . . . ," etc.) bore in on me, I lost heart. Twice a week I got dressed and went to Philippa's class—I couldn't stand to have her guess my humiliation—but otherwise, I haunted the dorm halls in my nightgown, unable to sleep or eat. When I did manage to confide in someone, it was my assigned faculty adviser, known for her feminist reconsiderations of classic works, her pleated skirts, and her long, horsy face with its large and strangely unsynchronized eyes. She was said to be living, *en ménage*, with two paleontologists, both uglier than she was. She flared her nostrils and asked me earnestly: "Why is sex so important to you?"

I couldn't say. I guessed that other people, the people for whom sex wasn't so important, just liked it when strangers touched where they were most tender. Or, maybe they weren't so tender there? I vowed to toughen myself, become more like them. I had to, if I hoped to grow away from my family and really become part of the world. If you can't rely on your kin, you must turn to your culture.

Wherein it was, somehow, always the first day of the rest of your life, the perfect day on which to love the one you were with. It turned out that Sid often had the recognition that he'd like to make love to this or that woman, that his declaration to me was not the amazing thing I'd taken it for, but more on the order of "Have a nice day." Not long after Cindy Crowe in the bathtub, came a new one, a small, earnest creature with a long braid like a rat's tail, who started most of her sentences by saying "Well, being the sensual type, I . . ."

I watched out the window as she and the others went along to their classes, tried a few steps to see if I could learn to walk their way. There, they were gone—I ran to the bathroom to study their cubbies, try to discover their secrets so I could imitate them. The shampoo I'd been so proud of was beneath them of course— Cindy Crowe's shampoo showed its price in francs. Turning over her jar of Tiger balm, to try to figure out what it was, I caught my reflection in the mirror and wanted to slap that frozen, cringing face. I'd let Sid inside me—of course he'd found me out. I woke up in the middle of the night (I'd slept most of the day), looked out at the hard little stars glittering in the sky, and swore that someday I'd be like them.

"You ought to connect with someone else, Beatrice," Sid said. "You ought to go to bed with Palomino—it would really be good for him." Palomino was the other boyfriend of the sensuous type. He had named himself for his hair, which was waist length and bleached an odd shade of buff. The next night he let himself into my room . . .

"Sid said this would be good for you," he said, applying a patchouli massage oil to my thighs. I was glad of this, as Palomino didn't bathe—in a museum of smells, his hair would nicely represent the seventies, full as it was of incense and hashish and Red Zinger tea, and, I first thought, falafel with tahini, until I realized that was just his own natural odor. I was lost and sad and all I wanted was to curl into myself and sleep, so I came as quickly as I could, after which he finished with a few thrusts, and went, finally, away.

When he called in the morning my heart jumped, though; maybe he really liked me.

"Are you on the pill?" he asked.

"I am," I said, proud schoolgirl.

"Is your roommate? I thought I might try her next."

To think I'd imagined a man's love would resolve all my troubles, to think I had been so naive. I deserved the likes of Palomino, for that stupidity. How I wished to go home, where there *was* no reality—I wanted my mother's fried puffball, I wanted my own bed. It was March and the fields of narcissus across the brook would be blooming in their brilliant defiance of the spring cold. I remembered going out one morning and finding them frozen—I'd flicked one with my finger and it shattered like glass. I warmed the shards back into petals in my open palm and knelt there grieving; I hadn't meant to wreck everything, really, no.

My schoolwork was suffering; I read whole chapters without taking them in. What was the point of reading, when the minute you shut the book, the world the author had stretched so beautifully open snapped back to its harsh, banal self? Imagine, that I'd been fool enough to believe these novels reflected something real. A guy like Henry James, who spent all day writing and all night making clever conversation, who had never married or had children or a job, was never caught in any of the webs of life . . . of *course* he saw everything in all its thousand delicate shades of meaning. He had nothing to do all day but turn one scrap of experience under the light. And I, who knew *nothing*, had been so stupid, I'd thought real people lived this way. I tore *The Golden Bowl* in half and threw it across the room.

Clearly, my midterm essay, "Fanny Assingham and Her Ilk," would not be in on time. So I had to slouch over to Philippa's office, where, having knocked, I stood at the door shivering, hearing her chair push back and seeing her silhouette come toward the frosted window.

"Beatrice Wolfe! A rare visitor indeed! To what do we owe such an honor?"

She stepped back to look me up and down, and didn't like what she saw. I'd started wearing a wretched black raincoat from the

Salvation Army, to hide my fifties dresses with their cabbage roses, their air of postwar fertility. I looked like a blackened tree stump in the midst of a poisoned rice paddy—finally, in step with my age.

"Beatrice, what did I suggest, about getting some more— form-fitting—clothes? And didn't you promise me you were going to look into some kind of pomade or something? Because the hair is—" She paused to search for a suitable adjective, but it was too late.

"Philippa . . ." I said, sitting down hard and covering my face with my hands, which did not prevent a tear from running down my chin and plopping onto her notes. She'd been working on her book, figuring out how all the little pieces of life fit into her over- arching theory, *her* key to all mythologies. One of her exclama- tion points swelled and blurred.

"Now. Beatrice. *Now* . . ." she said, looking very badly alarmed, as if she was afraid my tears were going to wash away all her efforts, and speaking to me like the unruly student I was. "Beatrice, we *must* not, we must *not* . . . we . . . What if soldiers cried on the battlefield? Where would we be? Enslaved! And cer- tainly if *soldiers* can keep from crying on a battlefield, *you* can manage . . ."

"Philippa, I love him!" I said, smearing the words together with sloppy feeling. "I need him, I'm lost without him."

She'd had a moment to collect her thoughts, now she could interrupt with confidence. "You *what*? You're "*lost without him*"? Beatrice, I find that very hard to believe. You weren't lost without him two months ago, why should you be lost without him now? Listen, males spill their seed and die. That's their purpose on earth. It's essential that a man spread his genetic material as widely as possible. Of course you received his nightmares by telepathy! Women are born to nurture, and nurturance depends on empathy, which, at its highest intensity, becomes telepathy. But you can't expect that in return, not from a man anyway. It's not what they're made for."

She hurried on, piling up intellectual sandbags against the flood. After all, she said, a man is aware that once there's a child, he'll be cast aside. Did I know, for instance, that female bees sting the males and stuff them alive into the honeycomb to protect the stores of food for their young? "Stuffing behavior" it was called—how loyal would *I* be to a gender that was willing to use me as a living bottle stopper? Of course I was distraught—quite understandable, but . . .

"Which one is it?" she asked. "The one you pointed out across the cafeteria?"

I nodded, miserably. It hurt me to think of Sid, his long bones that I'd felt were part of me, his air of living at a great distance from ordinary things.

"That one looked like a physics major!" she said.

"He *is* a physics major," I admitted, and after a minute, "What do physics majors look like?"

She drew back a little, twinkling all over, ready to press her point home. "Physics majors, my dear, are psychically extraterrestrial. They mean to impose a grand plan on the universe." (She gestured to show that I *was* the universe.) "They imagine they can *think* their way out of orbit!" She threw her head back, laughing, then reined herself in, pursed her lips, and added, in precise, campy diction: "However, they are wrong."

"He was my celestial twin!" I insisted, but it was my last sob of the day.

"I have never *heard* anything so preposterous!" she said, making a show of sputtering. "Your *celestial twin*? He is your *polar opposite. My God*, he belongs on Easter Island. No, no, I don't say he wasn't worth your while, it will serve you very well, in the end, to have had an experience with a type like that. You want to try *all* types. . . ." she turned to size me up again, and nodded briskly—yes, she had been right the first time, she was always right.

"Yes," she said, laughing a little nervously, "yes, I'm sure you'll try all types. I don't see any problem there."

And suddenly I was as curious as heartbroken; the process of my sophistication was begun.

Five

THE FINANCIAL aid director laid my father's tax return out on his desk, to show me an "adjusted gross income" in the minus six figures. A man who had lost two hundred thousand dollars in a year had once possessed that same amount. Did I understand?

I did not. My father only borrowed that money, I insisted, it had never really been his. But, this forbearing man asked, setting a box of Kleenex discreetly before me on the desk, could I see that this showed my father had spent two hundred thousand dollars in the last year?

At the sight of the Kleenex I, who always tried to do as expected, began to cry.

"Has there been trouble? An illness maybe . . . or . . . ?" Was there some other reason my father couldn't have spared a bit for my tuition? He looked at me with bafflement and concern. He was a ruddy WASP in corduroy trousers, whose handshake and ringing voice had come down to him through generations of wealth and confidence—such blessings can cramp a man's imagination. I went over the possible answers: Teddy had climbed up the ladder-back rocking chair, and when it started to tip, had clung to the television set, which came over on top of him. He needed *twenty-two* stitches. (Why does one boast of one's sutures? But one does.) The white pine that had towered beside the house, which Pop had been meaning to cut down, had come down of its own accord during an ice storm, smashing out the whole bedroom window. Days later Ma found a perfect bird's nest on her dresser top among the scarves. And the demand for ping-pong balls was not what they had expected, but Pop insisted sales would "bounce back."

That was the important thing, after all—to meet the vicissitudes with a smile. The sob that shook me arose from depths unfathomable. We were poor, poor, I insisted—my mother cooked on a single burner because mice had taken over the rest of the stove, Sylvie did without orthodonture though her teeth were crowded into her face so that, in just the moment of perfect delight when a woman is most beautiful, she seemed to turn into a vampire. After all, it wasn't as if I were an only child; the others needed things—*shoes*, for instance. A struggling ping-pong ball company absorbs cash like a sponge, everyone knew that. My God, if losing two hundred thousand dollars in a year didn't impoverish a family, what on earth would? Did he really think it was so important that I have the opportunity to explicate Sexton's "Ballad of the Lonely Masturbator" that I should take the bread out of children's mouths?

He sighed, he checked the clock, he began again.

"IT *is*, in fact, a lot more sensible for you to study 'The Ballad of the Lonely Masturbator' than for you to give up and go home," Philippa said.

"We can't afford this. They need me there."

"Water safety!" she said.

"Excuse me?"

"Water safety, ever studied it? What do you do when someone is drowning? Or, no, what would you do if you saw a number of people, all drowning together in the middle of a lake?"

"Sit on the bank reading 'The Ballad of the Lonely Masturbator'?"

"Well, better that than jumping in to join them!" she said. "They are drowning in American anti-intellectualism!"

"God, I thought it was debt."

"Same, same!" she said. "You could get a student loan. You should go forward, Beatrice.

"You should not go home. If you want to understand the disintegration of the WASP tradition, you'd do better to read Robert Lowell."

She was my thunderbolt; I loved to watch her teaching, her eyes darting as if thoughts were pinging back and forth in her head like badminton birdies, while she lit each cigarette from the last until there were too many birdies, and too many cigarettes, in play, and she blinked and shook the head to clear it, and rapped her pointer on the blackboard and asked, "Miss Wolfe, *may* we assume your full attention is focused on the text?"

It was, it was! "Okay," I said, and rushed to the library to get *Life Studies*, and to the bank to get a loan.

I'D STARTED sleeping in Sid's bed, since he was always with someone else. It was strange comfort, the smell of his shampoo on the pillow, the warmth of the down quilt he'd brought from home. But it was the best I could do. There, at 3:11 one morning, I was awakened by a full, soft kiss. I *knew*, I had always believed that a kiss like this would come, and that when it came, I'd be ready to give myself over completely, courageously. It was almost exactly what I'd imagined, this gentle responsiveness, a will to shape one mouth to the other again and again. I reached up tenderly, taking the dear head in my hands, eyes closed, lips parted to inhale the other, whose lips were cool and whose woolen coat smelled of the night air. Night air? I shook myself awake and pulled away, and the kisser stood bolt upright in alarm.

"Who are you?!" I asked.

"Who are *you?*" she replied.

It was Cindy Crowe, the girl from the bathtub, the one who was so free of the scourge of jealousy—I suppose Sid was spending the night with the sensual type. Cindy stalked out of the room and I heard her door slam shut—I pictured her taking Sid by the neck and smashing sense into him—in, of course, an utterly nonjudgmental and jealousy-free way. I turned over and pulled up the blanket. Philippa was going to *love this* story.

Six

*F*IRST, YOU must withdraw from that harem," she said, speaking the word *harem* with a relish that suggested she was as jealous of Sid's possibilities as she was disapproving. She'd shown us a slide of an Ingres harem scene to illustrate the romantic sensibility—the women turning their faces and their full, round breasts toward the painter without the slightest modesty, nor curiosity. They were so complete in their beauty they needed nothing else, while I ached all over.

"You don't have to prepare a legal brief, just explain that it is your unfashionable misfortune to have love and sex all tangled together, apologize, and let them go their enlightened way."

"Once I start talking to him, I'll accidentally throw myself weeping on the ground, grab his ankles, and beg him for love," I explained.

She started to laugh, because she saw me starting to cry. "No, you will not, because we will have rehearsed it and you will have practiced *not* throwing yourself on the ground!"

"I can't, Philippa," I said brokenly. "I love him."

A smile flickered on her face and I heard the drama in my voice, a strand I'd pulled out of the movies—a false strand.

"You will *act* as if you are above this sort of longing," she decreed sharply. "There's no need to actually *feel* that way. When you feel as if you're at his mercy you will—silently—repeat this mantra: 'I *want* you, and I *will* have you.' Just remember that, and keep cool. Do you think you can do that?"

I can do anything, I thought suddenly. "I want you, and I *will* have you," I said.

"That's exactly right, try it again."

"I want you, and I *will* have you," we said, together, with the kind of conviction that does not allow failure.

"You know, you could dance to that," I said. "Like, a tango."

I started to sing it, and she said, "Yes, Beatrice, I think you've got it!"

"The rain, in Spain, stays mainly on the plain . . ." I sang, really expecting her to sing along, but she remembered her professorial stature, opened the door, and I spun out into the hallway, breathing chalk dust and pipe tobacco and wondering, for the first time in weeks, what was for dinner that night.

DOTSY WAS moussing up her blonde helmet at the mirror. "It looks so *normal*," she said with furious frustration. "No matter what I do, I look like a Long Island housewife," she said, moving as if to tear the hair, and its ordinariness with it, out of her head.

"I mean, I *want* to be normal," she explained, with a sweet sigh. "Like *you*, you know." I could hear her condescension toward me, though it was very, very slight, and leftover, really, from the time when she had thought it ignominious that I'd never skied Gstaad. By now it was Gstaad that looked ignominious—the real action was at the edge of life, Avenue A or someplace. It was the same as I used to feel crossing the state line on the school bus—as if I'd gone over some edge into a more squalid—more authentic—world. Who could blame poor Dotsy for wanting to go over that edge? Or for thinking she could transport herself with a salon product? She grew up on Long Island, after all.

"I want to, but I'm not, I never will be," she said, with such breathy hopelessness that a man would have caught her in his arms to reassure her. I, however, knew too well that a determination on unconventionality could leave a person doomed to dine forever on puffball.

"I got into Arbileth's poetry section," she announced, very much as Percy Shelley may have announced he was sailing off to war.

"Congratulations, that's wonderful!"

"But, my hair."

"Come on, let's go get dinner."

"I'm not hungry," she said. She had passed beyond such things.

THANKS TO Philippa, *I* was ravenous. I walked into the glare of the cafeteria as if I were walking out on a stage, tray in hand, dazzled by the choices—chicken parmesan or vegetarian nut loaf, broccoli or carrots, peach cobbler or chocolate pudding. During my first weeks at school, I had been really overwhelmed by the bounty of the cafeteria, with its huge bowl of yogurt and all the different fruits and honeys and cereals. What would my mother have said? I wanted some of everything and my hunger embarrassed me so that I could barely peep out a request for "gravy" on my mashed potatoes. Tonight, I was a little different, because Philippa and I had nearly sung "The rain in Spain" together. Sid was eating with the sensual type, and I went out of my way to pass their table so as to smile with benign disinterest as if I were a completely poised and self-contained person and they had never feasted on my entrails while I looked helplessly on.

I want you, and I will have you, I thought, and when he left, I hurried to catch up and made my sex/love apology just as we'd rehearsed it. He looked surprised, but said he was proud I'd recognized my problem. In time, I'd toughen up and learn to conquer my jealousy, he was sure. I nodded enthusiastically, looked him full in the eye, smiling clearly, and repeated *I want you, and I will have you*, in my mind.

A few weeks later, I found him standing in my doorway with his guitar: he'd learned to play the whole Chaconne, and he sat on my bed and went through it very, very carefully, without feeling, but true to every note. As he passed over the place where he used to stumble as my dream carried him on, my eyes filled with tears—that melody seemed the exact sound of the project of belief I'd undertaken when I fell in love with him. But he hadn't, I reminded myself sternly, fallen in love with me.

"Congratulations," I said, with an appropriate amount of feeling—about one percent of the feeling I had. *I want you, and I will have you.*

"Thanks," he said, terribly shy suddenly, so I had the inkling he recognized the fragile thing that had grown between us, and still wanted it to flower.

"Would you like a back rub?" It was hard work for him to say this but he got it out.

"No, thank you." (I managed to speak drily here; Philippa and I had practiced.) "No, no, I'm fine."

"I've got patchouli massage oil."

"No, no, really." *I want you, and I will have you.*

"It's just that you look so tense."

"Oh, well, you know me." I laughed, and he looked up, our eyes met. "I've got a class, actually." I went on, lying, praying he'd go before I lost my resolve. "Oh, I'm late, late," I said *(I want you, and I will have you)*, backing away down the hall.

The next day he came again, and asked me to follow him back to his room. As we went down the hall, I looked out the window and saw the sensual type and some others lined up to get on a chartered bus; they were going to protest the new nuclear power plant, and it had been suggested—nearly been promised—that they would spend the night in jail. They were paying grim attention as someone demonstrated the use of Vaseline against tear gas, but it had an air of make-believe and I thought how sad it was that we had nothing more than nuclear power to protest when the generation before us had lived in such beautiful solidarity against an evil war.

Sid threw his door open: he'd turned the room literally on its head—the bureau, the bed, his desk, and bookshelf with all the books neatly upside down. On the turntable a bowl of red Jell-O was revolving at 33 rpm. Sid went into the closet and emerged a few minutes later wearing every single thing that had been hanging there.

"You mean to say you're sorry," I said.

He nodded, silent and baleful. A wonderful pride swelled in me—this, I thought, was my real gift: I could find my way into even the strangest heart. I would join the great explorers—Lewis, Clark, and that gang. They sought the source of the Nile, the Hudson, whatever—I just wanted to find the one secret in each human heart. I went to Sid, felt his arms, stiffened by all the shirts and sweaters he was wearing, close around me, told myself to take courage and venture on.

"I'd never looked at it the way you do," Sid said, and then, in such a low whisper that I felt he was trying to keep it a secret even from himself: "But, the more I think about it—I'd like to get sex and love all mixed up too."

The record on which the Jell-O was jiggling was Louis Armstrong, and Sid sang with him suddenly, in a deep bass that shocked me: "I'm putting all my eggs in one basket . . . I'm betting everything I've got on you."

He'd turned his life upside down, just so I'd feel more at home in it. He loved me and I knew it, which meant I'd escaped my mother's fate. I pulled him in and held him tightly as I could through all his layers, and we heaved the bed right side up and burrowed into it together.

But as badly as I wanted to fall into a mutual dream with him, I couldn't help feeling that he wasn't the man I'd expected him to be. He touched me with great precision, the way he played the Chaconne. He was proud of his acquired skill, but there was no anguish, no prayer in it. I threw my head back and cried out, most artfully aroused: I was skillful too. We fell asleep the minute we were done with each other, and when we woke up, it was dark and everyone else was up in the dining hall. I jumped up and got my clothes on. I wanted to catch Philippa while she was still in her office. It was as much her triumph as mine.

Seven

An apt metaphor, as far as it goes. But Lewis and Clark merely tried to enter the unknown; you are trying to let the unknown enter you!" said Philippa. "*Yours* is the more daring project," she added, with satisfaction—she saw herself, and anyone close to herself, as engaged in great endeavors.

The fact was, my courage was failing. I worked against myself to trust Sid, and I did manage to act properly, never seeming suspicious if he was out late, making sure he had plenty of time to console the abandoned girlfriends. But there was no more blurring of the boundaries between us, and his silence, which I'd assumed was filled with thoughts too deep for words, just felt like emptiness now. When his guitar faltered, I was secretly pleased; he'd hurt me and I wanted him to stumble at the same chord forever. At night I'd lie awake remembering those first days, praying we could find our way back, but seeing the cold stars out the window, I remembered how lonely I'd been, and I didn't dare risk relying on Sid again. Trying to love him was like trying to put my hand into a flame.

I'd come to see him as a specimen of manhood, rather than a man. Philippa and I were going to figure him out—with that we'd be on our way to mapping the territory of heterosexual love. I *had to* do this, to figure out where my parents made their wrong turn.

"Men!" Philippa said. "You—*yes, you*—gotta love 'em." She didn't, but she had to study them, if only to turn the tables. The poster over her desk was a Brassaï photograph of Henri Matisse studying his model. Impossibly lush, her one arm crooked behind her head, her hair falling in a thick dark wave, nipples wide and deeply colored, curves of breast, abdomen, inner thigh complementing each other, her lips soft, her eyes bored, and Matisse? A sharp beard and pencil, narrow little glasses, his lips pressed tight as he considered exactly how to distill her to a line. He would not be dreaming her dreams that night; he couldn't care less what they were.

"*Typical*," I said, telling Philippa how Sid was rereading all the same sci-fi novels he'd read the year before.

"It's the natural male genre," she said. "In science fiction *technology* is the dynamic force, there's none of this relationship stuff. It's all about . . . oh, *you know* . . ." (She whisked her left hand around in the air) ". . . escaping the atmosphere, if you know what I mean. Docking in space and all." She laughed. "It's a relief for them! Docking modules do not entice them, confuse them, docking modules do not ask for understanding, nor offer it . . . no, docking modules just do what *men* made them to do and then drift into some other orbit and spin."

"Yes, I'm sure it's restful," I said grimly, though I felt anything but grim. It was late winter, early evening, and the sun shone pale behind the low wet clouds. A blank canvas, ready for spring. The radiators were ticking and I felt drowsy and content, ready to talk the afternoon away.

"Where would we be, without them?" she asked suddenly, with a cackle.

"It's true," I said. "You wake up in the middle of the night and there's a snowplow going by, the lights are flashing on the ceiling, and the whole rest of the world is cozy in bed and . . ."

"*Men* are out there, working to keep you safe!" she said.

"Men Working!" I crowed. "My favorite street sign on earth!"

The conversation was arrested momentarily while she considered which was her favorite street sign, and whether everyone has a favorite street sign, and concluded, "But no, it's women who think like that; men just turn left or right or whatever." And we burst into laughter, me shaking my head at the hopelessness, she crowing at her victory over it—*it* being the arduous project of trying to love a man.

A man. Not Sid, whose metallic coldness I'd used to know for timidity, and taken into my heart along with his terrors and his persistence at the guitar. A man, a romance, a story for Philippa, to whom the heterosexual world was exotic as Tangier.

"Keep me informed!" she called down the hall after me, and that night, while Sid and I made love, I couldn't help noticing the way he kept his finger in me while he entered as if he was holding open a page; nor my disappointment that he couldn't catch me up and pull me under, overwhelm me like a wave. It was the wave I was looking for; Philippa understood. Of course, she'd said, one wants the incontrovertible force that holds you tight, pulls you under, tosses you onto the shore again, exhilarated, changed. Yes, *she* understood me, I was thinking, as I came; crying out: "Sid, Sid, oh Sid!"

As soon as he fell asleep, I'd be feeling around on the dresser for a dime—Philippa would be waiting for my call.

So, life stabilized. I had the man I loved after all, I had to consider myself happy. Spring broke up through the mud, patches of green appeared, and then apple blossoms and, by some miracle, they continued my scholarship. "I can't believe it," I said to

Philippa, "I thought they wanted to be rid of me."

She managed to look knowing and mystified at once and I went home for the summer with the knowledge I'd be back in the fall.

AND THERE they were, all of them—the cats hissing at me from the roof, Teddy and Dolly regarding me with huge eyes as if I were a member of that fabled species, the Visitors from the Outer World. The bedroom window was boarded over where the tree had fallen in. "Oh, we get the north light," Pop said breezily. "It might not be enough for a Sweetriver girl, but it'll do." He'd given up trying to placate Ma; now he was baiting her—she'd have her view over the marshland back the minute hell froze over. Valu-Spot was using our ping-pong balls as their in-store brand. Did I know how many thousands of sales that guaranteed? In no time we'd be on top of the world.

Meanwhile, my bedroom was full to the ceiling with ping-pong balls. "Don't make a *scene* about it, for God's sake," Ma said.

"Well, it's not like I could sleep on *the couch*," I sniffed. The living room was still empty, except for a baby rabbit Sylvie was keeping in a cardboard box (as one of the cats had eaten its mother), and a new concert grand piano. Ma wouldn't accept less than a concert grand, though our collective musical ability could have found full expression with a glass and spoon. The piano stood for possibility, on its wide ebony legs. Ma was taking lessons; she played "Danny Boy" by the hour, tears spilling down along her nose.

Who *were* these people? I'd expected to be welcomed back into this big loving family—the family we so *wanted* to be. Instead, I felt less at home among them than I had at Sweetriver, and I thought longingly of Charles, my Poet-in-the-Schools, of Philippa, and even of Sid.

"Listen to me," Ma said. "Just because *you're* having a love affair—"

A love affair? How romantic that sounded, how full of hope, of envy! I looked over at her—she was thirty-eight, she was well-nigh on fire. She had the car keys in her hand—she was going to pick Sylvie up at the ball field, wearing a halter top and a pair of cutoffs, though the decade of childbearing had exhausted her body. Her hair was raked back by her angry hand, her crow's-feet must have been deepening right then, so narrowly was she squinting; and there was such determination in her stance that she was absolutely beautiful.

I'd never seen this so clearly before—she didn't draw herself up this way with us, only with outsiders. With her rivals. I'd broken the circle and joined them and there was no going back. Tears rose in my throat but I was not going to let her see me in pain, so I turned to watch the bumblebees work in the mock orange. *June*—I knew it by the smell of mock orange. And if I woke from a decade's sleep and looked out to see spruce trees in silhouette against a red and purple sky, I'd know it was early December, around Teddy's birthday. The things we absorb, through the earth of home.

"Things fall apart, the center will not hold," said I to myself while I tried to cook dinner on the one stove burner that was still working. All over the world, families were in disarray, centers were not holding. It wasn't just us, it was a Subject of Literature. So, it was all right then, my pulse slowed a little. At dinner I told Pop that I thought they'd continued my scholarship because I was such a good student.

"It's an interesting question," he replied. "Does one prefer a smart woman, or a nice woman? I've always leaned toward the nice ones myself." It had never occurred to him that a woman might be more than the sum of the pleasure she gave to a man. But then, what chance had he had, for such thoughts to occur? Some guys went to school on the GI bill, but he couldn't; he'd had a new baby. I hung my head.

"HAH!" SAID Philippa, when I reported this and the rest of the summer's stories to her in September. "In fact, he does NOT, on the face of it, choose his women on that basis. Has your mother ever been described as *nice?*"

That dispatched, we went on to the next subject, which was My Summer at Sid's. I'd called him late that first night and told him I missed him too desperately to spend the whole summer away from him—soon I was on a train to Chicago, where his parents happily welcomed the chance to prove their progressive values by letting us shack up. They had mock orange bushes too, but when I bent into them I found they had no perfume.

"Really? There's a scented type?" Sid's mother said, trying to seem interested, as she had all summer, while I followed her from room to room describing the fragrances and enchantments of the home she had rescued me from. I was so grateful to be away from them, so I could love them properly.

Though being away from them meant I had to be *with* Sid, and his sci-fi, and his guitar . . . emblems of his coldness, reminders that I shouldn't dare open my heart. I'd learned, though, that it was possible to keep the legs open and the heart closed, and so we made our way.

"I don't know, I think I may be done with him," I said to Philippa, with studied ennui . . . feeling very superior to poor weak souls—like my old self. The threads between me and my family seemed stretched to breaking: Ma felt I'd abandoned her, and she could barely manage a few civil words to me on the phone. Pop was glad to be rid of me. Dolly and Teddy were young enough that I'd simply floated out of their consciousness. Even with Sylvie, the connection was fraying. She was there, immersed in the life I was trying to wrench myself free of, so we began to see everything differently and it was hard for us to talk. I was proud that I didn't need those parents anymore; I felt it set me above Sylvie. Now I had to learn to do without Sid too—to become cool and perfect, beyond love.

"*Done* with him?? Good *God*, after all we went through . . . !" But Philippa recovered instantly, saying, "Well then, on to the next!" with relish. We each glanced quickly, secretly, at the other, and so caught each other's eyes by accident, and laughed.

"Who shall it be?" she asked, scanning out the window for a likely subject. "Blond or dark? Artist, or critic? Student, or . . . You know, I'd think you might cast about among the junior faculty. Yes, that would provide the necessary substance; you need a guiding hand."

Of all of Philippa's qualities, the one I valued most was her sense that people might fall in love with me. She gazed into my face now, as . . . well, as a seer gazes into the entrails of a sacrificed chicken; she could not be passive, even when gazing. But whatever she saw there pleased her, and this, naturally, pleased me.

"Yes, junior faculty," she decided, glancing quickly away. She herself was junior faculty. I pictured a quick, serious man in a dark overcoat, who was opening a door for me—a door under a brick arch, such as you might find at Oxford.

"Why would someone like that want to go out with me?" I asked.

She cocked her head, and frowned. "Your *farm*," she said, "There weren't a lot of movie theaters close by, were there?"

"Well, there's one in Dover Plains." I'd been there two or three times, most notably to see *Gone With the Wind*, during which my mother kept pointing out how bold and dashing Scarlett was, just the way I was going to be. I'd sunk further into my seat, a Mole Who Would Be Queen.

"Have you seen *La Religieuse*? Of course not. *Les Biches*? *Persona*?"

I shook my head.

A terrible little smile played on her face. My ignorance, it was such a gorgeous, seductive thing.

"We have work to do," she declared. "The movies have taken up where literature left off, after modernism." She took a breath.

"My child, you have *many* pleasures ahead," she said, in a richly affected voice, and I started to laugh for some reason I didn't quite understand. I looked up at Matisse with his pencil scratching, and his model, whose job was simply to be fully, nakedly, herself. Then to Philippa, her oxford shirt . . . her eyes, resting momentarily on my collarbone.

She, *my teacher*, was studying *me*.

$\mathscr{E}ight$

*A*FTER *PERSONA*, I was standing at the mirror and Dotsy came up behind me, swept up my hair, and kissed my neck. I gasped.

"Does it make you nervous?" she asked me, steadily, as if she were the daughter not of Mr. and Mrs. Schuyler T. Maven III, but Mr. and Mrs. Man Ray.

"No, no! But it might make Sid nervous!" I laughed, skillfully deflecting the blame, and accepting a cigarette from the slim silver case Dotsy had bought after seeing *Notorious*.

The film series was a success, and from then on it, like my scholarship, was built into the Sweetriver budget. Every winter, as the snow damped us into quiet, we would gather in the auditorium to fall deeper into Philippa's black-and-silver world, infected with an erotic miasma which caused us to helplessly fill vases with calla lilies, wear tuxedo jackets with nothing beneath, carry whiskey in flasks, and gesture with ebony cigarette holders. How lovely we were, in our disaffection! We didn't *want*—not men, not anything. We were subject to no one. We drifted across the campus like so many smoke rings on the air, wearing the white silk scarves called Isadora scarves, twenty dollars apiece as advertised in the back of *The New Yorker*, and so long that you could wrap one thrice around your neck and the other end of it was still back there in Paris at the dawn of the modern age.

Esmé, the film projectionist, became fascinating by accident. Seeing her skillful fingers thread the film, we all fell in love with her. She could do something that kept us in thrall. Tall and certain, broad-shouldered, her thick dark hair cut like a man's, she had all the glamour of an RAF pilot, and it was hard to keep facing forward during the film.

Very early, the morning after *Salome*, the dorm phone rang and I shuffled out of Sid's room to hear a very husky-voiced Philippa, laughing and saying, "Well, Beatrice, I'm afraid the unforeseen has . . ."

"The Unforeseen" became our code name for Esmé, whose moods no RAF pilot could imagine, and who bedeviled Philippa for the next two years. Esmé had style, which is to say that about some things—her jeans, her boots, her slicked-up hair—she was enviably certain. About other things—her feeling for Philippa was one—she changed her mind every minute, but this only sharpened her allure.

"She's like Joan Crawford," Philippa would say to excuse her. If you were like Joan Crawford, you had license to transgress, because with every transgression you created a new story, you lifted your mistreated lover up with you onto the silver screen, and the thing would last, it wouldn't just evaporate like ordinary loves and angers. . . .

I, styleless, had to rub angry shoulders with the little people, in the cheap seats. Even if it was possible for me to become like Esmé, it would have meant treading perilously close to becoming like my mother. So I was not sorry when Esmé went to New York for the weekend and returned wearing a wedding ring.

"Back to her high school boyfriend!" Philippa sputtered. "This is *regression*, Beatrice, and I do not intend to be tormented by someone else's regression. *Some of us* do not allow romantic troubles to stand in our way. I mean, one is reeling, one is seeing double. But, is one weeping?"

She was not. In fact, she was rereading *The Importance of Being Earnest*, because she was my thesis adviser and the subject was Oscar Wilde. I loved him because he made sense of life by turning it upside down, and Philippa agreed that given the times we lived in (how the Puritans must have smiled, looking down to see their efforts bear fruit in the seventies: all the tight-lipped, denim-clad goodwives, pious about recycling and whole grains and sex!), Oscar was the right guiding star. Philippa was impatient with him for wimping out and becoming a Christian during his years in prison, but she could quote him, chapter and verse, and as the year went by, we could slap lines down on each other like kids playing cards.

I was still with Sid, still trying for some kind of purity in myself, a full openness to the world which would atone for my parents' withdrawal from it. At night, when Sid had put his guitar away, finished his quarks, and just wanted to swarm over me in the dark, I tried to offer myself wholly. He adored me in the dark, when his face couldn't betray his need. He was cold, so I redoubled my tenderness, determined that his strangeness would dissolve in my warmth, if only I could let him in deep enough. This had not, and would not, happen, but as long as I was narrating my quest for Sid's inner self to Philippa, it seemed within reach. She laughed about it—her own quest was to impose her will on Western civilization, and she'd never once thought about Esmé the way I did about Sid.

"But she's a woman, her essence is available," she said. "I mean, *was* available . . ." She laughed a little, and banished the thought. "She's already aging, losing her edge," she said with a shrug. "She's not what she was that first night.

"Wilde engineered his own fate," she said suddenly. "He had a thousand chances to avoid it and he let every one go past."

We were driving into Troy, New York—home of Boxers and Briefs, the nearest gay bar. Things are rough when your idea of excitement is going out for a drink in Troy, New York, but there it was.

Boxers and Briefs was up a back staircase above a pizza joint, a huge room with all the necessities: mirrored ball, a few plastic tables and chairs, four speakers, all larger than I was, and a few men and women scattered in small, awkward-looking groups around the sides of the empty floor.

"Predation is a part of gay culture," Philippa explained. "Yours is an agrarian attitude. You want to *farm* a love, grow it, tend it, and finally, pluck it. Not surprising, considering your background. *I* am more of a hunter-gatherer. I swoop down at midnight and return with my prey."

I nodded.

"Now," she said, "Have you ever cruised?"

"Cruised?"

"Yes, you know, cruising?"

"I think of it as kind of a man thing."

She drew back, one eye wide and incredulous, the other narrowed and calculating. This was her characteristic expression—a thing was only allowed to surprise her for a second before it went under the microscope, to see where it would fit into her theories.

"A 'man' thing, exactly. Because it's an eye thing. A woman's eye is the window of her soul . . . a man's is a *crowbar*. Do you see?"

She stood up and rearranged herself, adjusting a bra strap and pulling up her corduroys. "Watch closely," she said, and tromped off around the dance floor, stopping every few steps to cock her head like a robin listening for a worm. The only people dancing were two women in late middle age, both done up in perfect high-cowboy style, with brass-tipped boots and wide belts, doing a careful, slow swing to Donna Summer. The women our age looked wretchedly awkward, either gawky or massive, clinging to each other in the shadows.

"*Nuns!*" Philippa said to me as she passed. "They're a bunch of *nuns.*"

We watched a woman in a shiny polyester shirt as she crossed the floor to the bar, looking so self-conscious she seemed to have forgotten how to walk.

"Dowdy. Aggressively dowdy," Philippa cried. "Why?"

"Well, it's not exactly the Champs Élysées," I said.

"It ought to be the working-class version," she said, taking a long and morose pull on her Scotch. "They've been in the factories all day. This is their chance to express themselves, and look . . . Honestly, I think women become lesbians to *get away* from sex. I am *not* going to be able to demonstrate hunting and gathering here tonight."

A poignant slow song came on and the Westerners held each other like kids at a waltz lesson and box-stepped conscientiously.

"Straight out of the fifties," Philippa said, rolling her eyes.

"It's sweet," I said.

"Yes," she said, as if I had just tapped the definitive nail into some coffin. "Ready to go?"

There was a strange sort of claustrophobia in that room, the feeling that no one of real interest was ever going to walk into it, that nothing would ever change there. I felt crazily restless. What was happening back at school? Suppose Esmé had changed her mind and was sitting on Philippa's doorstep right now, or Dotsy had gotten a buzz cut? What if Sid had finally conquered the Chaconne?

We slouched away down the stairs. Even the fluorescent glare of the pizzeria looked cheerful now.

"Is there any hope?" I asked in the car. "Is it just foolishness to even imagine some deep, whole love?"

"If it is," she said, "everyone's a fool."

She sounded exhausted and resigned. "Work, you can rely on," she said. "Love . . . *ffff.*" She sounded too tired to lecture me. I almost felt like patting her shoulder, though I knew that if there was one thing Philippa hated, it was consolation. Dissolve the grain of sand before she had the chance to make a pearl of it? Certainly not.

"There are many feelings that take the name of love, but once you give it the name, it's no more than an idea," she said grimly. "*You* have your pastoral thing—you're infested by Jean-Jacques Rousseau. Which puts you in step with the rest of the country, God knows . . . it's not a bad thing. But . . ."

"But I'm trying to make a dream come true . . ." I said. "Without a wand."

"You do expect a lot," she said. She had too, once, and I was furious to think she'd been disappointed. Sweetriver had been one long ordeal for me—from that first day, it had been clear I would never be chic or bored enough to fit in. I wasn't yet a modernist, and the rest of them were postmodern already. I should have realized the night I dreamed I was spooning up a revolting bowlful of Jackson Pollock (turned out to be a stomach flu) that I'd always be on the wrong side, the naive side, of everything. But Philippa had looked so closely at me, and where everyone else wanted to see how small and dull I was, in order to feel bigger and shinier himself, Philippa had looked for exact, subtle truths. There was more in her than in most people, so she had seen more in me. And a ray of her intellect had glanced off the jewel of my ambition, lying there where I'd left it so no one would guess how it mattered to me—and in that light, I saw it, possessed it again.

"I'm going to find you a girlfriend, someone really wonderful," I said.

She checked the rearview mirror and turned. A fine rain was falling and the reflection of the stoplights ahead of us shimmered in the road. It was late and we were alone in a hopeless city, and she sounded almost wistful, as well as skeptical, as she asked, "You are?"

BACK AT Sweetriver I let myself into Sid's room, intending to slip into bed without his noticing, and found a stranger sitting there, reading Nietzsche. He looked up, throwing his wild curls back so I saw wild eyes glittering, a mouth whose deliberate curves made him look almost cruel, and—

"Don't tell me," Philippa said, "You recognized your celestial twin."

"In a word, Philippa, yes. I mean, there's this dark-haired stranger, sitting on *my* bed, and he looks at me as if *I'm* the intruder. And with this cool, appraising look on his face too. I couldn't let him get away with it."

"And, you just had to go to bed with him."

"I don't like to be dismissed, Philippa," I declared with a haughty wave of my cigarette holder, and settled one haunch on her desk. I sounded like Philippa herself, and this was a sound she loved to hear.

This guy whose arrogance permeated every gesture was Sid's old friend, Ross Symkowicz, who was transferring to Sweetriver. He looked up at me, his suspicion resolving into curiosity, and I saw some question rush across his face, which was not the question he asked—

"Is there a coin laundry?"

I took him over to the basement of Arbuthnot House, helped him get his laundry in, and then . . .

"It just happened, Philippa, everything was so beautiful. We walked up on the woods path and the leaves are just coming out—lit from beneath—you know, birch leaves are like little fans, and they're completely translucent, they were the tenderest green . . ."

She tapped her fingers: last night, we'd been world-weary and battle-scarred and everything that Troy, New York, inspired, but we'd been together. Now I was starry-eyed and she was still rooted—in her very hip and very heavy Frye boots—to the earth.

"It was the first time this year I could really smell the earth, you know what I mean, that real first day of spring? And we were just mesmerized by it, I don't even know what happened."

"No," she said irritably. "Birds don't know, bees don't know, why should you? But don't stop, not right there. What happened then?"

I went back and explained exactly—she didn't want rapture, nor theory, she wanted to know how each movement led to the next. I'd slipped on a mossy stone, and he put his hand out to steady me but I caught myself. After that it was impossible not to feel what we lost by not touching each other. Something went through me, coloring every cell; the gesture was uncompleted, and it was like Sid's Chaconne, my entire being wanted to see it fulfilled. We said not another word, for fear that speech, with its attachment to reason, would wreck it all.

"You know how it is—you get caught in this spell."

"You do?" she inquired.

"You know what I mean," I said, or squealed, coy as a teenaged girl. Which of course, I was—I'd forgotten.

"I mean, the moonlight, and the peepers calling, and a little splash on the surface of the pond, and you just want to throw yourself into it, become *part* of it somehow. Oh, Philippa, he *smells* so good!"

I sighed, swooning into her confidence, grateful to have the chance to go back over it all and solidify it in words. There had been the inkling, in the dark, that life was finally fulfilling its promise, sweeping me into the embrace I'd been waiting for. All that feeling I had to keep back from Sid for fear he'd hurt me again had surged toward Ross.

"Instinct took over, that's all, and we just . . . Oh, Philippa, to feel him inside me, I . . ."

"See," she said, "you remember. Women always remember. *Think*, just try."

"Well, Philippa," I said (with a giggle), "I wasn't taking notes!"

"And why not?" she asked, in a parody of the stern professor.

"I was otherwise engaged," I replied, gazing way down my nose in a parody of the sophisticated boulevardier-ess.

"Oh, Philippa, if you knew how it felt . . ." I went on, determined to give her a fuller, truer picture.

"With some small assistance, I might be able to form an image, partial of course, but still . . ."

"Making love to Sid, it's like he's doing some careful experiment on my body."

"I do not find this entirely unerotic."

"But with Ross . . ."

I looked over at Philippa. I was feeling awfully indiscreet.

"Yes? Complete sentences *please*, Beatrice!" she said. "But you might take a deep breath first. Your bosom is heaving!" She laughed, at herself—she wanted to know, and oh, how I wanted to tell her—we were girls together and any minute there would be a pillow fight. The subject of love was a kind of meal we were sharing—and Ross was a rich morsel, we couldn't wait to suck his bones.

"Oh, he touches me like he wants to *know* me," I sighed. But remembering how good it all felt, I had to remember something else. "I'm an adulteress," I said, with stagey contrition, hoping it would sound glamorous, but no. The smell of coal-tar shampoo made me want to cry. I knew Sid and all that troubled him; I couldn't make him suffer like I had when he hurt me. But to make love to him now was to sense the shape of some great void, which it seemed only Ross could fill.

In the light of day, Ross despised me. He couldn't believe I'd betrayed Sid so easily, my mind didn't have that edge he was looking for, and incidentally, my thighs were too wide. Around midnight, though, he'd forget all this and let himself into my room (I'd stopped sleeping at Sid's, saying mine was quieter). He'd slip into bed behind me, push his hand between my thighs to pull me in, with absolute authority, as if when he touched me, he turned into a god. Everything was there between us, in silence, until morning brought his reproaches and my tears.

Sid was bound to find out. A thousand times I imagined, with the deepest satisfaction, how he would ask: Are you lovers? I'd have to confess it, and the pain in his face would prove, finally, that Ross really loved me.

But Sid refused to notice. When I mentioned Ross, he automatically reached for his guitar case and, note by careful note, he crowded us out of his mind.

I dreamed John Updike tried to kiss me, but I pushed him away.

"That's out of character," Philippa observed.

"Oh, he strains the rapture out of everything. He makes adultery sound like a logistical problem, he never says how you feel as if you'll die if you can't make everything right for them both, that you need to spend your full heart on each of them. He doesn't say how *wrong* it feels, how sad you feel, and for all you're being greedy and stealing two people's love, you still don't have enough. I think Ross loves me . . . but it's like its a secret he keeps from himself, so I have to pretend I don't know it either. And Updike, he was supposed to be the Great Man, I trusted him!"

LATE THAT night I woke up and saw Ross standing beside me, wearing the velvet pants I'd taken off when I went to bed.

"*Très piquant*," said Philippa.

"And they fit him exactly, that's the weird thing . . . I'd never have guessed we were the same size. He was standing there so proudly, like a statue of Aphrodite."

"Wait, what statue of Aphrodite?"

"Unlike you, Philippa, I don't have a catalogue of Aphrodite statues in my head. I mean, he looked like he had a woman's pride, he carried himself that way."

"Yes, of course," she said. "Because they don't have it, no man feels that way about his body. They know they're lacking. A woman's body is a vessel in which a miracle is about to happen. I mean, a child is going to grow there. It's like being in possession of—"

"A crystal ball—"

"A volcano—"

"A nuclear reactor."

"You can see why a man would feel sort of intimidated."

"Yeah, I thought he was trying to get inside my skin."

"Like one of those serial killers," Philippa mused.

"Exactly."

"Men focus on things, like enigmas and women. They penetrate them, figure them out, which is to say, they're always just slightly behind us. We *are*, and they want to know why," Philippa cackled happily. Above her head, Matisse was squinting—he hadn't quite got the curve of the breast, the weight there.

"It was touching in a way. I did feel like he was trying to know me."

"So touching . . . he'll be getting out the chain saw next."

"Okay," I said. "I admit, when he realized I was watching him, he looked at me so coldly, it didn't seem touching at all. It was like I'd caught him stealing."

"I can see it exactly," Philippa said, shaking her head. She had worked her mind into synchronicity with mine, had tried to see the same image, even feel something similar. A man works to keep apart (until you fall asleep—then he runs to the mirror to see how he looks in your clothes), but women are always divining the common stream. The relation between a man and a woman seemed to me a pageant, a feat of choreography, but I wanted real love in all its organic peculiarity.

"Oh!" I sighed. "If only he *had* been a woman!" Then we'd have swum away together like a pair of dolphins, been happy all our lives.

Philippa smiled . . .

"I mean . . . not a woman, a *physical* woman." But the phrase "physical woman" made my cheeks blaze. "I mean, you know, just, less like a man."

"Of course, of course," she said, tapping her pencil. "Less like a man."

SHE WAS in the air, she was making me dizzy. *She* would know just how to touch me, *she'd* have that sixth sense that hears *more* than what's said, sees more than what's shown. The looks exchanged by the schoolgirls or religious novices or lonely young wives in Philippa's recommended films were rapacious and yielding at once: women have that full range of feeling, a harp with a thousand strings. Men need that music so badly! Sid and Ross had a rich source in me, but I lived in silence somehow.

I stood at my window, watching my classmates cross the common through the cold spring, and heard one of Ross's heavily inked sheets of notebook paper slip under the door. A love note, or a threat, it might be either. I threw it on my bureau; I'd get to it later. My thesis was nearly finished, the apple blossoms were opening. . . .

That night I dreamed of a woman, a pink-and-white woman from whose amplitude I would take the kind of satisfaction Ross had in me. Her heavy breasts and rough nipples, her sex so luxuriously swollen, I drew my fingers through it like a pot of thick cream. I woke up and ran my hands over my own body in amazement.

"Sid," I said. "Wake up!"

One of his eyes opened, incredulous. "What?"

"You've got to stop working at the guitar the way you do!" I said.

"Why?"

Because you're wrecking the music, was what I wanted to say. "I think it's counterproductive. I think you're sort of—squashing the impulse, the feeling—by being so careful to follow the script."

"It's not a script, it's a score," he said into the pillow, "and it's there to translate the music so a musician can reproduce it."

"It's there to suggest the feeling the composer intended," I said, "and give you the notes and tempo, but . . ."

"Beatrice, I'm asleep," he said piteously.

And I've been having an affair with Ross. He's cold and critical in life, but in bed he touches me as if he were blind and could only know me that way. With you—I'm like that damned guitar.

"It's important," I said. "Hold it with feeling!"

He put the pillow over his head. I had to get out of there, to find the thing I'd dreamed of. I looped my Isadora scarf around my neck and rushed down the hall toward the future, and as I passed the pay phone, it began to ring.

"Clearly, you're on a quest of some kind," Philippa said carefully, after I reported my dream. "And these things always have an erotic component. Now you will go to your own room and sleep because we have to go over the thesis in depth tomorrow."

THE KNOCK at my door the next evening was so tentative, no one would guess it was made by the fist of Philippa Sayres. "I just have a few suggestions here, for your final revision," she said, and held out the recent draft of my thesis, annotated in huge red letters with remarks like: "This ought to be *much* more lurid," and, "You are *missing* the *vampirism* here."

"Oh, God, I thought I got the vampirism in pretty well," I said, sitting down to look the thing over, irritated to be diverted by this from my obsessive examination of the vicissitudes of love.

Philippa sat down beside me. "Beatrice," she said suddenly, "this *dream*, do you think—"

"Do I think what?" I asked, stalling, because suddenly everything was crystal clear to me and every moment of my life was strung like a streetlight, leading up to this.

"Do you think that—if such a reality were to occur—do you think—?"

I had never known words to fail Philippa. Neither of us could really differentiate between thinking and talking, we just babbled along like a couple of torrents coursing into a common pool. There were times when only one of us was speaking (say, when the other was about to sneeze), and times when, having accidentally come out with the same idea in unison, we'd gasp at the spectacle of ourselves for a second before speeding on ahead. This, a real pause, was a first.

"I mean to say, you'd have gone through with *it*?" she said finally.

I couldn't bear the suggestion that I didn't have the courage for something, especially something in the way of love.

"Of course, I would have 'gone through' with *it*," I declared. "I always follow my instincts, you know that."

She looked down, shuffling her feet a little like a pitcher readying his curveball, and suddenly, in a voice as gruff and husky as that pitcher's, asked: "Well, what about it? Wanna fool around?"

"Oh, Philippa—I don't think . . . I'm not sure . . ."

I was surprised to hear myself demur, more surprised still to see my hand reach out by reflex and close around her wrist, as if she were a tuft of cotton, or bread, or cloud I was pulling off for myself, from the world of soft and beautiful and nourishing things. She was still arching an inquisitive brow and I was still shaking my head solemnly *no* as I sat her on my lap and kissed her.

But as our mouths met, she remembered which one of us was the teacher.

"Not like that!" she said. "No! You can't kiss that way right off, that's for later!" Her imperial confidence had returned and she pressed her lips tight together and gave me a hard little smooch.

"Have you had anything to drink?" she asked. I had not. She rummaged in the depths of her purse and pulled out a beer bottle—everyone should have a light sedative before lovemaking, she told me. She herself downed a little bottle of Bombay gin left over from her Christmas flight home, as if it was a nasty sirop prescribed for the nerves.

"There," she said. "*Now* we can . . ." She was on top of me, and I was wondering what on earth I had done. I reminded myself that I adored her—no matter how numb I felt lying beneath her. I kissed her again.

"No!" she said irritably. "This is *not* the time for that kind of kiss!" I tried to sit up, but it wasn't possible. "It is so!" I said. "I understand perfectly what you mean, it's horrible the way men try to stick their tongue down your throat and grab your breasts and claw their way into you right off the bat, but this isn't that way, it's a soft, longing kiss, a kiss of yearning, don't you see?"

"Lie back!" she said. "I am six years older than you are, I think I've learned something in those years, and the time for that kiss has not yet arrived!"

"Talk wrecks it, Philippa," I said plaintively. Then I remembered that as a child she had enjoyed reenacting Napoleonic battles. I decided to follow her will. *Trust in the physical*, I admonished myself—the simple warmth of her body against mine would counteract my discomfort, I thought, if only she could stop lecturing.

She could not. It was like making love to an owl—great wings enfolding you, brilliant eyes spying out every thought—and the beak and talons to contend with. When I finally got her on her back, kissing her neck and her breasts and brushing my lips down the center of her, she sat up suddenly, and said, "No, no!"

"Philippa? What?" I laughed a little and traced my finger along her thigh.

"No," she said, with finality. "This is your first time. That is *not* appropriate for the first time."

But I wanted to transgress, to declare that I was on a mission and would go where I pleased, that nothing would stop me. There were things I needed to know about love, and I was going to discover them. I had to. "I want, I want . . ." I took her shoulders and pressed my hips into hers with clumsy fervency, as if I could break into her and steal what I needed.

"Now there's something," she said, "*that* is quite enjoyable."

Afterward, as I tried to slip into a dreamy postcoital satisfaction, she plucked a tissue from the bedside and blotted her lips as if she'd just enjoyed a rare delicacy. I couldn't keep from laughing: such a gesture is unusual in a bird of prey.

She sat bolt upright.

"This is what those bunnies are like!" she exclaimed, pulling the sheet up to her shoulders, which left me completely uncovered so she could look me up and down.

"What bunnies?" Having just compared her to an owl, I felt strange being thought of as a bunny. I tried to sit up too but she pushed me back down.

"Playboy bunnies! You know! Like, 'Here she is, watering her plants!' and they'd have you bent over." She giggled lasciviously. "'She loves the warmth of the sun on her bare skin and goes through her yoga positions every morning to be sure of full exposure to the healthful rays.'"

She ran a hand over me, starting with the arch of my foot and going up over the whole moonlit landscape, fitting her palm to every curve, in wonder, as I looked on in even greater wonder. I thought she must be mad, but it was a madness I didn't mind submitting to. I'd never had any real idea what I looked like, in spite of the hours I spent at the mirror. Maybe I was ugly, or *maybe* . . . I stretched and reflected on my own beauty until, as she dusted down the side of my breast to my arm, she found a sticking point.

"Beatrice," she said, and I recognized the irascible humor she showed to a tardy or unprepared student. "Beatrice, there is *hair* under your arm. Why?"

Because we lived in a world that considered shaving one's underarm as the first misstep on that slippery slope that would eventually land one in the suburbs, barbecuing enormous steaks for some enormous husband, waxing floors, shaking martinis, and probably in the end even voting Republican. So this question came as a shock.

"Philippa!" I said, sitting up again.

"Lie down," she replied. "*Lie down*. A woman is supposed to be *smooth*, Beatrice. Sweetriver lacks depth in the art history department, so it's unfair to expect you to know this, but from the earliest days of classical antiquity, the smoothness of women has been one of the keys of our civilization."

So there, in the same moment that she was examining me with all the greed of a thief with a stolen jewel, she spied a flaw! So began the book of her disappointment in me, which, like everything of hers, was long and complex and comprised of thousands of details.

Well, I wanted nothing more than to be made over. I *knew* the ways I'd learned at home were wrong, that I'd have to shed them if I wanted to escape. And here she was, my teacher, and my lover, a woman who stood above the world, looking over it, into it, seeing it whole, instead of cowering in the crevices, weeping and raging by turns.

She was my inspiration, provenance, and terror. And I remembered how shy she'd seemed, knocking at my door. She *was* absurd, talking and talking, her mad firefly intelligence lightning now against this leaf, now there, and there, until the pattern of illumination, more vivid than the firmament it played against, was all that seemed to matter.

Of course. I was a lesbian, why hadn't I seen it before? The strangeness, the separation from the world, the bottomless yearnings—it all made sense now, as did the fact that I'd spent four years crammed into a dormitory phone booth, ruminating with Philippa. I'd be safe with her; she would school me until I was truly able to please her. Ross wouldn't be able to hold me in his arms and slash at my heart with his qualms anymore.

And I could leave Sid without seeming to do wrong. I made the devastating announcement the next morning. I have, I said, discovered my true way. Not the cruel, "I've fallen in love with another man," but "I've fallen in love with another species." It was a fact of nature: the climate had simply changed.

COMEDY, AS Philippa had explained in that freshman English seminar so many eons ago, is what happens when the body tries to follow the mind. Her mind was on the move between Aristotle's Athens, Paris in the twenties, and the Hollywood of Yvette Mimieux. Her body was stuck in the seventies in bed with mine. This ought to have been perfect: I was twenty-one, I had that fleshly springiness one wants in women and muffins, and I was her own creature, fed solely on her wisdoms these four years, bathed in the light of her favorite films, shaved by her own chosen razor, offering her exactly the type of kiss officially sanctioned by herself.

So, what was it that grated, that didn't quite fit? Twelve nights after our first, she came in through the doorway and some anxiety overtook her. "I don't think I'd better stay," she said. "It's that parking lot—someone's going to scratch the car."

"You park there every night," I said. My thesis, lurid or not, had gotten an A from the committee, and I had a bottle of champagne on my dresser. I was wearing a silk nightgown I'd gotten at the thrift shop that morning—someone's bridal nightgown, faded like old rose petals, with a dove embroidered on it, and fluttering from the dove's beak, a banner that read GRACE. Champagne, silk, petals, doves, grace—there was a lot of longing, magnetic longing, in that room, especially as it was only a small dormitory single. Philippa kept a vigilant hand on the doorknob so as not to be drawn farther in.

"Where are you going next week, by the way?" she asked suddenly.

Next week? But of course, I was graduating. Sid and I had

planned to go back to Chicago together, but obviously that was off.

"Maybe I'll stay in town for a while," I said. "We . . ."

"*We*, like you and me?" she said. "Together?" She looked mortally puzzled. "But, what would you do here? Surely you're off to the city, or . . . wherever . . . aren't you?" Then, suspiciously: "Beatrice, have you been boasting about me? Have you told other people we might be staying together?"

"No!" I said. "I mean, I hadn't even spoken to *you* about it."

"If this were me I'd have been boasting and had to cover my tracks."

"Well, as it's *me*," I sniffed—

"You want to live with me?" She was beaming all her hummingbird's concentration now on the strange idea that I might love her, as if it were the drop of nectar in a lily's throat.

"I think that is most unlikely," she said, with incontrovertible authority, so that I had to reconsider. Who *would* want to live with Philippa? She was a dictator in bed, barking orders just when I felt most tender, so that by now I felt tender at the very sound of her barking an order, which was, yes, unlikely, but didn't it prove *my* point? I adored her! And she—just that morning she'd turned up outside my economics class, saying that as she had nothing to do except comment on these last fifty essays, she'd looked up my schedule so she could walk me to lunch. Then, as we stepped over a drainage ditch, she stopped still, peered in, and accidentally delivered a lecture on the Roman aqueducts. How would such a thing happen, if not from love?

But she knew so much, about aqueducts and everything—she must know what we ought to do. She stood there cocking her head to the left and to the right, as if the idea that we might stay together was such a revolutionary upending of the laws of physics that she felt a pedagogical responsibility to follow out the whole

equation, lest she overlook the sort of astounding new theory
that would escape a more conventional mind.

Then she nodded, quickly and definitely—yes, I was absolutely
wrong.

"I really have to go," she said. "These dorm parking lots are
like bumper car rinks. Students are terrible drivers!"

So ardent, so vigorous, full of belief, full of longing—we made
terrible drivers, but as lovers, well, that was another thing.

"Philippa, are you saying that you're leaving me because you're
afraid your car will get scratched in the parking lot?"

She thought for a moment. "Well . . . yes."

I started to cry. I thought this was what one did under the circumstances. "But Philippa, I love you!" I said.

She smiled involuntarily, a sudden flash which was instantly
put out. Maybe she was touched, or maybe mocking, but whatever, those words had sealed my fate, because she picked up her
teaching manner where she had thrown it twelve days ago, and
proceeded to demolish my quaint little notion as quickly as if I'd
tried some deconstructionist foolery in class.

"We've had an affair, Beatrice," she said. "It was very nice. But
there's no real match here. It's in the pheromones, you know that.
The nose knows."

She paused appropriately but I refused to laugh. "Pheromones!"
she said, throwing up her hands, "What can we do about them?
Nothing! We'll still be friends of course!"

"Of course," I said, taking a deep breath. I knew that what
came naturally to me was invariably wrong. After all, I'd learned it
all from my parents. Philippa was a woman of the world, so if she
thought crying was inappropriate the tears would have to go.

"Okay, okay, 'bye!" she said, seeing headlights come down the
drive and fearing her bright little convertible was about to suffer
an insult. "We'll talk!"

"Okay, 'bye," I said. I felt dazed, as if a hummingbird had flown in one of my ears and out the other. I couldn't feel sad, though— Philippa had said not to, and she was my North Star. I sat still on the bed for a long time, until I realized I was waiting for her to come back. Then I got the champagne out of the sink, popped the cork, and drank some out of bottle, congratulating myself, though my A seemed meaningless suddenly. I'd only wanted it for her.

Nine

———

AND THEN, there it was, commencement. I'd arrived at the end of the journey I'd set out on that day fifteen years ago, when I'd hidden in my mother's skirt to peer out at the real children learning real things. Now, waking up to hear the tents go up, gears groaning to lift the poles and then the snap of canvas over commons lawn, I lay in bed breathing the June air as if it were a perfect drug, light and cool and scented faintly of mock orange. My education—my suffering—was over, my life was about to begin.

To the mirror! Yes, I was blooming in spite of my hangover— Philippa had been right, I *was* beautiful. Or almost beautiful; I lifted my chin, I smiled, turned slightly and there it was, that cringing inwardness in my profile, a sort of stupidity, the refusal to look at myself, at anything, for fear of what I might see. Just then, though, the tent swayed up into the view behind me, catching on something deep in my imagination: my mother's vision of my future. Tents had billowed there too, and ships sailed across the horizon with ropes of starry lights swinging, dancers gliding on their polished decks.

Ridiculous notion, but I was infected with it, so this glimpse of tent made my heart beat and my hopes balloon. One deserves an indulgence on such a special day. Mine would be expectation. I'd done what my mother needed me to do, so my reward had to come in kind—in a few hours I'd have my degree and the right to live among those people I'd seen only through windows up until now, the kind of people who always knew what to do. Tomorrow I'd be home! A thousand beauties burst into my mind, things I wouldn't have guessed I remembered—the creek that cut through the back field and the wild irises that grew there, which newly dazzled my mother each spring: "Beatrice, look, the blue flag!" And the bubbles in the glass of the barn windows, the light shining in through the cobwebs, the moths dead on the sill. My eyes stung with tears. How had I ever left it? I felt the enchantment of that place around my shoulders like a magical robe.

Which I needed, because as I crossed the lawn toward the Student Union I heard Philippa calling. "Beatrice Wolfe?"

How was it she always managed to sound as if she had a megaphone? I stopped in my tracks and looked down at myself to see what I'd done wrong.

And met Philippa's squint of amused irritation. "Are you really wearing *that* to commencement?" she asked.

"What?" I asked, though I knew she hated my dress—two layers of gauze that floated over me light as an apple blossom; Bette Davis wouldn't have been caught dead in it.

"That . . . that *dirndl!*"

"It is not a dirndl," I said, meaning to be dismissive but accidentally sounding defensive.

She drew back, hands on hips, the way she did midlecture when she was about to make a particularly savory observation. "As the author of the catalogue for the Costume Institute's *History of the Skirt* exhibition, I am afraid I will have to differ with you. And as your thesis advisor I must remind you that I have an investment in the way you look today."

She said this with affection; she was showing me she really *did* care. Which meant that it would be unseemly of me to shriek: "And as my *ex-lover* you can just keep your nose out of *my skirts!*"

"What's the matter with that black dress, and where are the new shoes?" she went on. (She'd insisted I buy a pair of stiletto heels, saying that if Nancy Kissinger was five inches taller than Henry it was only fitting that I should tower over her.) "This . . . this is a *schmatta!*"

"Well, it can't be a dirndl and a *schmatta* at the same time, can it?" I asked, exasperated, and found myself immediately waist deep in the history of the skirt and the relationship between German and Yiddish, and all the while watching with envy as my classmates slouched up the steps toward lunch. This commencement was not a momentous event to them. Next week they'd be in Paris, where some of them would eat in bistros so dreadfully out of fashion that the others would politely pretend not to see them as they passed. They were above haste, hunger, and sentiment, above any kind of longing. Philippa would never fit in with them, and thinking this, I couldn't help but feel a little spring of tenderness.

"I'll change," I said. "I'll change as soon as I eat. Okay?"

"Okay." And she went away happy. This was all she wanted, to organize the world into a picture that pleased her eyes. And to change—that was the easiest thing in the world for me.

SO AN hour later, seeing my family straggling toward me over the little rise, like refugees from an utterly senseless war, I was unable to take flight, for fear of turning an ankle. My father in his city clothes—sparrow-brown suit and wingtips—looked tall and decisive, like a real businessman. No one would guess trees were turning to molten filaments in his mind. Dolly stuck carefully beside him; he was our representative of propriety. She was just thirteen, but nearly as tall as he was, and thin, her long, straight hair tied quickly back. She refused womanhood and the madness that must come with it. Sylvie had accepted this—she was wearing my high school graduation dress, hemmed to a miniskirt, a pair of Ma's sandals (she walked with her toes bent up to keep them on), and over it all, a heavy, scarred leather jacket. The skin of some boy she'd captured, I thought.

And Ma, blazing with a near-atomic radiance—the look with which she declared that she had never, ever cowered in a linen closet, that she fed her family on tinned sardines and fried puff-ball because she was fascinating and unconventional, *not* because she was afraid to face the ordinary, competent people in the supermarket, who might see through her, guess all that was wrong. Her dress looked like a stolen flag: striped red, white, and green, and slit all the way up to her hip, a fact particularly notable because of the magnificent strides she was taking in her attempt to be the first one to reach me, so she could give me her side of the story.

A pace away, she stopped, leaned back and spread her theatrical arms.

"Sweetheart," she said, "Oh, my girl," and took me in, resting her head on my shoulder as if she had never rested anywhere before. Behind her someone else's parents came along, the mother in shell pink, her husband's hand at the small of her back.

"I'm *so, so* glad to see you," Ma said, with a certain emphasis that meant: *I'm the one who loves you, pay no attention to him.*

"Him" stopped behind her, forlorn. He didn't have the strength of feeling to pull him into a natural embrace. He wanted love, but he had to stand there still as a stone, willing me to approach him. I went and kissed him, with pity and a small defiance. Ma would not be pleased.

"What's the matter?" I asked her, as we turned to go on.

"Oh, your father wouldn't let Teddy bring his favorite chicken," she said in disgust.

Teddy was eight, with a head of sandy curls, freckles, a striped shirt—nothing to indicate he had the kind of second sight that's necessary if you want to tell one chicken from another.

"It's hopeless," Sylvie said to me once we got out of Ma's earshot. "Just ignore them."

This splendid suggestion would have been easier to put into practice if only we hadn't been made of their flesh. It was impossible not to feel their needs and wants, not to keep trying to fulfill them.

"Does Teddy have a favorite chicken?" I asked.

"He's afraid to go into the henhouse!"

"So he has some basic intelligence." We laughed, and it all came back to me, the brooding clucks of the hens, unseen in the stinking feathery dark, the chickenshit slippery underfoot— Sylvie and I with our pool of secret knowledge, the exact feeling of those days.

"A little," she allowed, grinning the way she used to, when she was going to do something like pour a bottle of perfume on the dog. "Might have been fun to have a chicken here."

Sweetriver's one formal moment, and Ma wanted to bring a chicken. Formalities, conventions, that old sense of everyone coming together, dressing alike, acting alike, speaking alike for that one instant in recognition of the importance of the day, of common ideals and beliefs, even among the most disparate souls—all this was gone. The last legacy of the war in Vietnam was the notion that conventions ought to be smashed regularly, like gongs. So they were getting increasingly hard to find, and the few that were left made a dull, tinny sound when you struck them. And I, who had grown up dreaming of the day when I would step finally onto the scaffold of convention, found only thin air.

A tray of intricate little hors d'oeuvres came floating along and I floated after it. How was the pastry twisted to make the bit of cheese inside seem delightful, and what about the little water-cress and brie *objet* with a tricornered hat of onion jam? I had to know. Ma had gone on ahead, striding directly into the path of Philippa, who stopped hummingbird-still to take her in, and flicked an incredulous gaze toward me.

"She does *not* resemble Mrs. Ramsey, dear," she said when I got closer, and I remembered some midnight when I'd tried to convince her that my family was just like Virginia Woolf's. "More, the Red Queen! Yes, yes, *definitely* the Red Queen." She laughed as discreetly as her nature would allow. It was her peculiar way of giving comfort—of showing me I had very amusing troubles, the best kind of troubles by far. Then she went off with Pedro de los Reyes, head of the Spanish department, to the buffet.

I gulped the onion jam thing (truly revolting) holding a shrimp toast delicately between two fingers, and, resolving to return for one of the cheese puffs later, performed a miracle of triangula-tion and seated my parents at opposite sides of the lawn from each other. Pop and Dolly were over near the Philosophy table— whose professors looked mangy as Rolling Stones—while I sat with the others near the Languages. Ma had her back to Philippa, and I was just about to bite the bullet and ask Ma how she was, when that famously penetrating voice began to speak.

"That thesis should have been *much more lurid*," Philippa was saying to Pedro. "And she can't wear short skirts with those legs— look at her neck, though, and shoulders."

"Very nice shoulders," Pedro answered mildly.

"You knew the mother would be a trip," Philippa went on, "but my god, *that dress.*" Her laugh went off wildly, like a champagne cork—a few more hours and she'd be free of me.

And though I hadn't yet asked my mother to explain her stumbled-up-from-a foxhole expression (she was placidly sipping punch but her eyelid had just twitched in a dangerous way), she began to tell me her story.

"The chicken is only the tip of the iceberg," she said. "*He* doesn't think we should tell you." ("He," spoken with venomous disdain, was understood to refer to my father.)

And from there she dropped her series of little bombs: *(1)* ValuSpot, the largest retailer of ping-pong balls on the East Coast, had found a cheaper source and stopped buying from my father, so that *(2)* they'd been unable to keep up with the mortgage payments, complicated by the fact that *(3)* they actually held two mortgages on the house, one from the bank, and one from the teachers' credit union, which had caused *(4)* two lending institutions to foreclose on the house at once, which left *(5)* bankruptcy as the only choice and, on another subject entirely, *(6)* Ma had lost her teaching job after she wrote a love letter to one of her students—well, not a love letter, really, just a term paper comment that had gotten out of hand—she'd been trying to boost his self-esteem. They'd wanted her out, now they had their excuse.

"Motorcycles are the only thing he's good at, Beatrice," she said (this "he" was spoken with aching devotion). "So of course, that's what he wrote about. He's not going to be a rocket scientist" (here she waved a hand vaguely in my direction as if I had discovered in Wilde's epigrams a coded formula for jet fuel) "but he *knows motorcycles* and I wanted to show him that's a worthwhile thing."

They had to be out of the house by the end of the month, and oh, they were divorcing—this at least was a bit of good news. "Out on the street," she wailed. "With three little children."

She gazed at me pleadingly. Surely I, the graduate, would have the answer. She'd do whatever I told her, of course, and if it didn't work out she'd be furious. I suppose that's the wellspring of my character—I expect my words to have an effect, usually a pretty bad one.

Therefore I said absolutely nothing, and made a flurry of eye contact with Sylvie. We never felt so cozy as when we were shaking our heads together over their follies.

And I felt again that wave of excitement I'd had when I heard the tents go up—here it was finally, the catastrophe that had threatened us all those years, that we'd hidden from and dreamed of, worked against, though we prayed it would come. The lightning would strike, the house would burn to the ground, and with it every bond that held us to each other; we'd be free. A shiver ran through me. What next?

Sylvie said, by rote, "It's all going to work out, Ma."

Fork poised, Teddy asked, "What *is* this?"

"Chicken," we all said.

"It doesn't look like chicken. It looks disgusting."

"It's creamed chicken, your favorite!" Ma said.

"No, it's not," Teddy said. "Pizza's my favorite."

"Your father likes pizza," Ma said witheringly. "Creamed chicken is your very favorite dish."

"It is?"

"Would I make up something like that?" she said, catching my eye as he poked his fork gingerly in.

Teddy looked at Sylvie, who nodded very wisely, so he tried a bite. And made a face.

"On your last birthday you *asked* to have creamed chicken," Ma said. "I'm your mother, I know."

He gave up, and began to eat, though without conviction. Olney and Dotsy floated by, she winding a ribbon around her finger and saying, "Well, it doesn't release until I'm twenty-five, so until then, I'm kind of on my own."

"So what's going to happen?" I asked Ma.

"*He's* going out west," she said. "And I . . . well, I have to see what . . ."

"Ma, this boy," I began.

"I didn't do anything, I did *not!*" she cried, so sharply that I had to stop and try to figure out what I'd accused her of. "What kind of monster do you think I am?" she asked.

I thought she was a very charming sort of monster—a monster who Meant No Harm. Just to sit close to her was to feel her panic in the face of life—to feel it exert itself on your own senses, pulling them into agreement with hers until everything swung wild and the air was full of unseen danger and you were alone and at its mercy and it was driving its needles in, and you'd do anything, break anything, tear at your own skin even, to escape.

I moved my chair a little. "No, Ma," I said quietly. I was exquisitely aware that Philippa was right behind us. "I didn't say you did anything wrong."

"Oh, my head," she said suddenly, dropping it into her hands as if it had grown too heavy with all the dread and woe. "Sylvie, go through my purse, would you, see if you can find my pills?"

Sylvie heaved the thing onto her lap. Across the lawn, Pop was talking with great animation, as always when forlorn, and Dolly cupped herself toward him, listening as if the force of her attention might hold the poor splintered man together a little longer. I tried not to look, to keep Ma from noticing, though of course she could see nothing else. If he stopped to pet the cat, she despised the creature for stealing the crumbs of tenderness that rightly belonged to her. And Dolly didn't have to stick at his side either;

he understood we ran an awful risk by being nice to him; he never pressed the point.

"Larry, that's his name," she said, as if those syllables proved something immense. "He's not a boy, he's nearly twenty. And Bea, he's so bright, if it wasn't for the dyslexia you don't know what he might have done."

Sylvie pawed in the bottom of the purse. "Here, here, I've got 'em," she said. "Is there water?"

Ma gulped them down with her wine.

What had I been thinking, when I said I'd go home? Of the mock orange, how I used to walk right into the middle of it, to smell the flowers, rain dripping down my collar from the leaves, bumblebees working around me. Beauty is an anesthetic, that's why we love it so. Mock orange smells so sweet, you can forget everything, including the reason why you're hiding from your family in a bush full of bees.

"What will I do? Where will I go?" Ma was asking.

"A liaison, a dalliance, that's all," Philippa was saying to Pedro across the way. How had she become such a dashing conquistador? What about those shy phone calls when I'd felt something in her creeping out to meet me, though she'd tried to lock it in? Or the way she'd imagined me as "one of those bunnies"?

"Though, the bosom," she added, in a tone of lascivious regret.

"Yes, lovely, lovely," Pedro breathed, sounding very deeply moved.

"I've hated him for twenty years," Ma was saying, ". . . since even before you were born. What they did to people, Beatrice, how they tortured them, despised them." You had to know her logic to understand this—*they* were the Nazis, my father's people. She shuddered. "That I *married* a torturer. And now here I am, alone with three little children."

"How'd you come by those children, by the way?" I asked,

thinking that it did look careless, this absentminded bearing of children by a Nazi year in and year out.

"Oh, for God's sake, *so* we had sex four times! So what?" she said, though some instinct caused her to pull at her hem. "You don't know—you really don't know, Beatrice—how I've suffered. And now, now what?" Her voice was heavy with tears again. "*I have nothing.*"

This was the first phrase of an aria whose crescendo might shatter the perfect bowl of sky above us, and I interrupted quickly:

"You have me, Ma."

"Thank God for you, Beatrice," Ma said, looking into my eyes so that I saw how badly she needed something, some thing she was sure I could give her. She took my hands in a gesture at once imperious and abject, and my heart swelled toward her against my will. She was awash in a torrent of her own making and I would have to fish her out somehow, and then would come the next flood, and the next, but I couldn't bear to see her drown.

"I don't know what I'd do without you," she said. "I knew, Beatrice, knew from the minute you were born."

That I would someday work the miracle that saved her from herself. "And now, look, all this." She gazed around, at the tent, the lawn, the stone chapel with its reflecting pool, and all the other parents, among them a couple of movie stars, a famous disbarred lawyer, and of course the modernist, Bill Canterbridge—as if the place belonged to me.

"Ma," I said, looking helplessly back at Philippa . . .

Who cried "Beatrice!" in apparent surprise at seeing me. She rushed over saying, "*This* must be your mother!" with a glance at Pedro: Did he see *now* what a peculiar conquest she'd made? Toward me she arched a brow—she'd seen, she was properly aghast, and in this way at least, she loved me; she wanted to know the story.

"You must be very proud of your daughter, Mrs. Wolfe," she said in a voice full of secret allusion.

"I certainly am," Ma replied, as if Philippa had challenged her to a duel whose winner would have the exclusive right to take pride in me. "It's an odd thing for me to say, I know," she went on, "but Beatrice is my . . . my role model. Through these *horrible* times . . ." (Philippa shot me a glance and I tried to signal—folly, destitution, divorce—with my eyes) ". . . she has been a constant inspiration to me. No matter what, I can always think, no, no, there's Beatrice, she's *your daughter*, and look what *she* can do."

Yes, surely someday I would lead a revolution, star in an epic, burn at a stake. Then, finally, everyone would know who my mother was. "I only hope I can follow in her footsteps," she summed up, as if pledging allegiance.

"I wish you every success," said Philippa with a very slight bow, and a glance at me in which the expression "*Off* with their heads!" could easily be intuited.

"She's my thesis advisor," I thought to explain, watching her go off toward the bar, but Ma had already forgotten her and was looking over at Dolly and my father. "I can't take this, I'm going to explode," she said—seeming to foretell a physical inevitability.

The provost came along, stepping aside so Philippa could pass, and stopped for a minute to congratulate me, gripping my arm and pulling me toward him to say, into my ear: "You look *savagely* beautiful."

I fell on this like a jackal—could it be, that there was some quality in me that I hadn't recognized? Because I really was savage, so mightn't he be right about the beauty too? If he was, the world would take me in, I knew.

"I can't be here with him like this," Ma said, louder, "*I am going to explode.*"

"Would you like to go to the library and see my thesis?" I asked, feeling what a feeble gambit this was. That I had written a hundred intelligible, if ponderous pages, *must* prove I had some inner compass and might be able to move forward instead of going around in circles all my life, but Ma could hardly be expected to see this. Was that thesis going to get up and pay her mortgage, after all, or restore her lost love? No, it wasn't lurid enough. It would lie there in the library, serving no purpose at all.

"My life is crashing down around me," she said, with angry tears, "I can't think about your thesis now."

Of all the things that rushed into my mind, not one could be spoken. Across the lawn I saw the provost lean in to whisper to Kitty LaWren, a modern dance major whose senior performance—"Bunny Life," for which she had worn only a pelt of white fur glued to her buttocks—had been hailed as a brilliant commentary on the way women are reduced by men to sexual playthings, and must certainly have had a salutary effect, since it had been attended by every single student and professor at the school. I read his lips: Kitty was looking savagely beautiful too.

My thoughts, torn so rudely from the mock-orange bower, took refuge in memories of Philippa. She had read everything, thought about everything. She was on intimate terms with Emma Bovary and Dorothea Brooke and all those women conceived not by mere parents, but by authors: ordinary women whose lives had extraordinary depth because they were lucky enough to work, love, connive, fail, and die in the warm light of their creators' understanding. How wonderful to have someone like Philippa studying you every day.

I'm a Lesbian, I thought stubbornly, and with this, a little wall flew up between me and my mother, and I felt safe for a minute. But I couldn't very well say it, and casting around to fill the silence, I found another way to prod her. "I guess I should go over and see Pop before the ceremony," I said.

Her eyes narrowed. So, it was just as she'd suspected, I was her enemy and like it or not she would have to order my execution. "Ask him," she said bitterly, "just ask him, if he thinks you're brilliant *now*."

"THE EARTH was formed out of chaos, honey," he said when I'd reached his side of the lawn. "It's solid." He put his foot down, to prove it. "Your life will be too." He was given to flights of philosophy, assays into this or that territory that filled in for conversation. In conversation, the other person gets to talk, and you don't know what sort of thing they might say. The person who knew him most intimately was my mother, and she used that knowledge of his tender spots so she could know where to drip her acid. And maybe it was true that only acid could burn through his thick hide to reach his heart.

I brought myself up—never mind, it was my commencement day and he was trying, at least, to say something fond. I saw in his face how much he wanted to love me—to butt through the big block of his disappointment in me and come out into sunlight again. Standing there in his suit, he looked like the man he had wished to become, the father he ought to have been, and I wanted to say, "There *was* a rabbit, I'm sure of it. You didn't mean any harm."

A great tearing noise issued from the orchestra. The graduation march had been written by one of the music majors, as a "realistic evocation of the great stress associated with growth and change." This was all explained in the program, as if it were a new idea that growth and change might be stressful. Oh, how had I gotten stuck here, class of 1978, the most ridiculous year of the most appalling century in history?

I shuffled into line with Sid and Ross, who nodded at me as if nothing had ever happened between us. They looked right together—Sid's angles and his stare against Ross's dark, plush absorbency. There'd been a swing band at the graduation party the night before, and the music had tricked us into acting like people from another era. Sid had asked me to dance, though I'd never even imagined him dancing before, but suddenly he was more than able and I laughed and twirled and even dared fall back into a dip, to see Philippa watching with approval from the side. Then the tempo slowed and I felt a tap on my shoulder: Ross was cutting in. He took Sid by the waist and waltzed him away. As they came back to me, he looked into Sid's eyes and said, "You know, I believe you'd kiss me now." Sid closed his eyes and bent toward Ross, and they had kissed softly as if in a dream. I'd closed the circuit between them; they'd gone to each other through me the way lightning goes through a body of water. Now they could court an intimacy that would have been forbidden, much more so than sex.

Philippa sucked the last butter off her fingers and adjusted her robe, ready for the processional. The thought that I was going away from her, that I might never see her again, opened in my gut with a black hopelessness like the thought of dying. What had I done, to push her away from me? I'd kept my bearings all this time by keeping focused on her—now I was going to career away, and collide with—I closed my eyes, I didn't want to know.

I always sing when I'm nervous: music makes an emotional context you can live in like air. So I took a breath and tried to call "Pomp and Circumstance" to mind—*it* was what I'd been waiting for, the elephantine cadences, the sound of tradition, of certainties passed down and down. I had studied, studied with all my heart, Philippa would confirm it—surely, after all my efforts, I deserved something solid in return? Against the scratch and whine of the orchestra my voice was lost, and the next thing I knew I was singing the "Marseillaise." It was sufficiently stirring, "*Le jour de gloire est arrivé.*" And it reminded me that there *was* something I could close my hand around: I was a lesbian. A little spring of something like patriotism welled up in me. The provost emerged at the head of the procession, and I fell into step with the rest.

Ten

POP AND Dolly drove home in the Jeep, while the rest of us
went in Ma's new Karmann Ghia : her motorcycle prodigy
had traded it for the family Oldsmobile. Teddy was on my lap and
Sylvie had to lie in the space behind the bucket seats, but the
squeeze was worth it: Pop and Dolly were so *morose*, we wouldn't
have had any fun with them. Ma was giddy—a blitz was destroying
her life, *finally*, and she was driving a little scarlet car, and everything was shattering around her and who could guess what might
come next?

". . . So," Sylvie continued, "She says to the man delivering the
telegram, 'Please sing it, I've always wanted to get a singing telegram.' And he says 'Oh, no, no, ma'am, I don't think . . .' But she
says, 'Oh please?' So he says, 'Well, okay . . . Da, da, da, da, your
sister Rose is dead, da, da, da, da . . .' "

We howled, I laughed until I cried—tears of relief, really: Ma
was back, not lost forever in the slough of despond. Sweetriver
had been a nightmare, but now I was awake. We were all together
and nothing else mattered. If we'd laughed earlier, we would have
been counted as heartless, but now that Ma was happy, laughter
was the only appropriate thing. It was proof we were family, that
we all understood life the same way.

"At least there's no chicken," Sylvie said in my ear. She was trying to stretch and lifted herself on an elbow, sticking her feet out Ma's window, and as we turned a sharp corner, one of her sandals flew off into a cow pasture.

"Now why would anyone put a fence so close to the road?" Ma asked, pulling over and backing up to the spot. The sandal with its thin white straps was on the wrong side of this fence, in the trampled muck. "This kind of thing must happen all the time."

"Not necessarily," I said.

Sylvie found a stick and tried to fish over the barbed wire, while a mildly curious cow chewed lazily and watched her from a few feet away. "Such pretty shoes," she said longingly. "That's not a bull, is it Ma?" It began to move toward us, maybe wondering if we had some corn.

"I'm going in," Sylvie said, pulling two strands of wire apart and squeezing between them.

"A bull," Teddy said—he was Ma's natural-born straight man—"has horns."

"Some cows have horns too," I pointed out, in my prim older-sister way.

"That's no cow," Ma harumphed. What an idea, a scenario of hers, peopled by a mere cow!

"My hair!" Sylvie cried. She'd gotten through, but stood bent to the fence, her fine blond hair snagged in the barbs. Ma and I started trying to untangle it but it was painstaking work of the sort Ma had no patience for, and the cow had begun snorting in a remarkably bull-like manner.

"It's pawing the ground!" Ma said.

"Come back through," I told Sylvie very calmly.

"I can't!"

"You have to."

"It's going to charge!" Ma said, abandoning her work in laughter. "Look! This is like my whole life, isn't it?" she asked. "Caught in the barbed wire with a snorting bull about to . . ."

"Ma, *work* at it!"

"And still I can't help laughing! When my life, my whole life . . ."

"*My* life! *My* life, mother," Sylvie said.

The bull or cow, unnerved by this creature with its three loud heads, had moved away from us and was looking off toward the valley, bashing away flies with its tail. Sylvie ripped her hair away from the barbs, grabbed the sandal, and flicked it out between two strands of wire, giving us a look of stubborn superiority, then climbed back through behind it.

"Why do these things only happen to *us*?" Ma asked.

The field curved over the top of a steep hill, from which we looked over the valley where those poor, beautiful, silly people had died in their little plane years ago, leaving their children to the fates. Now it was a settlement of ranch houses, and Ma flung her arms wide as if she expected that the people in those houses were all looking up at us. An audience confers respect on the thing it watches, gives it an extra measure of meaning. A mother feels her baby's forehead with the sympathy of the room around her, an old woman who has managed to pour tea in spite of her palsy knows her triumph is felt by all. All the excruciatingly ordinary crumbs, that one by one lead to the moment when you find your lump or whatever and begin earnestly to die: on stage they add up to something, they make their point. Then the velvet curtain closes, the squalid set is forgotten, the actors run out into the applause. Ma laughed in the sunlight—her life was as glorious as a truck full of fireworks at the moment the match is dropped. She might have seemed to rail against the heavens but in fact she was thanking them, preening before the gods.

Or before the people in the valley, it came to the same thing.

"These things only happen to us, Mother, because nobody else is trying to squeeze four big people into a Karmann Ghia," I said. Other moms might have lovers, but I was sure they didn't jam their huge families into the sportscars those lovers inspired them to buy.

"I suppose you're right," Ma said. "They have no joie de vivre." She went wide-eyed with sadness, like a princess visiting the poor.

"Beatrice," she said suddenly, "your knowledge, your wisdom is an amazement to me. I don't know where it comes from, but you say things I would never have thought of, you understand so much, honestly it's as if you were the mother and I were the child." She blinked dazedly, smiling into the sun. A Volvo came around the bend with a family nicely belted in, and she eyed it with pity.

"No joie de vivre," she repeated, gathering Sylvie and me in for the cast picture. Freedom had appeared to her suddenly; all the possibilities occluded by marriage—the loves, the professions, the plays she'd wanted to see, and the cities, cups of espresso, tangos, distant sails—they were out there. And we, as always, were filled with her feelings, here at the edge of the highway with the pasture arching up behind us, soft with timothy and buttercups and the yellow and orange flowers whose plain, clean smell meant summer to me, which Ma had called Indian paintbrush. In this as in everything she'd been wrong. "Hawkweed," Ross had corrected me with curled lip. I had to sentimentalize everything, didn't I, but he knew the shabby truth. And there was no point in replying that my mother had taught me wrong because she didn't know right, and because she was determined to deliver me into an entirely beautiful world. I had to start from the beginning, learn everything over again.

"HONESTLY, SYLVIE, I have *never* been so frightened as when that bull started charging, it was just like Pamplona!" Ma was saying as we turned up the driveway at home. She had not of course been to Pamplona but *I* must see it, and Paris, and fame, fortune, love with a capital *L*, and *all* the splendors of which she (who had so richly deserved them) had been deprived.

"It didn't charge . . . and we don't even know it was a bull," I said, but no one heard me. The house stood there forlorn, the paint not even peeling, just worn away, the screen door with its broken gingerbread, one window still boarded where the tree broke it three years ago, and books piled in a high jumble against another window so you knew no one ever opened it. Seeing this, you could tell there would be no freedom in this divorce, that my parents were bound not by marriage but by psychic disability.

The willow trees seemed to be pouring golden light into the brook, and my eyes stung with tears to think this had all been mine. I went up the front steps in a daze, as if I were going to meet a lover, but as I set my hand on the door Sylvie called out:

"You can't get in that way. It's stuck!" And indeed, the door hit some obstacle an inch or two in and wouldn't budge further. Teddy looked at me as if I'd just tried to walk through a wall, and Ma shook her head.

"I'd nearly forgotten there was a door there," she said, laughing. A low yowling set up overhead: a gray cat, not one I recognized, was glowering down over the gutter at me.

"It's *this* way," Teddy said self-importantly, a child playing grown-up. A child whose curls have been daily tousled, whose innocent observations have been repeated as bons mots, whose mother has breathlessly attended, for eight years, every movement of his face. A child like me.

"This is our goldfish pond," he said, acting as tour guide, pointing to the cracked cement pool where I'd tried to keep a goldfish years ago. The water had leaked out and with it the fish: I found the poor thing gasping, wedged in a crevice, the next morning. We went around to the back.

"And that's the factory."

The ping-pong balls—striped as novelties, yellow and orange, or red, white, and blue—were set out in the sun to dry like produce in a village market. Teddy gave one tray a knowing shake.

"They need turning every few hours or they fade," he explained. "Now, there's the brook."

"I used to live here myself, you know," I said finally, but he seemed skeptical. He'd been four when I left for Sweetriver and I was a kind of ancestor to him, more legend than reality.

"There's a tear in the pen," he said, stepping over a chicken to let me in the kitchen door. It was the same tear the chickens made use of when I was a child. The room was nearly empty and there was dust as thick as carpet where the sideboard had stood, grease stains furred with dust dripped down the wall by the stove, as if some awful truth of our lives was bubbling out from where we'd kept it hidden so long. Hope abandoned, a resignation to dirt, which, like failure, age, death, would creep over us, whether or not we fought it.

Walking into the living room with the late afternoon light slanting in felt like entering a chapel. They'd forgotten about the possibility of furniture; the piano was alone on the old blue carpet, an object of defiance like a boulder in the sea. My father's globe—the last thing from that solid place where Ma had fallen in love years ago—stood there, along with a papier-mâché sculpture Teddy had made in school. A leak along the west wall had peeled the paint off in strips and crumbled away the plaster so that insulation fell out between the laths, and the wide floorboards had warped and buckled, jamming the front door shut.

Ma had given up her piano lessons due to a foreboding about the instructor, who had not been sufficiently outraged about her job loss, and to Pop's sneering at her aspirations, which reminded her of Ivan the Terrible. She sank onto the bench now and rested her head on her arms, and Sylvie sat beside her, stroking her head.

"It's going to be okay," she said. "Really, Ma," but Ma shook her head, and, unable to speak, resorted to pageantry, folding up the piano cover and starting to play: "Lara's Theme." Lush, doomy romanticism filled the room, the house, the world—it was Ma's sense of the tragic ruin of her life, a sense she carried with her and could inflate fully in an instant, like an air mattress, except that this felt more like a full-scale replica of the cathedral in Red Square, onion domes and all.

"Why is she doing that?" I asked.

"She does it all the time," Sylvie said.

"It's deafening,"

"I think that's what she likes about it. Anyway it's kind of a step up from 'Danny Boy,' and beside that, Chopin's 'Funeral March' is the only other thing she knows." We ran up the stairs to escape the visions of lovers torn from one another's arms, and ragged children scavenging in the snow.

"You can have my bed," Sylvie said. "I've moved out, did Ma tell you?" She looked sweet and tender and very shy, the way she had when Pop had put the new lamb in her arms so long ago. "I'm . . . I . . . 'member Butchy Savione?"

"Sure," I said, thinking of him hunched into his jacket, shouldering his way to the back of the school bus on a cold morning. I remembered Donna saying their dad "went too hard" on him—

until one night when Butch hit him back, with a baseball bat.

Sylvie smiled joyfully. "Butch has his own place now and I moved in last week."

"Sylvie . . ." I said. "Are you . . . ?" She was sixteen years old. I'd never seen anyone give so much affection, or long for so much affection, as she did, with her broken-winged birds and orphaned rabbits and hangdog boys. The piano got louder—Pop and Dolly had just turned into the driveway.

"Where?" I asked, hoping I sounded happy for her.

"Back of the ball field, in the valley. I mean, it's a trailer—but, he *loves* me, Bea." She said these magic words in a fervent whisper as if afraid they'd evaporate with the breath she spoke them on. Downstairs the music swelled—old women were breaking up their heirlooms for firewood; the enemy marched through the frozen streets.

"We're home!" my father called in a parody of cheer.

Ma kept playing. Pop knew, as I did not, that "Lara's Theme" was also my mother's theme for her motorcyclist, who lived behind the movie theater, where she had gone to see *Dr. Zhivago* for seven consecutive days, hoping she might bump into him. Night after night, she sat alone, her eyes, ears, heart filling with music and color and feeling, all of which she attributed to this boy, instead of to Boris Pasternak or David Lean. And later, by flashlight, she wrote letters confessing her passion and trying to explain why it seemed such a wonderful, vital thing, though she knew it must be wrong.

She had not, of course, sent these letters. If she had they'd never have reached the man they were truly intended for, the man whose love had proved such thin shelter from a world of Muscovite cold: my father, who discovered them in her lingerie drawer only slightly less promptly than if they'd come in the mail.

She'd thought he'd be filled with remorse—how could he have let her live in such poverty of feeling, for so long? His heart would sweep open, spilling tenderness.

But no, he'd been crushed and appalled.

" 'WHEN YOU looked in my eyes I felt as if something wonderful was pouring out of you into me'?"

Pop sat at the end of Sylvie's old bed, trying to give us his side of the story, quoting one of Ma's letters with incredulity. "That she could write such a thing, to a boy, her own student." His voice was thin with grief and he repeated the words again and again as if hoping to dull them, as the music went on downstairs. She was playing with increasing violence, maybe hoping the music would change something. Her energy could have powered a mill, lit a city, defended a nation—but it was devoted to this, the larger-than-life-size model of her inner world, created to help us understand her. Did she need to play louder? All was lost, nobody loved her. She would live all her days in all the raging woe of a motherless child. The music reverberated through the whole empty, echoing house.

". . . that something wonderful was pouring out of *him into her!*" Pop said, and I thought how beautiful and right the phrase must have sounded, when she wrote it, and how it must cut Pop to the quick, though the more he repeated it the more ridiculous it rang. "This *boy!* I can't, I can't cope."

Dolly sat beside him, her arm over his shoulders, her face a pale mask of disapproval. Born into the world we'd made, she'd had to grow to fit into the odd bits of space that were left to her; we'd have crowded her out of existence if she hadn't been so prickly. She refused to live, like the rest of us, according to Ma's caprice. Looking for an alternate canon, she tried every rule she saw. She would be consistent, grave, cautious, she would speak no evil, she would do unto others, she would honor her father and mother, somehow. She was right, we were wrong. Wrong, silly, and false, but she would love us in spite of ourselves. And admire us, in spite of herself—how we shimmered, in our silly falsity!

"Ma doesn't know what she's doing," Dolly said grimly, and downstairs I heard her charge through a couple of weird chords toward the familiar refrain—that bloody torrent depicting a ghastly war. The worst consequence of war, of course, being the loss of safety, dignity, love. The wandering alone, longing to touch the stream of one's own life again where it flows through another being. It was impossible to listen without grieving.

Though there was no war, no cruel dictator, no great sweep of history at fault: we were hoist by our own petard. My mother was playing, for her husband, the music of her passionate lacklove, her anguished need. A need, like the leak in the roof that he had neglected until the door was jammed shut, the house beyond repair.

"My *children*," Pop said, as if he was standing over our lifeless bodies. "To lose my children . . ."

"Listen, you two can work this out," I said, feeling a dart from Dolly's direction.

"What would you do if you found a letter like this?" he asked. "A letter to another man?"

"He's hardly a *man*," I started, but of course this was the wrong tack. "She didn't *send* it," I tried. "If you found it, she couldn't have sent it."

"She *felt* it, honey. I guess that's what's important. She felt it," he said, with certainty as if he'd set his foot down on something solid and could catch his breath.

"She hurt his feelings," Dolly said plaintively. She hadn't fallen in love yet—she couldn't know.

"That happens," I said, and saw her mind snap shut. Everyone knew how coldhearted and ambitious *I* was. We heard a car coming down the dirt road, a sound so rare there that we used to dive behind the stone wall when we heard it, as if it might be the phantom of the world outside, come to steal us away.

Sylvie jumped up. "That's Butch," she said, "I've gotta go."

I followed as she ran down the stairs. Ma stopped playing and held her prayerfully for a minute, in a silence that felt like a fresh cold breeze, blowing the heavy music away. As soon as we walked out the door, she started again.

"You see what it's like," Sylvie said. "I had to get out of there." Butch was there in his little pickup, with a tough, defiant look on his face as if for him a smile was a sign of defeat. Or as if he was afraid I'd keep Sylvie from leaving. A little beige dog was sitting up front beside him like a good schoolgirl, and it leapt into Sylvie's arms as soon as she opened the door.

"Look," she said laughing, "this is Springtime! We found her in a dumpster!" She slid in beside Butch, with the dog wrapped tight in her arms. She wanted me to see this tableau, to show me that she was safe, and loved. They drove away under the thick, flickering masses of the June maples, the beauty that belied everything in our hearts.

"She'd have slept with him anyway. This way she doesn't have to lie." Ma missed a few beats explaining this, but turned the page and kept playing, so I couldn't point out to her that it's hell enough to struggle apart from a man when you're grown up and don't live with him, but when you're sixteen, and you don't have anywhere else to go . . .

As we got ready for bed, Dolly picked up my wheel of birth control pills and asked what they were. When I told her, she said: "So you'll never—you can't have a baby?" There was a shiver in her voice, a sense that I, having gone away, had betrayed them, had *become* the phantom of the world outside. She sat there with her Raggedy Ann doll on her lap as if it was her own child.

"Don't be silly," I said. "Of course not. Just not right now."

I'd been taking them since that day Ma sent me to the doctor and had nearly forgotten why. Now I supposed I could stop. Though Philippa took them, for the estrogen, she said. We'd stood grouchily at the sink together in the morning, swilling them down like a couple of cowboys in a saloon. Thinking of this, I felt how alone I was, suddenly—it was as if the wall beside me had fallen away.

We'd had canned mushroom soup for supper, because it was all we could find in the cupboard. Then Dolly had reached way in back and pulled out a jar of blackberry jam with a square of gingham over it.

"I remember the day we made that," I said. It had been much too hot but we'd been happy for some reason, ready to undertake something. Teddy was maybe three, hands and face stained purple and scratched all over from bumbling into the thorns. He rode on Ma's hip as Ma stirred the jam. I sterilized the jars and now was melting paraffin in the battered old pot we used, and Dolly cut the gingham. It was the life my parents had intended; we were managing it here, for a minute distilling the essence of goodness together and preserving it against the sorrows to come.

"Do you think it's still good?" Dolly was a nervous eater, she even hated things with raisins because they made her think of bugs.

"Probably," I said, but I didn't want to open it and be proven wrong. I wanted to save it so I could keep believing in it.

"I'll just have some yogurt, if there is any," I'd said, and Ma and Dolly had turned to me with the same shadow of suspicion on their faces. Was I turning into a person who liked yogurt? Because Ma didn't, which meant that by eating it, I would defy her, step outside the circle of her magic, and become ordinary, Midwestern, Republican, Nazi—who knew where it would stop? Seeing how things were going, Ma (who *did not* care about possessions) had gone back to the piano, while Pop threw his things helter-skelter into the back of the truck. After the temporary custody hearing the next day, we had to be out of the house for good. Ma had rented another one in town—old Mrs. Shipman, the cat-lady's place. Pop was just planning to get in the truck and drive as far as he could. Neither of them had invited me.

ALL NIGHT I listened to my parents berate each other in the next room, like a prisoner eavesdropping on a torture. The words were indistinct but the tones—of pleading, of the lash, and the cold hatred, sharp sobs and cruel silences—froze my blood. They couldn't pull apart without desecrating all the hopes and beliefs they'd used to share. Finally a barren silence fell and I could hear something running back and forth inside the walls. Only two weeks ago I'd been holding back the sweet viburnum branches so Philippa could stuff steel wool into the chinks of the foundations of her house, against mice. Then she'd settled back into her chair to read the Marquis de Sade.

IN THE morning, my parents took Teddy and Dolly, both cars, and all the tension and misery in the house with them to the County Courthouse. Sylvie and I were to spend the day packing, and waiting for Butch to deliver her, I sat on the back steps with my coffee cup, closed my eyes, and almost felt my mother's presence as I had years ago. The sun sparkled on the brook and she was the person she wanted to be, gentle and content: if you spilled something she wiped it up without thinking and absently kissed the top of your head. She brushed the grass back and forth in hopes of finding the four-leafed clover that would save her, make her gentle and content always. Where was it? Where?

"WHAT'S NUREMBERG?" Dolly asked me that night.

"A city in Germany," I told her. "Why?"

"The judge said we might have to have the next hearing there."

"He did?"

Dolly nodded gravely, and I looked at my father, who shook his head.

"He told your mother that accusations such as she makes against me are generally tried in Nuremberg," he explained. "Nice guy, the judge. Witty. In over his head."

The judge had asked Dolly her preference, and she'd chosen Pop.

"Well, he had to have *some*body," Dolly had said, setting her jaw. "Otherwise it's not fair." Teddy was to stay with Ma, and Pop was to pay her a thousand a month.

"*I* give *her* money?" he asked. "She's the one who has a teaching certificate. Anyway, she can live on the wonderful thing that pours out of his eyes." He—he and Dolly—were going west, where people laughed at things like child-support laws. He'd built a fire in the fireplace and was pulling out sheaves of old papers—the kind you save because you can't quite throw them away, though you can't quite bear to look at them again either—to burn. Ma, of course, was at the piano, and the music was aimed at Dolly now.

When the phone rang she kept on playing.

"It's not for me," Pop said, staying by the fire. Dolly looked from one to the other, and drew herself up, above their childishness, and went to answer it.

"It's for you," she said to my mother.

Ma turned a cold, blind gaze on her and kept playing. Dolly's existence had become too painful for her to acknowledge. It reminded me of what had happened after Forsythia died—I'd done something that tore through Ma's warmth into the black emptiness beneath, and she couldn't look at me anymore. I expected Dolly to crumple, though I remembered that I'd refused to. I'd drawn myself in and kept stonily apart, watching for the moment when I could get away. Dolly held the phone out stubbornly, two red circles blazing up in her cheeks, repeating: "It's for you."

"Ma," I said, over my shoulder. "Answer the phone."

She got up and went over to take it, saying "Hello?" and then an immediate soft "Hi. Oh, hi." One syllable. We knew then who it was. Pop stared into the fire, mesmerizing himself, and we all listened, as we used to listen from our beds for the sound of her voice in the morning.

"I can't . . ." she said. ". . . No, I . . . no . . . no . . . yes of course but . . . well . . . maybe . . . I can try, but . . . *you know I can't talk now.*" She listened a minute and her tone changed, the authority sifted out of it and she sounded jealous and wary. "Who's that?" Then calmer . . . "Oh, oh, I see . . . I'm sorry, all right . . ." To hear the longing in her voice, the anxious wish to please him, was like coming over a rise in the road and seeing the house in flames.

My father's globe still stood on the piano. It was fragile and he intended to take it in the front of the truck with him when he left. The world it showed no longer existed, of course, but the thing itself was handsome and solid, and I closed my eyes, touched it, and spun it around, feeling Ceylon and Abyssinia and Saint Petersburg pass smoothly by. Elephants, parapets, cinnamon, silk! Of course the minute television got inside them, they turned out to be Sri Lanka and Ethiopia and Leningrad, full of famine and pestilence and war. When I opened my eyes, I saw my finger was resting on—entirely covering—the New England states, and considered that I must be fated to stay close to home.

"No, it's *not* that," Ma said into the phone, "it's *not that at all*." She was trying to tell him something without letting us know, something that was going to change the course of our lives. I couldn't help thinking that this Larry had a place to live, even if it was only a wretched converted garage, and he had a motorcycle, and parents, and now our mother too.

"I will, I'll try," she said, hanging up.

"A student," she explained to us and sat back at the piano without playing. All that time I'd been wishing she'd stop, I hadn't realized that the music was like a wild sea swirling over a terrible arid expanse. Now I shuddered at the silence.

"Go ahead, Ma, you can play," I said, but she stood up suddenly, stepped over the heave in the floor, and went toward the kitchen as if she meant to go out the back door. Then came back and sat down again.

Then up, saying: "I'm going out," defiant as a teenager, so that I felt like a mean, straitlaced mother for wanting to restrain her.

"Can I come?" Teddy asked.

"No!"

"I never get to go with you, it's not fair," he said. "Pop wouldn't take me to the dump yesterday, he wouldn't take me for a ride in the truck, and it's not even a school night . . ." He looked around at us—he knew we weren't taking him with us into the heart of the story.

"Hey, they took you to court today and *I* had to stay home," I teased, and reached to swing him up onto my lap, but he twisted away.

"They didn't take me in with the judge! I had to go with the lady!" he cried, stamping his feet, but glancing over at me in fear and bewilderment to see if he was wrong. I looked back at him with a guilty bewilderment of my own. I'd joined the adults and betrayed him, acting as if the custody hearing was a family outing, as if his intuitions were all wrong. He peered into my face, weighing what I'd said against his own feeling.

"It's a terrible day, honey," I admitted. "I know it. We just have to bear it, and work hard to keep calm."

"*You're* not the mother!" he said. Startled by the truth this touched on, we all drew back for a minute and Teddy rushed on into his hysteria.

"You can't go, I'm not letting you go," he said, grabbing Ma's shirt and pulling at it as if he could physically stop her. He'd have done the same thing if she'd been going out for milk, but, for once, it was fitting. I felt his panic rise in myself too.

"Stop it!" I said, taking him by the shoulders. "Stop it right now, do you hear me?" I looked into his face with cold fury, thinking that really it was my mother who ought to stop it, that it was cowardly of me to be yelling at Teddy instead of her.

"*Stop* pulling at me! Let go!" Ma swatted at Teddy as if he were a bat that was clinging to her clothes. "*Let me go!*"

He let go, and stood there roaring, "I hate you, *I hate you*, you take me with you or I'm going to . . ." He stopped, teeth gritted, eyes wild. What recourse was there? "I'm going to hit my head, hit my head," he screamed, slapping at his head with the flat of his hands.

Pop, still on his knees at the fireplace, bent into himself suddenly, silently, like a monk in flames. "I can't do this, I can't do this," he wept.

"No, you can't do anything, can you? You never could," Ma said with cold, final contempt, while Dolly knelt to comfort him, looking up at her with venom.

"That's right, take care of *him*," Ma said to her. "Did he ever take care of you? Did he think one *minute* of your well-being? Do you really imagine he wants to have you with him, except maybe because it hurts me? '*Oh, my children, my children,*'" she mocked. "As if he had *ever* thought of his children before! My god, he tried to *kill* me when I was carrying Beatrice. When you fell out the window, Dolly, when you were two years old, he didn't want to pay the hospital bills, he'd have let you lie there with your leg broken."

He'd probably said something like: "Her leg can't be broken." Ma made something awful of everything, after all. But then he didn't seem to hear anything until it was shouted. He was cruel in ways no one else would notice, she had to make the scars herself.

"*I* watched over you," Ma went on, quiet now because she was saying the simple truth. "I was there for you, I carried you up and down the stairs for weeks. Choose him, then, go with him, but . . ." We listened. She was artful, she was always shaping whatever happened to suit her more fully, and if she'd used that extra dimension to work her life into a play or a painting, who knew; instead, though, she lived it out. Her voice turned to acid. "Don't expect my sympathy when you realize what you've done."

This made a good finish and she sat down, but the rage welled up and pushed her to her feet again.

"*Your* children?" she said to Pop. "Your children. Well, what about my *home*? *What about my life?* What did you do with that? Look at me, all this time I was patient, I told myself you were trying your best, I thought, 'Don't stand between a man and his dream,' even though you were dreaming of *ping-pong balls!* While you gambled with everything I had, and lost. And my youth is gone and what do I have to show for it, *nothing.*" She spat the word "nothing," then repeated it tenderly, comforted by it in some deep way. "Nothing at all."

And very, very calmly, as if she'd gotten her anger out and was returning to our task, packing these last few things, preparing to leave, she picked the globe up and carried it over to the fireplace. Teddy, astonished that his tantrum had not provoked the usual response, stopped crying and kept still with the rest of us, watching her.

"Everything I loved, gone," she said, sounding portentous, nearly Shakespearean. And then: "Everything," quietly, kneeling beside Dolly, laying the globe on the fire gently as if putting a baby down for its nap.

"Claire!" Pop said, but it was too late. The globe filled with fire, glowing like a rising sun for a minute before it fell in on itself and went gray.

"WAIT!" I said. I didn't know what to say next. My reflex was to keep Ma there a few more minutes and hope the centrifugal force of family would pull her back in.

She turned, irritated, curious, and, I could see, hopeful. I was the worldly one, the one who could always put things back together, what with my brilliance and my college education. If I'd said, right then: "Sit down and stop being silly. We need to put our heads together and work things out . . ." In fact, if I'd said *any-thing* in a tone of confident authority, I might have wound back time so the world bloomed out of the fire again and my mother took it up like a baby and they reconciled over its sweet head.

But seeing the hope on her face, I only wanted to dash it. Let it happen, the thing they'd been threatening all these years, threatening each other with as if they didn't know we felt it too. Let it come, let them see the consequences of their drama. Let them live in the world they'd made.

Oh yes, I knew what I wanted to say. When you take a person who has been nurtured in a climate of total hysteria, then pour her mind full of Great Literature with its pithy phrases, you may, reader, have created a monster. I faced my dear family as I was, stuck full of all the barbs from all the years, engorged with my education, ready to speak from—yes, my heart. It was a terrible thing to see.

"There's something I feel I ought to tell you, while we're all together here." I'd spent long enough cowering in a walk-in closet with these people, fearful so Ma wouldn't be alone in fear. I was getting out, I was going to blow the door right off.

"I'm a lesbian," I announced, in a voice that sounded strangely of TV-movie-heroine. Thank you for the tour of Russia, Mother, and the side trip to Pamplona. Now for the Greek Isles—there she is now, fair Sappho at her lyre.

The room went, finally, silent. Ruin, betrayal, heartbreak, divorce, poverty, despair—and one globe in flames—were forgotten, and all faces turned to me.

"I've *always* known it," I continued, trembling, fervent (every one of my mother's inflections was turning out to be useful). "*Now I see*—but it's only just come clear to me. I'm in love with a woman, I love her body, I *love making* love to her, and I'm not ashamed to say it. I'm *proud* to be a lesbian."

Dolly was looking very confused and Teddy had started repeating his times tables, but I had, for once, my parents' full attention. Philippa barged into my thoughts, gesticulating wildly in an effort to quiet me, but I showed her the door. I *did* love and want her, I did . . . and coincidentally, I wanted to slice my parents up with the very sharpest thing I could find.

I might have asked: *How can you have lied so, all your lives—pretending you knew what you were doing when really you were utterly lost, pretending you watched over your children when your children were watching over you?* But this was ever so much more deadly. It said: *You don't know me, in fact you don't know anything. If you're disap-*

*pointed because I love a woman, well then, you're a small-minded prig,
probably a racist, maybe even a Republican.* And: *Do you really think
that anyone who saw* your *example would be interested in heterosexual
love?*

I watched them like an assassin, to be sure my knife had struck
the vein. After a few beats—our family equivalent of a long
silence—my mother said in her voice of absolute loving toler-
ance, under which lay the same sentimentality I'd just put to use
myself:

"I believe that love comes to each of us in his own way. How
can there be such a thing as a 'bad' love?" (This a subject she felt
quite strongly about of late.) "No—and even if so, I would *never*
try to dictate my own children's choices . . ." Shooting that look
that meant: *"Unlike Herr Goebbels over there."*

"We'll support you in whatever you do, honey, of course," he
said, very quickly so he wouldn't have to think about it anymore.
No, I thought, it didn't matter whether I was hetero or homosex-
ual, whether I moved to Rome or Detroit, pursued a career as a
prostitute or a judge—as long as he didn't have to see.

"Follow your heart," my mother said vaguely, and went off into
the night, in pursuit of hers. Teddy sat stunned like the rest of us,
watching her go.

"We'd better get to bed," Dolly said, as Ma's headlights swept
over the room. "We've got to get up tomorrow."

Pop broke the fire up with the poker—trying to avoid looking
at me, I thought—and the three of them went upstairs quietly,
huddled together. I gave them the creeps. But then, I always had.
I'd hurt them by going to school, by liking my teachers. When I
asked for that yogurt, Ma just knew I was implying that some
other, yogurt-eating person was better than she. But I needed to
eat yogurt, lots of it, to keep up my strength, because every day
there was the quiet pressure—Did I really like school so much

that I wouldn't rather be home with my family? Did I really want to play with those children whose parents no doubt detested Ma, maybe almost as badly as she did them? What if I became like them, what if I broke the magnetic field around our family, and escaped?

But no simple friendship was going to accomplish such a feat—to do that, to really go beyond them, I needed a much more dangerous force; I needed to fall in love.

Sylvie had gone home to the trailer—little Springtime needed his walk and she didn't like to let him out alone because Butchy's neighbor let his dogs run wild. She'd left Butchy's leather jacket hanging over the stair rail, and I picked it up and held it as if it belonged to someone I loved terribly, who had died. It was big, to cover the wide shoulders of a man whose body was grown thick from work. It smelled of leather and oil and probably Butch himself, of the strength and safety a man can offer. That man was lost from our lives but he lived in our dreams, like the lost chord.

The room was dark except for the last embers in the fireplace, and outside, Jupiter was brightening in a band of azure over the crest of the hill. I was seeing this for the last time, and it made me feel strangely light—the empty house, the ruined hopes, the disaster finally upon me. I was young, I was just beginning; if I had nowhere to go, it only meant I could go wherever I liked. I slipped Butch's jacket on with a thrill, feeling myself tall and solitary, a sailor in a new port—a man, who can move in the world, and so, turn his back on love and walk away. Ma and Sylvie yearned for that man—they were both out hunting him now. Well, I was not going to search for him, pray for him, suffer for him, like they did. I was going to become him.

Part Two

O ne

M OVING TO Hartford was *in no way* tantamount to falling off the edge of the earth. Certainly not. I'd never been there, of course. New York was our city of reference, and we had the vague feeling that the roads marked for Hartford might, while not exactly falling off the edge of the earth, lead to a void all the same. No, *we* (the overweening, familial "we") did not go to Hartford; therefore *I* (self-made, rigged up out of bits of yarn and whatever) would move there, make my way in a real place, a place ruled not by a communal fantasy, but by supply and demand. I had about six hundred dollars in the bank, or less, actually, thanks to the Nancy Kissinger shoes. And my father had done some calculations on the back of an envelope, concluding that in Hartford I could get by on a hundred a week, while in New York, I'd need a thousand.

"No more than a quarter of that for housing, of course," he'd said, very knowledgeably.

I'd felt a little spring bubble in my heart then. The advice I'd had from him before was to take smaller steps, smaller bites, speak more softly, keep from raising my hand at school—try, in other words, not to act like the appalling chimera my mother was fashioning me to become. I caused a disturbance at the edge of his mind, and he'd wanted to help me quiet down so he could bear me. But being famished, desperate to get somewhere, and terrified no one would hear me over the general cacophony, I'd been unable to obey his injunctions. I'd disappointed him, he was going away, but in spite of his troubles, he'd stopped to puzzle this out for me. This envelope with his hasty figuring proved his fatherly concern.

"FIRST AND last, and one hundred security," said my new landlord, whose English was clotted with Polish gutturals, though he'd lived in the U.S. for thirty years. His name was Frank Prysznyrsny (pronounced *Pri-sneers-nee*), and his wife Henny shadowed us as he showed me the apartment, muttering with worry and suspicion as he demonstrated the makeshift shower and slid the tiny windows up and down in their jambs. Every time he spoke English, she shook her head and gazed heavenward as if ashamed of such affectation, and when I mentioned the lack of radiators, she gave a "*pffft!*" of disgust and explained in angry sign language how to shut off the front room and move the bed in next to the stove. The place had been their attic, but Frank had painted it (floors, walls, and ceilings, with a vivid aqua enamel that I imagined he'd gotten at a very good price) and put in the bathroom and kitchenette. I was their first tenant. As Frank smoothed the lease for my signature, Henny erupted in a cascade of anxious *zh*- and *y*-filled sentences, but he shook his head and hunched his shoulders, making a duck's back against her.

"And one hundred dollar, month," he said with satisfaction. An amount that would have changed his life, if only he'd had it when he was trying to get out of Poland. And which, as it matched exactly my father's suggestion, gave me a sense of holy rightness that I would, if I'd noticed it, have rejected as superstition.

But there's not time in a life to notice so much. As soon as
Frank and Henny went away down the stairs, I twirled in the center of the kitchen, arms open and head back, just like a figure
skater. Mine, *mine*, and the floors would always be swept, I'd get a
geranium for the window, and behind the bathroom door, there
was an ironing board. It was perfect here, perfect, like the places
I'd seen out of train windows—modest and striving, with old
women gossiping in bursts of evil laughter over the hedges and
children on plastic tricycles barreling down the sidewalks—not
unlike the neighborhood on Staten Island from which my mother
had been delivered, to which she longed to return.

"Oh, I can't wait for you to see it!" I told her as soon as I got my
phone. "There are all these little *pasticcerias* and delis, and everyone has a vegetable garden in the yard . . . it's just, so . . . *real*, do
you know what I mean?"

"No," Ma said, with irritation, reminding me how rude I was to
go on like this, with her so lost and sad.

"So, how are things there?" I asked, nursily solicitous.

"Fine, Beatrice," she said caustically. "Never better. I suppose
you heard about the accident?"

"No."

"Well, your father ran over a horse."

"What?"

"He *ran over a horse*." (So she'd been right, the rabbit was just
the beginning, and now he went rampaging through state after
state, murdering innocent creatures at will.) "In the middle of the
night. Outside Terre Haute, it belonged to some poor child there."

"Is he okay?" I asked.

"He's *dead*."

"No, is Pop okay?"

"Apparently."

"And Dolly?"

There was a long pause so I could ask myself if it was really necessary to torment her by bringing up Dolly, but she decided to be magnanimous.

"The truck is a total loss," she said. "But I gather *your sister* is fine."

"*Your father*" meant "this Nazi I've had to prostitute myself with for your sake." "*Your sister*"—not good. Pop would have made a very poor Nazi; he couldn't even bear to hear a mousetrap spring. Instead he'd put a lump of cheese in a milkbottle, propped at an angle. Once the mice were in, they couldn't skitter out. Then he'd turn them out into the field, and race them back to the house. I looked down at the envelope with his calculations and saw it was stamped FINAL NOTICE. Lucky he had Dolly beside him, I thought.

"BEACHY?"

The next call was from Dolly's careful voice, caught between truculence and apology. She'd promised to keep Pop awake by talking, but she'd closed her eyes for a minute and now—oh, *if only*—of course he'd been exhausted, who wouldn't be? They'd slept in the barn the night before, they'd been driving eighteen hours, and suddenly . . .

"Oh, Beachy, its head came right through the windshield," she said. "Everything was soaked in blood. I had to throw Raggedy Ann away. I mean, she's just a doll, I know that, but . . ." She trailed off, mastered herself, went on. "But the thing is, the insurance expired. I mean, they didn't give Pop any warning, he just missed one payment, it's *not fair*, but they say they won't pay. We stayed overnight here, we're going to rent a new truck in the morning—thank God I have my college money."

If only they'd hit a deer! A deer would have been okay, but a horse? That's what happens when things get past control. Bad luck, bad timing, bad judgment, they circle around and around, wrong leading to more wrong until . . . what? I didn't want to know.

And I didn't have to, I was on my own. That first weekend, I carried home a pizza and a quart of beer and ate on the little, tilting back porch in a heat so harsh and dry, it seemed like a physical force that held even the traffic on Wethersfield Avenue still. At first the only sound was the squeaking of a pulley as the woman across the way took in her laundry—the enormous panties and tiny dresses, the undershirts and pink uniforms and, finally, two sets of canvas overalls. Then the game, Red Sox vs. whoever, came on, and from every house I heard the organ huffing, the laconic announcer ticking off the plays as evening fell. Lucky, so lucky to look over this yard where so many lives feathered into each other, to feel the breeze come up with the darkness, see the backyard vegetable gardens below fade to shapes, beans laced over a teepee of poles, cornstalks in their ranks, tomatoes heavy on their vines. A cat leapt out of a copse of oregano to clap a grasshopper in its paws.

Then, thunder, and looking west I saw a cloud light up fitfully, as if it had a loose bulb inside. I packed up and went in to unplug things when I realized I could still hear the Red Sox game; the man across the way was not going to let the storm drive him in. He was still sitting beside his radio under the eaves as the first drops began to fall. I hit the screen door open with the flat of my hand and went back onto the porch, smelling the dust as the first drops wet the ground, and also the scent of oregano: the cat must have torn the leaves.

Suddenly there was an earsplitting thunderclap and the scene was lit so starkly that a brilliant, ashen afterimage burned in my eyes. I'd never seen the way things looked when they were lit up by lightning.

I'D TOLD Frank I had a job, and I meant to get one right away, but I hadn't counted on Henny and her world of foreboding. She lurked in her kitchen, boiling pierogies, watching the street from behind the curtain as if she expected to see tanks rolling in from the west. As I locked my apartment door, I'd hear her move toward hers, to listen as I passed on the stairs, then she'd go back to the window. And as she didn't let Frank smoke in the house, he was always on the stoop with his cigarette, waiting for something to happen, someone to walk by.

So I went off every morning dressed as if I were on my way to work, and didn't return until five. I'd take the bus up Franklin, and settle into a booth at Louie's, across the street from City Hall. Even the smells there—black coffee and eggs on a grill—were reassuring. The double doors to the kitchen bubbed open and shut as waiters pushed through with trays held high, to be set clattering on the other side. Glass domes sheltered piles of muffins and crullers for the businessmen in line at the counter. I stood, blessed, among the men in their dark suits with their decisive movements and great energy. Men going to work, going to make a difference in the world.

Soon, I'd be one of them. I'd bought a red pen to mark the ads I might respond to, and I had twenty résumés on vellum in a special folder. From the wooden phone booth at the back of the room I could dial prospective employers, and in the pink formica ladies' room I fixed myself in the mirror with the expression my mother used to meet the world—perfect moxie, a challenge:

"Strike one spark here and what a blaze you'll see." I was looking for work in the same superheated way I'd looked for love; I expected to stumble through some job opening into another life. If I didn't harness my genetic predisposition to hysteria and put it to some professional use, I was afraid I'd find myself playing "The March of the Toreadors" the way Ma played "Lara's Theme." I had to escape myself, to join the rest of the world.

The man at the next table was drinking black coffee, which proved that strong and able people did not need cream, and I would reveal my foolish weakness by asking for it. I drank. How bitter it was, but it was what real people liked.

Now the man folded his newspaper in quarters; again, I followed suit, going through job titles—financial assistant, payroll analyst, operations associate, systems coordinator, provider specialist—perhaps more black coffee would clear my head, because I felt like I was reading another language.

If I'd turned from the classified section to the front page, I might have noticed that unemployment was at a record high. If my father had known the things he'd pretended to, he might have mentioned that I'd have a hard time finding work, with few qualifications and no experience. If I'd had any experience, I might have realized the city of Hartford was dying. I had only ignorance to shield me, but thank heaven it was a very thick and impenetrable ignorance.

It was eight o'clock—time to cross the street and make my first application. I trembled, fishing out my quarters at the cash register. I was taking too long at it; real people had their change ready or threw a few dollars on the counter and went their way. There were two men behind me, with jobs to get to. The cashier counted the coins I'd dumped into his hand and returned two nickels, squinting at me with irritation. He knew I was an impostor.

The City Hall personnel office had me fill out a form and take a standardized test: my two best skills. There were sharpened pencils, little round circles to be carefully blackened in, a monitor who tap-tapped purposefully around the room, and who explained, once we'd finished, that the tests would be scored the very minute they lifted the hiring freeze.

So, on to the Gold Building, fifty stories high, its windows mirrored in gold instead of the common silver so it could be touted by the Chamber of Commerce as "the centerpiece of the Hartford Renaissance." The elevator went up along the front of the building so you could look out over the brave little city with its puffed-out chest and boarded-up storefronts, across the river which had none of the legendary might of rivers and just flowed humbly along as if it understood it wasn't needed anymore. On the thirty-seventh floor a pale man with small glasses and gray teeth shook his head in sympathy as he read my résumé over.

"Oscar Wilde and the Flowering of Decadence in the Fin-de-Siècle," he read. "What an interesting subject." I was afraid he was going to pat my hand, so sadly did he peer at me. "Not terribly helpful in the financial services industry, though. Do you follow the stock market?"

"No," I said, feeling very small. No doubt I was supposed to thank him and go, but I couldn't quite get myself to move. I looked over at him with what must have been naked avarice, because he said suddenly "Here, have one of our pens."

Having got me to stand up, he took pity.

"Have you thought of word processing? That would be the thing, I think, for someone of your background." Now he was cheerful, buoyant, even, jumping up to shake my hand. "Word processing. It's a coming field, just the thing for you."

To apply as a cocktail waitress, I wore the push-up bra Philippa had favored and the lowest-cut sweater I could find—in the mirror I saw the quintessential tough chick with a heart of gold. I'd move with quick grace between the tables, offering a smile to the regulars, who would love and confide in me, take comfort in the sight of me. When I tried this smile on the manager of The Inner Sanctum, a long, low place with flocked red velvet walls and an undulant bar, he looked into my eyes to see if my pupils were dilated. "I'll give you a call," he said, looking over my shoulder out the door.

At *The Courant*, though, I could see I really had a chance. The arts editor was so tweedy, even his beard seemed to be flecked, and his office smelled like Sweetriver: his pipe and the old books piled on the radiator. I was wearing a very tight shirt (I'd noticed that people paid better attention to me when I wore tight shirts), and I sank into the chair across from him, feeling as if I'd finally come home.

"It's been so long since I had anyone to *talk* to!" I said, giddily confiding my take on Wilde and the fin de siècle, humbly acknowledging my want of luridness, explaining that I thought the English language in general did not allow for the same lushness of decadence as French. When he checked his watch I talked faster, trying to squeeze everything in, saying how even though I'd never studied Shakespeare, I'd nearly memorized *Lolita* and *Portnoy's Complaint*. How I missed Philippa, missed the person I was when I was with her. Bubbling on, I felt I'd almost regained myself, but just as I was quoting Saul Bellow on Sweetriver girls—"Cold sweets won't spread"—I felt myself being helped into my coat.

I was not, apparently, "seasoned as a reporter" yet.

It was fate, I told myself, that was all. Really, public relations was the field for me, and had I been hired at *The Courant*, I'd never have seen the ad for an administrative assistant at Wings to Fly promotions. About public relations I knew only one thing: that my mother, for whom private relations had been so troublesome, held this profession in her highest regard. She pronounced the words "public relations" with portentous reverence, as: "*He's* in *public relations.*" So I had come to associate this profession with men who swashbuckled across continents with great long strides—the kind of man I was trying to become.

Just by saying the words "public relations," I seemed to become slightly more substantial, and as I walked down Belfry Street, the last cobbled street in the city, toward Wings to Fly, I knew I was going home. The brownstones with their carved lintels and leaded windowpanes, the gas street lamps fitted with electric bulbs—any minute I'd see Emma Bovary drawn by on her way to an assignation.

Yes, Wings to Fly was solid, it was real. I entered through the beveled glass door and smiled at the receptionist, who told me someone would be with me shortly. An hour or so later, a tall, slender man with a halo of silver curls came whizzing through the revolving door and fixed on me like a hawk on a vole.

"Why do you think you're the best person for this job?" he asked.

It was right out of a movie, so I knew what to say: "Because I'm smart and I'm a hard worker, and willing to learn the business from the bottom up," I snapped out, quick as a quiz-show contestant.

He blinked. "Oh, all right," he said, looking confused. "I'll be in touch." Then he turned his head and whispered "maybe," quickly, guarding himself against cosmic retribution, and disappeared up a flight of stairs. I reeled away into the dizzying heat outside.

Dizzying heat, dizzying hunger: as my money ran down, I'd stopped eating at Louie's, then I'd virtually stopped eating. I had a can of tuna, a few pieces of toast, and some celery every day: less than two dollars' worth of food, so I could count the gnawing in my gut as proof I was saving money, living within my one-hundred-a-week means.

The sun blazed down on me, and I found myself singing—the way people whistle through a graveyard. "I was a stranger in the city." There, a song about a person adrift, unconnected, who "viewed the morning with alarm . . . When suddenly, I saw you there." One was alone, confused, hungry, and then there was love, and everything was all right again. How beautiful—how transitory—loneliness seems in movies, with sad music in the background and the camera watching over every scene. The way Philippa used to watch over me.

A man and a woman walked past without seeing me, to examine a menu card in a restaurant window. I felt like I was watching them through glass—they were part of the world I'd meant to join, with its clear definitions and well-marked pathways, its long menus of delicious offerings.

"She-crab soup?" he asked.

"No, got to be gazpacho, on a day like this," the woman said, turning away. Her fingernails were pink as shells, her hair lay smooth at her collar; she was not wondering what was wrong with her, that she wanted gazpacho when the menu offered she-crab; she did not assume her date (*date*; a word from the language of her world, wherein men and women innocently, easily, took up relations with each other, as in, "I have a date tonight," then easily separated, as in "we decided to break up," freed in this way from swimming the ocean of glue I recognized as love) would discern, in her wish for gazpacho, a hidden shame that would instantly repulse him.

"Gazpacho it is," he said, and they went looking for gazpacho, and I went back to the air-conditioned lobby of the Gold Building and did what lost people have to: called my mother.

"Hello?" I seemed to hear her desperation in the one word. Which might have been exactly why I'd called her, as now I'd have to act self-possessed and might actually believe myself, if I was convincing enough.

"Hi!" I said, "How are you?" But when she heard my voice, hers turned to dry ice: so cold it burned.

"Hello, Beatrice," she said, with a very small, ironic laugh. I wracked my mind, trying to imagine what I'd done, but decided I was being silly.

"How are things going?" I asked. "Kind of rough, huh?"

She laughed again—no end to the indignity. "You have to ask?" she said. "But obviously you do, so let me tell you: I have no home and no job, a little child who needs me, whom I can hardly afford to feed. My life is *over*—I gave it away to a man who abandoned me, children who didn't love me. But thank you, Beatrice, for your concern."

"Ma," I said, in the most consoling voice I could manage, "it's *not* over, it's not. You can trust me, I *know* things are going to get better for you—for all of us." I heard a soft power in my cadences and began to feel what I was saying—as if there were a very strong and capable person in me, someone the terrified, disintegrated version of myself could rely on.

"Unlike *your father*," she said, "*I* have no one to take care of me. For instance, when I go out for groceries, I *walk*. It's two miles each way to the Grand Union. I do not have a car to wreck, but no one has thought to rent a car for *me*."

"Did someone rent a car for Pop?"

"*Your sister!*" she said, with a stricken, if triumphant, cry. "She gave *him* money to rent a *second* truck when I don't even have a bicycle, when I—" She gave a stifled little cry and I could see her pressing her knuckles into her mouth to keep from embarrassing herself.

"Ma, they were stuck on the highway. They couldn't just—"

"*They abandoned me,*" she roared. "And apparently you knew all along that she was funding this trip with her savings? What else do you know?"

There was a long silence, while she tried for self-mastery, or maybe for the perfect poisoned dart to blow at me. I was nearly relieved when I heard the click that meant she'd hung up on me. I knew what I had to do now, it was clear.

I had one dime, one hope left—NOW HIRING WORD PROCESSORS; ALL LEVELS. 555-3027.

"I'm a terrible typist," I told the woman who answered. There was something knowing in my voice, I thought, something quite authoritative. "That's why I thought, with my background in English literature, that something in the word processing field would be—"

So of course she hung up on me too.

Two

A TIDE of vertigo swirled over me. I'd probably have fainted, but the image of hundreds of insurance executives stepping over me on their way out for happy hour acted as a whiff of smelling salts might have, in the age I *ought* to have fainted in—Victorian. Instead I touched my forehead to the cool glass wall of the phone booth, closed my eyes, and waited for inspiration. Unfortunately the vision that rose in splendor before me was a cheeseburger. I'd stopped carrying money, lest I be tempted to spend it, but I had a bus token in my pocket, and I pressed it tight into my fist, standing at the stop as if the curb was a precipice that dropped off into empty space, thinking: *Home, take me home.*

And thought not of the old house, the fields worn threadbare over the granite beneath, the moths under the porchlight, but my matchbox apartment, tiny and perfect, a Fabergé egg upholstered in turquoise—my own. The bus came toward me like a big, friendly animal, the doors hissed open, I ascended, I was safe.

Frank was there as I walked up the street. He was leaning against the house, starting his next cigarette as he ground the last under his heel, but when he caught sight of me, he took a step forward into the sunlight and cleared his throat with a rich, complex cough.

"You got a job, Bee-trrrus?" he asked, "or you looking for job?"
I was taller than Frank, but he was standing on the top step, and
this, along with his smoker's throat and his thick foreign tongue,
gave his question a terrible gravity.

"Looking," I admitted, sure he'd evict me, half expecting him
to hit me. What would happen to my mother if I didn't find work
and she couldn't steady herself against my example? She'd slip
over the brink she had teetered on all her life. And take Teddy
with her, and—

"It won't be more than another week," I began, assuming that
he too saw each week as a fresh hundred-dollar bill.

"I can get you job," he said.

I dared look up at him. His face was the kind you see in old pictures, of a grocer in the doorway of his shop—there was pride
there and worry, sadness, resignation—compared to it, the face of
the woman who wanted gazpacho might have been a carnival
mask. He was concerned for me, and he wanted to help.

It was a job at the hospital, where he'd worked until he retired.
It paid well, there were good benefits and regular hours. I promised to meet him in the driveway, at 5:30 A.M. the next day, and
went upstairs to eat, in celebration—four slices of bread and butter and an entire bag of carrots—all the food I had.

There he was in the morning, cleanshaven and wearing a hat,
an old man's hat that was there only to be removed as a sign of
respect. He held the car door for me and waited while I settled
myself, with the awkward formality of a man on a blind date, and
as we drove across the sleeping city, he told me about Poland, the
war, and how he'd returned to Warsaw forty years later to find that
everything he knew was gone. He spoke the way brokenhearted
people do, as if life's purpose is to make peace with despair and
carry on.

We arrived at St. Gerasimus Hospital, and went immediately to the sub-basement, to the Dietary Department, a vast, chromed Tartarus where a conveyor belt snaked among steaming vats tended by small, dark, uniformed women. Hat in hand, Frank presented me to the shift supervisor. "I'll vouch for her," he said, with a catch in his voice that sounded like pride.

"Six A.M. sharp and wearing a hairnet and pantyhose," she snapped, and the thing was arranged.

Besides these items, I bought every single thing I'd ever wished for while musing amongst the liquefied celery in the refrigerator back at home: American cheese in thick perfect slices; pickled herring; peaches that glowed as if they each had a candle inside; a bag of caramels; a little brown chicken that had been turning on a spit. And a measuring cup (ours at home had fallen behind the stove, after which Ma disdained measuring cups, timid conventional people with their pathetic dependence on measuring cups, and rigid fascist types who were too good for a soggy muffin or a block of solid oatmeal), and . . . a soap dish! I could hear triumphant music swelling as I set *my* bar of soap on the raised ridges of *my* soap dish.

The phone rang so promptly that I tried picking up the soap again to see if that would stop it, but no.

"Great news," Ma said. "I've got a job!"

"Ma," I said, "guess what? Me too! See, I told you we were going to be fine, I *told* you! So, where are you working? The nursing home?" There was always a shortage of aides there and she'd mentioned it as a place she might try.

"No, not the nursing home, Beatrice," she said, aggrieved. "A *teaching* job. I'm a *teacher*, remember?"

"Of course, but—"

"Well, Silber Country Day is creating a new position, just for me! Just *right* for me! English and humanities, for seventh and eighth grade."

"They called you up?"

"No, I saw Sarah Randolph at the post office and she told me."

"And you called them up?"

"Well, not yet, I wanted to tell you first."

"Is Sarah Randolph doing the hiring?"

"Well, I'm not sure," she said, "but it's clear I'm the right person, and you know how much Sarah likes me. It's the trustees who really matter in these decisions . . . believe me, that's where the real power always lies."

"It's not exactly a bird in hand, Ma."

"*Well,*" she said, "if there was one person I didn't think would pour cold water on me, it was you, but I see I was wrong."

"I'm not pouring cold water, Ma, it's just—"

"Just what? Just that you don't think I can do it! You just snap your fingers and there everything is for *you,* but why would anyone want to hire *me*? Of all people, I thought you'd be glad for me."

"I *am* glad!" I said. "I just don't know exactly what to be glad about."

"Oh, no, you're just like your father, you think I'm exaggerating, you never believe me. It's one thing for you to have a degree, and a career." (I could hear her slashing at herself with the word "career." When she was young, careers had been for women who'd failed at love. She'd wondered what was wrong with her, poured her overweening ambitions into her children where they'd belonged, and when she looked up, motherhood was passé and she was unemployed.) "But not me, oh no, I'm not good enough, for me it's an exaggeration . . ."

"I—Ma—" How I wished I'd gotten the phrase "dietary assembly line" in at the beginning, because now it was too late.

"It's a terrible thing," she said tragically, "*not to be believed.*"

"I believe you, Ma," I sighed, wondering what stubborn lobe of my brain had demanded proof before it issued congratulation.

She needed to hear something in my voice, *then* she'd take courage, and who knew, then she might get the job, stranger things had happened. I knew what it was to be alone in hard circumstances, how much difference a kind word could make.

"It sounds like a wonderful opportunity," I said, but I didn't sound very convincing.

"I know, Beatrice, you have such a busy life, you don't have time to listen to my troubles." She was struggling to sound earnest, but bitter sarcasm seeped in everywhere. "I wish that just once, just *once*, a job, or a scholarship, or *something*, just *one* thing, would fall into *my* lap."

She fell silent, struggling with herself, and began again on a less accusatory tack. "I suppose I'm just too old, that's all."

"Forty-two isn't old, Ma."

"It's *too* old, Beatrice!" she said, in tearful fury. "You cannot conceive how old I am, after twenty years of marriage to, to *your father*."

She had bought my life at the price of her own, for my sake she had married—well, calling her relationship with him a marriage was like calling Hitler's march on Poland a parade! So that, being my father's daughter, I felt as guilty as if, in my clothes closet, behind the Little Bo-peep outfit my mother had so painstakingly stitched for my first-grade play, I was concealing a bayonet.

"I don't know what to do," she said.

"Do you have a résumé?"

She laughed. "What would *I* put on a résumé?"

"Your job experience?"

"I don't know how to do that kind of thing," she said.

"But, you're an English teacher. You teach kids how to write letters, how to organize essays."

"Oh, that's completely different," she said, then added, "I suppose you know how, though."

"Well, I mean, I can try."

"You write the letter," she said, with great excitement suddenly. "*You* can do it, Beatrice, I know you can. You'll know just what to say."

"Except the actual information."

"I can fill all that in later," she said.

"Well, you'd want it to be the basis of the letter."

"Really? No, there are forms you follow." (Spoken with an English teacher's authority.)

"You write it out, Ma, and I'll go over it with you, okay?"

"It won't work, Beatrice, I know it won't. Nobody wants *me*," she said now, in the voice of a woman who'd been around the block a few times and was qualified to sneer at the notions of credulous Little Bo Peep types like myself. "Even my own children prefer their father! He *never* loved you, but you love *him*! I know all about rejection, this is nothing new for me. All my life—*all my life*, Beatrice, I've let people use me and step on me and just push me out of the way when they're done. I'm damned if I'm going to be your sister's doormat too. She can reject me, fine, let her go her own way, but she should know what she's done. It's fine—fine—if Dolly doesn't love me, but *I like myself. I like myself*, do you understand? That much at least I've learned."

"Ma," I said, "Dolly didn't mean—"

"Beatrice, there comes a time when it doesn't matter what you mean or don't mean, when you are judged on the morality of your actions, it's that simple."

"Does that time come when you're thirteen years old?"

"Anyone who is old enough to make a decision like that is old enough to be held accountable," she said flatly, but when I didn't reply, her voice went dead.

"But I forgot," she said, "you're on his side too."

And despite, or perhaps because of, my calming noises and

murmurs of reassurance, she went on and on, building to such a pitch that I imagined her flinging herself against the walls and floors, before subsiding finally into the sharp sobs of a lost little girl.

"What am I going to do, Beatrice?" she asked, begged really. "What's going to happen to me?"

Oh, she was telling the truth of her feeling—that she was starving and alone, marching away from warmth, love, hope, marching through the snow with hatred at her heels and death before her. She'd felt this, for whatever reason, all her life. No soldier is more heroic than the mother who wakes out of her usual nightmare into her usual rage and grief, and sets it aside, to make a tender and patient and hopeful world for her children. In the time of Country Day school and bursting bladder, I'd come out to the car once and told her I'd never be able to hold it until I got home. "What's your reading homework?" she asked. "*The Yellow River*, by I. P. Freely?" And I said, "Don't make me laugh!" though already the urine was rising between my thighs and she looked over and said "Oh no, not volume two, *Swept Away!*" And we laughed, and nothing else mattered, it was spring and I was six years old, the sopping embodiment of all her dreams, proof that she'd transcended her madness and done good in the world.

I was her equivalent of sunlight, and if I failed to blaze out for a minute? She reacted as an aborigine would to an eclipse. As long as I was very, very careful, very, very good, though, I counted among the gods.

"Don't cry, Ma," I said now. I wanted to be the sunlight, to fill the room up with butterflies for her. I curled into myself as if her pain were in my gut, whispering the great motto of ineffectuality, the prayer over the head of every disappointed child: "Don't cry."

"Don't you *dare* tell me not to cry! *You've* never had to face anything like this, never. Oh! '*Don't cry.*'"

Anger, thank the heavens. Anger would keep her from crying her substance away. She hung up and I sank onto the bed and sighed. Maybe she'd stomp out of the house now and go look for a job. Maybe everything would turn out just fine.

Maybe, but there went the phone. It was my father, and immediately, I remembered how much I liked this poor guy, who was so absolutely cheerful in the face of penury and divorce that he could sing three verses of "Come-a-ti-yi-yippie-aye-ay" into a pay phone before he even said hello.

They were at the Palm Beach Motor Court, in Laramie, Wyoming. "How are things back east?" he asked, and I began to answer, but it turned out that this was actually the first line of a frenetic monologue on the rugged beauty of the West, the generosity of the people there, the steak, the sagebrush, the whiskey—ah, the whiskey—but here he lost his thread, and after a moment he took up again somewhere in the midst of an elegy: there had never been a happier family than ours, did I know that? Well, if my mother couldn't recognize it, he was better off without her. Fine, fine if she didn't love him (his voice broke), but surely she shouldn't expect his financial help then.

"I think they call that prostitution out here, honey," he said, and while I was trying to follow his logic he put Dolly on the line.

"How are you?" she asked, seeming to expect a lengthy and serious answer. They were doing very well, she said. Her savings would last them for at least a month. They were going to rent a little house—*unfurnished*—she said proudly, and I smiled.

"Have you talked to Mama?" she asked. "Is she okay?"

I felt a weight drop in my gut as if I'd swallowed a plumb bob.

"She's fine," I said, "she's going along step by step, you know. So what's it like, Wyoming?" I asked, to get off the subject.

"Well," she began, and in the one hesitant syllable I heard her little-sister's reverence, her sense that I was an august, austere figure, a judge or Buddha to whom one must speak only one's most illuminating thoughts—and her stubborn resistance to her own natural tendency to admire me. After a moment of reflection, during which I imagined her watching a tumbleweed roll down a long deserted street, she said wonderingly: "It's sort of like the moon."

When I was making enough money, I thought, I'd bring her to live with me. Under my wing, under Frank's roof, in this neighborhood where everyone tended his quarter acre as if Hartford had the world's most fertile soil, coaxing persimmons or bok choy or whatever fruits they most longed for into bloom—she would thrive. I pictured her figuring an algebra problem at the kitchen table while I stirred the soup at the stove. I made Hartford sound like the promised land for her, a cheerful polyglot metropolis where the cafés were strung with plastic lanterns and each national community had its own bakery and dance hall.

"Three associations just for Lithuanians, for example," I said. I'd noticed Lithuanians in particular because Ross was of Lithuanian descent, causing Philippa and me to do some research on Eastern Europe.

"Well," Dolly said solemnly, "You ought to join one, Beatrice."

I felt a kind of drowning sensation then: shame. She'd heard my tone, when I flew out of the closet at them that day, but she hadn't understood the words. Lesbian, Lithuanian—what did it matter? She recognized that I was declaring allegiance to something outside the family, something strange and probably terrible for which I was standing up with pride. So, then, she would stand behind me, she didn't need to know more. She was going to embody our parents' ideals, even though they themselves had never upheld them.

How I wished I had just shrieked *fuck you* at them, like any normal, rebellious daughter. I wanted to make manifest all the shame in that house, but our terrible secrets were not the villainies one finds in the newspaper, things like incest and physical cruelty, but weaknesses—ignorance, fear, paralytic uncertainty—that kept us from growing and changing and taking part in the world. So we ended up living together in a cauldron and exercising our miseries, with amazing ingenuity, on each other. I couldn't name our sins, so I found something else that dare not speak its name.

Three

I WASN'T going to be like them, crippled the way they were. I had honest work with a time clock and a paycheck and sore feet.

"This is the salt-free broth, this is the fat-free broth, and this is the salt-free, fat-free broth," the supervisor explained, nodding toward three chrome vats in which these identical solutions were boiling. "A heart patient could die from a single cup of fatty broth, and salty broth can seriously harm a stroke victim or *any-one* with high blood pressure. So this is a good spot for someone like you."

For someone who spoke English, she meant. My colleagues were mostly Filipino or Vietnamese. Daisy, who worked across the belt from me, had Down's syndrome.

"There, look. You've already missed one," she said. The trays were lurching by at a terrible rate and I seized a ladle of broth, but as I rushed to pour it into the cup I scalded my hand instead. Flinching, I spilled more of course, dropped the cup, and brought my hand to my mouth as if it were a sad little creature that could be consoled with a kiss.

"*Now* you've ruined the whole tray," the supervisor said, lifting the napkin from its puddle and holding it in front of my face like a soiled undergarment. "Reverse the belt!" she barked. Three trays had gotten past me brothless, now.

"*Concentrate*," she said. The forward motion began again, and, though my innards shriveled with each tray that came toward me, concentrate I most desperately did. When I missed one, Daisy would shake her head and point to the errant cup like a drill sergeant. My left hand was blistered and trembling. Now, when the broth burned my hand I felt a vengeful pleasure in seeing the clumsy thing punished. If it continued to betray me, it was going to starve with the rest of me, did it not understand?

"Get it right, get it right, *get it right!!*" Daisy screamed suddenly, and flung her dishrag, on which she had been obsessively wiping her face—at me. It landed in the salt-free vat, folding itself gently on the surface, then sinking, until the supervisor, who had come running upon hearing Daisy's shrieks, fished it out with her tongs.

I was gleeful at the prospect of seeing Daisy chastised, but she went after me.

"You are a probationary employee. People like you never work out. Daisy becomes anxious when there's a change of routine. Do as you're told or you will find yourself back on the street with your sandals and your degree."

Daisy shot me a malevolent glance. She knew full well how despicable it was to get things wrong all the time; here was her chance to feel contempt from the upper side.

Wounded, I became haughty. Fine, let them hate me. I was only there to begin my meteoric rise. I watched a tray of bright wiggly Jell-O make its way around the room in someone's hands: it was the only beauty I could see, and when it was carried behind a partition, I felt as if some last candle had guttered out and left me alone in the dark.

THE PHONE rang in my dreams for a long time before I realized it
was a real phone, and even then I tried to reach it without breaking into consciousness. I put it to my ear (1:14 A.M. the clock said;
it gave the only light in the room) and heard a stifled cry—my
father's. I clenched myself against this, the way you do when you
see a creature split open on the side of the road, and listened from
some high distance as he said how he'd imagined growing old
with his wife, looking back over the photo albums together. Now
he felt he'd wasted his whole life; he didn't know where to turn.

He'd imagined this all in a season of hope, when he was my age
and the world was in front of him. There *was* a photo album—it
ended on my first birthday. After that, we could never find the
camera.

"I—when I asked her to marry me, the look on her face. I've
never seen such, such—" He broke off in a sob, and started up
again, more plaintive than anguished.

"*She* was the one who wanted to buy the ping-pong ball factory," he said. "It wasn't my idea, she thought of it—now it goes
under, and it's all my fault. And she says that's why she's leaving,
so she can blame me, but she was dreaming of that boy all this
time. She felt as if *something wonderful was pouring out of his eyes,
into hers*—all that time she was writing to him, longing for him. I
can't bear it, I don't know what to do, I can't cope."

He'd lost his home and his family and he had only this phrase
from a TV commercial to describe his feeling. It was like fighting
a war with a can opener. Somewhere, Philippa was reading, she
was looking at something from one side and the other, she was
asking herself how Balzac would view it, what Woolf would have
said.

"You'll make yourself sick," I said. "Stop now. Stop and just
rest. Where's Dolly? Asleep?"

"Yes," he said, with a sigh. He'd protected her, she didn't know she was alone with a desperate man.

"You sleep too, Pop. You'll feel better tomorrow. Things always seem different in the daylight."

"I know," he said, his voice broken, "it's wrong of me to tell you all this . . . but I don't know where else to turn. A man can't live like this, sweetie, a man needs the feel, the smell of a woman he loves."

I shuddered, but it was only over the phone. He talked on more and more quietly until he'd talked himself to sleep like a child, and I hung up very gently, so as not to wake him.

HAD SWEETRIVER been only a dream? My paper topics: "The Mythopoeic Substance of Shelley's *Ozymandias*"; "Despair in Beckett \\ Despair in Brecht"; "Is Borges Kidding?" All of them written out over page after page, while I lay sprawled across my bed, thoughts, dreams, and feelings looping together in lovely patterns, to absorb me while I waited for the day I'd be released from literature and set loose in the world of love. Now it seemed no more real than the "farm" I grew up on. And Philippa too was gone, receded back into the shadow world with the farm and the education. The thought that she missed me was as silly as my idea that I'd find a niche in investment banking. She was a college professor. I was a Dietary Aide III. There had never been anything of substance between us. I must be as crazy as my parents, to have thought such a thing.

I pushed my cart down through the maternity ward into oncology and started taking in the trays. The uniforms and hair nets marked us, so the doctors, nurses, even most of the patients, acted as if we were invisible, discussing their private sorrows in front of us under the assumption we couldn't speak English. A young woman, pale and fearful, bandaged around the chest and arm, reached her good hand out to smooth the hair of her little daughter, whose face was the image of hers, but radiant, excited. "My mom had an operation!" she said, proudly, and in her mother's tender smile I felt her premonition of death, of leaving her child alone. An old man's cawing scream came from the next room. Thoracic surgery; the ribs have to readjust . . . I stood at the gap where the curtain's metal track ended: Did he have someone to hold him? Because that's the central necessity, I was beginning to see. I was alone, a ghost who peered into these lives, seeing, seeing, though they never saw me.

Now, a woman with bandaged eyes, whose husband was reading aloud to her from the bedside chair. I cleared a vase of tulips from her table, listening:

"The word 'presbytery' had chanced that year to drop into my sensitive ears and wrought havoc . . . I had absorbed the mysterious word with its harsh and spiky beginning and the brisk trot of its final syllables . . . 'Presbytery!' I would shout it over the roof of the henhouse . . . the word rang out as a malediction: 'Begone, you are all presbyteries!' "

He read in a fond, rueful voice, as if this was the story of his own youth, and I recognized the sentences as I might a lullaby my mother had once sung to me; my throat caught and tears sprang up, though I hardly knew why.

"*Habla ingles?*" the man asked me, kindly. I had, I realized, been standing there with the tray in my two hands, gaping at him, for a very long time.

I nodded, setting the tray on the table. I'd forgotten it was possible to answer him in words. Colette, that's who had written those lines—*My Mother's House*—I'd read it because Philippa said I ought to.

"Where do you come from?" the man asked me, and I looked out the window, over the ruined block beneath the hospital, the boarded storefronts, and the sidewalk that glittered with broken glass, toward the west, the land I grew up on. I remembered now that in my dream of Ross, we hadn't been in the dormitory hall but walking down the narrow dirt road toward home.

"Connecticut. I grew up in Connecticut," I said. It had been real once, it had, though now I saw it as if through the wrong end of a telescope, smaller and smaller, farther away.

"This *is* Connecticut," the man said, very helpfully, in the high voice people use to soothe babies and pets. "Hartford is the capital of Connecticut." He lifted the cup of ginger ale to his wife's mouth and forgot me, and I went down in the elevator back to the sub-basement, to the locker room where my face in the mirror looked so thick and plain and stupid with the hair drawn back in its net and the neat uniform collar, I understood why no one had wanted to look at me.

THE PHONE was ringing when I walked in the door at home. *Suicide*, I thought, though whose would it be? Ma, having prayed all her married life for divorce, realized now that it only proved she'd been abandoned. And Pop, who'd never dared open his eyes to see us, had suddenly realized he'd missed his chance. Dolly had bargained away her mother, to stay with him until that moment, when the affection she knew must be in him would finally spill. There she was on the edge of the desert, roasting in the hallucinatory heat, shivering through the vast frigid nights . . .

"Hello?" I said, my voice trembling.

"He is deranged!" Ma cried, as if we were already in the midst of the conversation. "Pathetic, limp, fearful, and deranged!" Suddenly she was sobbing. "I don't know what I'm going to do," she wept, at the thought of this pathetic, limp, fearful, and deranged person, and how he'd been torn from her arms.

"It's so sad, Ma, I know."

"It's *not* sad," she snapped, furious I hadn't read her mind. "It's revolting! He *owes me money!* How am I going to live?"

"What about the job?" I asked. "The teaching job."

"Oh don't be absurd, Beatrice," she said. "They don't want *me*."

"Did you call up?"

"There's no point in calling up!" She was truly exasperated now by my ingenuous optimism. "It's all gossip and backbiting around here, God knows what people are saying about me, but you know Sarah Randolph has heard every word of it. They're small-minded, conventional people and no one wants to know my side. Oh, my *head*. Teddy, honey, get me a hot cloth, will you? As hot as you can make it, and wring it out tight."

While the water ran in the background, I asked if she'd worked on her job letter.

"Yes," she said, a good schoolgirl, and began to read it out: "*I started teaching when I realized my husband was incapable of holding a steady job, and I would have to fend for myself and my children alone. I'd been teaching at Wononscopomuc Public High School for three years and never had any problems until another teacher's jealous vendetta against me—*" She broke off for a minute, saying, "Thanks, honey, you're so good," to Teddy. I'd brought the hot washcloth so often myself that I could feel her relax from miles away, and my own pulse slowed.

"You might want to take a—more positive—tack," I said. I liked the sound of my voice, when I was giving her advice. It reassured me to hear it.

"What do you mean?"

"I mean that they'll be looking to see what *you* can do for them. You want to show them what you have to offer, give some examples of what you've done already, stuff like that."

"You mean they don't really care how hard it's been for me."

"Exactly," I said.

"No, of course," she said with a bitter little laugh. "Of course." Then, marveling at the workings of a world that wouldn't concern itself with the perils befalling the innocent ex-wives of the pathetic, limp, fearful, and deranged, nor rush in to ease the sufferings of wide-eyed, altruistic teachers at the hands of their cruel, jealous colleagues . . . "It's *not important* to them. You see, Beatrice, that's the kind of thing I'd never have realized if I didn't have you to point it out. Why should it be that way, *why?* Now that you say it, of course it makes perfect sense: *Why should the world care about me?*"

The atmosphere of wonder was developing a charge and I sensed a thunderhead billowing, though her tone remained perfectly summer-afternoon, hazy and warm: "Beatrice, what would I do without you?" she asked. "I'd never have understood this on my own, but of course, it's childish of me to hope that anyone would recognize all I've suffered, would really care."

"Well, maybe to hope that some unknown personnel officer—"

"No, *anyone!*" came the wounded cry. "Anyone at all! *Who is there*, for me, *except* unknown personnel officers. I'm alone, alone in the world!"

A silence fell as one side of me twisted the other's arm. "There's me, Ma, I understand, I do," I managed to say, and truly. It was terrible, to have to blow every sorrow up until it loomed like a colossus, out of fear that no one would notice it otherwise. And then to quake in the cold dark of its shadow, defenseless against its enormity. She needed *me*, who, thank heaven, had been imbued in the womb with magical powers, to cast a spell on the monster, put it down.

"I—" I said, but nothing else would come. I could not spare enough of myself to repay her for so many tormented years. Hearing my hesitation, poison poured into her heart and she said coolly that she'd let me go, that obviously I (who *had* a good job, a good education, thanks to *her*) had more important things to do. How could I have become so stingy, unwilling to give what she needed, though it was only a few simple words?

"*Please* will you write the letter for me?" she asked.

"Of course, Ma, sure."

"Isn't it amazing?" she said. "It seems only yesterday you were born, you were the cutest baby, and now you're all grown up, *you're* guiding *me*."

I SAT down and wrote: "I've found I have an easy rapport with disaffected students. I can help them see their natural talents and gain confidence. Many of these boys—students—need only kind guidance . . ."

Her true accomplishment was quite different: she had withdrawn, in fear, into a raindrop-sized world, but she'd managed to endow her raindrop with such complex drama that it became a virtual sea. We couldn't tear our eyes from it, we had to find out what was going to happen there next. I tried to think how to phrase this on a résumé, but there was the phone again.

"Beatrice?" It was Sylvie. "I've been trying to get you for an hour."

"What is it? What's the matter?"

"It's . . . well," she stumbled, and then in a gust of happy excitement: "It's nothing the matter, it's . . . I . . . guess what? I'm pregnant!"

"Oh my God, Sylvie," I sat down hard on the kitchen chair. "Oh my God. What does Butch say?"

Her voice was soft, joyful. "He brought me flowers."

"So you'll get married?" I said, thinking, *Ah, a suicide in the family tradition.*

"Oh, no," she said sharply, "no, no. I'm never going to get all tangled up with someone else *that* way."

"Having a baby with someone can be kind of an entanglement, Sylvie."

"No, don't be silly," she said. "If I'm not happy, if things go wrong with Butch and me, I'll just go . . . wherever. *We'll* just go, the baby and me."

"Congratulations," I managed.

"Thank you, Beachy," she said, "thank you so much. I knew you'd be happy for me."

"Now you eat right, okay?" I said, to my own surprise. I must have heard it on TV. "Pregnant mothers need lots of—milk, I think, and leafy green vegetables."

She pulled on her cigarette and blew out a long, satisfied stream. "It sounds cozy, doesn't it?" she said. "Pregnant mothers?"

"Yes, honey, it does."

"DON'T FORGET, Gemini, the tide turns when it is low as well as when it is high," chirped *The Courant* astrology column, my best adviser, and the only part of the paper I could bring myself to read. I'd look away from the front page (CITYFEST PLAZA WILL DISPLACE TWO HUNDRED FAMILIES; YOUTHS ROLL VAGRANT ONTO TRAIN TRACKS, etc.). The classified was an endless list of the places I couldn't fit in.

The phone was ringing.

"I guess you've heard," Pop said, when I answered. There was a long silence, which I couldn't guess how to break. Parents and children are not meant to live by conversation, I thought. You can't have a sensible dialogue with anyone while some little tune in your head goes: "Without his sperm, I wouldn't exist. If he'd swerved farther, I wouldn't exist. If he had his wish, I wouldn't exist. But he secretly adores me." No, with a parent, you have to proceed by action: raising a timber frame or picking beans in adjacent rows.

"Heard?"

"I'm sorry," he said, "I can't help it." He was crying.

"I know," I said gently. I *did* know—nobody felt worse about this all than me. We'd known the parental lives would come to pieces, but that Sylvie too should be stopped in her tracks here, before she was even grown! She was only sixteen, she didn't realize what she was doing. She wanted something soft and warm in her arms, wanted to breathe life into that beautiful dream of family. Sylvie had worked at that dream; she was the one smiling there with firm, adoring belief in her parents, the one who picked up all the wormy apples and put them through the press so we could say we'd made our own cider, the one who'd been absolutely faithful to every tenet of the dream.

Of course he was weeping, who wouldn't weep? If only he and my mother had had a grounding rather than a consuming kind of love, their children could have stood on that foundation to reach up toward their own dreams. Or, love aside . . . but we were not able to put love aside; it was our ideal, our prayer and our best excuse, because in love anything is fair. The words "I love you" brought expiation, they healed wounds without a scar. If my parents had only been *able*, if they could have gone simply about the business of their lives, working ahead through difficulty, accomplishing some things and not others—if they'd been more like Frank and Henny, then they might have divorced, gone mad, died, for that matter, and left Sylvie entirely on her own, but she'd have had an example to live by. She'd be at school now, studying biology—she'd wanted to be a midwife.

"I don't know what to do," he said.

"There's nothing we *can* do," I said, thinking this mild consolation was the best I could offer. "She doesn't realize what havoc a baby will wreak for her."

Which was odd, because of course, Sylvie had seen babies wreak havoc before.

"It's not too late," I went on. "She's not even eight weeks along. You could talk to her, *tell* her."

"My *first* grandchild," he said. "And just when it seemed nothing good would ever happen again." He took a deep breath and continued. "You don't know, sweetie, you don't know what it means to me, to think that new life is coming, a fresh start where your mother and I failed . . . what hope it gives."

Of course. He'd been crying for *joy*. Thank God his hearing was so selective . . .

"*Anything* can happen, sweetie," he said, "anything at all. Nobody knows what's just around the corner. People make fortunes because they're standing in the right place at the right time, because they're cockeyed the way everyone else happens to be cockeyed at the moment. Look at pet rocks, for God's sake—it doesn't take a million IQ points to make a million bucks, no sir.

"And you know Sylvie," he continued, his voice swelling, so I remembered how he used to call her "little wonder" because she could skibble up a doorframe or scramble along the barn rafters as surefooted as a mouse. She was strong and agile and had faith in what her body could do. This was the first thing she knew about herself, because she could only know, at first, what set her apart from me. And her great gift, for him, was that she was so clearly *not me*. She'd grown, as children do, to fit the shape of his pride.

"She was *made* for motherhood," he crowed. "Remember how good she was with babies, from the time she was five or six!"

Yes, havoc was Sylvie's old familiar—she liked her lullabies in a mad patois.

"She's only sixteen now!" I said. "It's too young. And what about Butch, does he seem like a natural father?"

"Well, it's not as if she's *marrying* him, honey," my father said. I felt like the world's wettest blanket. Why not just let him enjoy?

"No, Butch *isn't* exactly who I'd choose," he went on, in his Voice of Clear Reason, his salesman's voice, "but he seems to love your sister and let's not forget *your sister loves him*. It's not up to us to dictate her life for her. She has to do *what feels comfortable for her*."

Had he been watching daytime TV? Whatever, it was easier to succumb to it, and let life roll on. It's exhausting to cut your own path, when the parental footsteps follow such a clear trail. Even if that trail leads to perdition.

"And you know, land's cheap out here, there's acres and acres, especially in the farther reaches—once you get a few miles off the highway, you can really get a deal. If I can just make a few thousand to start out with, I'll be able to buy a pretty nice spread. People commute into Laramie by small plane. So if things don't work out, and Sylvie decides Butch isn't what she wants, she can bring the baby and come out here. Plenty of wide-open spaces, fresh air, it's a great place to bring up a child. You know, I guess it's true what they say, honey: *Time heals all wounds.* I'm starting to see that just because I'm divorced doesn't mean I can't gather my children around me the way I always meant to. I've got my Doll here already, and if Sylvie and the baby came out, well, things are just looking up, I guess that's about all I have to say. But there I go, talk, talk, and I don't let you get a word in."

No, because after all, God only knew what I'd say. There I'd be, boasting about some book I was reading, that he wouldn't have thought himself fit to understand, and even as he hated me for it, he'd have to remember that he'd already wanted to be rid of me, and then a fog of guilt would rise up and make it even harder to look at me, or, God forbid, listen. So he talked and talked, trying to make amends. I responded with polite little echoes. At the end, we could both say we'd managed it, we'd acted like father and daughter.

So my heart sank when he declared his intention, after all these years, to listen. The last time I'd tried to get some message across to him I'd ended up flying out of the closet like Tarzan on a vine. I cringed and vowed to answer his questions honestly and fully.

"So," he said, while I braced myself. "How do you like Hartford?"

"It's kind of lonely," I admitted. "I get up in the morning and I can hardly get myself to go to work."

"Well, honey, no one actually *likes* going to work, do they?" he asked, warily. What was wrong with me, that I expected so much? "But we all *have* to go, that's what being grown up is."

Of course, he was right. Life was like this—meaningless, but crushing. There were compensatory pleasures—vacations, new stereo equipment, and stuff.

"We all feel that way sometimes," he went on. "But we don't just give in to it." The sound of his voice pleased him, the stern-but-fair tone, and the fatherly feeling it gave, of standing above me. "Without self-discipline where would the world be?" He got lost in his thinking and came up again to say: "Your mother raised you with the idea you were some kind of star—but the fact is, we all have to work for our bread."

True. Life depends on daily effort. There can be no giving in to the torpor that's always swaying beneath, calling you down. The strange thing was that he'd hardly managed to bear going to work himself. He said he was a lone wolf, an individualist—he couldn't take bossing. So he lay on the couch, combing the newspaper for new horrors, waiting for the next world war. When it came, all labors would be lost—so why labor? He fell asleep; his change slipped out of his pocket—we'd swarm the cushions when he got up. Suppose I didn't steel myself, and so followed him into twilight life? That would be awful. I squared my shoulders and changed my tone.

"It's a nice apartment," I said, "a nice neighborhood, lots of families—you know, gardens, and clotheslines and statues of the Virgin and everything."

"That's great, great, honey," he said, doing me the favor of forgetting all that went before.

"It's good to know you're nicely settled, sweetie. And about Sylvie—you know, Butch is just such a nice guy—*not* a genius, no, but a really hard worker, and he's had a rough time of it with his father and the problem at the Cumberland Farms and all—Sylvie's a godsend for him, and he loves her so much, it's wonderful to see."

"Wonderful," I said. The "problem" at Cumberland Farms had been armed robbery, though everyone said Butch was only the driver and then, only to spite his father, that he would never harm a flea of his own will. "Though I do wish she'd finish high school," I ventured.

"She's young," Pop said. "She's a bright kid, she's going to learn from everything she does. Look at the different kinds of people she talks to in the diner, people she'd never meet if she just went on in school. School's important, I don't deny it, but different people learn in different ways. The high school Dolly's going to out here, very few of these kids go further on. They're going to work on the ranches or the oil industry, they don't need Shakespeare. Life is full of surprises, sweetie, people take different paths. Look at Albert Einstein, he never got past the third grade!"

"Albert Einstein didn't drop out of school to keep house for an armed robber," I couldn't help pointing out.

"Well, you can't run the world, sweetie, and neither can I," Pop declared, in the tone of a man bobbing along on an inflatable raft while the world he couldn't run passed by.

He *might* be right, I kept reminding myself—Sylvie might have found a man who would love her and take care of her, Pop might strike copper or whatever it was you struck in Wyoming, earn back Dolly's college savings and more, get married again, live happily, die with money in the bank. Sometimes people who drop out of school discover the truths everyone else has been educated to overlook. Some armed robbers make excellent husbands. Certainly my father was statistically due for a break, and lots of people take dramatic turns in midlife, have strokes of fortune or understanding. The tide turns when it is low as well as when it is high.

"Isn't it exciting?" Dolly asked dutifully, when he put her on the phone. I replied dutifully that it was. Pop was teaching her to waltz, she said, to the theme music on Merv Griffin, which was about the only TV they could get. And they were moving into their rental house next week—it was on a cul-de-sac, like all the houses there. From the air, you could look down and see them, cut into the landscape.

"Pop's taking flying lessons. When he gets back on his feet he's going to get a small plane. You really need one out here."

"You do?" I asked, trying to sound normal. Did not the phrase "flying lessons" call to mind the people who bought our furniture and crashed in flames? Who abandoned their children out of folly?

"It makes him happy, Beatrice," Dolly insisted, angry at my hesitation. "If you could hear the way he talks about it, the way everything looks from the sky. I'm going up with him tomorrow, so he can show me," she said. "Don't tell Mama, I don't want her to get mad."

"I won't," I promised—quite honestly, as I didn't dare speak of her to Ma. "But Dolly, be careful, okay?" I said, as if a passenger in a small plane piloted by a man whose sheer empty optimism threatened to loft him into orbit could save herself by "being careful"! Very clever.

"So, have you joined any of those clubs?" asked my conscientious sister.

I HAD not. Everyone on earth belonged to something, except for me. Here were the Italian-Americans celebrating a festival, the bishop waving from his limo sunroof, the plaster saint bobbing behind. Saturday morning the whole West Side drifted along the sidewalk toward Temple Beth-El, fathers in suits holding the hands of their little girls. There was reggae night at the Haitian-American club, happy hour at The Hart and Doe, bingo for old ladies, and for the teenagers, rival gangs. For all I loved to go to church, to see people singing together with their egos quietly tucked away, I had no religion. Certainly no social class. Americans don't believe in them. And what would I put under ethnic heritage—Nazi?

In fact I was nobody, another American whose identity was to be read from the tea leaves, or changed with a surreptitious tap at the cup. Seeing a HELP WANTED sign at Kmart, I'd imagined myself standing at a cash register instead of over a soup vat, and it seemed a wonderful thing. I rushed in to apply and found myself at the back of an endless line. When I reached the desk and the receptionist said they'd run out of applications, I burst into tears.

She looked at me, incredulous: how did a person come to such ridiculous desperation?

Philippa would have known what to do, but I couldn't let her hear my cowed, shaking voice. She'd give up on me, and without her, without the trick I had of believing myself connected to her, I didn't know how I'd live.

To think that only weeks ago, I'd been the lesbian she had made of me: an electric, exotic creature, half-woman, half-serpent, known to most people only from fantasies they daren't even realize they had. When my freshman adviser asked me why sex was so important to me, she might have considered that every age has its form—the nature essay, the epistolary novel, the roman à clef—ours was bodily rather than literary. The sexual act—aka "the act of love"—was our medium; through it, each of us expected to have his/her own individual say.

Here dream and circumstance clasped hands and the circle was closed; my wish to be someone, belong to something, hear Philippa's rat-a-tat voice bringing down sacred cows like ducks in a shooting gallery—these were not peculiarities, they marked me as a member of a movement. I was lost, frightened, not to mention increasingly small-minded and angry, because I was part of a disenfranchised group, a group ignored and despised by the general run of Americans, who could honestly be counted among the meek, the deserving, the deprived. Why hadn't I seen it before? Of course I felt alien and misunderstood. I was a lesbian, a lesbian adrift in the heterosexual world.

Four

THANKS TO the film festival, and Philippa's photos of Paris in the twenties, I knew they were out there, the lesbians: sleeping by day, rising in the deepest blue of evening to shake out their marcelled locks, slither into their satins or buckle up their tweeds, and stalk out into the night (which they were not "taking back"; they had never let it slip through their fingers). Having whispered the password at the speakeasy door, they'd be dancing against each other, kissing the napes of each other's long necks, winding together like wisps of smoke, like vines; so beautiful, they'd escaped their bodies altogether. Drifting home at dawn, they'd nod their cloaked heads to M. Swann, off to Odette's by the back way.

I had only to find them. But how? Of course, the library—this was the only way I knew how to find anything. I settled in the most conspicuous reading chair with *The Importance of Being Earnest* and waited for someone like Philippa or Djuna Barnes to go by.

Some hours passed, but as I left, I caught sight of the Women's Community Bulletin Board, and there, nestled among notices for Cordon Bleu cooking lessons; Jazzercize classes; a lecture on Empowerment; a photography show: *Wommyn and Their Cats*;

the meetings for rape crisis and chronic fatigue; the number for
the battered women's shelter, there it was—The Lesbian Support
Group, 371 Hereford Street, #1A, Friday at 6 P.M.

I WORE the Nancy Kissinger shoes, of course, and black silk
pants, my shirt with French cuffs, because Philippa thought cuff
links were so commanding, and my hair pinned up loosely in my
great-grandmother's pearl and sapphire barrette, because she
had lived in the twenties so I thought it might help me fit in. At
6:15 exactly, I rang the bell at 371 Hereford Street, one of the
triple-deckers the city was made of, with a deep porch, front
doors with oval windows—a place where there had once been
lace curtains and probably a hydrangea tree in the yard, though it
was all ragweed and Queen Anne's lace now, with a half-full beer
bottle nestled in the mangy hedge.

They buzzed me back—I felt the current surge into the lock
and turned the knob as if I were about to enter one of the realms
children stumble into in books, full of wondrous terrors, true to
dream life rather than real life, but true all the same. At Sweetriver we'd played at being students, artists, lovers, protesters,
homosexuals—now I was going to be a lesbian for real: clear of
gaze, looking out from a chosen pinnacle instead of the swamp
I'd been born into; above the terrible longings I'd once felt for
men. I trembled on this threshold, closed my eyes for a second in
something like prayer, and opened the door . . .

To find myself face to face with a heavyset, middle-aged
woman who apparently acted as her own barber, and who, from
her solid vantage point (she was leaning on a very thick cane),
looked me up and down with something like suspicion.

"May we help you?"

"Is this the Lesbian Support Group?"

Her eyes narrowed. "And who might you be?" she asked.

"Beatrice," I said, feeling very small. "Beatrice Wolfe." At Sweetriver it had been Bay-ah-*trrree*-chay.

She stared at my outstretched hand as if a handshake was a custom she'd witnessed in an anthropological documentary but never actually tried, but finally she took it and gave it a squeamish squeeze.

"God, that makes nine!" someone behind her said. "Can you play second base?"

"I don't think so," said the first, with a smile that suggested her curiosity had been satisfied; she had divined all my secrets and would be willing, for a price, to keep them. "You don't play second base, do you, Beatrice?"

"No," I admitted, "I don't."

"I didn't think so," she said. "What *do* you do? No, wait, wait, you're a waitress in a soda shopp-ee, right? Or, a veterinarian's assistant? You're nice to little pussycats?"

I knew what she meant—I looked like Bo-peep dressed up as Vita Sackville-West. I was too pink-cheeked, too hopeful by miles, and while this might have counted toward beauty in another era, now it just looked naive. We're spinning through an infinite, sterile universe on a planet whose peoples periodically tear each other to shreds—and this is little Beatrice, all dressed up and wanting to shake your hand. At Sweetriver we strove relentlessly to gain experience—to rid ourselves of our tacky exuberance and replace it with the appropriate cynicism, contempt, boredom at the very least. Philippa used to accuse me of reading Wordsworth in secret when she didn't approve of my dress, and in a way, she was right: my obvious longing for a time when personal sadness, a betrayal, for instance, or a death, wasn't dwarfed into meaninglessness by a century of mass horror and grief was unseemly.

"Never mind," she said, as I fumbled for an answer. She stepped back and swung the cane aside for me in a gesture of chivalry, as if she was holding a door. "Come in."

I entered with eyes downcast, a pilgrim who'd finally reached her shrine. The air was rich with the smell of bean soup and apple pie, the windows were steamed over, a cat round and black as a bowling ball was kneading one of the afghans that covered the sofa and every single chair. The conversation had ceased on my entrance, and the faces turned toward me were as solemn as if I'd crashed an SDS meeting. Even their clothing—denim, flannel, a Guatemalan sweater, a T-shirt equating women with fish and men with bicycles, was earnest and serious and committed to social change.

"Welcome," the woman on the cane boomed, apparently speaking for them all.

"Hi, everybody," I said, "I'm Beatrice Wolfe."

"Pat," she said, so firmly that for a minute I wondered if *my* name was really Pat, and she was correcting my mistake. Then, looking at my empty hands, she said "It's potluck," with great disapproval.

"Excuse me?" She'd been drowned out by a burst of indignant agreement among the other women, who had resumed their discussion after giving me a quick look up and down.

"It's potluck," she said again. "*Potluck*. Everybody brings a dish. What did you bring?"

"Oh, I'm sorry, I didn't know. The notice just said 'support group.'"

"Fine," she snapped. "You can do the dishes."

"Okay," I said, taken aback. There would be a great many dishes to do, judging from the array of breads and casseroles on the table, the pots bubbling on the stove, and the sweets lined up on the counter in front of mason jars filled with whole grains.

Everything here was wholesome and maternal—it ought to be a pleasure to wash dishes in this warm, fragrant place.

A young woman, slim as a boy, with a cowlick and bowed legs, brought me a glass of wine and complimented my cuff links.

"I'm Reenie," she said. "I guess you don't play softball?" She didn't sound at all sorry—she touched my sleeve with wonder as if I were a tropical butterfly seldom glimpsed in these climes.

It was true that no colony of goodwives would have outdone this roomful of Sapphists for rectitude. Hair was cropped and fingernails bitten, the corners of mouths were pulled down and would not rise until peace, love, and harmony reigned over the earth. If any of these women had ever yielded to the sight of her own loveliness in the mirror, feeling simple, blessed happiness as if she were picking an armful of lilacs on a May morning, she had disavowed that pleasure by now. The pliant curves of cheek and lips, the soft waves of hair—the qualities that comprise the dream of woman, the longing for women—these had been disavowed in favor of a firm stolidity such as would be an excellent quality in, say, an ambulance driver during a world war. Their voices admitted no ambiguity, and their breasts swung under their turtlenecks, exciting as udders. Compared to them, I was a soap bubble, and Reenie gazed at me happily while the others talked on.

"Soup's on!" Pat said, and no one loitered.

"Sit anywhere?" someone asked as we approached the table.

"As long as it's boy-girl, boy-girl," I sang, and saw eight perplexed faces turn in my direction, deciding whether to take offense.

"It's come-as-you-are and sit where you please," Pat said, with a quick, resentful glance at me. "No *place cards*."

I spoke very severely to myself, asking whether I wanted merely to carry on the masculine tradition of objectification, or whether I cared about women's souls. After all, I was searching

for authenticity, and these women were resolutely without artifice; if they were to find one little tendril of artifice curling out of
themselves they would instantly tweeze it away. So then, they
were my people—genuine, sensible, down to earth. I must strive
to be more like them.

"And no *men*," Pat added, for good measure. A murmur of
assent ran through the room, and as the dishes were passed
around the table, everyone in turn had a story about the crass
gender we'd spurned. My cheeks burned. I must withdraw; watch
and listen more closely, try to transform myself. Reenie sat beside
me, and the neat, slender woman who took the opposite chair
glanced at me impassively. She hadn't said a word since I arrived,
and my imagination had leapt into the silence and turned her
accidentally into Françoise Sagan. I smiled and she quickly
looked away.

Pat hated men, she said, more even than the rest of us, though
her tense, pugnacious posture seemed a careful emulation of
them. As she helped herself to the cheese and onion pie, she
spoke of her father the butcher as if she'd been a slab on his hook.

"It was like he didn't speak English," she said, "like his language was *meat*. 'A nice brisket; a fine hind quarter.' He'd be full of
pride, roasting this thing that had been bleeding on the chopping
block that afternoon." She shuddered. "Barb, have some of the
nut loaf. . . . is the sauce down there?"

Barb pointed toward my right hand, which was resting near the
sauce. "It's not," she said, once the sauceboat was under way,
"that I haven't felt attracted to men, on occasion . . ."

"Well, *I* never have," I said suddenly, and extremely surpris-
ingly.

"*Never*," I repeated.

"Maybe I should rephrase that," Barb said. "Maybe attracted is
too strong a word."

"Attracted," Pat said, scornfully. If we knew, if we'd *only seen* what she had. Susan, her lover, who was as tall as a sunflower with the same bowed head, sat nodding. Susan's husband, Pat was telling us, had broken a chair across her shoulders and had, as she was leaving him, taped a sign to the back of her car: STRIP ME GANG RAPE ME FUCK ME TO DEATH. That's what men wanted for women, did we all understand? Pat had been working the desk at the women's shelter the day Susan came in, one eye swollen shut, her ineffectual fist jammed into her mouth as if it could keep her from screaming, her peace so fragile that the sound of Pat stapling forms into her folder had startled her into sobs.

"And the rest is history," Susan said, with a smile, because they were here, after all, living the happiest ending imaginable, seated at the head and foot of this oaken table, serving barley salad and stuffed squash. To a person as hungry as myself, just looking down over the landscape of casseroles was a great satisfaction. The heavy candles flickered as if for a séance, and we seemed like a party of spirits, lost children come back to rattle the nursery windows and avenge ourselves on our betrayers, our faces aglow in the soft light, our hands busy with knives and ladles as we passed the steaming dishes along.

What honest thing could I have said to them? "I came to transgress"? I opened my mouth and stuffed it with mashed potatoes, to prevent it from getting me into further trouble.

Now a latecomer, a tall woman engulfed in a cowled sweater, took the last chair. She maintained a stately, authoritative silence that slowly drew all the attention, the sympathy—all the energy— in the room toward her. Was she in mourning? She was dressed in black, but she looked as if she'd never cried in her life.

"Ginny," Pat said, as if the name itself spoke volumes, "I'm so glad." She sounded grateful, and Ginny nodded—gratitude was apparently the proper response. She would take just a little, she

said—the squash, and a drop of the soup—there wouldn't be any
animal products?

No, no, Pat rushed to reassure, of course not.

Nor refined sugar?

Certainly not.

Though there *was* fish on the table, Pat said apologetically. It
was sole. She would eat a placid fish, she explained—sole, or
flounder, or scallops, which were so far down the scale of sen-
tience and so delicious after only a minute under the broiler . . .
but never a valiant fish, a salmon, or God forbid, a skate.

"I don't know why a sole should suffer for its nature," Ginny
said, "Nothing that lives ought to be eaten." And she shuddered
as if she had narrowly escaped being eaten herself.

Pat, injured, countered that there were different ways to work
for the good of the planet, that she, for instance, would never use
water, a limited resource, to feed such a useless thing as a *lawn*. I
gathered from her tone that Ginny must have had a fairly large
front yard, perhaps even enough for croquet. Susan took up Pat's
cause, condemning ornamental growth, anything raised only to
be cut, and soon there was general agreement that lawns were a
brutal invention, grown for the pure pleasure of those who would
mow them down.

"In a word, *men*," said Pat.

"Better they take the testosterone out on the grass, than on
you and me," I said, by way of camaraderie. I had divined their
trajectory and was determined to follow it out.

At this, Ginny, who until now had seemed to be turning slowly
to stone, snapped to life as if I had slapped her. "This is *not* something to joke about!" she said.

"She doesn't know what she's saying, honey," Barb said, covering Ginny's hand with her own, glowering at me.

"It just makes me *so mad*," Pat started, "it just makes me *furious* to hear the things men do chalked up to testosterone. It's like people think there's no free will. There's nothing a man can do that a woman can't, and vice-versa."

I looked up and down the table. I'd expected the others would find it insulting to be lumped so summarily with a gender they felt they'd surmounted, but they seconded her loudly. They were like a school of fish, reversing direction in one unanimous flashing instant, so no matter what, they were all, always, pointed the same way. I was welcome as an eel. They were vying with each other, showing off how many rules they could follow, inventing new ones just to prove how obedient they were—even, swaggeringly, obeying two opposite rules at the same time.

"Women are just as strong as men," Pat continued. "I took down the Tae Kwon Do instructor at the Y on the *very first day*— and women aren't out there beating each other up, shooting each other. There's no hormonal reason a man *has* to mow a lawn, or kill a deer, or twist somebody's arm, or . . . hurt anybody. It's *not normal*, it's not, and it deserves to be *punished*. Yes, it does." She took a quick glance in Ginny's direction and Ginny nodded, relaxing until she almost smiled.

"Ginny, have some more squash," Pat said. "Really, I made it for you."

Reenie, the young one with the cowlick who had hoped I could play second base, was sitting beside me, eating so hungrily, she was missing the conversation altogether.

"I don't know why, but I'm starving," she told me, tearing off the heel of a baguette. There was a slight twang, Kentucky maybe, in her voice—like a squeeze of lemon. She laughed. "It's not like I didn't have a Big Mac right before I came."

Did she dare admit this? I laughed, and turned toward her, and as I did, I felt something ominous, like distant thunder. The woman across the table—Françoise Sagan in this epoch, but, possibly, Renée Vivien in the twenties (because I could see her in black tie and tails)—tensed, suddenly. Yes, I thought, she was dangerous and brooding, ready to try anything, her blank expression a mask covering the wild turbulence within.

"*Bonjour,*" I said, smiling—Reenie's ease had set me loose again, and I imagined Françoise would be delighted to meet another native speaker.

"Hello," she corrected. She'd seen that little spark jump between me and Reenie, and she was visibly troubled. She didn't like seeing me talk to Reenie at all. So she was interested! And my flicker of interest in her flashed over and involved, within seconds, the whole of my mind.

Her name was not Françoise, in fact, but Lee, Lee Schuyler. She was slender and modest with dark hair in what we'd have called a pixie cut when I was young. Her complexion was thickly pocked—a lonely adolescence, then, spent in her own bedroom mostly, wishing, of course, for love. When she turned her face, I found something like beauty in the shape of her eyes, and every time she turned I looked for it again. She was a mystery: *that* was what I'd been missing. And of course, it would be a love mystery. Men could drill through the ocean floor, pierce the atmospheric envelope, harness the elements, fuse the elements, and smash the elements back to their original smithereens, but they'd left barely a footprint in the world of feeling. *Mine*, I thought in triumph, forgetting Reenie and turning toward Lee with all the force of my curiosity.

The instant our eyes met, she looked away. So I'd been right—she liked me. And suddenly everything in Hartford was electrified by a divine battery that pulled all the scattered anxious atoms into orbit, and I felt that charge of attraction without which everything would fly apart into meaningless space. From that moment, I kept Lee in my sights, calculated my position according to hers.

The dinner had ended and Susan was pouring coffee while Pat cut her peanut butter pie into absolutely equal portions. Lee was looking down the table with some consternation; I couldn't bear to see her in want.

"What is it?" I asked. I'd had that vision that strikes with love—as if I'd seen an X ray of her heart and knew just where the scars were, what was needed to heal them. "What do you need?"

"Cream and sugar," she replied, perplexed at my urgency.

"Please pass the cream and sugar," I called. She must have the cream and sugar immediately. Her coffee must be perfect; I stopped just short of testing a drop on my wrist. I would fill every one of her wishes—she would have no choice but to love me.

"They're *in use*," Pat said, shooting me a derisive glance. At the other end of the table, Barb was refusing the bowl of grapes—hadn't we heard the boycott was on again?

"Could you send them down here?" Reenie asked. "I love grapes," she confided.

"Have mine," Lee said to her. "Do you want mine?"

"Well, okay," Reenie said, and giggled. "I mean, there's plenty," she said.

"Well, have these for now," Lee said. Her voice was quiet and certain, like a heartbeat or a metronome. She stood up, piled her plates together, and carried them into the kitchen, stepping softly and self-consciously, almost on tiptoe. I watched her the way I'd have watched a sunset, turning back to the table only when she was completely out of sight, shivering and pulling my sweater in around me again.

"Beatrice will do the dishes; she didn't bring anything," Pat announced, and I leapt up; Lee was still in the kitchen. But she passed me in the doorway, pressing herself against the frame lest our arms brush, and returned to the table to take my seat, and when I came back, she was talking to Reenie about the ball team.

I gathered up the dirty dishes. When in Rome one must follow the dictates of the Romans. And one way or another, I always seemed to be in Rome.

When I turned off the faucet for a second I realized they were discussing me.

"So *po-lite!*" Pat said. "It's the way they appease men," she added, "another way of wheedling, really. I mean," she said, with a little snort, "it's fine if you're that sort of person, like, a debu-*tante*. Okay then, purse your little lips and do-si-do, or whatever, and Daddy'll take good care of you. But for me, I don't have the luxury of mincing words."

I was scraping the last plate—the lima bean and barley soufflé, whose comprehensive protein everyone had extolled, sagged wearily into the compost.

"Sure," Pat said, "everyone's welcome here, but let her pull her own weight. Ginny, can I get you something else? More cake?"

"I'll go," I heard Reenie say. "Anyone else?"

She came into the kitchen and did a stagey doubletake when she saw me at the sink. "What are you doing?" she asked. "You're not actually washing all those?"

"I didn't bring a dish," I said.

"So what?"

"Pat said those were the rules," I said.

"Aw, don't go listening to Pat," she said.

Then I saw Lee in the door—or really, felt her presence. Most people are like children's drawings, the color flaring out beyond the boundaries all around, and least of anyone did I manage to keep myself inside the lines, but Lee was perfectly tranquil. My mother, I thought, would despise her, and at this, my pulse began to race—she was so wonderful and there she was, setting her cup on the counter beside me, so close I could almost have touched her.

"Are you all right?" she asked Reenie.

"Sure," Reenie said, sounding exasperated, and Lee tiptoed out again.

"Hey, it's eleven o'clock!" Reenie said, "We've got to go!" she said, taking my arm with the easy intimacy of a child, pulling me back into the living room. "Pat," she called, "this girl is actually doing your dishes for you!"

"Is she getting dishpan hands now?" Barb asked, with mocking solicitude.

I saw myself in the hall mirror, flushed and disheveled, my face pursed like a chipmunk or a squirrel: some anxious, hoarding creature that would bolt at the snap of a twig. No wonder they all despised me. Even my disappointment was proof that, unlike the others, I still lived in the luxury of expectation. Pat had been right, in a way, when she called me a debutante: I'd so completely adopted the protective coloration of a Sweetriver girl, you couldn't tell *who* I was anymore. I thought of Sylvie, smoking in her trailer, dropping her *g*'s, picking up the ways of her adopted people—such as working too much for too little and wondering when the car would give out. And Dolly, the little cowgirl. We had this notion that we could choose a life, walk into it through the front door, and make ourselves at home. But they sure did fit peculiarly, these lives.

"That's Iggums, and Poppums, and Missus Itsy Boodles," Pat was saying, introducing her collection of stuffed rabbits to Ginny, who seemed as nonplussed, for a moment, as I was. "We buy them for baby showers," Pat confided, "then we can't bear to part with them," and, succumbing to a wave of affection for one that had the big sad eyes of a thumb-sucking child, she picked the thing up and hugged it mightily, saying, "Oh, widdoo Poppums isa goodest girl ever, is she."

Then: "Eleven o'clock, ladies, let's go, please. The lights are

out, Susan? All right then, let's not leave the door open please,
very good, after you, Ginny."

KINGDOM COME was a former warehouse and Hartford's only gay
bar. The men there were perfectly turned out, costumed for
yachting or motorcycling or roping cattle, or some other little
boy's fantasy. The one thing they did not look like was real people—genuine facial expressions with all their intimations of longing and uncertainty would have wrecked the presentation. Beside
them we women shuffled like a herd of undersized buffalo, heads
down, hands in our pockets, ordering in whispers from bar-
tenders who handed us our drinks and took our money, looking
past us to the gods on the blacklit floor. It seemed as if the two
genders were such different species, we could occupy the same
space at the same time without ever colliding, almost without
seeing each other.

Everyone seemed different under the strobe. Pat leaned on the
cane and danced, from the waist up, with abandon, shaking her
index finger in parodic caution, throwing her head back and crying "*Yowsah!*" whenever the rhythm reached a certain pitch.
Ginny had withdrawn into a corner; her black cowl blended into
the wall so her pale face hovered eerily over the table. Lee leaned
against the wall, as laconic as a farmhand, drinking straight
bourbon, watching. I felt pulled toward her by a physical force,
so it surprised me to see people walk between us: Weren't they
defying the laws of physics? When a man lingered in front of her
for a moment, blocking my view, my instinct was to knock him
down.

"You know, you just don't *look* like a lesbian."

This, which would have been the harshest criticism from any
of the rest of them, came from Reenie in a tone of amazed rever-

ence, as if she were addressing the moon. I loved the version of myself I saw reflected in her smile: all dumb, slow, womanly flesh, swaying like eelgrass among the various currents. I remembered, bitterly, that I'd once hoped a man might see something like this in me.

Now I wondered if Reenie could help me become the way she was; like Tom Sawyer—someone who would never be mistaken for a girl. She was a welder at Ziptronix, which, she told me proudly, was a union shop—even the sweeper made sixteen dollars an hour. She'd just bought a house, a two-family in East Hartford across the river, and was fixing it up—maybe I'd like to come by sometime? Talking to her felt like talking to a man—not a Sweetriver man but a real one, a carpenter or a landscaper or something. There was the same pride: "See what I can *do*, to take care of you?" And I turned my nose up just the same as if she had been a man—I didn't believe in them, not even the female ones.

But I'd managed to angle her around so I could look at Lee over her shoulder. Sure, I said, I'd love to come over—meanwhile, did she want to dance? I wanted Lee to see us.

"Aw, I guess not," Reenie said. "But, buy you a drink?"

"Sure," I said, taking on a slight twang of my own. I could see Lee drawing on her cigarette, which she held between thumb and forefinger as if smoking was a very serious matter. She was drawing that smoke deep, deep into herself, and that must have been the way she felt about everything, and I wanted to absorb her, all her feeling and thought, just that way.

"So, how do you like living in Hartford?" I asked Reenie.

"I've lived here all my life," she said. "I mean, I went out to Chicago for a year a while back, but it wasn't for me. I liked Milwaukee, though. Milwaukee felt more like home."

"Have you been friends with Pat and Barb, and Lee and everyone forever and ever?"

" 'Bout ten years, I guess, for Pat I mean, and Susan. We started the support group just to meet some other women, really. We've only been meeting for a year."

"And Lee?"

"She's *brand-new*," Reenie said. "This is her third or fourth time."

"Did she just move here?"

"No. I guess she just kind of realized . . ."

"She just came out!" I said. A fact about her, gold in my sieve!

Reenie laughed at my excitement. "It happens," she said. "Now Pat, I got to know through the Women's Shelter, we're both volunteers." How she could have changed the subject from Lee to this matter of no importance I couldn't imagine. My attention faded and Reenie went off to get our drinks.

The minute she went to the bar, Lee approached me. It was what I'd been waiting for, what I expected. Once you were a lesbian, dreams came true. The other stuff—the misunderstandings, cruelties, broken hearts—came of the struggle inherent in heterosexuality, that bizarre process through which two antithetical beings attempt, over the course of a wretched lifetime, to fit themselves together. Lee set her hands on me with firm confidence—I thought with a thrill that this must be her nature: commanding, self-assured. We'd keep a salon like Gertrude Stein and Alice B. Toklas; soon Philippa would be coming down to visit.

The song was "Hot Shot," and it was a signal for the men: the night was reaching its climax, it was time to abandon their languid postures and immerse themselves in the beat. Around us, they danced by striking poses, passing poppers, and recoiling at each sniff like whips cracking. The back of a large, flat hand struck me in the mouth but its owner seemed not to notice, and I took it with pleasure—we were all swept up in the churning wave. Imagine, a few hours ago, I hadn't known Lee existed, and now here we were, moving together to the very same rhythm, though she danced without conviction, as if to deny her complicity with the throbbing music, its sexual vision. In the midst of her quiet assurance, I'd found it, a timidity, a need that would cling to me, draw like a soft mouth at my strength. I sang along—"Gonna be a hot shot baby this evening, hot shot baby tonight." Who cared if it had no meaning? It had a pulse, a pulse I felt in myself, and Lee would feel it in me and want me all the more.

It ended, we were dashed on the shore. "Thank you, thank you!" I said to Lee, laughing. "Oh, but let's not stop yet."

She was hardly smiling, I realized suddenly. Her expression was ninety percent tension, with some kind of entreaty just beneath.

"You were talking to Reenie," she said in my ear as a new song, a heavy, joyless pounding, began.

"Well, as much as one can," I laughed, happily disdainful of my one ally, now that I was with my heart's object. I remembered how Lee had looked at dinner and I wanted to set her fears to rest, to assure her I had no interest in Reenie at all.

"Did she say anything?" Lee asked.

"That she likes Milwaukee better than Chicago," I said.

Lee laughed, shy and happy. "She's so funny," she said, resting her head on my shoulder. "I've got a terrible crush on her," she admitted.

"Reenie!" I said, turning reflexively to look at her, so I could figure out her attraction and master it for myself. *What can she see in Reenie?* I thought, and at the same time: *Reenie sees plenty in me.*

"*Don't stare,*" Lee said, and out of fear of my "staring" pulled me in tight. We waltzed for a moment like a couple of prom dates, in time with some old song in our heads, while the disco music slammed on.

"Oh," Lee sighed, "it's such a relief to *tell* someone." She smelled so sweet, of laundry detergent, I wanted to gather her in and bury my face in her shoulder. Reenie was so natural—she said into my ear—like a colt, didn't I think?

"Yes," I said, thinking furiously that Reenie probably had about the intellect of a colt, and at the same time, that Reenie was at least perceptive enough to recognize *my* charms. I held Lee tight, tight as if I'd had a knife at her back. I already wanted her, but now I had to have her.

Five

I KNEW one person who had studied love in its every incarnation, from the time of immense, waddling fertility goddesses to the advent of leather and chains. One person who could have been curator in the museum of love.

"Philippa?"

"Ye-es?" (This spoken with her characteristic wary irritation.)

"It's Beatrice," I said, trying to sound as if I thought this would please her.

"Beatrice." Her wariness ticked upward: she thought she'd gotten rid of me.

"I wanted . . ." I said, but my voice caught in my throat. I wanted to show Philippa I was in love with someone else, so she'd know I didn't need her, wouldn't fear me and run away.

"Now, Beatrice, I thought we'd settled this."

"I wanted to ask your advice about something," I crashed in, but I was so hurt at her assuming I was calling to pester her, when I'd been so good, put my tail between my legs and fled the minute she told me to go, hadn't called her all summer even though I was lost and she was my guiding star, that my accursed voice broke and I felt a wave of tears rising.

"Beatrice, *Beatrice Wolfe*," she said. "Stop this at once!"

"You've already rejected me, Philippa," I said—drily, because I had a glimpse of some absurdity here that I'd never quite recognized before. "You don't have to repeat yourself. I'm calling for romantic advice—there's a *woman* here that I—well, Philippa, I've met someone wonderful."

"You've . . . you *have*? In Hartford?"

It did sound unlikely. "Yes," I said, smugly. Philippa might need Rome; let me show her what I could make out of the insurance city. "I wish you could meet her, Philippa, she's wonderful. So self-contained, so authoritative."

"Hmm, authoritative," she said. "That *does* sound piquant."

"But Philippa, she's in love with someone else," I moaned.

"Not insurmountable," she mused. I heard ice cubes—she was pouring herself a drink. Settling into her chair, ready for the next chapter. Now my eyes really did fill with tears. "She only just met you, you can hardly expect her to drop everything right away. In fact, you wouldn't want it—you need that tension."

"I do?"

"Yes," Philippa said, with sharp pleasure. She was an encyclopedia, she only wanted to be opened to the right page. "Of course! You want her to yearn, you want her to suffer the distance between you, so she'll feel the relief when you cross it! If she doesn't suffer, she won't know the strength of her own feeling."

"How can she have any feeling for me? She just met me last night!"

"You just met her last night, too!"

"But that's different."

"What's her name, what does she do?"

"Lee Schuyler, she works for the Aetna."

"Doing what?"

"I don't know. What does anyone who works for an insurance company do? They go there, thousands of them, every morning, and they don't come home until night. They must be doing something."

"It *is* mysterious," she conceded. "Where does she live?"

"I don't know."

"Well," she sputtered. "Do you have a phone book? Look her up, for God's sake."

"Willbrook," I read. "That's way south of here."

"You've got to go down and take a look at it," Philippa said. "Research is always the first step. Then you'll know how to proceed."

"I'll go down tomorrow, if I can find the right bus."

"And keep me informed!" she said. "Okay. 'Bye."

Keep me informed. I was just repeating these words to myself, in triumph, when she called me back.

"Where was she born?" she asked. "What sign is she? What does her father do?"

"I don't know, I don't know!" I said happily. I had Philippa back, what did anything else matter? I had Philippa back and I was going to make a good story out of Lee Schuyler for her.

AND THE next day, feeling for the first time in months as if I was doing something for a good reason, I left the hospital after my shift and walked straight past my usual bus stop to catch the number twenty-one for Willbrook. Dietary aides did not live in the suburbs; I waited with a couple of nurses, half expecting them to recognize my motive and turn me in to some authority. This fear—that I would overstep one of the boundaries that everyone else held sacred, and be discovered as an impostor, ridiculed and cast aside—would ordinarily have paralyzed me, but now I didn't care. My duty was clear; I had to keep Philippa informed.

Here it was! QUAIL RUN TOWNHOMES, A PLANNED COMMUNITY. A bank of steel mailboxes (Schuyler, 32B), a winding road with yellow speedbumps, parking spaces with stenciled numbers. I was at her door (dove gray, with no nameplate, no wreath of dried flowers, just a door). She was on the first floor, though, so I could look in through the slider, heart in throat, to see: white drapes, with a sensible thermal backing, an aspidistra, a round table on which stood a conch shell whose glossy inner surface scrolled open invitingly, and a photograph in a Plexiglas frame.

We'd had an aspidistra once, a gift from my father's sister. They're not very attractive plants, they never flower, but nor do they wither—to own one is to be certain that one thing in your living room is really alive. Ma saw hers as a bourgeois menace that would attract other conventional objects to itself until our world filled up with them and we became like everyone else. She'd tried to drown it but it only bloated, so she tried to parch it, but the water it had absorbed in the drowning attempt held it for months. Finally, she put it in the basement, and a year later it was, miraculously, dead, dry, and brown.

"I was not going to let *that plant* emerge victorious," she'd said, but I of course had been rooting for it. And here it was, sitting calmly beside a shell picked up on a beach vacation and a picture of someone Lee loved.

She loved someone; she might, possibly, come to love me. Waist-deep in the shrubbery outside her kitchen window, reminding myself to note for Philippa the feminine qualities of the conch, I felt determined that I *would* come to live with Lee and her aspidistra here at Quail Run. Live with her, live like her, my pulse slow, my thoughts calm.

I ran back up the long driveway to the bus stop, skipping over the speed bumps the way I used to skip down the school hallways when I was little. What a relief to be back on the old familiar treadmill, working toward love! The pounding pulse, the desperate inner pleading with a nameless god whose silence would leave me to learn the ways of another heart—the essential subject, the only one important enough to keep my attention. I took the bus back all the way to the Aetna Insurance Company, where Lee must be leaning in a doorway now, having a quiet conversation. Would she walk down the street for lunch? Was there a chance I'd cross her path? The idea of catching her in an act of normality, seeing her buy a pack of cigarettes or admire a dress in a shop window, made my heart jump.

THE SHOP I found myself standing in front of, called LaLouche, was a glass temple to the goddess of chic, and I imagined Lee going in there, choosing a few exquisite pieces and buying them without my million hesitations (were they too expensive, too pretentious, did they make me look fat, or silly, or like I had no idea at all what I was doing, etc.?). The faceless mannequins in the window leaned back against the air with their endless arms outstretched. One was carrying a stack of cashmere sweaters in muted, nameless colors, another was standing behind a card that read SALES OPPORTUNITIES AVAILABLE.

I imagined that if I went in to apply, the owner might become hysterical and try to chase me out with a broom, as a guest of ours had when a flying squirrel fell down the chimney one time. But whoever got that job would have a view of this intersection—she could watch all day for Lee. I didn't even dream of winning her, just of seeing her go quietly, competently by. Starvation hadn't done it, sweating in the bowels of St. Gerasimus hadn't done it—but now, for the first time since I'd arrived in Hartford, I really, *really* wanted a job.

So I pulled open the high wide door and strode toward the

counter, where a languid and infinitely supercilious man in a green silk shirt leaned against the wall and regarded me skeptically.

"You're looking for a job," he said, as if he were a soothsayer.

"How did you know?"

He laughed very slightly, tore an application form off a pad, and handed it across to me with a black and gold fountain pen ten times the weight of the St. Gerasimus ballpoint in my purse. It had a good effect on my handwriting, so that the application *looked* interesting. By the time I'd filled it in, I heard the proprietor's voice behind me, asking me if I could start that afternoon. He'd used the time to walk around and examine me from every angle, and he'd decided I would do.

He himself looked like a maharaja, or maybe more of a goatherd—someone from an exotic storybook. His silk shirt flowed over broad shoulders, and his jeans were pressed, his boots had brass at the toes. He had stubble instead of hair, like he'd shaved his head and then thought better.

"But," I said, "how can you tell I'd be good?"

"Instinct," he said, with amazing arrogance, and reading my name off the top line: "Instinct, Beatrice Wolfe." That was how he'd gotten so far in this business, he said, that was how he could know that, in spite of my apparent mousiness (he paused to let this remark sink in), I had potential.

"Stetson Tortola," he said.

"What?"

"That's my name," he said drily, stepping back, his eyes ticking over me as if he was registering my various capacities on some internal seismograph, then giving a quick nod. Yes, he was sure of it: he could *do* something with me. "Does it surprise you?"

"No, no—why would it surprise me?" I was always careful not to seem surprised—otherwise someone might guess I didn't know anything.

"Ever considered dreadlocks?" he asked.

I had not.

"Well, you ought to," he said, holding up a picture of Bob Marley that he apparently kept behind the counter for this purpose. "Dreadlocks would be just the thing. Sometimes a change of image is necessary."

I peered into the mirror, disappointed.

"I don't know." I wondered if he'd ever considered wearing deerskin, or an old T-shirt, because his face didn't go with his clothing— it was a wary, curious face, not the mask of narcissism I knew from Sweetriver and would have expected from a man in silk.

His eyes flicked over me and then around the store, looking for imperfections. He saw a sweater out of place and stepped around me to get to it as if I were a boulder in the road.

"What weekly salary would you need?" he asked.

Salary, my God. The word was barely in my vocabulary. Ma had made a salary, in her teaching days, but she took it in cash; she liked peeling off twenties to dazzle the pharmacist or the veterinarian with her insouciance, show how little she cared for it all. Money was the antithesis of love; so we didn't associate with the kind of people who made salaries.

But then of course, we didn't associate with anyone. "I'm not really sure," I said. Then I remembered what my father had said. "Would a hundred a week be okay?"

He darted a glance at me and I wondered if I'd asked too much. "Would ninety be better?"

"No, no," he said, "I'm sure I can manage a hundred.

"This a gift from Mom?" he asked then, plucking at my blouse. "Quite a look. Get something off the rack over there," he said. "I mean, assuming you can stay today."

Something in his voice mocked the idea that I might have anywhere else to go. He'd seen through me, knew more about me than I'd told him somehow. For him, fashion was art, and retail sales its attendant philosophy—and by this standard, I was an imbecile. LaLouche clothes did not stoop to flattery—no, they demanded that their wearers live up to their rigorous, if mercurial, standards. If you couldn't manage to look smug in a hacked-off sheath and furry leggings, pigment-dyed in two complementary shades of mustard, then you weren't the LaLouche type and would have to creep across town and get yourself something polyester at Sears.

And indeed, he shook his head sadly as soon as my hand closed on a hanger—"No *flowers*," he said, with a contempt almost as tender as affection. "Try the olive. It'll tone down the pinks." He pressed a finger to my cheek as if it was a muffin he was testing, and my heart leapt. I'd fooled him. I really did look as gentle and flowery as a woman. "You want to play *against* type, in this case.

"That's a little closer," he said, when I came out of the dressing room in something colored like a bruise, and stood in front of the mirror gawking—the dietary aide, the little squirrel, had disappeared. This person looked nearly like a predator, and seeing her I felt different than I'd felt in some months. Stetson had changed me into someone who might be attractive to Lee.

"I don't even know how this got in here—it looks like a table-cloth," Stetson said, carrying the dress I'd picked first, with its depictions of morning glories twining, into the back room. My first task was to pack it up to send it back to its maker, and I went about it with brisk efficiency, imagining Lee would walk by and see me, and be enthralled.

AT HOME, I called the hospital and told them I was quitting. I was shaking—I'd never dared quit anything before, for fear I'd get addicted to quitting and end up back home looking for a pencil for the rest of my life.

"You will *never, ever* work at St. Gerasimus Hospital again!" the supervisor said, sounding not unlike my mother. I felt responsible to seem undone, to weep and apologize and beg her to reconsider.

"Do you promise?" I asked. It was the first bridge I'd ever burned.

"LOVE IS a transforming thing!" Philippa crowed. "I must say, you've pushed the envelope in the stalking department, actually getting a job on her street. And fashion is an excellent field for you. We need bold vision, there's no appreciation these days of the way appearance can shape reality."

"There isn't?" The phrase "bold vision" described Philippa, but she always saw her best qualities reflected in me. I'd be startled and disbelieving, then I'd catch a glimpse of the corner of something, and there it would be—bold vision, or whatever. "Seems like people think appearance can replace reality."

"Which makes for absurdity. But it can *enhance* reality," she said. We were hitting on our basic argument—something about the role of glamour in life. Philippa's childhood had been gritty and glamourless and alleviated only by celluloid; mine was all show so that every time I got a clod of earth in my hand I was grateful.

I was going to flout her, and her damned precepts, from now until eternity. She could hardly expect me to live out her notions after she'd left me. I refused even to try to be lurid anymore, I was going with Lee and her aspidistra.

"And happily ever after too," I added, just to turn the knife.

"*But,*" Philippa said. "The aspidistra motif—I'm not sure I fully understand. I mean, there was the time I followed Tallulah Bankhead into Saks and watched her try on hats, but I didn't actually buy a hat myself."

"That's where we differ. I have a great sympathy for aspidistras." I told her how my mother had tried to extinguish ours, and she began to laugh like a mad gambler who'd put a quarter in the slot machine and gotten more than she could have dreamed. "I do believe, Beatrice, that this is history's first example of a really heroic plant. I see it riding into battle astride its noble mount. It *is* going to emerge victorious!

"So, how are we to accomplish this?" she asked.

We agreed that I had to get Lee talking, draw her out of herself and into my web. Reenie was the potluck hostess next week, which complicated matters, but Philippa delighted in thinking through complications. What if I became Lee's confidante, so that, as she poured her fears and longings into my ear, her affections were to change course, by degrees, and begin creeping in my direction? Would that be possible?

"I don't know," I said. "The thing is, Reenie keeps flirting with me."

"Now *there's* a twist!" Philippa cried. "This could be fabulous."

"How? It's just making Lee hate me!"

"It is making Lee rivalrous, and that alone is a fascination!" she said. "She's going to wonder what Reenie sees in you! Who knows where that could lead?"

"So she might fall in love with me to avenge herself on Reenie?" I asked, full of hope. I did not ask myself whether a love excited by spite was really the kind of love I was looking for; I was in no position for such a proud question.

Six

I'D GOTTEN *The Moosewood Cookbook* because the most upstanding of our last dinner's recipes seemed to have come from there, and settled on a "Comprehensively Stuffed Squash" for its enormous number of wholesome ingredients. Lee was behind me, quiche in hand, as I carried this masterpiece up the makeshift steps at Reenie's. I didn't dare turn to look back at her: she'd see I was casing her, planning to break and enter. She'd probably call the police.

The house was a shell, really, with a piece of plywood laid across two sawhorses for a table and a bedspread tacked up as a bathroom wall.

"You came!" Reenie said.

"'Course," I replied, stricken with shy happiness. So, it was scenario C: my favorite. I dared flash a smile at Lee, who looked as if she'd been run through with a bayonet. The others spilled in with their offerings while Lee busied herself setting out forks and knives from the drainer, with, I thought, a touching little officiousness, demonstrating what a very good little girl she was.

"Do you need help?" I asked, and she glanced up in irritation, wishing I'd go away.

"I could use some," Reenie said. She was sweeping up a pile of fresh sawdust, which smelled of pure hope, and I rushed for the dustpan.

"You did this all yourself?" I said. "It's amazing."

"She's an apprentice plumber, you know," Lee said with pride.

"You did the plumbing yourself too?" I said. Reenie nodded and offered to show me the bath/shower installation, and I was so happy, knowing this would trouble Lee, that I forgot whose heart I was pursuing, and bolted up the stairs behind Reenie with a thrill of expectation as if we were planning to kiss at the top.

Reenie, however, wanted to show off the plumbing. She demonstrated the valves and faucets while I staved off a terrible urgency; Lee was downstairs, this was my one chance to be with her and instead, I was accidentally learning the difference between copper and PVC. In the midst of it, Reenie caught her own eye in the mirror, pulled a comb out of her pocket, wet it, and slicked her hair back with a gesture she must have learned from the movies. No one had actually done that since the mid-fifties, when my father, in his high-motorcycle phase, had worn his hair that way. My blood jumped: she was so thin and long-limbed and her movements so boyishly utilitarian, but her throat was long and smooth and white as milk, no Adam's apple—that sign of a man's secret vulnerability.

"Paper cups?" Lee said, standing in the doorway. "Do you have any?"

"Oh, God, I don't know," Reenie answered, jumping up and brushing by us as she went down to look for them. Lee and I stood facing each other. She seemed to reproach me: she had dibs on Reenie, hadn't she made that clear? I did feel guilty—not for trying to steal Reenie's affections from Lee, but for allowing my own to waver. And out of that guilt, a thin tendril of sympathy began to grow.

"It's something to be proud of, building your own house," I

said, thinking that of course Lee loved Reenie—Reenie could *do* things. What skills did I have to show? My ability to keep the members of my family spinning like so many plates, so that as long as I kept running from one to the next, encouraging, consoling, nodding my head or shaking it, they would keep their precarious balance a minute more?

"I hope you two manage to get together," I said, with resignation. "For her sake."

And Lee blinked quizzically up at me, then her face shed its wariness and she nodded in agreement. "Thanks," she said. "We better go down."

By the time we got to Kingdom Come something infinitesimal, and essential, had changed. I'd told them all about my new job, and Pat had given the others that look she used to remind them not to trust me. "It doesn't bother you, perpetuating oppressive masculine ideals?" she asked.

Her tone made me feel so guilty and defensive, I barely heard her words. "It's a hundred dollars a week," I said. I could afford to buy Lee a drink. She talked about Reenie as we danced, but it was a different kind of talk, more a way of getting to know me. We were at one with each other, now that Reenie had enchanted us both.

"She's *strong*," Lee said, resting her head on my shoulder. "You should see her working. She just does the job step by step until it's finished, it's wonderful to see."

A slow smile, tender bouyant breasts, the ability to listen avidly and guess what underlies a conversation, a dreamy willingness to fall open in a man's hands; I'd thought I knew the catalogue of female beauties—strength, or effort? No.

"She's, she's just so . . ." Lee said, smiling hopelessly, dancing without reference to the heavy beat, as if to refuse its drive. Beside us Susan bopped miserably, like a chicken trying to fly, but the men around us seemed to be riding astride the music, and when the beat quickened they went with it together. I felt their vigor and loved it. I was skating at a rink once, falling down every twenty feet, when "You Beat Me to the Punch" came on and I did a perfect spin all of a sudden. The music had seemed to ask it, and I wanted to oblige. It was like love, I thought, looking up into the mirrored ball, feeling the bass thump in the floor. I was among my own people at last, and Lee was coming around, and Philippa wanted to hear the story. I glanced over and saw Pat flash a warning at Lee, and a dark glance in my direction. Guilty, without knowing why I should be, I stiffened, and bounced back and forth on the balls of my feet, dancing the way Lee did.

She was so quietly certain of everything. No, she said when I asked if she'd like another drink; she never had more than two. At midnight she said, "I'll drive you home," without inflection, as if this was just the next task on her list. Pat looked wary but Lee didn't register it and I decided I must be misinterpreting. We went out to her car, a fifteen-year-old Mustang convertible, gleaming like a new apple, confirming my every sense of her, and she unlocked the passenger door for me with an offhand courtliness worthy of James Dean.

TWO HOURS later we were still sitting in it, parked in Frank's driveway, with the engine off and the radio on. Lee was telling me about herself, or trying to. Her father was a certified public accountant, her mother a registered nurse. She'd grown up in Levittown, gone to secretarial school and junior college, moved up through the ranks at Aetna. She was in the education department now, teaching adjusters how to evaluate claims.

"Wow," I said, when she told me she had graduated from college in 1969, "You were *there*."

"Where?"

"*There.* In the sixties!" I breathed, my mind filling so full of images that Charles Manson, Abbie Hoffman, Bobby Kennedy, and Malcolm X all streamed together in a righteous, murderous procession. Straight out of the television and into my unconscious they'd come, while I worked my long division at the kitchen table, and what they had said to me, in unison, was: *Come, grow, and soon passion will blaze up in you and your life will begin to mean something. Make love, not war!*

"I can't believe it; you were there," I repeated, thinking that if Lee's hair had been long, which it must certainly have been back then, she'd have looked just like the woman at Kent State who had knelt beside her friend's body and shrieked at the heavens.

"I suppose I was," she said, writhing a little. "It didn't really get to us. I mean, there were some troublemakers. I mean, not troublemakers, I don't mean that, but you know—I wasn't in with that crowd."

I hadn't realized such a wave could sweep over a person and leave him or her unchanged, but looking at Lee—at her hairbrush, actually, which sat ready on top of her purse in case her inch of hair should become disarranged—I saw it was true, that she was more normal even than I'd dreamed. I'd kept my fascination with normality secret, even from myself—as one might when wishing for anything forbidden—to make love to another woman, say. Now I found I was trembling. Here was a gentle, quiet woman, the perfect antidote to myself. To touch her would be to lay hands on everything I'd ever longed for. Of course she didn't want me: Why should she? But I'd convince her to love me and when I had, I'd have conquered the world.

"No troublemakers in Levittown," I said.

"Well, not at Central Penn U." A light rain was falling, and with it the first yellow leaves from Frank's maple tree, which stuck to the windshield like paper cutouts on a schoolroom window. The comfort of fall—the chill, the dark, and the pleasure of drawing inward against them—came over me. Lee made no move to leave and I felt she expected something from me, but I didn't know what it was.

"Would you like to come up?" I asked, feeling finally that I'd rather take a chance on being rejected than disappoint her.

"No thanks," she said, with a faint laugh at my eagerness, though she still didn't move. I didn't like to get out and seem to reject her just when she was having the pleasure of rejecting me. So when she started to talk, I kept still and listened, even though the subject was Reenie.

"I think she does like me," she said, while I traced the shoulder seam of her corduroy shirt—it was as much as I dared touch her, yet. "But she's been hurt, she's afraid to let go. She's attracted, but she doesn't trust me—she doesn't dare trust anyone, really."

"It's sad," I said, despite the corrosive jealousy that was burning through me. "She doesn't realize her good fortune."

And out of the blue, Lee took my hand. We kept talking, to trick ourselves into thinking we were having an ordinary conversation, but, once we'd started touching each other it was impossible to stop, and we got twined around each other in an embrace that wouldn't have been possible in a standard shift. I wanted to give in, as I would have with a man, but she seemed to want to do the same thing. I waited to feel some urgency from her, for her to push her tongue into my mouth or make some other forceful gesture. Neither of us seemed to know how to do this and I wondered if we were doomed to spend all night in the car. I remembered suddenly a man who had thanked me profusely and earnestly when I unbuttoned his trousers—I'd thought it was strange at the time, but now I understood him.

"Who's Ginny?" I asked, since an unwelcome silence had fallen.

"She was raped," Lee said.

"My God. No wonder. She looks like she's just back from the dead."

"It happened fifteen years ago but she only just remembered. It's been very hard . . ."

"I imagine," I said, taking a luxurious pleasure in the centimeter between our mouths, knowing the distance would soon be closed.

"Mm-hmm." She responded to every move I made, but she made none herself. The rain had become insistent, my toes were cold, my neck stiff, and my bladder full.

"Lee, I have to say good night," I said, and now, without a word, she followed me in. We tiptoed up the steps to avoid Henny's notice, but as I fished for my keys in the dark hallway, my telephone started to ring.

"A wrong number," I said, hoping I sounded like the kind of person whose relatives didn't call with bizarre miseries at all hours.

"Let it ring," Lee said, but I was struggling with the lock, wondering which of them was alone in the night, hoping to conceal his or her desolation from the child sleeping down the hall, which of them was listening now to that godforsaken sound of a phone ringing in the empty room where they'd thought they'd find someone to console them. I was incapable of letting a phone ring. I fell in through the door and grabbed it.

"Sylvie's having a baby," Ma said, with Clytemnestra's grief.

"You know." I sat down and gave up all hope.

"You know? Who told you? *Your father*, I suppose. How long have you known?" she asked.

"She just called," I said, feeling my mother might otherwise have insisted that Sylvie was just going to have to get rid of *that* baby, and do it right the next time: tell *her mother* first. "Just this minute."

"I've been trying for hours."

"I've been in and out."

"Well, it doesn't matter. Beatrice, I'm going to give up, I can't go on with it."

"With what?" I heard my insolence as soon as the words were out. And I'd felt so sympathetic to her, before I answered the phone.

"Am I going to go through my life without being loved?" she asked me, her sorrow going over to rage. "Is that just my fate? Will I never—"

I'd been so alone with her all those years, I'd absorbed all her feelings and tried to filter the poison out of them, but it never worked and now I wanted to smack her for adding the sad violins and black borders as if I didn't know already that her heart was broken, as if I hadn't worked and worked to fix it all this time.

"NO," she said. "Of course *you* don't see what I'm saying. Why should you? Well, it's just too bad—if people don't understand, so be it. I've spent enough time trying to convince people to like me. I'm looking for money, now, Beatrice. Money and power. That's what it's all about."

Brassy dame—what'd she do with the weeping orphan?

"My life is over, *over*," she said now, sorrow gone over to rage. "But you wouldn't understand that, you with your *brilliant career*."

I put my head down on the table, trying to keep hold of my tongue. Lee sat on my bed, smoking, leafing through my *New Yorker*, and acting as if she wasn't overhearing my conversation. I wondered how much longer she'd wait for me. I willed myself to kindness; kindness saves time.

There *is* a divine presence in the heavens, I guess, because she said suddenly: "I hear thunder, I've got to get off."

"Things are going to be all right, Ma, really," I said.

"I said there's *thunder*," she said. "Good-bye."

And she vanished, leaving only some weird emotional residue, like the Cheshire cat. The apartment was damp and cold—when I'd left for the party it had been a sultry night. Now the windows were swollen in their jambs, but the phone call had given me a kind of desperate strength and I forced them shut tight one by one.

"Whatever the problem is, slamming things isn't going to help," Lee said, in the tone of a third-grade teacher.

"You're right," I said, and sat down beside her, expecting she'd kiss me, and that love would blot Sylvie and Butch, and their trailer, and their baby out of my mind. At least I would not be getting pregnant—using love as a trap, and getting caught in it myself—the way Ma and now Sylvie had done. This alone sent a wave of desire through me, and I imagined Lee and myself swirling into each other like two currents in a slow river. But she kept still beside me.

What was she doing here if she hadn't come to make love? What was she expecting? I lived to do whatever was expected of me—to succeed as my mother wished, or fail as my father wished, or hopefully both, so as to repair all the damage between them and keep everything whole. I knew a man would want me to switch off everything except instinct, lie back, give in, divine all his secrets, and transform myself without even realizing it, to match his dreams. With a man, you just take him into yourself, his gaze first, then his cock, then his heart. You feel him thrust into you, know he wants you. It's all so easy, I thought now, though of course I'd never thought so before.

I kissed Lee again, waiting for some vigor to seize us, feeling her stroke my arm, so gentle, so irrelevant. Where was Philippa, my hyperkinetic darling? She would never have just sat there—she'd quote something, she'd make love to me.

"Sometimes it helps if you push a window up a little farther before you try to pull it down," Lee said, trying to help, and a rough, angry instinct overtook me—I'd show her about slamming things! There was a vessel in her that needed to be broken so its essence could be released, like a vial of smelling salts. I clutched her suddenly, with a sharp, chiropractic snap—pure machismo. *In an emergency, break glass*, I thought.

And rightly, because she recognized the gesture and at once, her arms were around me in earnest. I took her head in my hands and kissed her for real. We had reached the necessary understanding, I hardly knew how.

"You're so beautiful," I said, and she smiled with kindly condescension—why did I state the obvious? Of course, I thought, there was nothing more to be said, and I unbuttoned her shirt—finally—to touch her breasts, her nipples, which were so exactly like my own that my body reacted as if it had been she who was touching me. Her cigarette was burning down in the ashtray. I crushed it out. From there everything was instinct—what a relief to be back in the land of eros, the one place where I knew what to do.

Seven

*W*E COULDN'T keep our hands off each other," I said in the morning.

"We?" Lee looked incredulous and pulled the blanket up to her neck.

I tried to recall our exact movements but could not. Had I forced myself on her? Probably. I was so greedy, had wanted her so badly, it was all too likely that I'd jumped in and overpowered her. I was like that, like a man: once I sensed a possibility, I couldn't hold back. It was *always* an emergency with me. Had she made love to me then from politeness alone? And I'd been filled with the joy of requited love when really I was practically raping her?

"I'm sorry," I said, mortified.

"You're impulsive, that's all," she said, as if she'd forgive me this one time.

She was dressed in seconds, in the clothes she'd folded so perfectly the night before. She wet her hairbrush, leaned down, and brushed her hair vigorously forward from the nape, then carefully back from her temples, craning her neck at the mirror and licking her fingertip to address some (invisible) trouble spots before sighing that this would have to do for today. In fact she

looked so neat and professional it was hard to believe I'd ever
touched her. It was Saturday, but she had to lead a seminar in Cost
Justification and Prioritization. She bustled in and out of the
bathroom on obscure but important errands, averting her eyes.

"I'm going to be late if I don't go this second," she said. I'd been
going to ask her for a ride to LaLouche, but I knew I had to let go
of her, if I ever hoped to see her again. She kissed me good-bye,
politely, and descended the narrow stairway. I heard Henny's door
click shut as she went down the path—there'd be a better view of
her from the front window now. From my own front window I
watched the Mustang go off down Prentice: Who'd have guessed
James Dean wasn't driving? So maybe she was a little like him, or
like the men Hollywood used him to represent—those wide-
shouldered men with such terrible longing in their eyes. It's hard
(Ma and Sylvie could attest) to keep away from men like that, who
seem to drink their life from us, so we can watch them grow
strong and marvel at all we've given them.

Nature made it so, I thought, sitting down hard on the thin cot
I used for a sofa, looking up at Frank's looping brushstrokes of
swimming pool paint on the ceiling. For a man, the words "I love
you" are an admission of weakness; for a woman they're a declaration of strength. I was right to love women, I knew it, but how
could I have wrecked it all with my unholy aggressions—why had
I tried to barge in on Lee's heart? I'd lost her; it was my own fault.

And into the appalling vacuum this thought created, rushed
the image of the joy we might have known if we'd really had the
chance to be lovers. How we'd have fallen with fear and delight
into each other's depths, kissed in slow defiance of the urgency of
desire, since we had months—years—ahead to satisfy ourselves
with each other. Last night's kisses had been movie kisses, show
kisses that looked better than they felt. And now we'd lost our
chance for the real kind. To lose something you've held in your

hands already is bad enough, but to see a hope fly up through your fingers while it's still shimmering, before all its truth, its ordinariness, is revealed—nothing stings so badly. Searching my mind for something warm to cling to, I found Lee's flannelly scent, and the one soft curl she had allowed her hairdresser to leave, at the nape of her neck.

She was gone, and with her, my chance for love. I'd thought she'd given in because my roughness excited her.

So much for my attempt to join the civilized world. I'd see Lee next week at the support group, if I dared to go, and we'd be awkward and distant and try to act as if nothing had happened. All the things I'd never get to say to her! This seemed the worst of it, because, unlike my mother (I kept turning the sentences from her love letter over, working to make them so meaningful that that boy wouldn't be able to resist her. If someone really, deeply loved her, she'd be healed and our center *would* hold), I could really speak my love. The phone rang; I jumped on it.

"I just wanted to say thanks, for coming last night," Reenie said. "It was really nice to see you."

"Oh, thank you for having me," I said, trying to imagine why she was taking up my phone line with unnecessary gratitude when Lee might be trying to get through. She'd been caught in the shower of stardust I'd been trying to sprinkle on Lee. But at least if Reenie was in love with me, Lee wouldn't be able to win her, so I could maybe catch Lee on the rebound.

"I was wondering if you'd want to go see the Paw Sox with me tonight."

"The Paw Sox?"

"The Red Sox farm team—down in Pawtucket. You ever been?"

"A sports team?"

"Um, baseball," she said, with a dry incredulity.

"Oh, thanks, Reenie," I said, "but I'm just so busy, I don't think I can take the time." I was going to spend the weekend with Lee, if I could wrest my phone line back so she could call me. "Thanks so much for asking, though."

"What are you busy with?" Reenie asked, with genuine interest.

"Work, in fact I'm late right now," I said, which, since I was going to have to take the bus, was true.

DRESSED ALL in olive and carrying my coffee in a Styrofoam cup, I strode up Aetna Boulevard. I was a working girl, I had my ring of keys; soon I would unlock the high glass door, punch in the code that disabled the burglar alarm, and flick on the banks of incandescent lighting. I'd sweep the sidewalk and wash the window with Stetson's telescoping squeegee, leaving not a streak: anyone walking past must be able to imagine reaching right through the glass to stroke the thick, soft cashmere sweater on the mannequin, whose posture Stetson had adjusted to perfect haughty languor, so you could tell she was above suffering. She lived in the gossamer armor of beauty and no man could resist her embrace. If only *you* could afford to buy a sweater like the one she had on!

That was the illusion Stetson used to tempt his customers: style, he suggested, could save you from the pain of mortal life. Passing between the racks, where pants and skirts hung each two inches from the last, an anxiety crept over you: Were you allowed to touch the clothes, or only to buy them? Approaching the triptych mirror that stood like an altar at the back of the store, you realized you *had* to buy something, or be doomed to remain a pouchy, stringy mess of flesh, a wretched thing that ought to have been aborted and would scuttle forever beneath the gaze of the divine.

I was to fix every rack the instant a patron walked away from it. If a sweater was disarranged, I was to take the pile to the counter and refold each one around a Plexiglas form. But Stetson tore his hair: I left the unitards stuffed into their cubbies, the one-of-a-kind ascots tumbling over each other on their pegs. I felt uncomfortable following people around and straightening up behind them, as if by trying on clothes in a clothing store they'd done something wrong. Perfection tempts vandalism: LaLouche was the physical manifestation of Stetson's pose, which, like all poses, infuriated me. It reminded me of my parents, pretending to be successful adults while they neglected all the small, true things and their lives eroded beneath them. Wherever I saw pride now, my lip curled and I considered what must be festering under it.

So I refused to give in to Stetson's aesthetic (his word, and if I heard it one more time I was going to dump one of the spare, cool Japanese flower arrangements over his head). This in itself was strange, since I was usually just looking for opportunities to give in (even by taking this job, I was continuing to reshape myself into the stylish woman Philippa had hoped to make of me). But there was a light burning in Stetson somewhere: when he looked, he really wanted to see, and this struck a corresponding spark in me. I kept pulling and tugging at the pose, hoping for a glimpse of what lay beneath.

As he did, in turn, to me.

"I'm glad for you, of course," he said, "I'd love to be happy enough to hum all the time, but I'm not, and exuberance is *not* the LaLouche mien." He marked a few pages in *W* magazine, so I could study the posture (disdainful, aloof) and facial expression (vacant, bored unto hostility) proper to haute couture.

"Sophistication, Beatrice, is about being above things like humming," he explained, seeing my eyes stray over toward

FrouFrou, the shop across the street, where a rainbow of feather boas was blowing in the doorway. The salesgirl stood amidst them chewing gum, wearing a bustle.

"Beatrice?" He snapped his fingers—satirizing himself, and I smiled. "Beatrice, a customer?"

Yes, another one of the depressed women who looked to Stetson's clothes for salvation. When I asked if I could help them, I really meant it: I was always hoping they'd ask me what they ought to do with their lives.

"Oh," I said to this woman, who was watching herself, and the infinite chorus line of identical selves, each wearing a jaunty but inexplicably buttonless alpaca coat, in the triple mirror, "Do you live in a warm climate?"

No, she said, she lived up in Colchester.

"Oh, well, that's a nice, sheltered spot," I said, having recognized my error and trying to back away. "I'm sure the winters in Colchester are very mild."

"Excuse me?" Colchester was about twenty miles north of Hartford.

"I mean," I said, "It's so hilly there. It's the winds, the winds on the plain, that you have to watch out for. In a climate like Colchester's, you could wear that right through November. And then by March, by March you'd be wearing it again, in a temperate place like Colchester. And it's so nice to have a dressy coat like that—not that it's *so* formal, just a little much for everyday, though now I think about it, not really enough for evening. And it can get cold in the evening."

I wanted to shut up, really I did. But I was coming to know too much about shopping. Nobody needed that coat, or this catsuit, no one would fall ill for the lack of one of the beaten gold necklaces in the locked case. You'd never guess it, though, from their faces—the men hunched and monosyllabic, grateful to be allowed just to buy something instead of having to speak their feelings. And the women, trying to believe in the gift, wrapping themselves in the heavy fabrics, turning at the mirror, joyful in the beauty the clothes seemed to give them without realizing it was they who were giving their beauty to the clothes. No sooner had I swiped the credit card than I would see the face grow uncertain: *Was* this that supernatural raiment, bound to confer grace upon its wearer? Or just another stretch of rayon under which the shoulders of its cowering owner, so confident in the mirror only a minute ago, would soon slump again?

I had to keep talking. There was very little I could accomplish on this earth, except maybe to save this woman from buying that coat. Our eyes met in the mirror. Hers glittered with irritation—just what was I trying to tell her? She ran her hand along the sleeve—it was so soft, and I guessed, looking at her, that she had not known much softness. She was not the glamorous customer Stetson imagined for himself (such a person did not exist in Hartford), she was heavy and in the middle of her disappointed face her lipsticked mouth glowed a brilliant cherry red—she'd come out this morning to try to feel pretty and hopeful—why did I want to wreck it?

"I love it," she said with defiance, and twirled like a little girl, a smile lighting her face for a minute while the unsecured lapels flew out. "It's so luxurious, but it's not too dressy, you could wear it with jeans, you could wear it with a suit," she piped—almost exactly the copy from the *W* ad—and she pressed her face into it, inhaling the jasmine scent Stetson steamed into everything so that it would still smell of LaLouche as long as it was new and full of possibility.

"Have you seen the hats and mufflers?" I asked. She was determined, her Visa was platinum, and once she crossed that line and handed it over, she'd be good for another fifty at least. "Hand-knit from the wool of free-range llamas, all vegetable dye, and very warm—they'd fill up that open spot in the coat."

She took one of each and grabbed a cashmere lap robe as she passed the display. Total: $675, and it wasn't yet noon.

"Which is marvelous, Beatrice," Stetson said. "It is, but it *does not* fold the shirts. I mean, what is this, an origami elephant? Is this the trunk flapping here?"

It was a sleeve. Sloppy folding, secret reading, casually reminding a customer that his magnificent purchase must never be exposed to sunlight or soapy water—with these amulets I tried to ward off mercantile despair, the sense that the whole world might be as cool, precise, and empty as LaLouche.

"*No reality*, Beatrice," Stetson had said when he found the radio on. "Shoppers torn between alpaca and vicuña should not have to listen to the news from Zaire."

"I *like* reality," I'd countered, though this, like most sentences spoken on earth, was wish presented as fact. The news frightened me to death and I just hummed all the louder when it came on. I couldn't listen, couldn't look at the world outside, for fear of what I'd see. Still, though, I *dreamed* of being the kind of person who read the newspaper, who dared to find out things—I aspired to it, badly as it frightened me.

He'd smiled, ruefully—he was getting to know me a little, he sensed the layers of meaning under the things I said; he liked knowing those layers were there. "Here's a little reality for you, dear," he said, opening *The Courant* to show me a man who'd strangled his girlfriend's seven-year-old daughter when he discovered she'd been unfaithful.

"I'll take vicuña," I sang.

"That's my girl," he said. I rearranged my posture to look more like one of the mannequins, then started laughing and gave it up, so he had to laugh too.

"That's my boy." His eyes flicked wide at the condescension before he remembered I was repeating what he'd just said to me.

"One thing I do know about is the vise grip of love," I told him.

"I believe you," he said, with surprise. I didn't usually speak with so much authority. He turned his wide brown eyes on me with warm curiosity, so I was moved to grab a bunch of sweaters and fold.

"SO, BEATRICE, have the waves rolled over the shore, as it were?"

"I suppose you could say that," I said.

"And you haven't called to report?"

One didn't admit defeat to Philippa, only triumph. I decided to try and distract her.

"Too busy," I said. "I've got a new job. Selling *very chic* clothes." Her silence seemed to have a dry quality.

"It's true," I piped, aware she'd find it bizarre. "At the most fashionable store in Hartford."

The silence became somewhat dryer, as if I'd said "the warmest beach in the arctic." But this did make it seem more likely that a congenitally styleless person like me might be an acceptable salesgirl there.

"Well. Congratulations," she stumbled, but caught herself. "I expect you'll make an excellent salesperson. You're so—natural."

"Natural" was *not* her highest term of praise. Lee, I thought, would value my artlessness properly; she herself had such simplicity. And I gave my memory of the night with her another little tweak toward the good, and missed her even more. Who'd have guessed that by flouting my parents, I'd find a way to flout Philippa too?

———————

"YOU DIDN'T call me," Lee said.

The woman's not supposed to do the calling; seeing my nature, my mother had drummed this into me early. "I thought you didn't want me to," I mumbled. I'd just gotten home from LaLouche and I was a different person than I'd been when I last saw her, four whole days ago. Hearing her voice, I felt ashamed all over again of the way I'd forced myself on her.

"I did—want you to," she said, or this is what I thought she said, but she was barely audible and this gave me some courage.

"I thought you said I overstepped—"

"Should I bring a pizza over for dinner? Would you like that?" she asked.

"Lee, I . . . I'm so sorry about last night. It was wrong, so wrong and I never will again if only you'll give us the chance we deserve. I hardly know you, but there's something between us that's . . . transcendent, I guess you could say. I feel so much when I look in your eyes, I know there's such a wonderful possibility there. Please forgive me, please give me another chance. You have such grace and intelligence, there's a deep understanding in you, it would just be terrible if I never got to know you."

I felt all this just then with such fervent intensity that I didn't care whether or not it was true. Love is the most important, most elusive thing there is. You only had to take one look at my parents to see this. If they'd been murdered, I'd have become a detective. If they'd been paupers, I'd be a banker. But they were victims of love, so this set my course: through vigilant scholarship, innate talent, and plain hard work, I would become an expert on that subject. Then I could bring it down from the mountains, or up from the canyons, or wherever—see there was enough for everyone, that no one was left stumbling parched through a desert again. I'd be the woman who found the cure.

Hearing Lee's step on the stairway, I opened the door to a face I had to struggle to recognize, after all the permutations it had gone through in my mind. She kept her eyes down, afraid of what she'd see in me, but she needn't have worried. We were women; our weakness was attachment, not isolation.

"You're sopping," I said. It was raining and her trenchcoat with umbrella to match was streaming. "Let me get a towel." I dried her heavy dark hair as I'd used to see Ma do Teddy's when he was just out of the bath, and kissed the top of her head for good measure. Then I wrapped a blanket around her shoulders, lit a candle in a beer bottle, opened the pizza box, lifted a piece out for her with the cheese trailing; here we were together, safe. The rain drummed on the roof, the maple tree scratched at the window. From this moment on we were lovers, without question. My physical presence was enough to drive her dreams of Renée away.

"I will think of myself as an archaeologist," I told her, "and of you as the City of Rome."

"Don't be silly," she said shyly. "There's nothing to discover."

"What *can* you mean?" I asked. "We're just at the beginning, We have whole nights' worth, years' worth of talk coming. I mean, what's your favorite supper? What's your idea of God? What weirdo things can't you bear, and what do you love for no reason at all? Are you superstitious? How do you suppose you came to be a lesbian? Where do you see yourself in five years?" I saw myself flowing beside her and into her like streams becoming a river, all the currents of feeling and philosophy rushing together.

"What is this, a job interview?" She meant to be saucy but her voice turned fearful. Her eyes were not brown as I'd remembered but a pale milky blue like a kitten's; they weakly appealed to me to stop the interrogation.

"It's the beginning of a lifelong conversation," I said. "What do you dream about? What are you most curious to know?"

"It's the kind of stuff *kids* talk about, in college," she said, squirming. "Spirituality and stuff."

"What do you want for yourself?" I interrupted. "What do you long for, more than anything?"

She shrugged. Finally, in a voice so small it was almost inaudible, she said, "A girlfriend, I guess." Then, looking down at the floor, she said: "That was my first time, with a woman, I mean."

"Lee!" I said, but she kept her eyes fixed, and I saw that I shouldn't press the question. "Well, you've got a girlfriend," I told her. Philippa had said I had a bold vision.

She drew back, shaking her head.

"Trust me," I said, full of feeling—feeling that had been lying around in my heart for years. "I just want to know everything about you, Lee. We're at the frontier together, we're pioneers."

She looked desperately uncomfortable—but her eyes broke free of her qualms for a second and I saw a flash of light in them, as if she'd just seen something from a dream. "I love you," I said.

People are always saying things they don't quite mean, things they only wish were true. They're likely to deny love just when they feel it most deeply. I despised this convention and was determined to flout it. "Never doubt me," I insisted.

"You're nice," Lee said, gazing upward in discomfort. "You're very nice to me."

"I'm not nice," I said, blazing suddenly. "I love you, I want you, I see my future in you, I feel at the brink of something so amazing between us." I was boiling with sentences like these, passionate declarations. It didn't matter what I was declaring, really, or why.

I wanted to hear myself say the things people dare to, when they're loved. Lee's face went through some stage of incredulity and then broke open suddenly, and I thought—*of course, she's waited all her life to hear these things, and I can say them.* I didn't ask myself whether I meant it—was only proud of my daring and its effect.

In bed later, wearing the nightgown she'd brought in her overnight bag, she told me in a childish whisper that there was one story that might give me some insight into her—one detail that had always seemed to her revealing. Then, with pride, and shame at being so proud, she told me that she held the all-time attendance record at Clear Springs Central School. She had not missed one day of school, from kindergarten through eighth grade.

She believed in order, in lawful simplicity. She didn't care about the mysteries that make people so different from each other, even though we're all so much the same, nor the memories, if they were really memories, that can haunt a person and alter the course of a life. She suspected that it was dangerous to think the way I did, trying to follow all the subtle strands of thought and feeling that wove through every moment. Things are as they are, who can really say why?

Life is to be lived, not deciphered. Lee would rescue me from all my figuring; she'd welcome me into her world, the ordinary, unexamined world whose windows I'd only peeped through before. The rain coursed down over the window, and I rested my head on her flanneled shoulder, and slept as deeply as a fugitive, safe in his cell finally after years of running. The unconscious life was the only life for me.

Eight

————

MY FIRST paycheck came as a revelation. It was $77.32.
"Stetson, we said a hundred."

"That *is* a hundred." He looked uncomfortable, though, as if
I'd touched on something he was ashamed of.

I held the check up for him to read. "See, it says seventy-seven
dollars."

He winced. "You don't know about taxes, do you?" he said,
with tender incredulity.

"Of course I know about taxes," I snapped, though I'd completely forgotten about taxes and it had never occurred to me that
taxes might consume almost a quarter of my wage. Seventy-seven
dollars was less than I'd made at the hospital, and I owed Frank
two months' rent.

"I'm sorry," I said. "You're right, I didn't realize. This is fine, no
problem." It was all written on Stetson's face—that he knew the
money wasn't enough, that he couldn't afford much more, that I
wasn't doing a very good job and he couldn't very well fire me but
could hardly raise my salary. If I started to cry, which I was likely
to do if I admitted to myself that it *was* something of a problem,
that would make him more unhappy and I didn't want him to
despise me.

"A sweater!" he said suddenly. "You need a new sweater! Look at these, have you seen how soft they are? Have one, take the raisin-colored one there, it's you."

I grabbed it as if it was edible. "You, in that sweater, Beatrice?" he said, sounding sarcastic because he sounded that way even when he was sincere—"Now that's class."

One afternoon while he was out pricing display racks, his mother called. I'd never considered that he might have a mother, but he did, and she, having lost a leg, and most of her vision, to diabetes, was lonely and needed someone to talk to. So she talked, chewing too, or so it sounded, while *Wheel of Fortune* played in the background, interspersed with commercials for hospital beds and orthopedic pillows. Josip, as she persisted in calling him, had been such a nice little boy—did I know, she collected commemorative plates and Hummel figurines and even as a two-year-old he had never so much as chipped one? After his father left, he'd done everything with her, even watched the soaps every day. Then he'd figured out how they could make ends meet, when she was desperate and he was hardly more than a boy—that was how he got into trouble, it wasn't his fault. She talked on and on and I listened with all my heart, as I did every time I got my ear to the world's door.

"How much?" Stetson asked, holding up the pink "*while you were out*" slip where I'd noted her call.

I tried to act mystified, but he waved a hand. "She always tells the sales clerk, Beatrice," he said. "Otherwise I might be able to wiggle out. How much?"

"Seven hundred," I said, "though . . . she said . . . it might be closer to a thousand, really."

"A thousand it is," he said, writing the check. "Anything else?"

"I think she's lonely," I said.

"Very astute of you, Beatrice," he said, "but I meant, were there any other messages?"

I shook my head. I shouldn't have peeked behind the curtain. He loved clean, well-lighted places, he was determined to raise himself into the lifeboat with the survivors and leave the wreck behind. And the survivors, you *know* they'd been traveling first class. If he wished to live among them, they must never guess about the Hummels, the sweet, greasy smell of the little apartment, any of it. No reality.

"When I first saw you," he told me, "I said to myself, 'That's class. That's old money, man. She's a woman of wealth and taste and all you need to do is dress her, Stet.' "

So, I was pulling it off. Or rather, as Stetson was also an impostor, he had to live by the impostor's code: believe in the disguises of others as you would have others believe in your own disguise. Expose another, even in your own secret heart, and the whole house of cards comes down. If Stetson had had the good fortune to matriculate at Sweetriver College, he might have become friendly, as I did, with Thaddeus Standish Alden, whose father, the lumber magnate, had singlehandedly deforested an entire northern range. Thad's paintings were the pride of the school, proof that Sweetriver was at the cutting edge of the postmodern, not at all mired in Abstract Expressionism like people said. His taste ran to the color black, whose many forms and depths you would not, if you didn't know him, have guessed. He used to knock on my door at midnight to borrow ten dollars and offer confidences, such as: he loved his dog better than any human; they slept curled together and even smelled alike; he painted only with black because it was the last color in the school bookstore display, and so the easiest to steal; and he had to steal—he refused to take money from his father's filthy hands. When his mother was taken ill one night, he came in to borrow bus fare home, swearing that modern life was to blame for his troubles—in an earlier era she'd simply have been left on a north-facing slope to die. When I thought of old money I always thought of Thad, and the things that got caught in his beard.

"Then," I said, "why the dreadlocks?"

"You know, who else would look fabulous in dreadlocks?" Stet said, "Princess Margaret. I swear, if I could get Princess Margaret in here I could really do something with her. It's that whole Ivy League thing that makes the dreadlocks matter, it's seeing them where you expect a tiara. They do the same thing as a tiara, shapewise, you know. And that's the kind of thing that suits you."

I knew he meant this as a compliment, but I was tired of having him lean back and gaze at me as if I was one of the mannequins. I turned on him.

"What's going on with your hair?" I asked him. He'd been letting it grow a little, and now it was all spiked up with gel, some new thing he was trying. "I thought you must have just gotten out of the shower, but that was hours ago."

"It's the wet look," he said. "It's what they're wearing—I don't like to shock you, Your Majesty, but powdered wigs are passé."

But his sneer failed him and he sounded mostly hurt. I'd violated the impostor's code and let him know I could see through his disguise. He checked the mirror fifty times that day and by the time I left I was feeling like a vandal.

And why? So what if Stetson had seized with earnest solemnity on "the wet look," or any look at all? Surely everyone ought to be able to worship as he likes? I was ready to turn out the world's closets, upending bureaus and slitting mattresses until I found the jewels life was hiding from me, and I was infuriated to see Stetson's devotion lavished on superficial things. Because I'd caught a glimmer of something deeper in him, and when it seemed to fade, I felt he'd betrayed me, sided with Lee to show me that the precious essences I'd dreamed of, the deeper insight and broader understanding, were no more than figments of a naive college girl's imagination.

Next morning he came in with the hair soft and dry, sticking up in little tufts. "Like it, Beatrice?" he asked, with his usual lofty acidity.

"I love it," I said, because he looked sleepy and rumpled like he'd just woken up, and because I knew he'd done it for me. "You should grow it out a little."

He smiled, almost shyly. "Nah, it gets unruly," he said.

"God forbid," I said, fluffing up my own mop. "Wouldn't do to let it run wild." But since I spent most of my waking moments trying to change myself to meet somebody else's ideal, I was terribly struck by his changing something in himself for my sake.

"Did you used to wear it long?" I asked him.

He almost flinched, for some reason, then got himself together and smiled. "Yeah," he said. "It looked just like yours."

"Horrors."

He smiled immensely. "Then it got caught," he said, keeping his eye on me to see my reaction. "In the axle of a car I was stealing."

"Why were you stealing a car?"

"Had to get somewhere," he answered, happy to have shocked me.

"Like, a hospital?" I asked. He held back a minute more but then, the pressure was getting to him—he wanted to tell his story.

"To see Jimi Hendrix," he admitted. "I saw this Jeep just sitting in a driveway, the houselights weren't on. I knew the back door would be unlocked, I knew the keys would be hanging there. That's how people are, they can't really believe—"

"Some guy is just going to drive off in their car." I looked at him sternly, like a third-grade teacher.

"Exactly," he said, laughing. "But I just got on Eighty-four, in the pouring rain, and I got a flat tire. Man, you have never seen anyone change a tire so fast."

"One of those miracles of strength, like guys have in a war," I said.

"Exactly. Except, I try to stand up, and my hair is wound in the axle. And while I'm lying there trying to get it out, there come the police."

"What happened?"

"Guy had scissors in the glove compartment, cut me loose, wished me well."

"He liked you," I said, thinking this cop must have seen the same thing I did in Stetson, a vital goodness that would make it impossible to imagine him a thief. "He just naturally helped you."

"Or, he was just stupid. Anyway, the next day, I left the car up the street with the keys under the seat. I'm sure it worked out."

"So, does this mean I have to watch my purse?"

"No, no, of course not." He looked protective, as if I could count on him to keep me safe from that old self of his. "I don't do stuff like that anymore."

He was even talking differently, his irony was gone and he was watching my face like a guy watching a slot machine, to see how I'd take the story. I took it very well—like the money for his mother; it was a glimpse of something real, something solid in Stetson—something that wouldn't change with the fashion. Just the phrase "stuff like that" had an adolescent ring that touched me. He could have been some guy on my school bus, before Sweetriver got me in its clutches. I disapproved of myself, but I couldn't help liking his criminal spirit—I recognized it as if it were my own natural way.

"No, now you're a fashion guru," I said.

"Oh, I'm just a drunk, Beatrice," he said jauntily. "Recovering, but basically, a drunk."

"Stetson!" His mother had hinted at this, and he probably knew it, but his telling me meant something different. It went into my heart like a hatpin.

"Once maybe, but not now." I swept my arm out to remind him what a palace he'd made. "It's impossible for me to think of you that way!"

"Then you're wrong as usual, Beatrice," he said, ducking into the back room.

*N*ine

*I*F IT's a girl, we'll name her Seraphina," Sylvie told me. Her voice had a child's confidence—a thing so fragile, anyone could crush it—but she trusted me, she put it in my hands. Our hearts still contained the same vision, like two lockets with matching pictures enclosed.

"Butchy's making *a lot of* money," she went on. "You know the old drywall plant out by the railroad tracks, the Nubestos plant? Somebody's bought it, they're going to make running shoes or something in there. But they've got to get all the old junk out of there and they pay in cash, no taxes!"

"But Nubestos abandoned that place. They just laid everyone off and closed it overnight."

"Yeah, there was some kind of change in the law."

"Yeah, that Nubestos was going to be liable in about a billion dollars' worth of lawsuits when all the workers died. Sylvie, that place is poisoned, that's why they're paying under the table."

"Butchy's not afraid of it, not at all," she said stubbornly. She'd not hear her man called a coward. She'd taken up his life and that meant taking up his views, his ideals, even his ignorance—something unmanly in the fear of ingesting poisons, and, I supposed, something unrealistic. Butch was going to die in a fight or a car

crash; asbestos wasn't *quick* enough to kill him. Sylvie always said
"I don't know" so sweetly, with such generosity: she was happy
not to know, so someone could have the pleasure of explaining.
She *did* know what could be accomplished with an admiring
look, how much would be given to the girl who stepped back and
seemed to want nothing at all.

"Sylvie, you've heard of mad hatters, right?"

"Like, in *Alice in Wonderland*?" she asked, sounding out of her
depth. I *would* have to bring up English literature (that is, her lack
of education).

"No, or, yes, but, do you know why hatters used to go mad?"

"No," she sighed. "You mean there was more than one?"

"They lost their minds because they worked with arsenic
every day!" I said.

"That's terrible," she said politely, without seeming to make
the connection. Who can really imagine everyday actions—good
things like hard work—as harmful? The history lesson of the
Wolfe dinner table had been that the past was a hellhole, not to be
peered into. Suppose you lost your footing on the bank? No, you
lived with your back to it, and all its mad hatters.

"I put geraniums on the front steps, and yesterday I put Con-
tac paper with pictures of flowerpots on the kitchen walls; I just
couldn't scrub them really clean, you know?" She drew on her
cigarette and I heard real happiness in her voice, the unfathomable satisfaction manifest in domestic particulars: the geranium at the window, the patchwork quilt, and under it, the man
and woman, lost in each other's love. She'd never guessed she
could have it all so easily, so soon.

I HAD flowers too—a pot of calla lilies Lee had brought me as a
gift—a secret apology for being the kind of person who had never

wondered about fin-de-siècle Paris, I'd thought, when I saw her standing there in the door, wearing her corduroy pantsuit and carrying these flowers.

"I don't need calla lilies, not when I have you," I'd said.

"You always say the right thing," she mumbled, as I took her in my arms. I was never, ever going to admit that I knew there was an aspidistra on her end table at home. I was going to help her make lasagne and then we were going to get in bed and watch a *National Geographic Undersea Special* together, if we could manage to keep awake. Sleep pulled on us irresistibly now, as if by finding each other we'd done our work on earth and were folded into comfort, away from strife, for evermore. Every night I dreamed I was walking the dirt road home.

"TEDDY GOT me a new lamp, from school, so I can work at night now," Ma said.

"Did they have some kind of a sale?"

"No, he found it in the faculty lounge."

"Found it?"

"It was in the back corner, no one used it."

"You mean he *took* it."

"Well, found, took—you wouldn't understand this, of course, Beatrice, but people in our situation have to live by their wits."

"I guess that's true," I said. What did it matter to me whether Teddy found a lamp or stole one?

"Without Teddy I don't know what I'd do," Ma said. "*No one else is helping.*" Then, suddenly, she broke into flirtatious laughter. "Larry!" she asked, in a dramatic whisper, flaunting her divine secret, "what are you doing back here?" Then came some kind of muffled struggle and the phone crashed to the floor.

"Is somebody there?" I called into the phone, telling myself that Larry is a common name, and this was probably a much older and more distinguished Larry than the one whose eyes had poured something wonderful into hers.

"No, no, nobody," my mother said lightly, "Thank you, my darling, it always helps me *so much* to talk to you. You give me hope, and strength. Don't forget, sweetheart, no matter what, *never, ever* forget how *much* I love you . . . good-bye, good-bye."

"YOU HAVE to have faith, Beachy," said Sylvie, when I repeated my conversation with Ma to her the next day. "Love overcomes all obstacles."

"I do, I do, I have faith in love," I protested dully, thinking that Sylvie was never going to read *Madame Bovary* or *Anna Karenina* and so would be unlikely to get any great perspective on love—its sources, its consequences, its sacred power. I could still hear her wistful twelve-year-old voice singing: "Ta-a-mmy. Ta-a-mmy, Tammy's in love." That was all she had dreamed of—being precious to a man. A man full of strength, grace, and a certain suppressed rage—and in his eyes, that longing a woman knows she can fulfill. (Hubris, Sylvie, is the pride that goes before a fall.) Once this longing sucks all a woman's love and effort into it and is still not filled, and there's no hope to keep the rage in check anymore, things get broken, whole lives get broken. If there was money—but in Brimfield Valley there was no money, only television, alcohol, and faith-in-love. Love, a wheel worth breaking yourself on.

On the other hand, Ma had read Flaubert and Tolstoy, and all she'd noticed was that Madame Bovary was the heroine, the eponymous *main character* of a Great Work, while the others, the good and happy wives and mothers, were part of the scenery against which Emma's drama played out.

"He's not really her boyfriend," Sylvie cajoled me. "He's her assistant, more like."

"And with what does he assist her? Overcoming obstacles? They've already overcome two fairly large obstacles: her marriage, and her job!"

"You're such a know-it-all, Beach," Sylvie said, with admiration and disapproval at once. Not only had I stepped beyond the family pale; now I went so far as to question Ma's supreme right to map our moral territory according to her own caprice. There was that choice to be made—Ma or reality.

"Larry's really nice, *really*," Sylvie said. "He's sweet, you know, in a hulking sort of way, and he's thoughtful—he stacked all Ma's wood for her without her even asking—and he's good with Teddy, just like a big brother."

"Which makes sense, really," I said, "in that he and Teddy *could* be brothers."

"How do you mean?"

"I mean he's not that much older than Teddy! Ma is dating a boy!"

"No," she said, "*not* dating, not the way you mean . . ." her voice trailed away and after a moment she said, "Butch turns twenty-one next month, imagine! He'll be legal. I wanted to have a party but he got all huffy and said what did I want, everyone to figure out he's been using a fake ID?" She laughed. "Not that anyone doesn't know it now, it's just so Don won't lose his license if the bar gets busted. They'd just say Butch tricked them, that's all. But the cops won't bust Butchy. Like Don says, Butchy knows when to trickle and when to pour, and they never bust a pourer."

For the first time in her life she knew things I didn't. She *was* somebody—the bartender's girlfriend, as fine a position in the valley as the mayor's wife held on the hill. The old ladies there fussed over her pregnancy, telling her to put her feet up, knitting afghans, all the things she'd dreamed of, watching those *Tammy* movies with Ma through the endless insomniac nights, learning that love existed over bowling alleys and out back of the auto body shops, not behind the leaded windows of the fine homes. That—marrying up—had been Ma's mistake, but she wouldn't make another, now that she knew where she'd gone wrong. And Sylvie had collected her fallen hatchlings and abandoned kittens and now this stray man, one of those outlaw men whose feelings were stronger because they're never dispersed into language. It was almost like the love and need bottled up in there made them big, because it made them restless, they had to spend huge effort to get rid of it, by lifting enormous beams and hauling in giant tuna and whatever. Sylvie had a man she could take shelter beneath, and she was fitting herself to him in every single way, becoming his comfort, his only luxury, picking up his mannerisms and habits of speech, withdrawing into his world, giving up everything else.

"No, I like a *real* man," she said, with a deep laugh of satisfaction, of knowledge beyond her years. "Though, I wish he was more excited about the baby," she said. "He cares, I know he does, but, it's like he doesn't dare love anything for fear it will hurt him in the end. Oh, Beatrice, I just know I can make him happy, we'll be such a nice family, don't you think? But he's so tense now, he gets mad at the drop of a hat—it's the money, and we need a bigger place, and—"

Little Springtime was barking wildly and she told him she'd take him out in a minute. "The neighbors have these huge dogs and they just let them run. He's afraid of them," she said. "I mean, I don't think they feed them . . . they're stoned all the time.

"I saw the Mushroom in the Grand Union yesterday," she said, getting off the subject. She meant Mrs. Markham, the ninth-grade teacher who Ma suspected had turned her in to the principal. "She didn't even say hello to me, just stuck her nose in the air and walked right by, just because I'm pregnant. Jealous old prude, she can't stand the thought of it—I've got Butchy and she's all alone."

Ma had called Mrs. Markham a "poisonous old mushroom" in front of a room full of boys on detention, which had caused Mrs. Markham, who was in fact short, pale, and large-headed, to develop this nickname, a problem exacerbated by the fact that Sylvie had, purely by accident, called her "Mrs. Mushroom" to her face. So there was no room for question about the reason for the angle of her nose.

"Why is everyone so small-minded?" Sylvie asked in a tone of perfect bafflement, Ma's habitual tone. "Why can't they just be happy for me, that I have a boyfriend who loves me, that I'm expecting a baby?"

And so she sped happily, gloriously, even, toward her precipice, waving to those poor crabbed souls who, unloved by Butch, unpregnant, refused to wish her godspeed. As our conversation wound on, she lit the gas ring to start a new cigarette, praised her midwife ("She asks me—'Did you eat your yam?'— can you imagine that, someone worrying over you that way?") and told me more about the neighbor, whose idea of a family outing involved giving his two kids psilocybin and taking them to see *2001: A Space Odyssey*. "And, did Pop tell you he's teaching Dolly to fly?"

"DON'T TELL *Mommy*," Dolly said.

"I won't, I won't, but Dolly, he doesn't know how to fly a plane yet himself. How can he teach you?" It was one thing for him to *take* flying lessons—but to give them?

"You have to promise. I don't want to upset her." Then she paused, listening: "It's okay," she said, hushedly, "he's taking a shower." She listened again, and, satisfied, began to explain. "He's so depressed," she said, "that's the thing. And the flying makes him feel hopeful. And if this deal gets, you know, off the ground, he's going to buy a plane—it's the best way to get out to the site, really, so he needs to know how. He *is* good at it," she insisted. "He picked it up right away. Peabo says he's natural."

"Peabo?"

"Corwin Peabody—he's the teacher," she said, a bit stiffly—she sensed my skepticism and was defending my father against some charge I hadn't yet made. Or, she was doubtful herself—but doubt was a sin to her and she refused to recognize it. "He's teaching Pop, and Pop's teaching me. I mean, just showing me a few little things. He loves to take me up there and show me what things look like from the sky," she said, and laughed happily all of a sudden. It was the first time I'd heard her laugh since they'd left. "You'd think he owned the state of Wyoming, when he's up there," she said.

She was there beside him, asking him starry questions, taking him more deeply into her possession every time he answered one. This was to be her consolation, for the loss of her mother—she would own her father absolutely, and forever.

"It's not expensive?" I asked, looking for a way to discourage her without seeming to speak against Pop.

"No, it's not, Beatrice," she said sulkily—did no one trust her? "Flying lessons do cost a lot, usually, but Pop made a deal with Peabo—he's helping him get in on the ground floor of this mining deal, so the lessons are reasonable . . . actually they're free."

And how was school? She liked school very well, she said primly—true, she had studied these same things last year, but there was nothing wrong with a little review, and it meant less homework so she had the time she needed to keep up the house. The real education was the new geography, the culture of the West—who had known about all of it, the Indians, the Spanish Catholics? There was so much she was learning by living in a new place, meeting new people, seeing a completely different way of life, and goodness, learning to fly.

"How many fourteen-year-olds have the chance to do that, after all?" she asked me. "No, we have a wonderful life out here, it's great!" she said.

"I'm so glad, Dolly," I said.

After a long pause, she added, "So I don't know why I feel so awful, just so dull and gray all the time—I shouldn't talk about it, I don't mean to depress you," she said, but having started, she couldn't help but continue: "I'm ruining this great trip he brought me on, I try to only cry in the shower so he won't see me, but now he thinks I've got some cleanliness fetish and he keeps telling me not to waste water." She laughed—we laughed together.

"You must miss Ma," I said, thinking that one's mother is one's lantern, and if you can't see the way forward by her light, you're likely to lose the path altogether. But I had said, as usual, the wrong thing.

"No! No no no, it's not that. I'm old enough to do without Mommy, it's not that at all. I don't know what it is," she said. "I've always been this way, you know that." She spoke with disgust, certain that if only she were more vigilant she could beat the misery out of herself. She'd decided to stay with Pop and would stand by him even if it meant forgetting there was any other choice. She refused to miss her home, her school, her friends, her sisters, her mother, and she was left explaining to herself over and over what a fascinating life she was leading, castigating herself for her failure to enjoy.

And the one clear, beautiful moment in the midst of this was her pleasure in flying, that is, her pleasure in Pop's pleasure in flying. I too remembered those times when he stepped out of his gray sadness into the light: suddenly the world was full of possibility. Then he'd fade again and with him, whatever the hope of the moment had been—maybe something as simple as the stair rail he'd meant to fix, still rickety months later so that Teddy toppled off and came up holding a piece of it in his hand—was gone. If I'd been alone with him, in Wyoming, a state situated exactly at the edge of the earth, I supposed I'd like flying too.

"It's exciting about the baby, isn't it?" Dolly asked, in the voice of a very good girl, who would always put her own little troubles aside to rejoice in the happiness of others.

"*Very* exciting about the baby," I said. Far too exciting. Or maybe I was just killing the little bit of joy my family had managed to scrape together, acting like a stuffy, disapproving old spinster aunt.

"It's not like people can't change," Dolly said. "And Butchy's a nice guy, underneath it all. He'll love the baby when it comes. He's just nervous beforehand, you'll see."

"You're probably right," I said. There was a black streak through Dolly, along which, if we weren't careful, she would some day come apart. We allowed for it without thinking, worked around it and so were shaped by it ourselves. Not Pop, of course— he was sealed into his own world, opposed to coddling the quirks of other people's personalities. This trait made him consistent, though—reliable. If Ma was careful of your tender spots one day, then she'd be at them with a hammer the next, and if she was supposed to pick you up at three o'clock and arrived at six, you'd better admit your watch had gone berserk. Pop would be there on time and in person—only his self was missing. So Dolly had taken him as her own. This had been fine when we were all together, and the rest of us could keep her in mind, but now?

"It's like you don't have any faith in us, Bea," she said sulkily. "How are people supposed to manage without that? Ma didn't believe anymore, and that was when Pop lost his nerve, he didn't have the touch like he used to and the business went down. That's why flying is so important, do you see? When he's up there, way up over everything, with all the controls in front of him, when he can look down and see the whole world below, then he can feel the problems fall away, that he's onto a good thing. That gives him the confidence he needs so he can spread the good word about the mine. So the flying would be worth any amount of money— it's an investment. Do you see?"

"Yes, I do," I said. I saw that she was speaking in his phrases, filling in all of his blanks. Her life depended on it.

"It's so hard for him," she said, "without Mommy, you know, anything that cheers him up is important. Family is everything to him. You should come visit us, Beatrice, it would be good for him."

Somehow this reminded me of Sid's saying it would be healthful for Palomino to have sex with me. "It's expensive," I said.

"But, you can afford it, Bea. You have a job." She figured that people who had jobs could afford things: I used to think like that too. Our ignorance, how immense it had been. I glanced at Lee's Burberry umbrella in the corner, the proof that she'd be back. I wasn't alone.

"No!" I said. "I can hardly afford . . ." But what was I thinking? Was I going to tell Dolly the truth? That I hadn't been able to manage the job of dietary aide, and so had given it up for a position as a shopgirl that paid even less? That I spent most of my time cowering in my little apartment, dreaming of a lottery win or a disaster, anything that would save me from having to figure out how to live? Tell a bunch of people who have nothing but faith to sustain them that their leader has no idea where she's going?

"It's the time," I said. "You come see me, can you?" I asked, so heartily I sounded Texan to myself, and was tempted to add: *I'll show you a fine time, little lady*. I felt better just hearing myself confirm Dolly's notion of me—a competent, admirable person, someone who knew what to do, living proof that members of our family could, with some simple training, creep in from the mad ledge and take part in life. Infatuated with this image of myself, I happily suspended my own disbelief and thought how nice it would be if Dolly came to live with me. And if things didn't work out for Sylvie and Butch, she and the baby could come too, and maybe my mother, which would mean Teddy, and then I'd *have* to pull myself together and act like the person they thought I was— there'd be no other choice.

Until then, Ma would be reading by stolen lamplight, Sylvie would follow her heart, Dolly would be learning to fly. But I was here, safe, with Lee. The picture I'd seen the day I peeped through her window was of herself, age six, standing very straight in front of a neat little Monopoly house, unsmiling but content, firmly planted in that earth. Neither smiles nor beauty were essential in Lee's world—in fact, these were luxuries that suggested a lack of humility, a dangerous inattention to duty. I smoothed the hair down at the nape of her neck—she was pocked even there; acne must have plagued and mortified her, but the thickly scarred complexion left behind didn't blush to reveal every emotion, like mine.

Every morning I drove her to work, bidding her goodbye not with a kiss (we didn't dare), but with a complicitous glance against which no kiss could measure, a glance that set us above the rest of the world, and suggested that our love, with its backbeat of secrecy, was for all its mundanity a great, important drama, something much more exciting than any mere man and woman could achieve. On Monday, my day off from LaLouche,

I'd return to the vast Aetna parking lot to wait while the claims adjusters and actuaries streamed past me through the dusk, meeting their wives and husbands, going to pick up their kids at day care or shop for groceries or any of those activities that illuminate ordinary lives. Here Lee came, in her pants and blazer, and the wire-rimmed glasses she'd gotten because she admired mine—lately we'd been asked several times if we were sisters. She hugged her leather "organizer" to her chest, stepping around a puddle with self-conscious care.

"Do you want Chinese?" she asked. And the city faded to lavender, the streetlights blinked on east to west along the avenue, and the evening began to shape itself in apartment after apartment, in each of thousands of orderly lives.

Ten

"S TET, ARE these twenty percent off, or thirty?" We were doing markdowns, many, many markdowns. The fall season had not been what Stetson had hoped. I pushed through the curtain into the back room, carrying an armload of lime and mustard djellabahs, and found him standing on his desk in the dark, to screw in a lightbulb above. His hair had grown an unruly inch, and this change had seemed to bring another—he moved quickly and unself-consciously now, and he had a strength I'd never have guessed. The day before, he'd picked up the triple mirror and moved it across the room as if it was made of cardboard. I couldn't lift the corner of it myself.

"How many alcoholics does it take to screw in a lightbulb?" he asked.

"Thirty-five?"

"None. We prefer to remain in the dark."

"Stetson, that is just not you," I said.

"Oh, but it was, it was," he said. "Honestly I feel like just giving those djellabahs away," he said. "Even I don't like them."

"Why did you buy them, then?"

"It was *the look* for fall," he said, derisively. "Flick the switch, will you?"

I did, and there was light. "There, a miracle," I said.

"They look even worse with the light on," he said, with a sigh that reminded me ugly djellabahs might be his undoing.

"It's one season, that's all, Stet."

"Josip," he said suddenly.

"What?"

"Josip Dinge. That's my name. But Stetson Tortola sounds better. Josip Dinge sounds like the name of a drug addict."

"No, it doesn't," I said.

"It is, though," he said. "I mean, I say alcoholic to pretty it up." He laughed, then looked straight at me—he wanted me to know. "An honest man would say drug addict, because that was what it was."

"Once, maybe."

"A desperate, pathetic man," he insisted. "It's something no amount of silk can cover. Something you spend the rest of your life working back from, every minute of every day."

He took the djellabahs from me and carried them into the half-price bin, his mouth set with workman's stoicism: salvation would come to him through diligence, if it came at all. Watching him, I felt pure light, as if his confession was a sun rising in the corner and its light was flooding in on us, changing everything, so next minute the haughty mannequins would turn from the window and embrace each other with faces full of grief and hands trembling with tenderness.

I thought: *He's just like me.*

"STETSON," I said, a few days later. "There's something I ought to tell you."

He'd heard the catch in my voice and looked up. "What?"

"I, I'm a lesbian. I'm gay."

My pen was shaking so that it suddenly made a little graph on a silk jacket, which shocked me. Why should a person as gay and proud as I was shake so, over the revelation of a perfectly natural thing?

"What do you mean?" he asked.

"Well, you know, don't you? I like women—more than—you know."

"Really?" He looked more baffled than anything else. "You sure?"

"Well, yeah I'm sure," I said, taking offense, as if he were questioning my credentials. "I mean, my girlfriend's pretty sure."

"Your girlfriend." He sat back against the desk, crossing his arms and taking stock of me, and his manner, which had faded since the day he told me about the drugs, returned. "And who, pray tell, is your girlfriend?"

"Lee Schuyler. She works for the Aetna."

"My," he said, looking me up and down the way he had the first day. "I wouldn't have thought—I mean, not that you can tell—" He was stumbling all over himself. In one minute I'd gone from being someone he could say anything to, to someone he hardly dared look at. I'd only wanted to match his own confiding honesty with my own, and instead I'd opened a door on something far too private—as if I'd tried to send him a valentine and given him a real gory, fatty heart instead. I dropped the pen and put my hands out as if I could grab the words back.

"I'm sorry, Stetson. I shouldn't have told you."

"Don't be silly!" he said, hands to his heart. "You know I'm not like that!"

I knew he wasn't going to like me less—if anything, he'd like me more—I was a representative of a type of person he *of course* liked and would stoutly agree with. But I wasn't Beatrice anymore. Our little alliance, which had developed in its own natural and peculiar way, was irradiated by this news.

"I know you're a good liberal, Stet," I said. "It's not that."

"It's just not very Princess Margaret, I guess," he said.

"I told you I wasn't Princess Margaret," I said grumpily. "A princess! Stet, I got on the wrong bus the other day and didn't have the courage to get off again, so I rode it to the end of the line and took a taxi back for fear the driver would look down on me."

"You *project* Princess Margaret," he said, overruling me. Then he added: "*My* girlfriend will be interested to hear this."

Here was a revelation. I wasn't going to take the bait and ask about her. I felt like bursting into tears and making some angry accusation—though what on earth would it be?

"Why?" I asked, sullen.

"She just will," he said. "She wants to be a social worker."

"Oh, so you think I need her help?" I asked with a bitter laugh.

"No, no!" he said, but we couldn't look each other in the eye. "Of course not!" he protested. "Everyone has the right to love in *whatever* way—"

"*Whatever* way," I echoed, so he could hear his condescension, his little push away.

"I don't mean it that way," he said, though. "You're deliberately hearing something I'm not saying—why?"

"Because you're saying something you're not hearing!" I said with great anger. But it was five-thirty. "Go on," I told him. "I'll lock up. Go away."

"LIKE ME? They *loved* me," Ma said on the phone. She'd made some revisions to the job letter, and the guys who were developing the old Parkington place as townhouses were considering her for the front office. "Nobody else can give them the kind of class I do, and that's what they're looking for, style, someone who will define the way people see the place. They need chutzpah, and if there's one thing I've got, it's chutzpah!" She belted this out so grandly, I expected to hear a big chorus come up behind her—*Fiddler on the Roof* meets *Anything Goes*.

"It's the red suit," she said. "That's what carried the day." I heard a thud in the background: her kicked-off pump hitting the wall.

"The red suit?"

Honestly, how did people like me, people who had no sense of showmanship, survive in the modern world? "Red denotes power," she explained. "A woman in a red suit shows a man she can hold her own, that she's got the confidence, the ability."

I saw, in my mind's eye, a woman in a power suit cowering behind a desk in fear of a ringing phone.

"So, they implied you had the job?"

She laughed. "I showed 'em what I can do for 'em, that's for sure. They're the right kind of people—*powerful* people. Everything clicked, we're made for each other. Perley took me aside and said he was very impressed. Then he put a piece of ice—out of his bourbon—down the back of my jacket! Now, that's what I call a good sign . . . don't you?"

I took too long to answer.

"Well," she said, "*I* think it's a *very* good sign."

LEE TOOK me out to dinner: she loved to drive me out along the highway service road and let me choose between the steakhouse with the huge neon cactus, the Swiss Chalet, Moby Dick's, which was built to look like a clipper ship, or the Shamrock, with its real thatch roof—this was the America I was dying to be part of, a vast paved landscape studded with bright plastic replicas of exotic places.

"Tiki Hut!" I said, Tiki Hut being the most ornate, a green pagoda with a dragon breathing real smoke beside the carved doors. Inside, it was lush and dark with a real waterfall at the back surrounded by palms heavy with plastic coconuts and mechanical macaws.

"What do you think?" Lee asked.

"I love it!" I breathed. Before I met Lee, I'd been out to dinner maybe three times in my life. We had a scorpion bowl—rum and tropical juices served in a hollow coconut with two red-tasseled straws. And a pupu platter: crisp fried wontons tied with ribbons of chive, pork pinkened by a sweet marinade and laced on skewers, tiny pancakes, some kind of glistening red roe like beads—a two-year-old's paradise of edible toys. I twirled my paper umbrella like a top on the table.

"I've heard of pupu platters, but I've never had one before," I told Lee, who smiled with secret delight and said, "Try the rangoons." She had eaten hundreds of pupu platters, she went shopping at the mall, she traveled for work sometimes and thought nothing of landing in Indianapolis or Little Rock, checking into her hotel, ordering room service, or maybe going down for a drink in the bar—unheard-of sophistications.

"Did you call your mother?" I asked.

"Mm-hmm. The blood pressure's down and they say if he walks a mile a day, everything ought to be fine." Her father had a little heart trouble and they worried.

"Anything else?"

"No, everything's fine. She was sewing the badges on Jennie's Brownie uniform." Jennie was Lee's niece, daughter of the CPA brother whose wife, to everyone's bewilderment, didn't sew.

"Do you want to drive up and pick apples on Sunday?" she asked.

"You're amazing," I said. "How is it you can guess just what I'd want to do most?"

"You're not hard to please," she said tenderly.

This was why she loved me. I worked hard to phrase things the way she liked them, to say, "Well, she disagrees with me," instead of "She's psychotic!" or "He has a little heart trouble," and not, "He is doomed, doomed!" She appreciated my effort. It left me without stories, though, so we ate in silence.

"Will you come by LaLouche tomorrow?" I asked.

"Do you think that's wise?" Lee said. "Wouldn't it—?"

"Wouldn't it what?" I said. "I want Stetson to meet you."

"Why?" she said with a little grimace. I'd made the mistake of repeating his confession to her, because I'd wanted to relive the warmth it had raised in me, but she found it repugnant and had suggested I look for another job.

"Because I want to show you off!" I said.

She shook her head, but a smile of broke over her face, seeing I wasn't ashamed of her.

"Don't be silly," she said. "I'm nothing special."

It was her ability to say this, to think it, to move through the world every day in the quiet, calming belief that she was nothing special, that fascinated me. I'd had no idea a person could think such a thing and survive.

"Don't you want to meet him and see the store?"

"I've been in there before," she said.

My fortune cookie said: PEACE AND COMFORT, ALL THE DAYS. I read it with a prick of fear.

THE NEXT day, awkwardness made friends of Stetson and me—we banded together against it. He got a phone call and I heard him talking quietly and intensely, soothing, pleading, then obstinate, so that I couldn't help wondering.

"*Women!*" he said, seeing my curiosity, and I laughed.

"The impossible gender."

"You said it, not me."

"It would be sexist if *you'd* said it," I said.

"We wouldn't want *that*." We laughed, together.

"I am *not in love* with her," he said, and he looked to me with a plea. "I'm not. I mean, I love her dearly, but there's not that—" He searched for words, finally put his hand up and yanked a fistful of air as if it was a rope let down from a helicopter—a saving thing. I knew what he meant: love that goes beyond reason and pulls you into a new realm—and you're frightened, and more alive. In all the recent commotion I'd nearly forgotten about this kind of love, but the sight of Stetson's gesture was such a visceral reminder I had to look away so he wouldn't see how it moved me.

I nodded. "What way is it?" I asked.

About to answer, he looked with sudden anger at his hands, as if they had betrayed him.

"I don't know what way it is," he said. "I think, is it just me? Afraid of commitment, the typical thing? I mean, my *marriage* (he gave the word marriage a mocking emphasis) lasted six weeks. I *was* in love with her."

I smiled ruefully. I knew what he meant, too well.

"Then there was Lisa—we lived together three years . . ." He shot a quick glance at me, trying to guess how much further he could go . . . and paid me the huge compliment of continuing. "Though I barely remember it. *Junkie love* . . ." He laughed and shook his head. "We were so busy looking for the next fix we never paid much attention each other."

"That's a help," I said, and he smiled to himself, looked down, then gratefully up at me. I loved to hear Stetson confess. He trusted me to trust him. We seemed to be on a brave errand together: trying to step into the swirling mess of life to try and retrieve a few small truths. We had the time for this because few customers ever stepped into the store.

"Now," he said, "It's all calculation—will she make a good wife? A good mother? I hate 'dating.' I'm always thinking too hard to feel."

"I know just what you mean," I said. "And you know, you probably do love—"

"Tracy."

"Tracy. More than you know." I was folding sweaters, making a show of competency. So like a man, to torment a woman with an ideal of love like that. He looked at my pile of sweaters with resignation.

"She's a great little worker, I have to say," he said. And suddenly. "I love this! You are a woman, and you love women. You're the perfect adviser." Stetson was thirty-five years old, but I seemed to know more about love than he did, because he'd lived in twilight so much of that time.

"Well, I wouldn't say I've been a great success with women," I said.

He smiled at me. "Aren't we a perfect pair?" The word "we" went straight to my heart. I looked quickly away from him, not wanting him to see he'd made me happy.

"But you think about women all the time," I said. "You have to, to run the shop. You think about what we want, what makes us look good, how to trick us into buying it—Did you always want to own a clothing store, even when you were little?"

"Nah," he said, making a face. More and more, we talked like teenagers together, dropping our *g*'s, saying "yeah" and "nah" and generally acting as if we were leaning against our high school lockers. Not that I'd ever been like that in high school. "I wanted to be a doctor."

He looked down as if he'd expected me to laugh at him. "Kids always want to be doctors," he said. "I'd never have got through the math."

"You're a whiz at math!" He'd do the week's accounts in the time it took me to change the vacuum cleaner bag.

"I failed it big-time," he said. He shook his head. "After my father left, everything was so screwed up, I couldn't think about stuff like that." Then he gave me his sidelong, preconfessional glance.

"I always felt like a doctor, with my needle," he said. "Sooo skillful, tap, tap at the syringe, getting it all just right . . ."

"Mixing up something for the pain," I said.

"Idiot."

"Lost kid."

"An accident waiting to happen," he said, but he was looking at me with his eyes wide and his hair sticking up so funnily, he made me think of one of Sylvie's baby birds, and I wanted to feed him something.

"You've done your penance, don't you think?" He'd worked on a road-paving crew in Kentucky, to pay off his debts after rehab; that was where his physical strength came from, and why it embarrassed him.

"You never finish a penance like this," he said grimly.

As he walked away, though, he suddenly stretched his arms out and did an effortless pirouette—arms spread wide, head back—in the middle of the store.

"How'd you learn to do that?"

"I didn't know I could," he said, looking at me in surprise for a second as if maybe I'd put a spell on him.

Eleven

"BEATRICE, DO you have a minute?"

"Philippa, why are you whispering?"

"Because—well, I'm not sure," she admitted, beginning to speak in a normal, piercing tone again. "I was wondering if you could give me a few details, pertaining to a rather delicate matter."

"What?"

"How long is an erect penis, exactly? I mean, I came into contact with them occasionally back in college but I'm looking for a more recent example. And there's the matter of oral sex—is it a lollipop-type arrangement? And circumference . . . circumference is very important."

"Why?"

"I've decided to try an experiment," she said.

"What do you mean?"

"I have a date," she said. "With a man."

"What for?" I asked. I felt like suing her for breach of contract. *I* did the living, *she* provided the commentary. This was one thing I'd thought I could count on.

"I'm just giving up on women," she said. "They're so lumpen, so predictable."

"Tallulah Bankhead wasn't lumpen. Nor predictable, from what I can tell."

"Tallulah Bankhead is dead. *Now* for some reason it's not about sex, it's not about love, it's not even about dreams and fantasies—it's about politics, or some kind of moral superiority. You can't just be fascinated, you have to *agree* with these women to go to bed with them, you have to hate the same people they hate, it is so *boring*. Lesbianism is just not what it used to be."

"Agreeing with people has never been your strong suit," I said.

"Why are you whispering?"

Lee had just come in and she didn't like my talking to Philippa. She said that it made my voice get hard, that we laughed in a mean way. "I'll send you a little diagram," I whispered, hung up, and ran to kiss her.

"BEA," STETSON said, in his hesitant, penitent way, and I turned toward him expectantly. "Beatrice, I—"

"What?" I asked. Usually we both loved his confessions. He'd save things to tell me, for the pleasure of shocking me or making me laugh, and because, as he put things into words for me, he took them out of his imagination, where they were formless tormentors, and turned them into solid objects, things we could examine until they lost their power. He'd watch my face as I listened, and that alone must have given him some kind of absolution, because I was fascinated with his determination to face his failures, and grateful that he trusted these stories to me.

"I'm running out of money," he said, eyes closed, and shoulders squared. "I can't—"

"Now, Stet—Josip—" (we'd agreed to try going back to his real name) "it has *not* been that bad this fall, and we haven't even started the holiday season yet, not really. Don't let your confidence down now—you need it."

He swallowed. "I can't afford to keep you on," he said.

"Stetson!"

I was doing a good job, by some strange accident. People could tell I was sincere and they wanted to buy from me. What other salesperson had ever tried to talk them out of a purchase? Sometimes they just wanted to stand up for a sweater I'd shaken my head at—they'd buy it out of stubbornness.

"I've told you I was barely making it," he said.

"People are always saying things like that," I said. "I mean, look at this place!" There wasn't a smudge; the offbeat neckties hung just so on the tie rack, it was all so muted, sophisticated, expensive, meant to catch the eye of such a superior class of people that I wondered how many of those people there were. "It's magnificent!" I said.

"Exactly. It cost money, too much money—I had to have everything shiny and new. I borrowed from this guy Duane who was in rehab with me, he'd gotten an insurance settlement. Now he's married, he's got a kid, he needs it. And I don't have it. If I let you go, I can pay him a hundred dollars a week."

"But Stet—"

"*I can't run out on anything more*," he said, fists and eyes both clenched shut. He was afraid to look at me because if he saw my disappointment, he'd give in. I looked at him; I'd never seen a man who couldn't run out on things before.

"How will you manage? You can't be here all the time, you have buying trips."

"Tracy can sit the shop for me, when she's not at school," he admitted. "She wants to. She can do her schoolwork between customers." He glanced down, remembering the "No reading" edict. "Listen—here's three weeks' pay, this week and two more. You go, right now, you start looking for a job, you'll have one before you know it. You ought to be putting that education to better use, your parents can help."

"My parents don't send me money, Stet."

"Come on," he said, "You cannot be living on your salary here; it's a hundred dollars a week!"

ON THE bright side, this meant I could pay my back rent. Dear Frank was smoking the eternal cigarette, leaning against the corner of the porch, when I got home. Corn sheaves had sprung up on every one of these little city porches, as if the people here had meditated so intently on the superabundance of American grain that their collective dream had materialized right here in Hartford.

"Chome ear-r-r-rly," he said as I came up the walk. He sounded uneasy, but I knew that if I sank down on the step and told him I'd lost my job he would only be sorry.

I took the mail—a shampoo sample which made my heart leap as if the universe must finally have sent me the precious little gift I deserved, and a postcard from Dotsy Maven, who said there was nothing like reading the Brontës when you were actually living on the moors.

"It's a nice spot, isn't it," I said, "it always feels cozy on this street." It was a good feeling, saying something honest to Frank.

"One block from the bus," Frank mused, "and a big basement, good drainage, not so cold in the winters, not with the stoves." After a short silence, during which I searched unsuccessfully for some kind words about the plumbing, he seemed to make a decision.

"You like the new job?" he asked.

"It's great," I said. "I have a really nice boss, that's the best thing really."

"You found a place for yourself," he said, nodding as he thought it over and decided that this was the important thing. "That's good. You got pension plan?"

"Oh, yes. And I've got the rent for you. I'm sorry I was so late."

"Beetr-r-rus," he said then, in a voice so serious that I immediately realized that my mother had killed herself—the police had called and that was why he was being so nice to me. Unless Sylvie had gotten arrested . . . or my father had crashed the plane.

"Beetrus, that guur-r-rl . . . she sleep on the couch, or, she sleep with you?"

He had dropped the cigarette and was crushing it with his heel, and while he spoke he looked down, but when he lifted his eyes I saw only consternation, and the prayer that I'd go for door number two: the couch.

"With me," I admitted. I couldn't let him think he'd imagined it: he'd be too ashamed.

"You got to go, Beetr-r-rus," he said.

"Okay, Frank, I will."

"But," he said. He'd expected an argument, and he'd hoped I'd win. "Where you go?"

"I'll find someplace," I said, "don't worry."

But of course he'd worry. He had worried about me from the day I signed the lease.

"Henny," he said. "She—" He looked up toward the kitchen window and the curtain twitched. Henny would have heard our voices, or felt them—Frank's vibrato always hummed through the walls. I wondered how long she'd been nagging him to get rid of me, whether he'd put her off in the hope her suspicions were unfounded, or that I wouldn't pay the rent and he could evict me for that instead.

"I understand," I interrupted. I'd wanted to shock someone, after all. And to shock someone, in the year 1978, when every bourgeois idiot was out proving himself daring and open-minded, was no mean feat. The protest years were over and there was no clear division anymore between peaceful, loving people and the kind of hateful, stodgy, warmongering racists who'd made the rest of us feel so good about ourselves when we scandalized them. So here I was, shocking Frank, who'd last read a newspaper in 1941. This was his house, his piece of the dreamland America. I was the spider under the bed—the creature from the sphere of wrongness just the other side of the veil, where everything works in reverse and kindness is really cruelty, and love, hate. Frank knew nothing of the culture whose bonds I wanted to slip. For him my little shock came in at 20,000 volts.

"I'll be out by the end of the week," I said.

He looked straight at me, and I realized that until now, he had always gazed down or up or past me, as if he'd have felt rude meeting my eyes. Perhaps he'd known I'd see too much in his glance, and now I saw profound disappointment, confusion, and embarrassment. I searched his face for disgust or contempt or something else that would help me feel anger instead of guilt, but I couldn't find them.

"I understand," I said. "Really." His face softened, and he closed his eyes for a second as if he was trying to recall the way he'd used to think of me.

"YOU'LL HAVE to move in with me."

Lee said this the way she said everything, quietly, calmly, and finally, as if she were snapping a little purse shut after counting out an exact sum of change.

I hadn't dared recognize my predicament, until she solved it for me. Now I realized how frightened I'd been and my knees nearly buckled. "Lee, you don't know—" I could hardly believe her kindness.

"It's just good sense," she said, embarrassed. "Two can live more cheaply than one."

My eyes filled. I loved her. "Lee, you are the most wonderful person I've ever known," I said, feeling a tear slide down along my nose. "I'll find a job," I said. "I can pay half the rent, for sure."

"We'll think about that after you get settled," she said.

A qualm passed through me like a shiver, too quickly to be understood. "As soon as I get a job, I want to pay part of it—it wouldn't be fair."

"All's fair in love," she said, the loaded word dragging her voice under so I caught it out of intuition rather than sound.

"No, it has to be fair," I insisted, meaning *Because this isn't love, really.* But we wanted it to be love, love it would have to be.

"We'll be *so* happy, Lee," I said.

"It's the practical solution," she said manfully.

"It does seem sensible," I agreed. With this we tiptoed past Aphrodite and crept into each other's hearts by the side door. "You're my soul," I told her. "My heart and soul." If I was unfit for any occupation, that left all the more of my ambition to be spent in the service of love.

"The things you say," she mumbled, and I knew what she meant. A man would never admit such a thing. He'd see any bond as a chain, then have to prove himself by breaking it, setting out for new lands. For women, love *is* the new land.

"I say what I feel." Truly, though, I amazed myself with all I could say to her. It's human nature to conceal love, which leaves us open to such pain—but with Lee I could somehow speak what was in my heart. Because she was a woman, I could trust her. We had a secret inner language in common, a language I'd waited years to use. "I felt it the moment I met you," I went on, "that fate sent me to Hartford, because you were here."

She looked terribly shy, embarrassed, frightened to death. "Don't be silly," she said, looking down. Suppose I suddenly realized who I was talking to? She needn't have worried. No fisherman tends as carefully to his net as I did to the vision I had superimposed over Lee's face.

MY POSSESSIONS made two loads in the Mustang, and the thing was done. We were together, Lee and her aspidistra and me, in her apartment with the white, white walls.

"Rest," she said. "Just lie down and take a nap. You've been through so much."

I pulled the duvet (the place was entirely outfitted in things whose names I'd only seen in catalogues before) up over my head and slept. She was making bean soup in the kitchen—the smell itself was nourishing, the windows steamed over and outside, the rain kept streaming.

"Have you seen the classifieds?" I asked when I woke up.

"It's on the étagère," Lee said. She said "étagère" the way Ma said "public relations"—as if it was a key to the domain of legitimacy. It set me on edge, but everything set me on edge now. What I was searching for was not to be found in a catalogue. I looked for it in Lee's eyes and she averted them for fear of disappointing me. She was afraid I'd see her reaching for something that was beyond her, that was ridiculous to try for. Our neighbor upstairs had come home the day before with a reproduction of a spinning wheel, which he'd carried up the stairs on his back. I'd mistaken it for a harp at first.

"He got a good deal on that," Lee said, "they go for thousands now." She didn't think it a forlorn thing, standing alone in a suburban living room far from sheep or wool. She didn't wish it was a harp, she liked it as a spinning wheel, a reminder that peace, prosperity, happiness might be attained, so long as one kept the proper schedule—spinning, dying, weaving, and so on. I wanted transcendence; she preferred to do without aspiration, to keep things small. She was looking for the daily effort, the weekly result.

I took the classifieds down from the étagère (freestanding bookshelf) and admonished myself to emulate her.

"Don't get hung up on looking for a job right away," she said. "Take your time. You're not a shop girl, you'll find something that fits your talents. Here . . ." She took the newspaper out of my hand and folded it back to the front-page photo of Anita Bryant looking so complacent, so comfortable in her hatred. If she despised homosexuality, then homosexuality must be a great thing. I took Lee's hand with a sudden spring of pride. "*Relax.* You've got plenty of time."

But I'd dreamed I was on a voyage across a thick, oily ocean, carrying my mother's head in a sack. She wouldn't be able to hear, see, or breathe until I could fit it back to her body again, but I was afraid to open the sack, because suppose the head got lost? So I lay in a deck chair in the sun, with the water roiling, trying to forget this responsibility and feel how beautiful everything was, though I knew something incomprehensibly awful was ahead of me.

"Why do you dwell on these things?" Lee asked me, when I told her the dream at dinner. Yesterday she'd found me sketching a penis, now this.

"I don't dwell on them," I said, guiltily—I had never thought of it that way, but no doubt she was right. The thing to do was look ahead, not back. "You're not interested in your dreams?"

She looked quickly away. "Not particularly," she said. "Not with a *burning fascination*."

"Burning fascination" sounded suspiciously like a phrase of mine, and she said it with queasy condescension. She was guilelessly buttering a biscuit—and the soup smelled so good, and soon I'd be back under the quilt, dreaming again.

"It's delicious," I said.

"It's the slow cooking," she said. "I don't have those kind of dreams."

"What kind of dreams do you have?" I asked, with too much interest, so that I got a quick shrug, and after a long pause, an answer spoken so softly I could hardly hear:

"I dream I'm flying, flying with women, over the housetops, over the ocean, you know, it's always the same."

"Always?" I asked.

She nodded. "It's beautiful," she insisted, "it's not carrying my mother's *head in a sack*." She glanced heavenward. Was this what she had been doomed to, through homosexuality? To associate with morbid persons like me?

I wanted to stop dwelling on things, to look away from the abyss at the center of everything. One was supposed to ignore it: to work, shop, and cook, and then there was television, and nice dinners out. This was real life, just what I'd waited for. Every morning Lee cautioned me not to tire myself as she left me alone in the little apartment for the day. I'd water the aspidistra, read the want ads, circling the ones I might call when I got my courage together, then fall, exhausted, back into bed. When I awoke I'd search the drawers and cabinets, looking for the key to Lee's soul. I knew there must be more to her, some kind of secret, maybe something sinister and exciting but more likely just something sad: a packet of old love letters, or some memento of Reenie. The kind of thing my father found in Ma's drawer. I wanted to feel the knife of jealousy against my bone again, the better to savor my new satisfaction. But I found nothing. Had Lee lived thirty years without accumulating any ticket stubs or pressed roses?

I put a sheet of paper down on her desk blotter and did a rubbing with the side of a pencil. A phone number! I dialed with my heart in my throat, and got the dry cleaner. I went to the mailbox and brought the day's catalogues in to revel in the array of duvet covers, the models striding through the wheat in their "field jackets," standing at their easels in "poet shirts." Under the duvet, imagining myself at an easel in a poet shirt, I fell deeply asleep and dreamed spiders had spun the bed into their web, so that if I dared move I'd be trapped. And woke when I felt Lee standing over me, holding a hand to my forehead as if I must have had a fever, gazing at me with something like awe.

"I can't believe it," she said. "I just can't believe you're here."

Twelve

"BEATRICE, I am calling to lament the state of American manhood."

"Oh my God, you had your date."

"Yes, and he didn't, well, he didn't. He didn't do what normal, red-blooded American men are supposed to do, he completely let down his side of the deal."

"What was that?"

"He *just sat there*, Beatrice. He *made no move*."

"Maybe he was shy?"

"What if we were at war? Would you be saying 'maybe he was shy' while he ran away from the battle?"

"I like to think that's not the right analogy," I said. But I was afraid I was wrong.

"If you look back over history . . . even prehistory, the pattern is clear. . . ."

"Philippa, did you let him get a word in?"

"W . . . of course . . . I . . . of course. I always let you get a word in."

"You listen, when I interrupt," I said. "Which is a noble quality; I wish I were able to do the same. But on a first date . . ."

"A man has a responsibility to . . . shall we say . . . put the ball into play . . ." she said, with professorial authority.

"Philippa, did you smile up at him and say dewily, 'I had a wonderful time'?"

"Well, no. I mean, I didn't have a wonderful time. Why would I say I did?"

"What did you two talk about?"

"The Crusades," she admitted.

"Did you think of changing the subject to something more personal?"

"I love talking about the Crusades."

"So, you admit it! You had a wonderful time!"

"I was able to correct some of his information," she said grumpily.

"Oh, Philippa, what am I going to do with you?"

"He's six foot two, Beatrice. He has a Ph.D. in political journalism. He's been to Moscow five times. Surely he can get up the gumption to make the first move. What is going to become of this country? And then there's the whole question of lingerie."

"What would that be?"

"Oh, *you know*," she said, sounding sweetly, utterly vanquished, in despair at herself. "Little lace insets here and there, that kind of thing."

She pulled herself up short, though, in soldierly fashion. "An interesting experiment, but lingerie is in the ascendant here, I'm afraid."

THERE WAS no law against walking down Aetna Boulevard, I said to myself stubbornly, and one afternoon I went in early to pick Lee up, left the car in the staff parking lot, and strode along the sidewalk toward town as if I had every right to be there. I couldn't bring myself to turn my head (it wasn't like I wanted to see Stetson), but as I walked by LaLouche, he came to the door. It was December. Silver reindeer lifted candelabra antlers in the window behind him and the mannequins were offering each other gifts wrapped in white silk.

"Is that you?" he asked, and my first impulse was to say "no."

"I had to get a lightbulb," I said.

"Oh, yeah, you went to Hazleton's? They've got an amazing selection. I got the fixtures for the dressing rooms there, they cast a really flattering light, warm—"

I had no idea how long a person could go on about light fixtures, nor did I expect *myself* to have so much to say on the subject, but I did, and finally had to stop myself in the middle of a sentence about wattage, asking—"So, how are you? How's it going here?"

"It's okay," he said. "It's the holidays and that always helps."

"Tracy likes working here?" I asked.

"She likes being a part of it," he said, with a little sigh. "And she loves the clothes. Which does help." He pulled the steamer out of the back closet and I could see that tension in his back and shoulders that used to precede one of his confessions. "She's in class now," he said. "I have to admit it brings us closer, working together."

Now this, for no reason, made me feel so terrible that I had no choice but to say, with wholehearted happiness: "That's wonderful, Stetson. She's so pretty. I'm sure she's a great saleswoman."

"Thanks," he said, sounding sort of disappointed. "And—how are you?"

"I'm good, good. I moved out to Willbrook with Lee. No job yet, but I've got some interviews coming up. I'm doing fine."

His smile was no less radiant than my last one. He was grateful for the chance to show his open and liberal nature, and determined to be happy for me. "Congratulations!"

"Thanks, Stet," I said, though there's nothing more infuriating than having all kinds of people rush out to pat you on the head when you're right in the middle of a transgression.

"You lucked out when you got rid of me! I'm sure Tracy understands all this in a way I just don't." This was *(a)* an insult cleverly disguised as a compliment, and *(b)* a lie. I'd never lied to Stetson before and it made me feel as sick as when I'd dreamed I was drinking the Jackson Pollock painting.

He'd smiled sadly down at the floor when I said he'd lucked out, but now he caught himself. "Hey, you'll need some new clothes for those interviews," he said.

"Well, Tracy's the one to help me pick them," I chimed. Let those two fold shirts together until the end of time.

"Beatrice, I owe you an apology," Stetson said suddenly. "I should never have hired you; you quit your other job for this and then—"

"Oh, don't, Stet," I said. Because I didn't want to remember how warm it had been there, steaming out djellabahs and waiting for his next story.

"Can I take you to lunch sometime?" he asked. I must have looked perplexed, because he started explaining that I'd given him insight into the kind of person who didn't buy from LaLouche. "And Tracy won't object, seeing—"

"That I'm a lesbian," I snapped.

"Exactly." He caught my eye and smiled, and I felt, as always, that we had a body of secret knowledge between us that we acted on even though we couldn't have said what it was.

"Close to You" was playing on the radio and I said, "Oh, Stetson, I *love* this song!"

"It's the Carpenters," he said, peering into my face as if to check for dilated pupils. "Are you okay?"

We laughed, and suddenly everything was easy. "It's like—" he said, glancing at me for reassurance, so I nodded and made a reflexive beckoning motion with my hand, coaxing his thoughts toward me. "These songs that run in your head, when you remember the words, you know why you're stuck on the tune."

"Yes!" I said. "I never thought of it, but you're right"—that expression of raw need crossed his face, so I continued—"that is *so* true."

"You know that old Isley Brothers song, 'She's Gone'? When you left . . . I'd come in every morning, and . . ."

"Lunch, yes, let's have lunch!" I said, to divert the freight train that was heading straight at us, and ran out into the blue evening. Across the street two little girls in velveteen coats stood on tiptoe before the Christmas village in the toy shop window, and everywhere there was an air of extravagance, haste, anticipation. People were rushing along with the sense that something glorious was about to happen—it was going to be Christmas and love would assert itself over the foolish angers and wrongheaded notions that bound it in chains the rest of the year.

"I'll call right after Christmas," he said as I went off up the street to Lee.

Thirteen

LEE AND I drove out to Dunbridge to the Christmas tree farm.
There was a dusting of snow, and two kids with red mittens
ran ahead of us, pulling an old wooden sled. All around us were
excited children and beleaguered parents, people looking for the
same communal reverence as we were, though their city shoes
were too cold and wet to allow rapture.

"Come on, Lee," I said—feeling that all the trees, or all the
good trees, were going to be spoken for if we didn't act quickly—
and that she was purposely keeping just a few steps behind me,
pulling on some invisible harness to slow me down.

"These look kind of small," she said, and looking around I saw
she was right. It was a field full of dollhouse trees that would be lost
in Lee's big white living room. "Maybe farther up." We tramped on,
leaving behind the heterosexuals who were willing to settle for little scraggly Christmas trees; we were entering unbroken territory,
a brave new world of love. It was only a few weeks since Harvey
Milk had been shot in San Francisco, and his kind, smiling face
haunted me. ("Antinous, the beautiful martyr," Philippa had
explained. "It's a natural response.") In another year I'd have
dreamt of bringing him back to life by making love to him, but

really this was better: the immense, silent candle-lit procession through the San Francisco streets reminded me that I belonged to a great movement, that I—*we*—were on the side of good.

High up, the trees were taller, fuller, and you could lean into them and close your eyes and smell the pine.

"This one!" I said, standing beside a very full one, all spangled with snow.

"Do you think . . . ?" Lee asked, with a child's happy disbelief: Can it be, really?

"Yes!" I said stoutly, feeling it was my gift to her. I reached deep into it, took the trunk in my two hands, and realized it was growing there and could not just be picked up and carried away. "How do we do this?"

"I don't know."

"Well, what do you usually do?" I asked, thinking that this was the sort of thing she was supposed to know, and that my toes were getting cold and it wasn't fair that there was never anyone to give me a little guidance, even about such a thing as picking out a Christmas tree.

"I don't," she said. "I've never gotten my own tree. I go home for Christmas."

"You do?" She'd seemed so grown-up and self-sufficient.

"I mean, I already have my plane ticket," she said suddenly, and her face, whose stillness always had such a calming effect on me, crumpled into tears.

"You mean, we won't have Christmas together?" I was actually relieved to hear this because my mother would have gone crazier if I didn't go home to her at Christmas.

"I can't bear it," Lee said.

"Lee, it's okay. We'll have a celebration before you go. We have our tree." But she was really crying now and I let go of the tree and put my arms around her. She shook me off, taking her hands from her face for a minute to gesture toward the families farther down the slope who mustn't see us touching.

"We'll make cookies," I said. "Would you like that? Real Christmas cookies with sprinkles. And cocoa, and we'll sing carols!"

"No," she said. "That stuff only makes me sad."

"Why?"

"It just—it's not Christmas. I'm afraid to leave you," she said, and sniffled, stood up straighter. "That's all."

I looked into her face, trying to see what she meant. "It's just for a few days," I said.

"I just, I have the feeling you won't be here, when I get home," she said.

"Lee, where would I be?" I started to say "I don't have anywhere else to go," but changed it quickly enough that she couldn't feel it, I don't think. Though I know people do feel things the people they love don't say. "I live with *you*; I love *you*. I'm not going anywhere."

She shook her head vehemently, like a child. "It's such a strong feeling."

And strange, here in the midst of a Christmas tree farm, coming from someone who seemed on an even keel. There was something stilted about it: she was trying to show me a piece of herself that she usually took pride in concealing, so it sounded awkward and false. And I, who'd insisted she open up to me, wanted to shake her now she had—she'd tricked me into thinking she was one of those strong and able people I longed be, and now she was sobbing over nothing on a freezing hillside. As I listened I watched a mother hold a snowsuited baby up over her head to smell its diaper, then tuck it resolutely under her arm and head down toward the parking lot.

288 · Heidi Jon Schmidt

I took Lee's wrists and pulled her to face me. "I will be here when you get back," I said, in a voice quiet with conviction. It was amazing how clearly I knew what to say. "I will be right where I am now, right beside you. Okay?" She nodded, head down, an abject child. "Okay. So, what about this tree?"

"I guess you're supposed to bring a saw," she said. "Maybe they have saws in the shed. I'll go see."

I stayed by the tree, to protect it—it was the last vestige of some old dream and I felt I'd kill anyone who'd try to take it from me.

Lee came back with a rough-toothed saw and knelt in the snow, but after much effort she said, "It's not really working," in the droopy, disappointed way she had, so I realized she'd never expected it to work and was pleased now to see she'd been right all along. I got down and saw she'd only scarred a wide section of bark, without even cutting through.

"Let me try." I might have been irritated with her ineffectuality but I was used to it. It was the pleasure of my life to sweep in and fix everything while the lost souls stood by in awe.

The saw jumped back at me. "Jesus, this tree might as well be made of marble!" I said.

She looked pleased. "I guess we'll have to get one already cut."

She wants me discouraged, I thought. Otherwise I might escape her. My response was a flash of defiance. I'd seen my father cut our Christmas trees on the hillside behind our house. And whatever he could do, I could do better.

"Here," I said, and holding the sawblade straight between my hands, I pulled it back and forth and felt it grip, finally. I sawed on with raw determination until my fingers cramped, and the cut went halfway through.

"Now." (I thought of Pop's hands reaching through the branches to pull the trunk back and keep it from binding the saw.) "Take the tree like this, okay? Just pull gently." And the saw went through, and Lee staggered back under the weight of the tree. "We did it! We did it!" I said. "Do you see?!"

"It's not a big deal," she said. "Everyone else did it too."

Everyone else, though, was a man. "But you didn't think we could!" I said. I'd fallen back on the ground and was sitting there in the snow, catching my breath. Dusk was coming on, a wintry flush at the bleak horizon, and the lights—those strings of big, round lights that automatically go with Christmas trees for sale— blinked on. Lee smiled down at me as if my excitement was adorably naive.

It was more expensive than we'd thought, and it took a huge effort for the farmer to get it tied to the Mustang's roof. We drove home in evergreen splendor, our tree branching above us, ready to bless our home.

"My God," Lee said, when we got out of the car.

"What?"

"Look."

The tree was about the right size for Rockefeller Center. Stag- gering beneath it, we approached the front door; the first two or three feet of the thing went in with no trouble, then caught on the doorframe and we were stuck.

"You pull, I'll push," Lee said.

"The branches will break!"

"No, they'll snap back," she said, in a little singsong like a nurs- ery rhyme. Was she really so ignorant? One rarely feels such per- fect rage as when carrying an unwieldy object with another human being.

"No, *no.*" I condescended to explain. "The branches will *break off. Don't force mechanical things.*" My father's adage: his way of communicating was to explain how things worked. He'd be telling me about carburetors and I, listening for any way in to his heart, had memorized every word. I was starting to feel like crying myself. This big, soft, fragrant tree seemed like the physical manifestation of all the love and unity I'd wished for back home, and we'd gone to such trouble to get it, and now it wouldn't fit through our door.

"It's a tree," Lee said, infuriatingly. "It's not mechanical."

"It's going to be kindling in a minute," I snapped.

"Beatrice, I can't . . . hold it up anymore," she said, and dropped her end—the heavier end (somehow we'd agreed that the heavier loads belonged to her) on the stoop, so that my end had to follow, and I slid down along the wall and sat beside it, in comfortable despair.

"What next?" Lee asked, from outside.

"I don't know." I felt stubborn; I blamed her. We were not going to become a family, we were just going to stagger a drunken path under the weight of some damned enormous symbol.

"The slider," Lee said, from way down at the other end.

"What?"

"It would fit through the sliding door. I think."

It did, and miraculously it stood, it stayed, it took up no more than a third of the living room, it smelled sharply of fresh hope and expectation.

"We did it," I said, falling back on the couch. "*We* did it."

I was glowing with victorious, exhausted pride. *Our love* could fell mighty trees.

"We did," Lee echoed skeptically. She couldn't imagine why I felt such triumph. Then: "But we don't have lights, or decorations."

"We'll string popcorn!" I said. "We'll go out and get some cranberries and popcorn to string!"

She looked pityingly at me: "Do you know what time it is?"

"No." The tree was in front of the clock.

"Almost midnight." She had to get up at six-thirty.

"I can't believe it. We never ate supper."

"No," she said, with some delicate irony. I'd gotten carried away again, and she'd forgive me as many times as it took for me to learn to moderate myself. She tousled my hair; she knew I didn't mean to be difficult; it was my youth, my inferior upbringing.

"Nighty-night, sweetheart," she said, going into the bathroom. I'd always despised the phrase "nighty-night." What can it mean? But my mother had hated it, along with "fridge" for refrigerator, "cukes" for cucumbers—"To make a lasting connection, one has to be open to the Other!" said my inner Salvation Army volunteer.

"Nighty-night, hon," I said. "I'll be in in a minute." I was going to respect her difference—to try to live up to it by giving up some of these notions of mine.

She went to bed; I sat a long time in the middle of the white room, in front of the bare tree. No Christmas tree, however fragrant and perfect, was going to re-create the past—because that past hadn't existed. Those wide-eyed children sitting beside the fire, listening for reindeer, were phantoms from my parents' dream. They'd thought it would save them, and I could never help secretly hoping they were right, that if my eyes were bright enough the dream would flood in finally through the windows. But no, so I had to find it some other way now. My head ached to think of all the billions of parental longings carried by billions of children, all over the world. Bleak it was, alone there, knowing how little I could do.

Fourteen

"THE ROCKING chair is for the little mother," Ma said, pulling it out for Sylvie, who smiled so happily it frightened me. I remembered when she was little and Ma gave her a puppy—she was so stricken by its softness, she hardly dared to move. I'd thought then that it was awful to love things the way she did—it put you in such danger.

"I'm not tired, Ma," she said. "I can help. Do you want another Scotch? Then I'll set the table." She was showing, but nothing like I'd expected. I knew nothing of pregnancy, except whatever I'd gleaned as a child, watching Ma—I'd never imagined having a baby myself. When I thought of babies I thought of that instant of pure silence after they fell downstairs, before the shock wore off and they started wailing. Sylvie bustled back and forth, while I sat down heavily in the rocker. Ma's rented house was small and cut into odd-shaped dark rooms—it was a good thing she hadn't brought anything beside the piano, which filled the living room almost completely.

"Use the poinsettia plates," Ma said, nodding toward a package of Chinet. "Your father took all the dishware," she explained. She spoke the words "your father" as bitterly as ever, and Sylvie caught my eye. We both knew he had the china because Ma had refused it.

"Doctor Mengele," Teddy said happily, wanting to please her. I laughed politely, wondering if he had any idea who Doctor Mengele was, and knowing Ma would be on guard to see if we properly despised our father.

"Teddy tells me I'm drinking too much," Ma said, turning her bitterness on Teddy now that Pop was gone, gazing into her Scotch glass as if it were a crystal ball with all her miseries swirling inside. It was a mood I knew, and I could predict its outcome—she'd go silently up to bed, leaving us wondering how we could have hurt her so, all feeling guilty and sniping at each other. In the morning she'd say she didn't know why she should make breakfast for people who despised her as we did, and Teddy would blow up and say if she thought he despised her, she must really be as stupid as he'd always suspected, and Sylvie would apologize abjectly for the misunderstanding, and Teddy would accuse Sylvie of caving in, and I'd demand that Ma tell us how she could fall into such a state over a nine-year-old's remark.

"Oh, pfff! What does he know?" Sylvie answered, folding a paper napkin as a coaster and taking the drink out of Ma's hand.

"Top it off, will you?" Ma said, with a saucy glance at Teddy, who obliged:

"Glad you don't drink too much."

"Oh, do you *have* to?" I asked him. "You know perfectly well that she—"

"That she *what*?" Mother asked. "That she's an old drunk? That's what you were going to say, so, say it. We can't all be perfect, like you."

"That she is *psychotic!*" I said. "That she's psychotic and that even though you, Teddy, are nine years old and *she* is your mother, *you* are the one who has to watch what you say around her because she is insane."

"Take that back," he said. "Take that back! She's *my* mother and I won't let you say that kind of thing about her! After all she's been through. Take it back or I'll—" he'd picked up a knife from the counter and was holding it over me like an ice pick, and, reader, I'd only been home for an hour. Shortly, he dropped the knife, as if the force of absurdity had broken his grip on it, and was sobbing in the next room, and Ma was begging me to go in and apologize.

"Why?"

"Because he's just a little boy, Beatrice," she said. "He's just a little boy who's had a terrible year and has gotten so worked up over Christmas, because he wants it to be so nice, such a warm family thing, he gets disappointed so easily. I *know* how he feels, I *know* what it is to be like that. Can't you just tell him you're sorry? Christmas will be ruined for everyone."

"Ma, he was threatening me with *a knife*."

"Oh, for God's sake, it was only a butter knife!" she picked it up and poked her own arm with it, the skin springing back, healthy and pink.

So, I begged his forgiveness. "Apologize to *her*," he said into his pillow. "She's the one you insulted." But his sobs were subsiding, and soon I heard the strains of "Lara's Theme" from the living room.

I went to sit with Sylvie in the kitchen, where the music wasn't so loud.

"When you set such store by a piano, wouldn't you think you'd learn a couple more songs," she said, shaking her head and blowing a smooth stream of smoke upward. I felt so happy here, full of energy, ready for the next challenge, whether it was delivered by

tongue or knife or bolt of errant lightning. If I were back in Hartford I'd have been wanting a nap. Here we were all shrieking at
each other, wonderfully at home.

"I think she's found the one piece that most completely
expresses her inner being," I said, and we laughed, in horror,
because the lugubrious melodrama of that song, the aura of
splendor in travail, was overwhelming.

"Maybe *that's* why they're evicting her," Sylvie said. In spite of
the great simpatico between the real estate developers and the
woman in the red suit so ably portrayed by my mother, the job at
Parkington Estates had gone to a man. She was going to sue their
pants off, for sex discrimination, but until it came to trial she was
the pantsless one. On examination of the housing code, she'd discovered that her landlord couldn't even press a charge for six
months, and even then would have an uphill battle against her
and Teddy, these wretched refugees from the siege of Moscow. So
she had an enemy to butt against, an explanation for her misery, a
dear little home with crooked (i.e., illegal; don't think such a
thing would escape her) stairs and sad old Masonite paneling, she
had Teddy, and she'd put Dolly out of her mind. She had a pretty
little spruce for a Christmas tree whose trunk was suspiciously
similar to the stump sticking up beside the front steps.

"We're getting a donkey," Sylvie said, changing the subject and
getting up to stir the pot. It was venison stew—Butch had hit a
deer up on Breakneck Road the week before.

"Why?"

"Butch wants one." This—the ability to supply all of Butchy's
wants—was the small but constantly pulsing power cell of her
life. She did not suffer indecision anymore—her ends were clear.

There was a tap at the back door—businesslike, accustomed—
and Sylvie put the outside light on and gestured through the window to the boy who was standing there. He made a quick, frantic

motion with his hands, meaning that she had to come out instead. She opened the door. "Don't be silly, Larry. It's fine."

He was tall, one of those boys who gets his height so suddenly, he can't quite bear it and stoops over to show he's still partly a child, still in need. His cheeks were brilliant with acne, his hair black as his jacket and hanging in his eyes. "She won't like it," he said, looking as if he wanted to pull himself into the jacket like a turtle. "She's playing that song."

"Oh, she's had too much to drink, that's all," Sylvie said. He shook his head emphatically, and jerked it toward the back steps so that Sylvie handed me her wooden spoon and went out with him. Behind my own reflection in the glass I could see them worrying something together, and I saw how it might be to have him hulking over you, cupped like a hand around a match, wanting to protect you so you could keep him warm.

"Well, I'll tell her you were here," she said as she came back inside, but he looked straight at her and shook his head no. "Okay?" she said, questioning, but he ran down the steps and around to the street and was gone.

"*He* thinks it's something *he* said," she snorted. "He brought her this, to make up for it." A small gift wrapped in red and green paper. "It weighs a ton," she said, putting it in my hand.

"A sculpture," I said, remembering a nude Philippa had as a paperweight that had been cast by some girlfriend long ago.

Sylvie smiled. "Lug wrench, I'll bet," she said, bending down to hide it under some dishcloths in the bottom kitchen drawer. "Some kind of a tool. I'll put it under the tree after she goes to bed. Ma, Teddy, it's dinner." The piano got louder and I looked around the door into the living room to see Ma turn the music back to the first page again.

"I'm not hungry," she said, as if I were too low on the evolutionary scale to understand her dedication to art.

No one likes to be called psychotic, no matter how deeply one believes madness is essential to brilliance and to love. (She did believe these things, and I'd absorbed them from her, the stories of women leaping into fountains, women who'd gone beyond life's rules. She wouldn't mind my sleeping with women, only my sleeping with *bourgeois* women. *That* was the betrayal. And in my mind I gathered Lee's duvet tighter around me.)

I closed my eyes; the music swelled, and Sylvie came out with the ladle and said, "Butchy's here, Ma, time to eat. Please, Ma?" With that entreating child's voice that said Christmas meant everything to Sylvie, and the threat that if Ma didn't come to the table, Butch would know she was crazy. Ma cast a quick (defiant, of course) glance at me, stood up, lifted her chin, and went in to greet him.

Everything about Butch was squared off—his shoulders and fingertips and his chin. His hair was wet—he must have showered after his day at the old Nubestos plant, and he was wearing a canvas jacket. His face was so bright and eager to please that I was determined to be pleased by him. And was reminded that I was a lesbian and didn't—so there—need love like his.

"Butch," Ma said, looking into his eyes with abject, drunken gratitude, "what would we do without you?" Sylvie went over to put her arms around him, bracing her feet against his. He curled an arm around her waist and picked her up suddenly, so she started giggling and cried, "Put me down, put me down!" And he carried her into the living room, dropped her on the couch, and started kissing her, while she squirmed and squealed with joy.

And Ma, looking left out as always, hurt to the bone, went down the hall to call Teddy and returned on tiptoe. "He's asleep," she whispered, beckoning us into the kitchen again.

"There," she said, when we were all sitting. She still sounded prickly but she was doing her best. "Christmas Eve. Dinner. Who'd believe it? Beatrice, will you say grace?"

"Dear God, thank you for blessing us with so much love," I said, meaning it, in part, ironically: Hadn't she repeated again and again that love was the only important thing on earth? And did we not love each other? We did. So all must be well, and these soup bowls of meat (stewed for hours and still I could barely chew through it) had not been ladled out to illustrate Ma's hopeless hungers but the ingenuity of her satisfaction. She was clinging here, in this dark-walled kitchen with worn-through linoleum, the Formica singed and bubbling, while I had a home to go to where the walls were white and the carpet was thick and soft.

Butch said, "Amen!" and tore off a chunk of bread.

"So, how's the new clothesline working out?" he asked, and Ma took up where she'd left off.

"Where would we be without you?" she asked him, with a seriousness usually reserved for questions of theology. "The venison, my clothesline—you know, Beatrice, he replaced the leaking window on the south side, he's been my angel and protector, and that's the truth." I saw Sylvie there across from me, my little sister, who had been dumbfounded by the softness of her puppy, and tears sprang up and I didn't know whether to rescind the ironic grace I'd offered and replace it with something earnest, or to crash out of the back door to escape all the need in that tiny room.

THE FIRST thing I heard next morning was Teddy, wailing that he wanted to open his stocking. It was still dark. I was on the living room couch and I felt deeply, utterly, comfortable, as if I were about to find out that Hartford had only been a dream. I listened for Ma's voice. It was Christmas, so she'd want more than any-

with my coffee, hearing, *It's only a but-ter knife*, in my mind, to the tune of "Paper Moon." I filed this away; I knew Stetson would like it.

Sylvie and Ted were playing Parcheesi (Butch had had to leave to open the bar), and she crowed wildly just then; she'd gotten a blockade. Our disaster had saved her from having to push ahead into the world beyond our family, which might, for all any of us knew or understood, have been outer space. Every time Pop lost a business or Teddy went to the emergency room—with every reversal, we had to give up whatever love or accomplishment we'd been pursuing and return to familiar territory, start over. Sylvie was safe under the quilt here with a baby floating inside her; she was where she belonged. It was I, with my striving, who'd gone astray.

The phone rang, and kept ringing, though Ma fixed it with an icy stare. Sylvie answered and managed to speak with great warmth while maintaining a posture of irritation, then rolled her eyes and gave the phone to me. Pop and Dolly both said how happy they were; they were going to Peabo's for Christmas dinner, his tree was built of antlers, yes, real antlers he'd collected over the years—he did a good business flying hunters to the more remote areas of the state. That hollow, lonely feeling began to settle on me, the feeling that nothing was solid or true anymore.

"Ma, talk to Dolly," Sylvie said.

"That's what everyone wants, isn't it?" Ma said, pouring herself a Scotch with a little glance of defiance at her fusty, disapproving daughters. Well, she was a free spirit, she drank when she liked. "Everyone wants me just to forget how she's rejected me. Her lungs were weak when she was born. I slept sitting up with her in a sling around my neck . . . for six weeks. . . ."

"It's Christmas, Ma."

"Here," I said, "Ma wants to talk."

thing to be happy, and this meant that if the least thing got out of kilter she'd panic and fly into a rage. She dialed the phone and I heard her reasoning with a bewildered Sylvie.

"He just wants things to be the way they used to be, honey. He wants to run in and sit on your bed and open his stocking with you." The whispering continued, I dozed off and when I woke up, Butch and Sylvie were at the back door. It was a quarter to six.

"Merry Christmas!" Ma said. She sat down at the piano and started playing "Deck the Halls." Butch stood behind her looking like he'd been blindsided by Christmas in the middle of the night, but the music was rousing and Ma's determination on good cheer was incontrovertible. The room was freezing because the landlord had let the oil run out, but she'd gotten the woodstove blazing and I sat up with my blanket around me, took the cup of coffee Sylvie held out with two hands, and kissed Teddy, who cuddled in beside me, and sang.

Nearly every gift was intended for warmth. Ma had gotten me a printed shawl, soft green with big, loose heads of pink and ivory hydrangea. It was as if she'd managed to save me a square yard of the past—the next thing to uprooting the hydrangea in front of the old house for me. Unwrapping it, I looked up with a real shock of joy on my face, saw her smile with love, and felt as if I'd filled her room with butterflies at last. She was like a child; when she was happy she truly believed in a beautiful, innocent world. Which meant that she was doomed to disappointment. But for the moment, the room was full of her happiness; it was a bright soft, intoxicating thing.

"I was afraid you'd wake up with a headache," I said.

"No, I feel fine," she said. "That's the good thing about bein drunk—you don't get sick in the morning." The sun was up few last oak leaves were rattling on the tree outside. I leaned b

"Merry Christmas," Ma said. Then, "I'm glad to talk to you too." Then a long, listening silence, with a shadow deepening on her face. Then, stonily: "Well, you've made that choice, haven't you? And I didn't stop you, did I?" She thrust the receiver at me and stalked away.

"Someone had to tell her that what she's doing is wrong," Dolly said to me primly.

Ma was crying softly in the corner.

"Eva, I should have named her," Ma said later.

"Eva?" Sylvie asked.

"Hitler's mistress," Ma explained, and Teddy laughed and laughed.

"WHEN YOU said it was a trailer, I thought you meant it was a . . . trailer," I said.

Sylvie had wanted me to see her new home, so there we were, out behind the ball field, where Butchy's trailer, a rounded beige model, such as families towed behind their cars during some inconceivably happy earlier age, was parked here between two real mobile homes and an old schoolbus up on blocks.

"It *is* a trailer," she said. Inside it, Springtime was yapping wildly. "It's nice neighbors mostly, but Ed in the schoolbus, I don't think he feeds his dogs. Here, Springy," she opened the door and he leapt out and raced around and around the trailer, causing furious, hoarse barking behind the bus.

"Shut that dog up, he's getting them all going!" a man shouted.

She wheeled around to shout back, but shook her head and stopped herself. "Come on, come on, little silly," she said. Springtime sprang up into her arms and she carried him inside. "No point arguing with crazy people," she said, as if repeating a lesson. "Just keep your distance, leave them alone. Oh, it's freezing in here!" She turned all four of the gas burners on high and very soon the top quarter of the room was stifling. "I've got to get a little fan," she said.

"Is it safe to use the burners like that?" I asked.

"So far . . ." she said lightly. The linoleum was worn away underfoot, as we were standing in the only patch of real floor in the room, in front of the stove, between the table and the bed. Sylvie bent to look out the back window, where a hillside of low brush was filled with candy wrappers blown in from the Little League games. "See, that's Butchy's father's land. The goat'll keep the weeds down in there."

"I thought you said a donkey."

"You have to get a goat, with a donkey. Or the donkey gets lonely."

"Oh."

"Let me just grab the shampoo and we'll go back to Ma's."

THERE WAS no shower in the trailer, and Sylvie had never cut her hair because Pop loved little girls with long hair. So she washed it at Ma's after Ma and Teddy had gone upstairs to bed that night, and then she sat with her back to the stove to dry it. There we were together, the two of us who remembered all the same things—the blue-and-yellow spider spinning in the clouded window of the henhouse, the sprinkling of violets in the grass, Ma bringing out a pitcher of lemonade, Ma's eyes gone dead suddenly because she'd glimpsed something wrong, something despicable, in one of us.

"The trailer's cozy, don't you think?" she said. "I pretend we're on a boat sometimes, when it's windy." She smiled and tilted her head back, lifting her hair to get the heat under it, about to tell me the story of her love, which, like all such stories, seemed amazing to the two people involved in it, and completely ordinary to everyone else.

"He doesn't know," she began. "He doesn't really know what he's feeling, but I do, I can always tell." She looked down quickly. I was the older sister, the one who explained everything . . . I had a Voice of Experience, and my experience in Matters of Love was vast. Sylvie only had Butch, and now his child.

"Beatrice, he's *so good*, that's *why* he gets in trouble the way he does. He tries to make everything work for everyone and when he can't do it, he gets mad, and you know the rest," she said, with a combination of shy pride and resigned embarrassment. "His parents . . . you know, they're just lost, it's hard for people like that. His mom was born Jewish, but Butchy's father was Catholic and she converted when they got married, and she raised Butch Catholic (which is I'm sure why he's the way he is), and now, she's born-again! They baptized her and fifty other people, in Mudge Pond, last August."

"Nice, stable family," I teased.

"Well," Sylvie said, palms up, "I feel at home with him!" and we laughed happily at the thought of these two families joined together and the stories that might result. Then she turned serious again so I could feel all her longing and how it must seem to be fulfilled now. "It's like he's always been there, like a shadow in my dreams."

The shadow of some boy on a motorcycle, my father, maybe, except this one was hers, and always would be: her face showed his feelings, how could he leave? Now she knew what it was to be the ray of magic in a man's darkness, have him grateful, *to you*, for everything he sees.

"He's not the kind who'd ever notice me," she said shyly, as if he were Adonis come down out of the sky.

"The Cumberland Farms thing, the B and E, he feels so bad about it," she said. "He was a kid, he'd seen it in the movies, that's all. But of course, if he'd never done it he'd always have gone to Cumberland Farms for his coffee and I'd never have gotten to know him. (She'd been working at Odge's Variety, two blocks away.) So I guess God works in mysterious ways, just like Ma says. There I'd be, watching Carrie Listel scratch lottery tickets, which is a hard thing to watch, and he'd say hi and I'd give him his change. I didn't really notice him, until he didn't come one afternoon. Then I realized I'd counted on seeing him. Carrie Listel came in and bought her tickets and she stood there scratching them off—she won ten dollars, she bought ten more tickets, then she won two, bought two more—I couldn't stand to see it, she worked at the nursing home, she needed that money, and I felt like I'd run through all my chances to see Butch the way she was running through her chances at winning the lottery.

"So the next day I said—very lightly, like it was something I'd noticed in passing—'You didn't come in yesterday.' And he looked *guilty!* Just for a second, like he was sorry to disappoint me. And then he got terribly shy and gruff and gave me exact change and went straight back out again and I thought 'He must really like me!' " She looked down and played with the fringe on the afghan for a minute, as if she'd just said something conceited and was waiting for me to reprove her.

"It's written all over him, how he feels about you," I said.

"It's funny with a man, isn't it, Beatrice? All the things they can't say, so they just radiate them instead. I figured out ways to let him know without exactly telling him—like one day I said his coffee cup had been in my dream the night before. If you could have seen how he smiled—I could tell it really made him happy. After he left that day, Carrie Listel won a hundred dollars and put it in her pocket and went home, satisfied for one minute out of her life, and just as she was leaving she turned around and said, 'Watch out, young lady,' in a very severe and kind way . . . like a mother, and I said, 'I will, Mrs. Listel,' and I wanted to pick her up and twirl her around, because I knew she'd seen that Butch loved me. The next day he was going over to help his brother put on a roof, and when he said he wasn't coming in, I made sure to sound disappointed (usually I'd be careful *not* to), and then he said, "I'll be back by dinner," and I said, "I'll be off by then," and he said, "I know," and then there was this long silence and I said, "Thank you, Butch, I'd love to have dinner with you."

She opened her hands as if to let a pair of doves loose, and gave her brilliant, jagged smile. "You know, I think men want sex so much because they have to let their tenderness loose that way, before it, kinda, drowns them," she said.

"I wouldn't know," I tried, in my Voice of Experience, but the irony curdled and I missed my mark.

"After that first time, he jumped up and said, 'I gotta go,' and I thought, 'What happened?' And then I thought, 'I know what happened.' I did! It was too good, too right, the kind of thing you have to get away from before something spoils it, and I sat up and looked around and I thought, 'This is the nicest trailer I've ever been in' and I just burrowed back under the covers and slept there and I thought, 'I'm home.' And when he came back, he lay down and looked in my eyes and he didn't say anything, but I knew, I could feel it, and I said, 'Oh, Butch, I do, I love you too.' And he hugged me so tight, I knew, I *always* know, what he's feeling; it's in his eyes, in his hands, but he can't say it."

She was quiet for a minute, luxuriating in her thoughts, remembering. I considered telling her my story about Lee, though I knew it would embarrass her. I used to love embarrassing Sylvie, because it proved how much more worldly I was, but now I didn't have the heart.

"Which is why I knew it was okay to get pregnant," she said, stubborn, and pleading. Wouldn't I please see that she was following her inner compass, the only reliable guide? Didn't I also live this way? I nodded. I wanted her dreams—these soft little girl's dreams—to come true.

"What do you mean, you knew it was okay?"

"I knew he wouldn't mind in the end. He saw it as more work and worry, but I knew."

"So you convinced him."

"I think I've convinced him," she said. "I mean, I told him it was the safe time of the month, that's how it happened. Then I acted surprised. I mean, I *was* surprised! There's somebody else inside me. I knew it right away; my period was two days late and I knew it, I could feel I was different, some tiny change in the taste of things, and then I just felt a change sweeping through me like a wave. But I acted like it was an accident, and he believed me." (She pursed her lips to contain a smile, and I thought how true it was, that if you wanted to feel a man's love, you had to trick it out of him. I was so grateful to be away from that now.)

"He believed me, and he was worried, but I could see he was happy too—proud, like. He knew in himself that we'd accomplished something together. You know when you love a man and you feel him inside you the first time, you know how it seems to be a . . ." She got shyer and shyer, but more and more determined to say what she was thinking, even though words couldn't really touch it. Still, by speaking, she could begin to turn a mercurial feeling into a solid reality. The sentence she spoke, she would remember, repeat it to herself—and when everything went awry (as it would, because it always does), she'd still have it to bring the past to life again, nearly as reliably as if she could save the essence of that day, that love, in a bottle, to be opened in the depths of old age. ". . . like, a *holy* thing? And you're so tender and amazed and you can hardly believe you're together and you're facing the wildest danger—the danger of being seen, *known*—facing it *together*. You're full of daring because you love each other, and you look in his eyes, and you feel him—well, you know what I mean."

Unfortunately, I did.

"And out of that comes, a, a . . ." She started crying; out of happiness, because she was knocked up by an ex-con bartender from the valley and every night she could touch him and feel him want her and she was going to be poor and worried and probably increasingly angry, but this was the price you paid for having just a month, a year of this feeling. She was amazed to have such a lucky fate, and though I could see the troubles stretching ahead, I mostly envied her. She was so happy in her illusion, and as it seemed to me there was no happiness *but* in illusion, I prayed hers could be preserved.

"He *will* love the baby," she said. "He already does. Because he loves me." She was tentative, waiting for me to contradict her, but when I nodded she said firmly and quietly, "I know he does. And Bea, I wouldn't have been any good in college . . . I was never that good in school."

She'd fallen behind because she missed so much, staying home to keep watch over everything. The teachers would say "Beatrice Wolfe's little sister," and she'd panic at having to live up to me because I loomed so large in her mind.

"You know, with this Nubestos thing, maybe we can save some money, and who knows what then?"

"Oh, my God, Larry's present!" she said suddenly. "I forgot!"

"What do you suppose it is?"

Sylvie looked up at me with big, naughty eyes, not unlike the eyes of a child who has just decided to spread peanut butter on the cat. She'd done that once, and another time had pushed an impeccably dressed real estate agent off the little log bridge into the brook, because Ma didn't want the house to be sold. "It felt so good," she'd said both times, when I asked what had possessed her. Simplicity was allowed to Sylvie. Being a good student, a good girl, had left me without the satisfaction any natural human would feel, kneading peanut butter into fur.

"Let's open it," she said.

"No!' I already knew Ma's longings too deeply; I didn't want to see them in the flesh. Sylvie went to get the package out of the cabinet.

"I guess he couldn't find a box." It was an awkward shape and the thin paper printed with jolly Santa Clauses had been wrapped around it like a tourniquet, secured with yards of Scotch tape. "We'll wrap it up again. She won't know."

"Sylvie!"

"He'd have told me what it was if I'd asked." People had always confided in Sylvie—everyone has so much to tell, and when you find someone who'll be honestly fascinated, of course, you're only grateful.

"Really, I think we *ought* to look," Sylvie said, "in case it's something that's not such a good idea. They're on the outs, him and Ma."

"So I gathered. Why?"

"Oh, who knows, with her? He did something, or said something . . . I don't know, and neither does he but Ma won't talk to him and he's just desperate to make things right."

At this, she tore off the wrapping, abruptly, like a child stuffing a cookie in his mouth before Mother can say no. And there it was—

"A gun?" Sylvie said.

"No," I said. "It's chocolate, and you take off the foil." But Sylvie was shaking her head and the minute I set my hand on it I knew it was real.

"Why?"

"I cannot guess," Sylvie said.

We looked at each other with as much excitement as alarm. Mine, of course, was an educated excitement: I had studied Chekhov and knew that a gun over the mantelpiece in the first chapter will go off by the end. We both knew that a gun added something to a story, and this one was bound to add a new chapter to our lives.

"YOU KNOW, *I* think your mother has made an *excellent* choice," Philippa observed. "Most men don't have a clue in the gift-giving department. This guy obviously loves and understands your mother and knows exactly what sort of thing will please her."

"Philippa!" I said (in a shocked whisper; I was huddled under a blanket on the couch so Ma wouldn't hear me), but I had to laugh. Philippa's parents lived in her mind as vengeful gods enforcing immutable laws. They did not suffer drunken brainstorms and rush out to buy flocks of sheep or ping-pong ball factories. They'd never asked themselves if they were happily married; they'd never dreamed of divorce. They didn't fall desperately in love with figments of the imagination, nor fly into sobbing rages when those figments failed to come alive . . . banishing the former beloved back to the netherworld, only to lie pounding their fists on the ground, hoping to raise the dear figment again. But if they had done all this, and one or another of their shades had arrived on Christmas Eve with a gift-wrapped pistol, they would have *given the pistol back*. What good were they, to a woman whose term of highest praise was "lurid"? None.

"HE MISSES me," Ma said, with tears in her eyes, turning the thing in her hands. "He misses me; he wants me to know he's thinking of me."

"Flowers are more customary," I said.

"Oh, flowers! Oh my God!" she said. "What an idea! I cannot even imagine Larry carrying a bunch of flowers."

"That is the *point*."

"Oh, Beatrice," she looked at me with great tenderness—not maternal feeling but the sympathy of a missionary toward her dear aboriginal flock. I did not understand love, did not understand men, the way she did.

"He knows I've been frightened here, all by myself," she said. Having so few resources, she made use of everything. The fear would draw Larry to her, make him feel stronger and more confident, less her student and more her protector. Soon he would forget that *she'd* been supposed to guide *him*. "He wants me to feel safe."

"Ma?"

"Don't you see, Beatrice?" she asked, gazing intensely into my eyes. "*Don't you see?* He's giving me something from *his* world, he's showing me what he can do for me. It's a token of *love*." What depths this word held for her; I could hardly look. "I sent him away," she whispered. Her tone was from the wrong movies: tearful, overwrought. Philippa wouldn't have let these films into her festival. But poor Ma had only been to the teachers' college. *I* was the one whose mother made sure I got a *real* education. "I told him to get out of here and never come back. I told him he was a boy with a crush on his teacher, that he'd misunderstood me. I told him everything I told Jeff Rush." Jeff Rush was the high school principal.

"Why?"

"Be*cause*," she said, angry at my stupidity, or her own—who could tell, and anyway what was the difference? A daughter's idiocy is only her mother's brought to bloom. "Because he doesn't love me, not really. He has some kind of fantasy, but it's not *me*. I need someone who loves *me*."

"Well, you can't expect—"

"I know!" she said, with the sharpest grief. "I know. I can't expect anyone to love me."

Why did she have to grab half a sentence and jump off a cliff with it like that?

"So there," I said gently, pointing to this gun. "He *does* love you. He brought you a gift."

She nodded, looking down at it as if she wanted it to promise her something, so that I knew she'd put it in a drawer like her love letters, and consult it daily or hourly as a talisman, until she'd gotten used to it and it lost its power. She cried so sadly, I was afraid I was going to cry with her. And then what? We'd be lost. We were clinging by our fingernails already—we had one job, Sylvie's waitressing—between us. By some accident of grace we had roofs over our heads. We had venison, thanks to Butch's reckless driving, and Teddy had liberated a bit of light.

"You've got to give it back to him," I said.

"What do you mean?"

"It's a gun," I said. "You need a license for it, and you don't have one. So it's illegal to have it, it's a crime."

She laughed, incredulous at my naïveté. "Innocence is a lux-

ury *some people* can't afford," she said, worldly-wise. "We can't all
be like you."

Oh, she was proud, and with good reason—her spirit, her intelligence were immense. And what strength she had needed, to keep herself perfectly still as one era after another bound her to the rack! But she'd been good, she never struggled, never let her ambition surface except when she looked into my eyes.

As she did now, her mascara leaching into her crow's-feet with her maudlin tears, ridiculous, yes, but not without magnificence. She was a giantess of promise, struggling up and out of the depths, dripping with the old notions of femininity, bellowing her fury and confusion that something so potent, so able as herself should find no path forward in the world. And to see her, to feel all the pity and admiration, yearning and fear, that I did in her presence, was to be very, very glad I had Lee, and the strangeness and forbiddenness of my own life. It worked against her like garlic against a vampire.

"You don't understand," she said.

The gun was an appeal to her true spirit, I knew that. There were a lot of laws she wanted to break, and Larry had sensed that, found her an instrument. He was only in remedial English; he did not know that a gun that appears in the beginning is bound to go off by the end.

"Don't let Teddy see it, okay?" I asked.

"I won't," she said, and smiled over me with the maternal tenderness of the ages. Her dear daughter, who understood so little. She put the pistol on top of a pile of towels she'd just folded, took it upstairs, and came down looking ten years younger than she had that morning, and brushing away a tear. "*Love* is the essential thing," she said. "And of that, we have plenty, *plenty*. Larry's coming over," she said, the way she used to say "all clear" before she let us out of the linen closet.

I felt all my good sense twisting to splinters—she loved him, he made her happy. Against that, what argument could I make? Larry was the age she'd been when she met my father, and he came from *her* side of the tracks. She saw in him everything she'd given up when she married. Well, she was going back to the beginning, she was going to get it right this time.

Part Three

One

I DROVE Lee's car up to Bradley Airport, feeling the excitement associated with such places. Real people, who steer their stately and impressive lives along the wide boulevards of authenticity, often have to meet their comrades at airports. Here was a real person now, coming out through the automatic doors with his briefcase, checking his watch (he had to be somewhere, they needed his expertise).

"Hi!" I said, as one real person to another, and he blinked in confusion and looked away.

I sipped coffee at the coffee bar, stirred by the sound of the jet engines but acting preoccupied, as if this was just part of my ordinary day. And here came my very real darling, looking more dedicatedly prosaic than before, as if she'd just had a refresher course in keeping down to earth. But when she saw me, she broke into a huge, delighted smile.

"You came!" she said.

"I told you I'd be here."

"I know. I just never—oh, I don't know," she said. "Hi." She gave me our look, the one that hinted at the amazing kisses, way beyond the ordinary heterosexual kisses, we'd give each other if only we were allowed.

"Home," she said, when we got there, turning her key in the lock and pushing her suitcase through the door with her foot. She reached behind the tree to turn up the thermostat, then turned to me in the stale cold and said, "Really home, now you're here," and kissed me, clinging against me, and I folded her in, to protect her, the way you do with women.

Then, shy: "I got you something."

"I got you something too!" I said, as if it was an enormous, telling coincidence that we'd both bought each other Christmas presents. Well, to me, it *was*. Sid gave me one gift in our three years together: a string of coral beads. Seeing them, I'd known he meant them to represent all the things he couldn't say . . . and that he knew he'd lost me. I wanted to cry every time I put them on.

Lee had set a small box on the coffee table, wrapped in hand-made rag paper and tied with raffia, as suggested in a *Courant* feature on gift wrapping a few weeks ago.

"Mine first!" I said. Stetson had given me a deal on a silk shirt she'd admired.

"Oh, sweetie," she said, holding it up and then turning away from me with reflexive modesty to slip it over her head. "Oh, I didn't mean for you to get me anything." She was sincere, I realized. She honestly did not require a gift from me. I repeated her sentence—*I didn't mean for you to get me anything*—in my mind, to catch her inflection, so I could use it sometime. And fixed myself on the tiny box with a quick prayer that I'd say the right thing when I saw it, since it was going to be a ring.

"Oh, Lee, diamonds!" My eyes sparkled, my voice was hushed and joyful, both. "Are they *real?*" I wouldn't have asked except I knew they must be, and that she should have the pleasure of affirming it.

"Of course," she said softly.

"Oh, Lee. Lee, I love you so."

"It's like in a book," she said. "A happy ending."

"No," I said. "A beginning."

Lee smiled patiently and I felt the foolishness of my youth and idealism. No one seemed to feel the sacred mystery of love as I did . . . but everyone believed in sex. And Vitamin C.

"Come into bed with me, my rose hip," I said. "I wanna touch your nipples." I could say forbidden things to her, and affect her terribly. I was taking her where she'd been told she mustn't go. I dusted a finger lightly where her nipple touched the silk shirt, and she pulled away, smiling. She was always trying to domesticate sex with those smiles. I understood. I was used to leaving the knife edge of wanting to the man, but without it, we wouldn't continue, so I caught her around the waist and cupped her breast and dared her to refuse me. She was not one to accept a dare.

The ring was from the nicest shop in Hartford. It was hand-made, of white gold with the diamond chips inset, and once it was on my finger, I never took it off. It was ugly, unnatural to me, but I didn't let myself dwell on it. Lee had picked it out and I was going to love it, just the way I loved her.

"AND WHAT, may we ask, is this new accountrement?" Stetson asked, with his old edge of satire. We were having our lunch, at the Chanticleer, where some dizzying length of time ago I'd seen a man and woman talking about she-crab soup while I leaned, faint from heat and hunger, in the shadow of Wings to Fly Pro-ductions. Stet had insisted on bringing me there, to remind me those times were really past. So here we were, embarking on a bowl of lobster bisque together, like a pair of beggar children who'd got into the palace banquet by a hidden door. I wouldn't have had the courage to walk in if he hadn't been with me, but our friendship made all things possible. We felt smart and beautiful and good, entitled to love and happiness, when we were together.

"Which fork do you use?" he asked, in a stage whisper.

"It's *soup*," I whispered back, and we giggled tipsily. I remembered those mornings, him with his squeegee, making certain no flyspeck marred the windows while I refolded the sweaters, the aimless talk that would lead to some surprise. Every time we found something in common it was like a glint of gold. He'd gone camping in the park near our house when he was a Boy Scout. Amazing, that he'd been just down the road and I hadn't know. We counted back—it was the same year Forsythia died, so I got to tell him that story, and he shook his head, saying he'd have been the same as I was, heartsick *and* fascinated. It felt like he'd pulled out a splinter that had been festering in me for years.

"Soup. Thanks, Princess," he said now.

"It's nothing, Your Majesty." We smiled at each other a beat too long; he rushed to the rescue, pointing to the ring again.

"I got it for Christmas," I admitted, seeing he was still looking at the ring. "You must be doing really well, to bring me here."

I meant to distract him, and it worked. He smiled in spite of himself and looked around the place like he owned it. His pride gave a little tug at my heart—it was so earthly, transitory, masculine, and so well deserved. He might seem to be lost in the vapor of chic (to be perfectly chic would mean being hard and still as a mannequin, and above all earthly pain, not unlike the feeling of being perfectly high)—but he'd earned the right to eat here, day by sober day.

"It's going a little better," he said. "Now about this ring, Beatrice. Is there something you want to tell me?"

"No," I said, with a strangely flirtatious lilt. "No, there isn't."

"This came from Sandalwood, didn't it?" he said, taking my

hand, which looked like a water lily cupped in his. "Not one of their better efforts, I'd have to say."

"You're jealous!" I teased, and to my amazement he blushed.

"No, no," he insisted, "of course not."

"I mean, you can't bear to see anyone wearing something that doesn't come from LaLouche."

"Oh, oh, I see," he said, with an embarrassment that engulfed us both.

I wanted to push away from the table and run out the door. But Stetson summoned himself—his very beautiful, thoughtful, open, searching self, over which the cynical manner sat like a porkpie hat on a marble Apollo—and said, with his dark eyes wide and earnest: "I meant to say that this shows a commitment, right? Congratulations. I'm about to undertake a commitment myself, so it's kind of cool we're doing it together."

"What's that?" I said.

"We're getting married," he said, in about the same tone he'd used to confess his drinking.

I forced a generous and proud smile right over my face, instantly. "Congratulations!"

"Thanks," he said. He sounded relieved. I made the smallest questioning look, wondering if it was polite to ask whether this meant he'd fallen in love, finally, and he must have guessed this. "Well, it's the natural next step, I mean, we've been seeing each other a year, she wants kids, you know—"

Not . . . "We can't live without each other"; not "We want to spend all our lives trying to do our best together." Just—"It's the next step."

Fortunately the waiter was sliding a glazed breast of squab onto my plate.

"She really loves me," he said, as if this was surprising.

"Smart girl," I said. He was smiling with such a gentle humor. I looked around the restaurant, which was supposed to be the best in town and was filled at that hour with people who felt themselves lifted above the ordinary for a moment, just because they were eating there, at cherry-wood tables with thick linen cloths, under an avant-garde chandelier of blasted steel—even the pigeons here were squab. But Stetson and I, we continued to be our ratty, hopeless, laughing selves.

He reached for the butter and I caught sight of the edge of something under his cuff.

"Is that a tattoo?"

"Yeah," he said. "Sorry. I try to keep my sleeves down."

"Doesn't that sort of defeat the purpose?"

"Purposes change," he said. Shaking his head—"There was a time when I'd do anything to get near a needle." He laughed. "I *still* look forward to my flu shot every year."

"You know," I said, shaking my head, "I just do not get it."

"No," he said, "people don't—the gratification." A look of deep, secret need passed over his face, a look I recognized. Even in our deepest insanities we seemed to be kin.

"It is *so* good to talk to you," he said. "I think it's because you're *different*, so you understand . . ."

"WHERE WERE you?" Lee asked, when I met her in the Aetna parking lot. She looked so upset that I automatically lied.

"Looking for a job. Where would I be?"

"You didn't tell me."

"Well . . . you didn't tell me you were going to work today. Why should you? I know you're going to work."

"The next time you're going to be out of the house for the afternoon, you call me," she said. "I was worried sick. I couldn't imagine what had happened."

"I'm sorry," I said, reaching over to squeeze her hand. "I didn't want to bother you at work, that's all."

I'd intended to tell her Stetson had taken me to lunch, but now I couldn't. Which was silly, because she'd have been pleased that I was safe and taken care of. It wasn't like I'd had lunch with Reenie or another woman. But instinct kept me quiet and I rooted around for another subject.

"Do you usually get a flu shot?" I asked her.

THE NEXT day I did penance by keeping right at home where she wanted me. The phone woke me at noon and I answered briskly for fear the caller would guess the truth—that I was a very small, inconsequential being at the helm of a very large and unwieldy personality, who had to cling to her mattress so as to be ready for the inevitable smashup.

It was the City of Hartford Personnel Office, and they were offering me a job.

"We're bound by law to call the highest scorers first," the man said hopelessly. That test! I'd forgotten all about it. "Though I'm sure you've already found something . . ."

"No, no," I said happily, "nothing at all."

Just what he'd suspected; even the highest scorer hadn't managed to find a job in nine months. Poor little Hartford, whose civic grandiosity would never be fulfilled—it was destined to sit there on its bend in the river, nervously reassuring itself of its own importance while on the highways that swirled over, around, and through it, streams of traffic carried all the vital, intelligent people back and forth from Boston to New York. Hartford had to rely on people like me.

"When do I start?" I asked, hoisting myself up on the pillow. A wardrobe was blowing up in my imagination, a closetful of pale, flowery dresses like an avenue of cherry trees in May, dresses in which I would look so lovely, perfectly in bloom, smiling like some girl in a pantyhose ad—a smile without complications.

"Did you want to know what the position is?" the dry voice asked.

"Oh, yes, of course!"

"It is a Library Technician III position, at the Oxford Branch of the Public Library," he said, slipping into his vernacular. "City benefits, and after a period of probation you will be eligible for yearly raises, performance-based of course. You can come down to City Hall to fill out the paperwork any time, and you can start as early as tomorrow."

"THE PERFECT place for you to begin," Philippa said. It had certainly made for a good excuse to call her. "Government would be an excellent arena for your talents. The civil service is strangling for want of fresh thinkers. It is a very good sign for the City of Hartford that they had the foresight to hire you."

"It's a library technician, it's not—"

"In fact I wonder that I never thought of politics for you! You're interested in people, you're open to things, and you have a natural authority—from managing those parents, I suppose . . . but why stop with them? Yes, yes, I see it quite clearly, Connecticut politics, that's the place for you." My heart was sinking; she sounded just like my mother.

"Philippa, it's a CETA job . . . its make-work for pathetic people . . ."

"Beatrice, it's a *beginning*," she said, and I thought of her back at home, watching her father with his bricks and planning her own life accordingly: upward, course by course by course.

"CONGRATULATIONS, HONEY, it's wonderful," Lee said, sounding crestfallen. Driving toward City Hall next morning, she stopped to wave in every other car, and for pedestrians who looked as if they might consider crossing.

"Drive! Just drive the damned car, will you!"

"There's nothing wrong with careful driving."

"If we go any slower we will be in reverse!" Now she decided it was her civic duty to stop and pick up a rolling trash barrel.

"Imagine, I did the best of everyone who took the test," I said, and she looked over at me with a tight little smile.

"Yes, and what stiff competition."

"What do you mean?"

"Well, it's not exactly the Harvard entrance exams," she said, as we approached, finally, and I saw what a beautiful building City Hall was, modeled on the Acropolis, stately and graceful, built before anyone could guess that the city would rot away around it. "Do you really think you should take this job? We don't need the money, and now, if something better comes up you'll miss it."

I hadn't seen a paycheck in three months. When I needed a new bottle of shampoo I agonized over putting it on the shopping list and going deeper in debt to Lee. She protested that we lived together and these things didn't matter, but I felt she was trying to buy my soul.

"This so-called *job* doesn't even demand four years of college. It's not your level, and it's in a terrible neighborhood, and you'll be there until eight o'clock."

"Which everyone knows is when the ghouls come out."

"I can't talk about this," she said suddenly. "It's not a good idea, that's all."

"Lee," I said, "this is the first time anyone has ever suggested to me that library science was a high-risk profession."

After I filled out all the forms, they told me I had a month to move back into town—"City employees have to live in the city," snapped a personnel receptionist, drunk with her power over me.

Two

WE'LL BE SO happy, Lee. We will," I said, standing at the window of our new place, three blocks from the library. *The Courant* had done a feature story on the neighborhood, describing it as an "urban oasis, vibrant with growth and change . . . holding the flavor of the islands from which so many of its residents have recently arrived while benefitting from gentrification, thanks to the new population of 'young professionals' (this, as we knew, was a rhyming euphemism for "homosexuals"). Looking down Hereford toward Governor, we saw the emphatic lettering ("Your Problem All Solved!") of the signs for Capitol Jewelry and Loan, Casteneda's Furniture—("No Payments till Fall") and San Juan's, a convenience store with barred windows where young mothers could exchange WIC vouchers for rum. And out the side window, the curved iron gate of the cemetery, flanked by a cedar whose two trunks diverged from a single root.

"Look," I said, "just like us!" Though the cedars were not softly merging but struggling apart.

She smiled, embarrassed. "You're crazy."

"Crazy about you. Our own place. Together," I said, and she relaxed a little. She hadn't wanted to move, of course, but she'd understood it was necessary for "my career" and she was a very good sport, always. "We'll go to the Symphony and be home in five minutes," I said.

"Three minutes to work," she replied, without much conviction, but then, conviction seemed loud and impolite to her. Her voice was always faltering in the middle of a sentence as she asked herself whether she was saying the right thing.

"The woodwork here is amazing," I said. She loved woodwork, and our landlord, a Baptist minister who was so busy in the right-to-life movement we figured that as long as we didn't have abortions he'd let us be, had left it the natural wood color she liked.

"It really is nice," she agreed.

"Lesbian Nation!" I said, fist up. Pat and Susan lived up the block and had had us over for dinner once already, Susan wearing a nightgown of flannel thick as velvet and Pat pouring cocoa with curmudgeonly good will, saying she'd never, in all her days, expected to find herself amidst such a hen party, next we'd be doing each other's hair.

"I love it," I proclaimed, settling beside her on the couch we had miraculously pushed over the stair rail into the room. "It's so cozy, like off-campus housing," I said.

"It's off-campus all right," Lee said, getting up to look out the window. "We better get the curtains up before dark," she said.

"Why?"

"Because we don't want to incite . . . well . . ."

"Incite what?"

"Did you read the paper?" she said. "The Canyon Rapist? He'd see women through their windows and know they were alone. We have to get curtains up right away."

"Lee," I started, but she wouldn't have it.

"It's a risk," she snapped. "It's just that simple."

Blame the insurance industry, all those actuaries sitting there calculating risks all day. But looking over at her, I closed my

mouth. Her face was tight—exhausted but resolute. My idea of
city life came out of *A Tree Grows in Brooklyn*—I saw myself reading on a fire escape, with a big geranium beside me and my hair
pulled back in a bow. For Lee the move was in every way a step
backward—a huge risk—but she had taken it because she was in
love. Thinking this, I closed my eyes and saw us sweep each other
into an embrace so graceful and muscular, it must come either
from a dream or Nijinsky. I owed her an immense debt, and I was
going to love her the way I'd always wanted to be loved.

"Oh, Lee," I said. "I swear, fate brought me to Hartford so I
could be with you."

She squared her shoulders a little against sweet talk.

"Honey, it's going to be fine," I said. "No risks for you, not here
with me." I reached to pull her in but she stood up instead.

"I'll just tack up a sheet for now," she said, carrying a chair
over to the window. "Have you seen the hammer?"

The window shattered in front of us. A wheel of flame opened
beyond it, and we ran screaming into the stairwell, where we met
our new neighbors, the Lopez family, who were screaming too.
Out on the street, someone shouted: "It's the transformer, the
transformer blew," and we began to understand that the world
hadn't burst entirely into flames. Lee sank onto the steps—her
knees just buckled. Three hours later, in bed, with cardboard
tacked over the window, I held her as tight as I could, arms and
legs around her, and felt her shaking so hard I thought her bones
would break like cups in an earthquake.

"It's over," I said. "It's over, there's nothing to be afraid of now."
But even I knew that in truth, it had just begun.

"SHOTS RANG out on Hereford Street last night," the newscaster
said, very brightly, on the next day's news, as if he had forgotten

that gunshots meant anything except higher ratings. It had been a kid with an air rifle, trying to hit a squirrel on the wire.

"We have to get a deadbolt," Lee said, turning away from the TV. It was the first thing she'd said for hours. We'd kept unpacking by rote. The landlord said someone would be over to measure for new glass the next day and the plywood would be off by the end of the week. For now, the television was the closest thing we had to daylight.

Lee sat on the sofa, then jumped up and went to the kitchen and looked out through the little porch over the garage. "It's getting dark," she said, with dread. Her face was set like her mother's, in the pictures I'd seen—a face that seemed to have become sadder and sadder, year by year, until the mouth turned down even when she smiled. She had absorbed this blow, would absorb others, but beyond that, there was no energy, no desire.

She's old, I thought. She was thirty-nine years older than me, but if expectation is the measure of youth, she was ancient. She looked forward to nothing—she had no obsessions, nothing she was determined to see of, or say to, the world—she'd be content, as she had told me many times, if we could just live here, safe and together, for the rest of our lives. Once I said, "Lee, when you love somebody you want to love their history too, their whole family, their town, and their ambitions, because it's all a part of that person—don't you understand?"

No, she'd said, shaking her head fondly at my little eccentricities. She did not understand.

"I'll call a locksmith tomorrow," she said.

From that moment, she shrank and shrank. Loud noises gave her palpitations. If I got home a half hour late I'd find her in tears. She refused to ride the bus because of the gauntlet of doorsteps between our house and the stop, populated by guys with boom boxes and beer cans in paper bags.

"Don't go down there," she said. "If you need to go somewhere, I'll drive you."

Suddenly she stopped still and her face went white as if she'd just heard a scream.

"Lee," I said, "what is it? What's wrong?"

"My heart," she said, pressing one hand, then both, to her chest. "I don't know." She lay down on the couch and closed her eyes. "Feel how it's beating."

I found her pulse—it was wild.

"Should I call a doctor?"

"Just don't go down there," she said, in a broken whisper. "Don't go down there. Just don't go down there again."

Three

C, or B?" This was the question posed to me, with liturgical solemnity, by Cyril Tremblay, Branch Librarian, my latest supervisor.

"Excuse me?" I smiled enormously. He was testing me, I guessed; he wanted to gauge my bibliographical knowledge somehow . . . "*C*, or *B*?" I repeated.

"*C*, or *B*?" he affirmed, with great irritation, as if I was a lackadaisical student stalling for time. He was a tall man, his square head jutting forward, a vein pulsing in his forehead as if thought was heavy labor for him, each idea a new stone to be lifted to the top of a high wall. His question sounded like the great ones—to be or not to be? either/or? *C*, or *B*? I could not answer.

"It's simple enough," he thundered, coming so close I could smell his winey breath, holding a copy of Ivy Compton-Burnett's collected works up in front of my face. "*C*, or *B*?"

"Do you mean, how should you file it?" I asked him.

"What else would I mean?" he said, with a small fury.

"*C*?" I asked, bracing for a blow.

"Do you think so?" He squinted at the book, touching the *C* of Compton and the *B* of Burnett in some kind of bewilderment.

"We hardly have room in the *C*'s," he said, and then sadly, acquiescing, "But, you think *C*?"

"I do," I said, feeling I'd spoiled everything. He disappeared into the stacks with the book and when he returned, he seemed winier yet. I was helping a woman who wanted to read *Gone With the Wind*, but I didn't understand how the interlibrary loan procedures worked and I asked him to explain. He looked at the loan form vaguely for a long time and said finally:

"You don't want that."

She looked perplexed.

"It's soap opera," he said. "You don't want it. I have the definitive history of the Civil War. It's a personal copy, but I'll bring it in for you tomorrow."

"*Gone With the Wind?*" Mrs. Arruda persisted. She was from El Salvador and she worked at the bakery up the street, selling brilliantly colored, cloyingly sweet cookies that were hard as flint. She had very little English but here she was at the library, determined to get some.

"You'll actually learn something," Cyril said, giving her a hard look—was she going to sink into philistinism, when he was offering a chance to learn as much as *he* knew? The more Cyril drank, the more censorious he became somehow; it was strange.

She faltered, glancing over at me, properly embarrassed. "Thank you," she said with confusion. She'd come over from the bakery, with its portraits of Christ in thorns on one wall and Frank Sinatra on the other, looking for something romantic that would pull her into the new language—she couldn't live up to Cyril's standards.

"Shall I send for *Gone With the Wind* too?" I asked. Everyone else wanted Harlequin romances and auto-repair manuals.

"Oh, yes," she said, "thank you."

When she was gone, Cyril said, "I don't bother with interlibrary loans. Too much paperwork and they always send the wrong thing anyway." Seeing my face, he said, "They don't read them, they don't return them, then we're to blame. If I see one in the thrift shop I'll pick it up for her."

I frowned; he became exasperated.

"We can send for it," he said, "but it will not come. Interlibrary loan is a good idea. The world is full of good ideas. Urban renewal, for instance; an excellent idea."

He looked out at the concrete square across the street. No one even wanted to walk there—they kept in the shade of the buildings and strode through only if there were no other choice, hunched as if there might be a sniper on one of the roofs nearby. There was a dry fountain in the middle, but not a single tree.

"Busing was certainly a very high-minded idea," Cyril said. "Look at this—" he held them up, a thick pink sheaf of overdue notices. "Some of these are a year old. The people they're addressed to don't live here anymore, or they took out the books when they were in detox and now they're using again, or, now here's one—what do you suppose that address is?"

"115 Spring Street?"

"The homeless shelter," he said. "The book was due in January. What do you suppose the forwarding address might be? Oh, and here's a favorite: 'Undeliverable, Building on Fire.'"

"There," he said, chuckling—sad things cheered him up, they proved he was right about life. "You're beginning to see. You did the chairs back there, did you?"

Mr. Klipsch, in his many overcoats, sat at the back table all day when it was raining. He was incontinent and his urine took the finish off the chairs. It was my job to wipe them down after he left. Lysol in one hand, lemon oil in the other, I headed to my task, but heard a loud, importunate voice behind me suddenly.

"A meatloaf special please, side of mashed, extra butter."

"Stetson!" Had he crossed the city, just to come see me? I looked up into his eyes and saw he had.

"*This* is a library, sir!" I huffed like a cartoon librarian, giggling like a girl.

"I'm sorry!" he said, and whispered: "I'd like a meatloaf special, please, side of mashed, extra butter." His eyes ticked over me like always, accounting for my breasts as if he was afraid they might have escaped since he last saw me. It seemed a lucky thing to be able to give comfort so easily.

"What are you doing here?" I asked.

"I have a reference question."

"At your service," I said, saluting with my rag.

Then, in the tone of soft amusement he often used when admitting something: "It's an excuse to come by. I called up and your girlfriend said you were here."

Girlfriend.

"I missed you too," I admitted, and he smiled without meaning to, looking down at the floor.

He leaned against the shelf while I washed the chair, and eagerly shook Cyril's hand. "You're a lucky man," he said. "She's a great salesperson."

"We're not selling anything," Cyril said, walking away.

"I think I have just the book for him," Stet said, pointing to the AA manual under his arm. "Everyone comes to it in his own time, though, I know." Dear Stetson, he was radiant with AA. "Actually, Bill W's not a very fluent writer," he said.

I looked up at him, and saw from the tilt of his head that he was saying this because I was a lit major and still a relative of Princess Margaret in his eyes. This sentence was a stepping-stone on which he meant to cross the gap between us. The gaps between people are so immense, but who ever looks for a true way over?

"God, is that what it's all about at AA? Bill W's prose style? You go around in a circle and pick apart his metaphors, and somebody says 'reminds me of Camus' and someone else says 'derivative, *I think*, of Faulkner'? I thought you got to tell your old stories over and over."

"There is that," he said and I smiled at him, looking down so he wouldn't see how ravenous I was for his stories. He had so many, starting in his parents' house, backed up to the Saco River ("You never hear people fight down here the way they do in Lewiston"), his escape, life on the road with Carrion, the band he'd been sound man for, rehab (waking up on a rubber sheet, the wreckage behind him, the daily fight to come). Stetson had failed so badly. And risen in glory, because he looked that failure in the eye.

"By the way," he said, and I saw he was sparkling all over with something he'd wanted to tell me.

"What?"

He took that second glance he always took before daring to say something . . . "I brought something we can both enjoy," he said, looking around and seeing we were alone (it was a library, one was always alone there). He pulled out a *Penthouse* magazine that advertised "Open crotch shots of Germaine Greer."

I gasped, as I knew it pleased him to shock me.

It turned out there was more than one Germaine Greer on earth, and this one had an ex-boyfriend who needed some cash. Her breasts brimmed up as she parted herself, head tossed back on the pillow with a smile that said you could use her any way you liked, if only you'd love her.

"That is *not* Germaine Greer," I said. "Germaine Greer does not smile that way." But I was blushing to the roots of myself, because it was exciting to see her revealing all her secrets. And because Stetson was watching my reaction so closely.

"Philippa always said it's really the womb men want to see—
that's where the action is," I said. Lee got nervous when I talked
about Philippa, so I could only mention her with Stet.

"I guess I can see that," he said, still gazing on Germaine. "Did
I ever tell you what my father said, when I asked him about
women? I said 'Dad, what is it, between a woman's legs, that's so
important?' and he looked me in the eye, put his hand on my
shoulder, and said 'Son, it's like the American flag.'"

"Ought to be inspiring," I said.

"But tempting to defile."

I nodded, laughing with rue, though I'd never been happier.
"Look," I said, because the winter sunset was hitting the red
brick rowhouses across the square, and even though one of them
was boarded up and they were all covered with graffiti, they had
the feeling of 1910 about them suddenly. I could imagine a milk
truck, and the immigrants of that time coming home from the
typewriter factory.

"It's beautiful," Stet said. "It's like a ruin."

We were drawn to the front window together and stood shoulder to shoulder, watching a hamburger wrapper blow across the
square in the cold, rosy light, feeling so like a couple looking over
their newly planted acres that I had to resist the urge to put my
arm around him.

"It's a shooting gallery over there now," he said.

"Remember when drugs were like a promised land you
could find in your own self? All the visions appearing? Everything seemed so much more intense and important after you
had some dope. You were finally getting into a deeper dimension. It was more like what I'd expected from life." Or rather,
from love.

"That was an illusion," he said sharply, and just as I was

heartily agreeing (having remembered what deep water this was for him), I saw Lee drive up in front. It was five o'clock. I grabbed my coat and ran out to her, feeling as though I'd been caught doing something awful. "Stetson came by," I said, hoping for absolution. The tiniest change came over her, some variation of her breathing. I switched the subject. I didn't want to tell her about "Undeliverable, Building on Fire," either, so I asked how her day had gone, and she said tiring, but good. I looked out the window and started humming, not thinking, until the words rose into my mind suddenly. "I get no kick from champagne . . . mere alcohol doesn't thrill me at all . . . I get a *kick* out of you." I pushed the door open with my foot on "kick," and saw that it was our sunlight hour—the time when the sun came over the crest of the roof across the street and shone right in through our windows.

"Sweetie, don't do that," Lee said, "it makes a mark."

Four

SYLVIE'S BABY was a boy, seven pounds five ounces, named
Jesse, not after anyone, Sylvie explained—it was just that
Butch like its sound. He'd taken an extra shift at the bar and wasn't
around much, but the money was great, and little Springtime
kept Sylvie company at home. Peabo, Pop's flying instructor, had
given Dolly his frequent flier miles so she could come back to
help out, but after she was there for two days Butch said he was
sick of tripping over her, and when Ma heard Dolly was at Sylvie's
she pulled out the baby blanket she was knitting and reworked it
into a sweater for Teddy instead.

"I suppose you've been planning this little visit all along," she
said to me, bitterly. I didn't answer. I was contemplating the vision
of myself as evil genius, devoted to driving my mother out of her
mind through stratagems as devious as persuading the bad sister
to guard the good sister's doorway and so, cruelly separating a
woman from her firstborn grandchild.

"I suppose your father will be here next," she said. Yes,
Mother, and after that, Albert Speer—I got him a weekend pass;
I've got connections in Hell. I sighed, and this was apparently an
incitement, because Ma said suddenly, and with great force, as if
she'd been holding her tongue all this time: "His first act toward

you was an act of murder! And now somehow he comes out smelling like a rose, you're willing to shelter him, to care for him, you don't even care what he did to me."

My heart filled with sympathy for this poor aspiring murderer. I was the author of his troubles, but I hadn't meant to be, and I wanted *something* to come out right for him, someday.

"I guess I should have learned by now that no one is going to understand me, not even my own child."

After she got off, I held the receiver button down for a second and then dialed Sylvie, to ask Dolly to come visit me, so I could take her under my wing. I was going to build a perfect replica of childhood for her. I put an old patch quilt on our guest bed, and turned it down the way Ma used to, when she had a moment of respite and was trying to make things nice. And I made Ma's spaghetti sauce for dinner, and planned a trip to the aquarium the day after she arrived. I went to five different florists looking for Queen Anne's lace and bee balm to make a bouquet like the ones we used to pick at home.

"Those are field flowers," a clerk explained, looking at me strangely, so I could see I'd violated some florist etiquette that everyone else understood. "You know, the kind that grow wild. There's no point in selling them."

"Well, unfortunately I do not happen to be in possession of a field," I huffed. The nerve of her, acting as if just because I didn't have a field I was somehow less of a person and not entitled to the same flowers as everyone else. I felt like bringing her up on a civil rights charge. "I mean, look at this! You have a special on Asian terrestrial orchids!" Was this what was left to the poor and unlanded, a bunch of expensive and probably carnivorous jungle plants that looked like mutated sexual organs and smelled of mouthwash and paint thinner? I turned on my heel.

And there she was, my sister, alighting with her many parcels from the bus across the street from the florist, dropping one glove, then another, bending to retrieve them and losing her glasses, the scarf sliding from around her neck, then, her face lit up as soon as she saw me and she ran toward me across the busy street, though her shoes stayed behind and the bus driver was holding out the purse she'd left on her seat.

As I hugged her I felt her steel herself, as if I were holding her too tight or too long. I stepped back. I had so much to say to Dolly and none of it could really fit into words. We stood there at the curb, looking at each other with hope and suspicion, like people on a blind date. When I last knew her, before I went to Sweetriver, she'd been a mystical nine-year-old who lived according to a mad Talmud of inner rules: she couldn't go to school without a little bracelet she'd woven for herself out of cherry twigs, and she'd counted Ma's goodnight kiss as an amulet and refused to speak afterward, answering any question with a flurry of frantic hand gestures meant to illustrate the dangers she'd face if her silence were broken. Since then, I'd seen her once or twice a year in the midst of the squabbling parents, flapping chickens, and barking dogs that constituted our family. I had no real sense of her. And here she was, tall as a woman, uncertain as a girl, scratching the back of her left ankle with her right foot like an ibis or flamingo or some other bird that seems, though it spends its life in water, not to care to wet its feet. A spark of confidence and her face would have been beautiful. What struck me about her, though, was her inquisitive silence: she was full of questions she didn't dare ask. She'd stepped on too many land mines in her life . . . maybe that was why she stood on one foot.

"I hope you haven't been waiting long," she said.

"No, no, only a minute . . . I'm so glad to see you."

"Yes," she said, looking left and right as if now that she had crossed the street, she remembered she ought to watch out for

342 • *Heidi Jon Schmidt*

cars. "Yes, it's really nice of you, Beatrice . . . This is just great."

She might have been reading from a phrase book. She knew there was some proper way to address formidable me, with my degree and the terrible shadow cast by my sexuality, and now my great big-shot job at the library—but who could guess what it was? I felt terrible for her, having to look up to me, but I knew I was the best she had.

"Welcome to Hartford!" I said.

"Thank you," she said earnestly. "Oh, you should see the baby! He's so adorable, his little eyes are so dark and round and curious. You'll love him, Beatrice, and the trailer is just like a little playhouse!"

"Cramped, though," I said, in case she was hurt that Butch had sent her away, but she frowned and insisted the place was lovely and spacious, that you'd never guess it was only eighty-four square feet, and furthermore, she could completely understand why it might have been hard for them to have her there, with a brand-new baby and all. "It's perfect! He's the most beautiful little baby," she said again, as if she had to prove it to me, since I was on the Pill and probably believed all babies ought to be killed.

"All they really need is money," she said. We were back at the apartment and she was looking around at all of Lee's furniture. "It's hard, with a baby—they're doing the best they can, Butch works and works, it's a hard life."

"No," I said. "It's not money that's lacking, it's *emotional* where-withal," I tried to explain. "They're totally at sea, how can they support each other? How can they make a good foundation for their child?"

She looked at me without comprehension. "I suppose the library hired you because of all the college?" she asked.

"I suppose that had something to do with it," I said.

"Not everyone has to go to college, Beachy," she said sharply. "Plenty of people do just fine without it. They learn a trade, they work their way up."

Was she turning into my father? She'd failed to mold herself completely in Ma's image, and look what had happened. Dolly had to listen to him, all day, every day. She didn't know a single person west of the Mississippi, except Pop, and she was in danger of becoming lost in him, of knowing the exact labyrinth where his heart and mind came together, and not one other thing.

I'd escaped; Dolly had followed him into the fire. I wondered if I could pull her back somehow without falling in myself.

"Lots of people do fine without college," I said, carefully. "It's absolutely true that there are all kinds of paths through life."

"Pop never went to college," she said, recognizing my wariness and resenting it.

"Indeed, Pop never went to college and look at all he's done," I said.

"Right!" said Dolly, who was unaccustomed to irony. Her face relaxed. I felt her tension drain away. "I wish more people could understand that, Beatrice," she said.

Lee came in with a folded towel and washcloth for her, in a very tasteful shade of eggplant—she'd bought them when we moved in, to complement the pink and gray tiles in the bathroom. I checked Dolly's face—yes, she was properly impressed, she had never seen towels like this. And she seemed slightly uncertain— wasn't it wrong somehow to have nice towels? I myself had always had a secret lust for towels, and thick rugs, and rose-printed curtains like the ones from my mother's girlhood, before she got lost in her jungle of rage.

"It's very nice of you to have me," Dolly said to Lee. "I'm so glad to have the chance to get to know you." She opened her bag and set her things on the dresser.

"You look beautiful, Dolly," I said, because she did, in a very cool way, and because we always said this, out of love, to each other.

A ray of hope shone in her face but immediately vanished. "I can't look in the mirror, Beachy," she said. "I know I look just like Pop."

Like the exact sort of person her own mother despised. She got into bed and Lee and I moved around the kitchen, setting out the breakfast things. "So, I'll pick up juice at San Juan's tomorrow," I said. "And you'll get the fish at Louie's?" We'd already planned this, but I wanted to feel like the head of household, whose child was settling down to sleep. It was an accomplishment, this calmness. It was worth the sacrifice.

"Good night, Dolly," I said at her door, but she didn't answer, and I thought, *She's at home here.* I intended to keep her.

Lee always seemed anxious when she found me reading, as if I might find something in a novel that would turn me against her. She never said as much; in fact, she'd often bring me a cup of tea, or ask if my light was bright enough, but I could feel her discomfort. Once, when I was involved in a book and read right through breakfast instead of looking at the paper, she asked, "What's it about?" with a kind of irritated disbelief, and later used the phrase "the life of the mind" as code for "an affectation." So I didn't read when we were at home together, and once we lived in the city and I began to feel really guilty toward her, I stopped reading at all—I was determined not to betray her. Now, though, I picked up my copy of *Middlemarch*, with all the notes I'd taken in Philippa's class, and brought it to bed with me. Lee was asleep. It was dark and quiet, and the bouquet of anemones I'd settled for hovered there in the vase. The étagère stood as serene as if it had been passed down to us through the generations, and I thought for a minute that there might be real possibility in my future, that my promise might be more than some fantasy my mother had cooked up. Stetson saw it too, after all. Falling asleep, I thought of him.

"IT's so nice to have a sister who can take me places, like this," Dolly said, as we got on the bus to go to the aquarium. I, who'd been planning it all month, was excited as a child, but she sounded mostly dutiful. It occurred to me that she was constantly pretending—to be excited and happy, to rely on Pop, to be fine without Ma . . . until the pretense took on its own life, protected her so she didn't have to see herself alone in a desert. She could tell I was happy to be the big sister, the guide, so she was playing the little sister for all it was worth. Well, I was going to show her a better way. There'd been a photograph in the paper of a tank full of billowing jellyfish, "moon jellies," whose transparency held light so they seemed to glow in the dark. When Dolly saw this, she might know some of the things that were possible if you broke through the invisible barrier around our family.

I'd offered her yogurt for breakfast and she'd looked at me as if I must be out of my mind. She'd keep Ma alive in her absence by keeping to Ma's ways, and this meant despising yogurt and persons who liked yogurt, and other foods or habits or words. As we walked down the sidewalk to the bus stop, she stepped conscientiously over each crack.

"I've never been to an aquarium," she said, with assiduous awe. If only I could act the parent, and she the child—well there was safety in that, for both of us. The bus ride might take us exactly where we wanted to go, and when we stood before the enormous tanks in the dim undersea light, watching the fish flash by, we'd become the children we were supposed to be, amazed and joyful as the world opened out before us.

"You're going to love it," I said, thinking how damned inept our parents were, how *I'd* show Dolly the world.

I'd seen the aquarium from the bus before, at the intersection of Park and Vine, but there was a new subdivision going up along Vine Street, and where I remembered a little corner gas station set in a tangled woodland there was a landscape of sandy canyons now, with backhoes grinding over them on heavy treads. The light was green, and the other direction seemed to lead straight into the woods, so I pulled Dolly along westward.

"It's just the next block," I told her. Vine Street had no side-walks, just a wide drainage ditch with lengths of plastic pipe laid beside it. One or two houses had already been built—a little boy was trying to pedal a tricycle in a muddy driveway while his mother smoked a cigarette in her open door. I nodded to her and a shadow crossed her face—I felt as if she'd laugh at me if I asked her for directions, and if she laughed at me I'd probably disinte-grate, leaving Dolly all alone. We walked on along the street, which had widened to four lanes and curved assuredly through the empty land—it must lead somewhere, and the aquarium seemed the likeliest place.

"It's kind of barren here," Dolly said, "I mean, in a very nice way—because they're improving it." We could hear the heavy equipment downshifting to climb the hills, which were several stories tall.

"Is it like Wyoming?" I asked.

"Oh, no!" she said. "You know, Wyoming's got the richest min-eral stores in the whole country. There's no sand there at all—it's all rock and clay and if you dig down just a foot the earth is all red and gold and green."

"I meant, is this a little like where you live—a development?"

"I guess," she said, not wanting to contradict. "Maybe it will be, when it's done." We rounded the corner with no sign of the aquarium. We seemed to be in the midst of a choppy sea of sand with no compass, and on the horizon a lowering sun. I picked up the pace, determined on the next curve. It was the middle of March and the pastel sky promised spring but the wind was from the north and right in our faces.

"Do you think maybe it's moved?" Dolly asked. (In our family it was considered very impolite to suggest someone had taken a wrong turn.)

"God, how would you move an aquarium?" I asked, though if they had moved it, this wouldn't be my mistake. "No, it's right around here, I've seen it," I said. "Not much farther now." The suspicion that I might be walking in the wrong direction only spurred me on: I could not, I would not, be the latest person to lead Dolly into the wilderness; she trusted me and it would be too awful to disappoint her. "Just another minute," I said.

"It's nice to have a little walk," Dolly said. "Stretch my legs."

"I wish the wind would stop," was the next thing she said to me. Besides its being cold, the wind was full of sand now, which meant that either it had switched direction or that we had. We'd come to the bend I'd pinned my hopes on, and could see down a long stretch to the light at a distant intersection. There were no longer any trucks or cranes working, and the land was churned up with the trees still rooted in it. We'd walked more than a mile.

"It's just up at the light," I said. It was right near a stoplight, I remembered.

"Do you think they'll have a water fountain?" Dolly asked. I looked over at her—her cheeks were flushed and she was beginning to limp a little—her shoe had worn through the heel of her sock.

"Oh, they have a whole cafeteria," I said. "We'll sit down and have toast and tea!"

She smiled in the deepest way—toast and tea was a phrase from our childhood, or really from my mother's childhood, during which there had been, she told us, department store lunchrooms where tea was served with cream cakes and fresh strawberries. She spoke of it with such longing that we'd longed for it too.

"I don't know why Pop wants to live way out West," she confessed suddenly. "It's not like there's anything for him to do, really, just sit by the phone and watch the news. I don't really understand." She worked at understanding, for a second, but in the end, the idea didn't appeal. "We're together, that's the important thing," she reminded herself.

We'd reached the intersection, and it was just that—eight stoplights strung up across two four-lane thoroughfares, surrounded by more raw land, with nothing else in sight except one of those impregnable telephone company structures that confound the romantic by being at once so mysterious and so dull.

"I don't know, Dolly, I can't find it," I said. I could hear the disappointed, querulous note in my voice and I stopped talking instantly because I was afraid I was going to cry and I knew there was nothing worse than having the person you rely on fall apart that way.

"It's okay, Beachy," she said. "I don't have to see the aquarium."

She was so sweet—I wanted to smack her. How wrong, how perverse of her to keep renouncing and renouncing, first for my father's sake, now for mine. I had promised her something I couldn't give her, pulling her along the side of a sewage gully to bring her nowhere, and still she refused to be angry, or even disappointed. I sat down on the bank of the ditch and rested my head on my knees. The great flood of cars that had been dammed up at the light gave way suddenly and roared past us.

"I've screwed up," I said then, trying to sound lighthearted. "It must have been the other way. We'll have to turn around," I said. "I don't know what else to do."

She nodded. "It really doesn't matter, Beachy," she said. "It's just nice to get to spend some time with you."

She meant to mean it, I knew. I stood up and dusted myself and we started back. We'd come much farther than I'd guessed— miles. I'd dragged her along, walking and walking as if no map were available and no one else would know the way, searching for an aquarium as if it was a single flower in a twenty-acre field. How long had it been since we got off the bus? It seemed to be rush hour already.

"Let's hitch!" I said, and we stuck out our thumbs the way they do in the movies, but no one even slowed. They didn't see us, or maybe we looked so pathetic no one dared to stop, lest they find themselves saddled with a pair of foundlings. I began to run, backward, with my thumb out, and to edge into the road as if I might throw myself in front of somebody's car. Now they swerved in wide arcs around us, eyes still averted.

As we came back to the bus stop, I saw the sign for the aquarium over the trees, about half a block away—it hadn't been visible from the other angle. Neither of us cared about it anymore, but we did want a drink. As we went up the steps, parched and covered with dust from the excavation, a young woman came out with a ring of keys.

"We close at five," she said, looking at us sadly. She could see something about us that we could have kept hidden if we hadn't been running through a dust bowl for hours. She pointed to the clock inside, which showed the time as 5:02. Beneath it was a tank the size of a small room, filled with fish in shades of azure and silver-green. I thought of smashing down the door.

"It's okay, Beachy," Dolly said. "We'll come another day." She sat down on the step and wiped her face with her sleeve.

"It's *not* okay," I said angrily.

She blinked, and looked at me in wounded surprise—how

could it be, when she had done everything just as I'd asked her, and really, she was as good as gold, polite to Lee even while our being Lithuanian was so strange and unnerving to her—rushing to wash the dishes after dinner—she had even insisted on paying my bus fare. How could I answer her so sharply?

"The important thing is that we're together," she said.

"That is *not* the important thing," I said, through my teeth. "The important thing is . . ." but I couldn't think. Maybe nothing was very important. I felt the impulse that had just arisen—to tear all the veils and set my hand on something true—recede. What did it matter, after all, any of it? Nothing would change. We would all go on spinning outward, away from each other, each foolish hope failing, each desperate move leading to a worse consequence, whether or not Dolly and I saw the jellyfish in the Hartford Aquarium.

"You're right, of course," I said. "It's just, I'm so sorry." My voice, infuriatingly, was breaking. I tried to cover it with a laugh. "Oh, dear, why do these things always happen to us?" I said. The afternoon would shrink away; we would turn it into a neat anecdote that confirmed our sisterhood; we'd laugh to think what we must have looked like to those drivers who'd passed us. It would be funny one day, it would, and we both laughed dully in anticipation.

"If we could just get something to drink," she said then, wearily—no one could accuse her of complaining. But the museum was closed, the woman had disappeared back into the building, there was nothing in any direction but the lees and swells of bulldozed earth. Thousands of cars sped out of the barren landscape now, heading, it seemed, nowhere, the bus among them. It picked up its passengers and took off again before we could brook the traffic to reach it. the driver staring stonily ahead while I tried to signal him, the passengers looking on mildly, full of their own thoughts. They had seen many more curious sights than this bedraggled woman, waving her arms on a street corner as if she thought she was drowning. We got the six o'clock bus and rode back to Frog Hollow in a silence broken only by Dolly's earnest expressions of gratitude for the wonderful afternoon she knew I'd meant her to have.

Five

*L*EE HAD made baked stuffed flounder for dinner. "Finally, a fish," I said, but no one noticed the joke.

"If you'd called I'd have started it later," Lee said as she spooned the gelatinous stuff onto our plates. "I've been working on it ever since I got home." No doubt true, I thought—she was convinced that all foods needed to be chopped, marinated, and sauced until they were completely purified of any trace of their vulgar roots. She could make a vegetable terrine that tasted exactly like fish and a salmon pâté that tasted just like broccoli, and then there were the tomato roses or the pureed turnips or the veal birds. Usually I liked this, since it meant we spent hours in the kitchen together with only the simplest conversation, grinding garlic against sea salt, sifting cornmeal over a boiling pot—it was all abundant, fragrant, warm. Sex was nearly behind us—we didn't seem to need it anymore and were only moved that way when we'd been out in the straight world and remembered that for us making love was an act of rebellion. But the food, the food proved how lucky we were in each other's love.

"What's in the sauce?" I asked, thinking it looked like disintegrating cardboard.

"Shallots, in a cream reduction with a little vermouth," she said, and I had a guilty flash of memory: Ma, getting Thanksgiving dinner with only that one stove burner working. "And paprika, and celery salt, and I put in a pinch of curry, I don't know if you can taste it.

"And it's the tamari-sesame dressing," Lee continued, pushing the salad toward me. "Look at the cucumbers—I used that julienne blade."

Dolly's good humor was running low and though she praised each bite, she only got through three or four before she excused herself, asking if we'd mind if she took a shower. This time tomorrow, I thought, she'd be on the way back to Wyoming. I was counting the hours.

"She's sort of sullen," Lee said, as soon as we heard the shower. My blood leapt—"What do you mean?" I asked.

"Look, she hardly ate a bite. She doesn't smile, she just sits there making little judgments. She has no spark," she said, and went silent.

"She's depressed," I said, standing up to clear, moving gently so as to keep my speech light. "Would you smile, if you were fourteen and your mother wouldn't recognize you and you had to move two thousand miles away from your family and all your friends so you could live in a godawful tract house with your lost, dazed father, and the mountains went up like a cliff to the west so you never saw the sun after one o'clock in the afternoon?"

And if your older sister, your one hope, was so inept she couldn't manage to take you an afternoon's outing, never mind saving you? I thought.

"And what's your wattage, anyway?" I asked suddenly, and Lee gasped as if I'd struck her and started to cry.

"She's a guest in our home," she said. "She ought to make some effort." And then, as if she'd only just truly heard what I'd said, she sat down and wept in earnest. In my anger I'd jabbed her right in the big secret we were keeping from each other.

"Three bites, and I worked on it all afternoon."

"It's not about dinner!" I roared, but I realized she'd been offering me an olive branch, a chance to pretend it *was* about dinner, and not about whatever it was I was desperate to get from her, that she didn't have to give. I heard my mother's ghost in my voice . . . and *that* I refused to accede to.

"I'm sorry," I said. "It's just been such a bad day . . . and you made a wonderful dinner, and if only I'd called, everything would have been fine."

"Accepted," she said, turning both faucets on to fill the dishpan. She took care of me all day, every day—whether or not I needed it. I owed her gratitude at least. Slender though she was, she seemed like a pudgy boy, her shoulder blades moving like a pair of tiny, useless wings as she soaped the dishes and set them in the drainer. Then she went into the back room, where she was refinishing a chair. I ran my hand along the surface of the dining table, her last project; it was like satin, you could almost feel the grain. Wind, water, and Lee Schuyler, I thought—they all know how to wear the things they touch smooth.

Dolly came out in Lee's bathrobe and made for the refrigerator. "My stomach feels funny," she said. "Do you have some ice cream or something?"

We never had ice cream.

"How about some cheese?" I asked. It was moldy but we could cut that part off.

"I know," she said, "I'll eat that yogurt. I think that would help."

"That's Lee's," I said, wanting to bare my teeth and ask how the yogurt had changed since breakfast, when she'd found it so revolting. Spinning into a rage, I caught a dizzied glimpse of something—she meant to eat the yogurt now to make amends for her earlier refusal. She looked up at me in hurt surprise.

"For her lunch," I said, "That's what she has for lunch—she's worried for her heart."

"Well, can't she get some more?"

"Not before work," I said piously. "Have some cheese."

"It's all moldy," Dolly said. "Don't you have cottage cheese, or cream cheese or something?"

"What is it, do you think food just grows in the refrigerator? Well, it doesn't. Someone has to go out and buy it, someone who *works*." Someone who had spent hours making a special dinner that tasted awful to me, who wanted only one thing—my love, which I could not seem really to give her . . .

Dolly shot me a despising glance and quickly looked away. Her lip was quivering, and I saw the moment of her indecision give way to anger—"You're my *sister* and you won't give me a cup of yogurt out of your refrigerator!" she said. "All that time living out there and not once, not one time, did *you* call *me*, to ask how I was doing, to say you'd do anything to help, nothing, *NOTHING!*" A sob shook her, and she bent into herself, holding her own arms as if that were the best embrace she could hope for. "Abandon us all? When just a few thousand dollars would mean so much—for Sylvie and the baby at least—he's just a baby, he hasn't done anything wrong."

She immersed herself in weeping, repeating "my sister, my sister" in sarcastic misery. If her mother was an implacable, avenging whirlwind, her father a wisp in the breeze, then, I stood *in loco parentis*. On this we had both, without thinking, agreed. Sylvie and I were the only ones who had so much as a job, and everyone knew Sylvie needed every dollar, while I lived in comfort and ease.

"One goddamned cup of yogurt," she said again, and I grabbed it out of the refrigerator, ripped off the lid, and pushed it at her.

"Here," I said, "have it, if you think a cup of yogurt is so important, eat it then!"

"I don't want it *now*," she said, pushing it away and burying her head in her arms to cry so quietly, I could hear the faithful, exact strokes of Lee's sandpaper in the back room.

"No, I insist, *you* eat the yogurt."

"I don't *want* it!" she roared, striking out at it as if it were a cup of hemlock, and it went flying across the room, spilling its pale pink contents in the most vibrant, painterly way. She waited for me to respond, and I thought that we were at the brink of the familiar, that I could almost feel my mother's presence. Ma would have raged at Dolly, or splashed a dishpan full of water down on the mess, or whatever would most completely electrify us. And afterward, we'd feel we'd witnessed an act of nature, been washed clean by a furious storm.

"I want to go home," Dolly said. "I want so much to go home."

"You'll be there tomorrow." This was the cruelest thing I could have said. She didn't mean Wyoming of course, but our home, or the place we had tried to believe it had been, the beautiful farm on the hillside where the girls with their long hair cradled the little lambs in their arms, while in the valley below us, the evening lamps blinked on and the stars grew brighter in the sky. Why couldn't that place have existed, when we'd wanted it so badly, had worked so hard to make it real? She cried at the table as I sopped the yogurt off the floor, listening to Lee's sandpaper, thinking of that poor lost place, our home.

"I'll never be there again," she said.

"And in fact, you were never there in the first place," I snapped.

She looked at me as if I'd lost my mind, but I didn't care, so long as she didn't grab hold of me now and pull me down. It seemed possible to me that, with great effort, I might be able to shed my own meshugas—my family—accomplish this or that, keep out of debt, go to the supermarket without being fearful of the cashiers, love someone—all this might be in reach, but just barely, and not with Dolly holding on to my skirt.

Dolly took a deep breath and sat back in her chair. "But it's true," she said. "I'll be home tomorrow." She was giving up on me, and the minute I felt her grip loosen I was filled with regret.

"Dolly," I said.

She waved a hand, sniffed, and even smiled a little. "I took pictures of the baby. Pop said he can't wait to see them. There's a store out there that develops them in an hour."

Lee came in peeling her rubber gloves off like a surgeon and went to the sink to wash her hands.

"I think that was shellac I was stripping off there," she said. "I closed off the back room."

Her face was so closed against us, it seemed I'd need a can opener to reach her.

"What were you two arguing over?" she asked, when Dolly was tucked in and we got into bed.

"Yogurt, strawberry yogurt," I said disgustedly. "Really, about the past and the future. The thing is that she can't bear to admit what's happened to her, that she needs her mother, that she made a mistake going with Pop, she can't bear to see it and the mistakes just snowball." I talked on and on, about my family, all families, the human entropy by which each wrong turn leads you further toward the edge of life, generation after generation, until you're lost.

She laughed. "My little dramatist," she said, with kind condescension, patting my hand. "Go to sleep, things will seem different in the morning."

"Your little *what?*" I asked.

"Don't be offended," she said, still smiling. "It's cute, I mean of course it gets on people's nerves, your intensity, you know—your way of thinking too much—but I think it's cute, it's part of why I love you."

"Cute?" I said. Well, what if I roared from the depths of myself, and bit off her head? Because that was what I, cute little pie that I was, felt like doing just then. There was, I thought, a superciliousness to Lee's humility: a contortion of ego. Hers was all the larger for managing to appear so small. "I do not *think too much,*" I said, with Churchillian composure. "I am trying to figure my way out of a mire."

"I know, sweetie," she said. "I know it's hard for you." The pity in her voice revealed to me a small and peculiarly simple landscape that I'd never glimpsed before—her view of me.

"How about a little back rub?" she asked me. "Or a cup of chamomile tea? You know how I like to indulge you."

"*Talk* to me, then," I said.

"Sweetie, there's no use examining everything the way you do," she said. "This, too, will pass, as they say" (she faltered, afraid of misquoting). "No use crying over spilt milk," she said, to make herself clearer. "You're still young, you like to be *philosophical, mystical*" (strange emphasis, as if these words were pornographic). "And that's fine, it's sweet, really, but—"

"But what?"

"Well, I guess I just forget how young you are," she said, "You'll cool down, and it's refreshing, your being so, you know, naive. Let's go to sleep. I don't care about the yogurt. I just want you to be happy, that's all."

"You hypocrite! You just want me to shut up. I don't want a cup of tea, or sleep, or a little back rub, I want to reckon with life, can you possibly understand?" How loud would I have to scream, to make her turn into Philippa?

"What is there to *say?*" she hissed, all her patience finally sparked to anger. "What do you want *me* to say? Tell me, and I'll say it! You want more, I know, but there *isn't* more. *Accept!* Content yourself with what is. *Grow up*."

We lived in a world where growing up meant giving up—abandoning your own aspirations, laughing a little at all those silly hopes and dreams, mummifying yourself in layers of fat, or television, or golf. No wonder everyone was obsessed with youth!

"I'm not smart enough for you, that's all," she said.

"Lee!" I said, "that's not so. That's not what I mean." This was much too cruel, I would never have allowed myself to think such a thing. "You're so smart, Lee, you are," I said. "Look at all you've done, how far you've gone at work." I apologized on and on, forgetting that she had meant, smug creature, to save me from all my thinking, as I (smug creature) had wished to save her from the desperate ordinary darkness of her life. Now she lay pressing her hands to her heart as if she could slow it that way, or as if I needed to be reminded how fragile she was, how easily I could hurt her. I took a deep breath and tried to be understanding. "We're different people, we want different things, that's all," I said. "I wish you'd talk to me more, and surely there's something that you wish from me, something you would change about me too?"

No, she said, accusingly—nothing, *she* loved *me* the way I was.

"Please, I want to know," I said. "If we're going to live together we're bound to have problems, differences, and how will we ever work them out if we can't make our feelings known?"

"I don't see why we're 'bound' to have problems," she said stiffly, but after a few long minutes she admitted that, yes, there was something that troubled her.

"What?" I felt a great weight drop from me—there was hope, we would talk things out, we'd be fine with a little give and take. . . .

"You could. . . ."

"I could what? Don't worry, silly thing, I won't get mad, this is all part of getting to know each other, it's part of the fun of it, don't you see?"

"You could—" and the words rushed out as if she could hold them back no longer: "You could use your own towel!"

"What?"

"You could use your own towel," she said, swallowing. "I put yours on the top bar, you know? It's just more sanitary."

No doubt, but the request seemed to make the world go black. "All right," I said. "From now on I'll use my own towel."

"It's no problem about the yogurt," she said. "I'll eat in the cafeteria tomorrow." Her voice was blank—she was tired of me and my family, my insistence on tracing the byzantine labyrinth of life. "Let's just forget it now, and sleep," she said, and a minute later I felt her twitch as she dropped off. She was good at forgetting things.

I heard something from Dolly's room—was she crying? I went to her door, but she was silent, even when I called her name.

I stood at the window in the living room, pressing my forehead against the glass. It was a perfectly clear night; I could feel the universal emptiness, and I was glad to think how accidental we all were, a species born by accident, our language and sympathies so well developed, by accident, that we're doomed to live lives whose hope and despair are equally illusory. How is anyone supposed to live, knowing all the time that he'll die? It was a great comfort, the pointlessness of everything. In such a haphazard world, no one could be very much in the wrong, my mother might ride off on the back of some kid's motorbike, my father might blow away in the wind, and if I lay here in Lee's bed and did nothing, so what? We're ants, all of us, teeming, industrious, utterly expendable. Someday we'll be relieved of the burden of life; until then . . .

Then something moved in the cemetery. An apparition in a

long white gown stumbled into the street below me, seeming to run and cower at once, falling against the wrought-iron cemetery gate and resting there as if she was a rag that had been tossed over the rail.

It was Susan. After a minute she lifted her head, cringing at first, but seeing she was alone she looked quickly up and down the street, into the cemetery, and finally directly up at the window, though it was dark and she didn't see me. Her feet were bare and she crossed her arms for warmth. She started across the road, but changed her mind and with a sudden resolve scooped a handful of gravel up from the cemetery drive and aimed it straight at me.

"Susan!" I called, putting up the window.

"No!" She put her finger to her lips and pointed to our back entrance, and I unlocked the kitchen door, waiting at the top of the stairs while she tiptoed up with such elaborate care for silence that when a step creaked I felt like screaming.

"What is it?" I asked her, closing the door with the same exaggeration. "What's happened to you?"

She had a split lip and a black eye. The heavy flannel nightgown I'd envied was torn down the front and she held it closed with her hand. It was old and worn, she said, and it had just given way at a tug.

"Who tugged it?" I asked her. "Pat?"

Yes, she told me as I wrapped ice in a towel, things like this had happened before, though not this badly. She held the pack to her eye and winced. Her own tears were salting her wounds.

She didn't seem angry, only sad. I had to understand, she said, that Pat never meant to hit her—Pat had been kinder to her than anyone she'd ever known. It was her natural response to stress, that was all. I didn't know how hard it was, when you grew up that way—sometimes things just got out of control. That was why Pat went to work at the women's shelter—because she knew it all, she understood, she really could help. When she was at the front desk everyone felt safer—she wasn't one of the poor shrinking violets like Susan who quavered when they tried to ask the simplest question and practically asked to be pushed around. Pat protected them, lied for them—once she had knocked a pursuing husband down the stairs! And then, one by one, they betrayed her: they went back, they loved those husbands *all the more*, they turned around and blamed *her*, Pat, saying she'd blown everything out of proportion, that she hated men, that yes, they were bruised, they had, certainly, fallen, but it was more a slip than a push—who can tell what's happening in the thick of a fight? Everyone makes mistakes, everyone gets angry, just because he waved the knife and said, "I'll put this through your black heart, you bitch!" didn't mean he didn't adore her. Or, more to the point perhaps, it didn't mean he didn't need her absolutely, as badly as if he'd been a tiny, lonely child. And Susan made a cradle of her arms to shelter some tiny, lonely child in her imagination and began weeping again.

Imagine how Pat felt, Susan said, when she remembered her parents, the way, once her father was done with her mother, he'd come after her with his belt, as if his anger was so enormous, it could never be assuaged. You had to sympathize, you had to see how brave Pat was, how staunch and true, you had to love her, and with love came anger, tearing jealousies, misapprehensions—in love one must be doubly understanding.

Lee had set the breakfast things out, orderly as a Japanese garden, on the sideboard as always. I put the teakettle on—I was going to let Susan talk herself out, comfort her, draw her out, sneak into her heart and see if I could fix everything there, but I felt Lee's silent presence in the doorway.

"What happened?" Lee asked, pulling her bathrobe sash tighter, bending over to Susan to look at her face in the light. "My God, Susan. Beatrice, she needs socks, and a robe, or something . . . can you get her something warm? Where's Pat? Is she all right?"

"She's fine," Susan said cautiously. I felt a change in her, the slightest turn toward the ordinary, the expected—with this calm voice she would move her story a little closer to the center, toward the stories we'd heard before. "We had a fight, that's all. I got mean—I do sometimes, I just get mad—and we had a scuffle. I'm so sorry I woke you. I'm fine. Really, I'm fine."

"You get the things, would you?" I asked Lee. "I'm just making tea." I wanted her out of the room so I could gain Susan's trust, but no sooner was Lee down the hall than Dolly appeared in her place, wearing my nightgown, which left her thin legs exposed.

"What is it?" she said, and Susan looked up.

"Susan, this is my sister Dolly," I said, grateful as always for my long study of Emily Post. Introductions should give an entrée into conversation: "Dolly, this is Susan, our neighbor, she works for the phone company."

"Glad to meet you," Dolly said, standing like a flamingo again, looking from one to the other of us in puzzlement—was this just an ordinary night for us? What did we do, really? Why did we live like this, on the edge of shame? Dolly had absorbed my father's feelings; he'd passed his dread of me on to her. Here, in the middle of the night, all life was reversed so the dreads were realities, and hope, calm, comfort were shadows we couldn't really believe.

Lee came back with some clothes, which Susan let rest in her lap like a strange, foreign gift she didn't know how to use. Lee and Dolly kept silent—the deepest sense, for both of them, was that words were dangerous and might shatter the fragile peace. I believed fragile things deserved to be broken. So they withdrew and I took over, pouring the tea out with a confidence I'd forgotten I could feel. The extremity of everything, bare feet on asphalt, doors pounded on in the night, sobs tearing up from something infinitely deep—these things were familiar to me, as was the silence that necessarily surrounded them. It was like being home again.

"Put the socks on," I said softly to Susan, and she obeyed, pulling Lee's sweater on too and wrapping it tight around her. Softer still, I asked, "Shall we call nine-one-one?" I knew it would have been wrong to say "the police."

Susan said nothing, but seemed to be listening. Then she shook her head. "There's no emergency," she said wearily.

"Do you want to look in the mirror?" I challenged her.

She laughed. "You don't know the half of it," she said. Suddenly her voice was full of life: "I wish you could hear what she says to me—'I'd like punch your teeth right down your throat, you filthy whore'—she sounds like a sailor. She even looks a little like a sailor, don't you think?" and she giggled: "Bowlegged! Oh, no, I've seen a lot worse than this, let me tell you."

She was boasting. Something had happened to her, she was at the center, and we were witnesses to *her* life. She was richer, in experience, than we. It wasn't much, maybe, but it was something, something she was not going to let us take away.

"Is there film in the camera, Lee?" I asked. At least we could take some pictures to show her the next time, remind her that this had happened before.

"I've got mine," Dolly said.

"Bring it, honey, will you?" I said without turning, keeping still so Susan wouldn't startle and flee.

But the phone rang. I looked up at the clock: 1:15 A.M. For the first two rings we stayed still, as if pretending we didn't hear. As it continued it seemed to become more insistent, and Susan hunched in on herself, covering her face.

"It's not that late in Wyoming," Dolly said, leaning toward the phone as if its power was too much for her to resist.

"Answer it," Susan said suddenly, with absolute authority as the center of the drama.

It was Pat, as we must all have known. She did sound chastened, apologizing for the late hour, asking in a voice of well-rehearsed, innocent concern whether I might have seen Susan. She had gone out earlier and hadn't returned, and she was ordinarily so reliable, it made Pat worry.

Susan took the phone from my hand.

"Baby, I'm right here," she said, and I knew my chance had passed.

"I'm sorry, honey," Susan said, "I know I was wrong." There came a wail from Pat, a cry of wounded rage we could all hear. Lee and Dolly and I turned and tiptoed away to the living room like the three blind mice, though we didn't need to go. Susan had forgotten us, as she crooned a lullaby of forgiveness into the phone. There's great strength, in forgiving, and she sounded more confident than she ever had before.

Lee and Dolly struck up a real conversation, trying to leave Pat and Susan in privacy, though I'd hoped to overhear them. They started by bemoaning lost jewelry. Lee had been trying to skip stones off the Acadian rocks and seen a bracelet go flying into the waves; Dolly had lost her ruby ring down a storm drain—this went on until I hated them both, for their lack of ferocity, their determination not to intrude, which was wrecking my chance to get to the heart of it all. I heard Susan avow her love to Pat, and when I turned back, Dolly's eyes were shining—she was talking about flying, a subject she hadn't dared discuss with me. But then, Susan was in front of us, thanking us in a way that seemed to plead that we forget it all, and she rushed out the door as if she couldn't bear one more minute away from home. Downstairs the door locks opened and shut with reports like gunshots, and the house was returned to its midnight silence.

"There's nothing you can do in a situation like that," Lee said. "It's their private business."

"They seem okay," Dolly said. "Everyone has a little fight now and then."

"I think Pat might really hurt her someday," I tried, but Lee pointed out that Susan was not only a foot taller than Pat, but eight years younger, and so the case was closed.

"No one can ever really see inside anyone else's marriage," I said.

"Well, it's not a marriage," Dolly said, puzzled.

Lee pointed out that Susan was a free agent, and we all agreed that we should honor her wishes and forget it.

And, having agreed not to discuss the only thing that mattered at the moment, we found ourselves in an awkward relation. "I'd better get to bed, the bus goes early," Dolly said.

LEE'S SOCKS and sweater fell into the black hole. Susan couldn't have returned them without admitting what had happened, and for us to ask about getting them back would have seemed terribly rude. I saw Susan buying milk at San Juan's a week later, but when I asked how she was, she said she was fine, just fine, in a tone of perplexity as if this were a prying question. Later I saw her dodge through traffic, trying to cross Park Street to avoid me. After a while I learned to give her a quick friendly nod when we passed, as if she was someone I'd met at a party once years ago. That frozen night, the ghostly vision of her stumbling through the cemetery, came to seem like something from a dream. How could such a thing have happened in our world, our refuge from the violence of men? It wasn't possible; it didn't make sense, and the incident was washed out of memory day by day until all that was left was a slight uneasiness at the sight of Pat's car with its WHAT PART OF NO DON'T YOU UNDERSTAND? bumper sticker, parked in the handicapped space at the Y. Months later we went to the grand opening of the Wives and Mothers Thrift Shop, which had been set up to support the battered women's shelter, and there were Lee's things all nicely laundered and displayed. We bought them back for $3.75.

Six

I STOOD up on tiptoe, so as to make eye contact with Mrs. Arruda over the bakery counter. "We haven't seen you for weeks," I said. "Is everything okay?"

"Oh, yes, yes," she said, smiling with some distant El Salvadoran humor I didn't recognize.

"Well, I wish you'd come into the library sometimes," I said. "We miss you."

She took a quick, puzzled glance at me. Why would we miss her? People never guess the effect of their own qualities—Mrs. Arruda's matter-of-fact manner, her determination in the face of difficulty, had given me an inspiration I didn't find anywhere else. Whenever she came in and I talked to her, I always felt like my job at the library was worth it, that I was doing some good.

Now her shoulders sagged and she admitted she couldn't make her way through Cyril's Civil War history. And Cyril having honored her, by lending her one of his own books . . . she didn't know what to do. She couldn't just put it back in the return slot, but neither could she bring herself to come into the library and confess that she'd failed.

"When a man has learned so much," she said, "and wants to give some of it . . ." she ran out of words and extended her open hands to try to show all the loan had meant to her. "And then I don't read . . ." she said. "I was a doctor, in El Salvador," she said, suddenly, to counter her shame.

"You were?"

"A . . ." she needed courage to pronounce it, "pediatrician? For children?"

"Yes, yes," I said.

"I went to take the test, here, I study and study—and, no pass," she said, "—the language—You don't believe me," she said sadly.

"I do believe you. Why wouldn't I? Can't you work on your English and take the test again?"

She smiled and shook her head. "Will you give the book back to Mr. Tremblay?" she asked me.

Yes, I said, of course. When she brought the book back to me in the library, all wrapped in layers of brown paper and twine, I felt like beating Cyril to death with it: he'd wanted to show Mrs. Arruda how much more learned he was than she, as if that learning had been put to any useful purpose! He'd isolated himself with his reading, as my parents had living on their farm.

"She's from El Salvador, Cyril. She doesn't need history lessons," I said. "Did you ever look for it, *Gone With the Wind*? It can't be very hard to find."

He was sitting at his desk, checking through a batch of overdue notices, and he held up a finger so I would see he had to get through the job before he could give me his attention. When he finally looked up he seemed to have forgotten the question, so I repeated it, but his answer was a slurred dismissal. I started to speak to him angrily, but what good would that do? He'd be hurt and he'd get even more pompous.

His young self was still alive in him, alive and fierce and disgusted with the old, beaten inebriate he'd become. This angry young idealist had to be kept in check somehow, hence the wine, which didn't, in the end, subdue the young Cyril, but went straight to the frustrated old pedant's head, giving the young Cyril all the more opportunity to savage the poor old man. I knew, though we never mentioned it, that Cyril was gay, and that his own times had not provided him with the flying-closet-ejector system available to people like me. He'd just suffered the little jokes about his extended bachelorhood, then the waning of those jokes and the silence that replaced them. Now he was twice isolated—neither his love nor his intellect dared speak their names anymore.

"It's a *book*," I said. "It's our job to get books for people—the ones they ask for, not the ones we think they should read." How amazing to hear myself, addressing the good side of Cyril.

It was my night to stay until eight, though after Cyril left at five, the only other person in the building was Mr. Klipsch, trying to sleep off his desolation in the back, and taking the finish off the chairs. Without him I'd have been lonely. With him, I was competent: shelving books, typing up the new cards, recognizing myself for once as essential: I kept the world going here. When I went to empty Cyril's wastebasket, I found it full of torn-up interlibrary loan forms: in spite of all his demurrals, he had been trying to get *Gone With the Wind*, but each time, he had gotten confused—first he'd filled in Mrs. Arruda as author; then he'd asked for it to be sent *from* our branch rather than *to* it; then he'd sealed the receipt in the envelope and kept the request in the file; then he'd given up.

He didn't do it because he didn't know how. Cyril knew a great deal; he knew that a general looking down over the Charge of the Light Brigade had said to his companion: "*C'est magnifique. Mais ce n'est pas la guerre.*" He knew that the great works of literature had already been written, because actions don't have clear consequences anymore. "Anna Karenina risked the loss of her child for 'love'!" he'd say. (Certain words he always spoke with implied quotation marks, as if he was above using them himself.) "What would she risk now, less alimony?" He knew all the odd alleys (the *lacunae*, he said with relish) where a man might relieve himself in some privacy, walking home from the bar. He didn't go to Kingdom Come, of course, but to Sallie's, which he called a "wrinkle bar" because it catered to men his age, who had grown up "effeminate." No one at Kingdom Come was effeminate, styles had changed. But he couldn't write out an interlibrary loan form. So, although I'd dreamed he would take me under his wing, I realized now that I had to take him under mine. I'd been trying for so long to find people to teach and protect me, as if I weren't a fierce and learned being already. I was full of answers but they weren't the answers people expected, so I hadn't dared give them. I'd rather believe myself a fool.

I pulled out a new form, filled it in, and sent it to the main branch. Just like that.

So I was humming "Summertime" to myself, imagining calling up that freshman adviser of mine and saying, "Listen, a few years ago you asked me why sex was so important to me, and I feel I owe you a fuller response . . ." when I heard a clear voice singing the words behind me:

"One of these days, you're gonna rise up singing . . ."

"Stetson!"

"Sorry, I couldn't resist," he said, "I didn't mean to intrude."

"How did you learn to sing like that?" I asked him.

"My father sang," he said.

Of course, I thought, *that's how people learn things.*

"I'm so glad to see you!" I said, "I've been dying to tell you . . ." About my interlibrary loan victory, though it might have been anything interesting and true. He'd want to know those things, think about them, try to see them clearly. His career of mistakes had brought him here, to a place beyond pretense, where life in all its infinite variety was to be gazed at with tender fascination. Everyone else I knew had a persona to tend to, a hypothesis to prove. Stetson was just *interested*, newly born out of rehab, with a bad headache, a fierce curiosity, and the knowledge of his own— of everyone's—terrible fragility. A man is only the sum of his fascinations, I thought—Stetson was a giant.

His sleeve was pulled up so I could see more of his tattoo: something like a dagger curving up his left arm, the initials ATWHHC lettered crudely above it. "What do the letters stand for?"

"I don't tell people that," he said, yanking the sleeve down again. "A youthful indiscretion," he explained. "Like everything else in my life. Listen, I just wanted to tell you—I've got to go away for a few days—a funeral."

"Not your mother?"

"No, no," he said. "My friend Duane, remember? The one who lent me the money for LaLouche?"

"What happened?"

"Relapse," he said.

"A relapse of what?"

He glanced at me with puzzlement for a sec. "Of shooting up," he said. "OD."

"But he had a new baby, he was fine!"

"I know," he said, angry at my innocent assumptions. But, of course a Princess Margaret type like me would need more explanation.

"It happens all the time. They—we—can't take much stress. You put one foot wrong and that's it, out you go." I remembered him singing "She's gone," when he missed me. And how the next verse of that song began "I need a drink." I touched his sleeve where it covered the tattoo, but he pulled away with something between a shrug and a flinch, saying "Gotta go."

Seven

"ELEGRAM," SYLVIE said, rather drily. I'd picked up the phone on the first ring.

"Is it a singing telegram?"

"Oh, Beatrice, you're too close to the mark."

"What do you mean? Oh, he crashed the plane." Why would he have studied flying otherwise? That was what he did, that was his calling. He crashed the car, he crashed the house. And Ma, she was like some souped-up race car he'd saved up for, the kind with flames and teeth on the sides: he totaled her.

"No, he didn't crash anything," Sylvie said, laughing sadly. "He's fine."

"Well, if that isn't just like him! But, what then?"

"Dolly was struck by lightning."

"What do you mean? What was she doing outside?"

"She wasn't outside. She was inside, on the phone. There was a thunderstorm and it made her think of Ma, and she decided to call her up and try to mend fences."

"Wait a minute, she had a radical personality change due to an electrical disturbance?" (Yes, reader, I was capable of making a mean joke about my sister even as I waited to hear if she was still alive. And Sylvie was quite able to laugh at it; we're sisters, we were both feeling the adrenaline high of bad news.)

"I know," Sylvie said, "but that's what Pop says she was doing. And now she's in the hospital."

"... IN A *coma*," Ma spat, when she called a few minutes later.

News can never, apparently, be so bad that it wouldn't benefit from a little tweak, a layer of gloss here or there. The word "coma" has an authority that mere unconsciousness cannot approach. It's much better to be washed away by a hurricane than some pointless little tropical storm.

"Not a coma," I said. (Ninety-nine out of one hundred women prefer it when their children are not in a coma.)

"What do you mean, not a coma?"

"Well, she's in and out of consciousness, but a coma is . . ."

"I can't believe you're accusing me of exaggeration when my daughter is in a coma!"

"I'm not accusing you of exaggeration . . ."

"Well, the semantics don't matter. What matters is that *he* killed her."

"Ma . . ."

"I *never* would have let that child pick up the phone during a thunderstorm," Ma said. "I told your father thousands of times that lightning travels over the phone lines. He probably *told* her to call me. He used to make phone calls during thunderstorms just to defy me. Oh, why couldn't it have been *him?*"

DOLLY WOKE up in the ICU and tried to lift her hand, but her arm wouldn't obey. Her body was feathered over with a pattern like a frosted window, Pop said, and there was a strange new turn at the corner of her mouth. It made her look sardonic and removed. I remembered how I'd felt that first night in Hartford, standing on the fire escape with my arms held out toward the oncoming storm. How good it felt to have escaped from the linen closet and feel the wind in my hair. And yet how good it had felt *in* the linen closet, when we were little—to know our mother was watching over us, keeping us safe. Dolly had been there in Wyoming, yearning for her mother, and determined to hold firm against her mother, and the storm came over the plain toward her, and she went to make the call.

She was discharged from the hospital. They said she was fine. Except for the blinding headaches, the strange slow heartbeat, and the loss of all hearing in the ear that had been pressed to the phone.

"LICHTENSTEIN'S FERNS, they're called. The filigree pattern on a lightning victim's skin, I was *just* reading about it, Beatrice. *Literally*, this was *yesterday*. Listen, they follow the perspiration, that's how it happens."

Philippa had to be given credit here, for adding fuel to a drama by *reading*. "I'd love to really see it. Do you think your father's got a picture? And what was she doing on the phone in an electrical storm?"

"I don't know. You can't blame me!" I said. (Though of course, if I hadn't been conceived and refused to be miscarried, if I hadn't abandoned them for college when I knew they couldn't manage, nor been such a disastrous surrogate mother to Dolly . . .)

"You have to admit it's odd," she said, laughing. "I mean, how often do I make a special trip to the library to research the effects of lightning strikes? How often have I done that? There is *obviously* a connection here."

"You're right!" I cried, because Philippa loved to hear this, and because it was so, so comforting to believe that while my family was dialing for thunderbolts, Philippa was studying them, getting it all figured out.

"When did it happen?"

"Around four."

"That is *exactly* when I was in the library," she said. "I was reading that the highest incidence of lightning strikes is in the late afternoon and I looked up at the clock and—how extraordinary, Beatrice. *Little* did I know."

"OH, THE doctor can't get a word in edgewise," Sylvie told me. "*You* know how they are. Ma wants to be sure Pop gets blamed for it all. He wants to prove the doctors don't know everything . . ."

She took a deep drag on her cigarette and laughed, awfully huskily for a girl of seventeen. "On the plus side, Ma's eviction seems to have been staved off," she said. "You can imagine it, can't you?

" 'Your honor, I have noplace to go, I've been abandoned by my husband, my daughter is lying in a coma, and *this man* wants to evict me, turn us all into the street.' "

Springtime was barking wildly, a high-pitched little yap. "God, I just took him out," she said. "No, Springy, you're going to wake baby Jesse up. No. Shhh," she said, to no avail. "Okay, okay, wait a minute, Bea." I heard the front door squeak open and then silence, and she came back and said, "All right, now everyone's happy."

Then she was screaming, and I heard her fly out the door screaming "No, no, no," and a furious, snarling chaos, and she came back and wailed into the phone, "Beatrice, Beatrice, they killed him, they tore him apart."

"Call the police!" I said. "Call the police, and get out of there!" but Springtime was dead, and she was sobbing as if she'd lost her whole family, and I was a hundred miles away on the other end of the phone.

THE POLICE came and shot the neighbor's dogs, and the next day they came back to search the trailer. The neighbor had told them Butch was selling cocaine.

"They're going to take the baby, Beatrice, I'm afraid they'll take the baby away."

"Sylvie, what do you mean? Who?"

"Butchy is clean, Beatrice! He'd never do anything like that. The cops have it in for him, that's what it is."

"Sylvie, what happened?"

"They came in the middle of the night," she said. "He had some dope—joints rolled up in the drawer—maybe five or six. Bea, he likes to have a couple tokes every once in a while, the way some guys have a beer."

"Where is he?"

"Police station," she said.

I heard the baby crying—a persistent rasp like the sound of a rusty hinge. She picked him up and the cries became louder, frantic, as if the baby had just realized what kind of life he was facing.

"I won't let them take him, that's all," she said, with that forlorn toughness I'd come to expect from her, but she began to cry again, so deeply. All this time, she'd been winding the rope for her own noose—and she was surprised to find herself swinging from it now? But seventeen-year-olds do that—generally it means they end up losing a driver's license, not a child.

"It's my fault," she said.

"What do you mean?"

"I shouldn't have called them, about the dogs. Oh, I wish I didn't do it, Beatrice! I wasn't thinking, and it's a violation of parole!"

*E*ight

———

STETSON DROVE us to the bus station to get the Pride Charter to New York—ninety lesbians in lavender—a beautiful thing. I could barely sit still in my seat—the parade would start at the Stonewall, where *everything* had started, where we (that's right, finally I was part of a great, vital tradition) fought back against oppression and set off on the road to equal rights. Grace Jones was going to sing at the rally in Central Park. Pat came up the aisle with an air of immense self-importance; Susan behind her was wearing a T-shirt with a peace sign/woman's symbol on it. The men were taking a different bus, which caused a stir as we debated whether we'd been excluded.

"Honestly, didn't we get into this so we could escape from men?" someone said, and I answered with asperity. "No, we got into this because we loved *women*."

"*Please*," Lee said under her breath, and faced forward sharply. "Do not make a scene."

From behind us someone said: "They're our brothers, but they don't welcome us."

And someone else reminded her that it had been decided there would be no male children allowed on our bus.

"That's different," Pat explained. "We are asserting our right to our own lives and bodies."

"But to pay for babysitting . . ." someone said, "when it would be a good lesson for them to see us, to recognize right from the beginning that this is wrong . . ."

We were cozy together, huddled away from the hateful forces outside. We *knew* everyone despised us and that made our hearth-fire blaze all the higher. I'd not been so snug since the last thunderstorm I'd spent in the linen closet with my mother. The world was divided into two camps:—people who killed defenseless animals for fur, dumped toxins into reservoirs, and hated lesbians; and those of us who were sensitive to the myriad needs of the world and hated no one, absolutely no one, except those people in the first group.

The bus started and Stetson waved, looking forlorn, I thought—left behind, all alone. I blew him a kiss. (I'd come to transgress.)

Someone started a chant and, clapping, stamping, we pulled onto the highway and out of poor little Hartford toward the real city.

"I'm hyperventilating," Lee said.

"Okay, okay. Breathe nice and slow," I said. "I'll count with you."

"There," she said. "That's better." She squeezed my hand. "What would I do without you?" she asked.

She'd have stayed home, and felt fine. Instead, two blocks into the march, she sank onto a doorstep and said she couldn't go any farther. "It's a virus," she said, "the nausea, ooof." I rubbed her back. A man went by wearing an enormous ostrich feather fan on his penis and nothing else, thrusting as if to fuck the whole world. Colonies strutted past, shouting out their pride—proud to be gay, proud to be bi, proud to ride motorcycles—What would Cyril have thought? I wondered.

"Tens of thousands of amazing lesbians, seas of them," I wheedled, with the sinking sense of how alike they—we—all looked, how exactly we'd fit ourselves to the mold. So righteous in our unconventionality; so perfectly the same. "We don't want to miss that."

Lee's panic attacks had eaten further and further into her life until she didn't dare take a plane trip or ride in an elevator, and if we tried to go out to a friend's house, she'd end up bent double with stomachache and have to be taken home. Also, she'd become acutely self-conscious, so that she sometimes seemed to be performing a mocking pantomime of whatever she meant to be doing—mincing between her plants as she watered them, or washing the windows with large, unnatural strokes. She was trying with all her might to act like the person I wanted her to be, but when she tried to speak, her mouth would go dry suddenly. Her anxious voice quivered in my mind all day, saying: "You won't go down to Washington Street, will you?" "You'll call, when you get there? You'll keep the door locked? You'll be home before dark?" Once we went swimming at the Y together and she cried out in alarm when she saw me swim toward the deep end of the pool.

The transsexuals, pre-op and post-op, pranced by. They dressed as if they were turning themselves not into women but dolls. What, I wondered, would make a society think its fantasies *ought* to come true? What if people dared speak out the desires of their hearts as fully as those of their bodies? Still, the transsexuals knew how to carry themselves—*they'd* show *us* a thing or two about women! Lee pawed through her purse for the little pink pills the doctor had prescribed for her palpitations, and took one with a gulp, leaning against my shoulder.

"That's a little better," she said.

I was beginning to feel a great sympathy with, of all people, men. Why hadn't I been grateful to those boyfriends when they leapt up from the bed and rushed to the ball field or the library or whatever arena of striving and conquest was furthest from the foggy tide basin of female feeling? If not for men's ridiculous qualms, I'd have stuck right to them, lovely, sticky creature that I was, so partial to those long looks, long kisses, long, long afternoons of ardent dishevelment, after which I could rest amidst the tangled bedclothes in the satisfied exhaustion of one who has been most deeply, fully, properly used. I'd have married any one of them, with my arms open, my heart open, my mind open as a sieve. Thank God they had done me the favor of resisting, letting me live a little longer before I folded myself into someone else. Lee loved me as completely as I could have hoped, and I was stuck like a sparrow on the lime twig of comfort, beside her. The parade passed by, traffic surged in behind it, and I hailed a cab for Central Park.

What a day! Frisbees sailed above us. Men strutted in leather harnesses. Women caressed each other's naked breasts in the sun. And here was Grace Jones, tall as a man, sleek as a woman—she looked as if a committee of gay men had designed her, like the huge golden Oscar statue at the Academy Awards. Everything stopped; we stood at attention, she took the microphone, and into it she snarled transcendently: "*I need a maa-aa-an.*"

Faces froze, the women near us looked to each other for guidance. Was this a slap? Was it all right? We looked around—what should we do? She had been named Entertainer of the Year by the Gay Congress of the City of San Francisco. We applauded, but our smiles showed mostly consternation.

Back home the song rang in my ears as Lee and I tried to make love in honor of Gay Pride Day: it seemed the hardest work I'd ever done. I always had to remember to touch her gently—though the delicate little caresses she wanted would have driven me up the wall—but now I could barely keep myself from hurting her. I bit her shoulder, as if a bolt of pain would awaken her, engage something passionate, but she said, "Now, no biting," like a coy kindergarten teacher remonstrating with a child. I ran my hands roughly over her, wanting to take her like a lump of clay and wrench her into some more satisfying form. Her nipples tasted as bitter as iron—*I hate you*, I thought, but I managed to make myself call her darling.

After she fell asleep I went out to the living room to read *Middlemarch*, and watch Dorothea struggle to properly love her husband, to honor him even after his death. She was conscious of everything, examining all the moral questions, striving to live up to her beliefs *and* her promises, even when they ran counter to each other. The promises I had made to Lee clanged in my mind suddenly like all the church bells in a mad city, drowning out everything else. I closed the book and set it on the parsons table, and Philippa's voice spoke in my thoughts as clearly as if I were sitting in her classroom. She was quoting George Eliot: "There was not room enough in poor Rosamond's mind for furniture to look small in it," reminding us how tender Eliot was toward her characters and all their mistakes.

One small thing became clear to me just then: Philippa Sayres was the closest I had to kin. I tiptoed into the kitchen for the phone.

"WHAT DO you mean, you're in love with me?" She laughed, after my lugubrious confession. "It is *most* unlikely, Beatrice! You're in love, I don't doubt it, it's in your nature." Here she laughed in tipsy appreciation: "But with me? Me? I really don't think so, Beatrice, no. You're onto *some*thing, though, something . . ." She paused to parse this latest feeling, and after a moment in which I could imagine her consulting her inner oracle, she said, "Yes! That's it! You need to go to graduate school!"

"Graduate school?"

She was paying me a compliment, in her own idiom. She saw me (oh, I did love her) as a dashing figure, and so accorded me her highest honor. To Philippa, scholarship was a fine steed for a good joust, and she welcomed me into the battle. She'd been my knight on a white horse, no question.

"What would I study?" I asked her.

"Goodness, Beatrice, surely you can figure out *something* for yourself," she said. "Listen, I can't talk, *Gone With the Wind* is on."

I watched it too, and when it was over I kept staring, until somewhere in the middle of the night I woke up to see the Israeli Philharmonic performing live in Tel Aviv. The volume was down so far that I couldn't hear the music, but the sight itself was beautiful—all these musicians working as a body. How well they must know their conductor—they were attuned to the slightest change of his face. How lucky, to be a strand of that music, a member of an orchestra, to bring all of yourself—every instinct, thought, and movement—to work, toward a beautiful end, studying and studying, trying and erring until there was no further need of thought and it was natural, it was music.

The eye of the camera closed in on a bassist, a young man. He was too tall, with a raw, alert face that seemed to be watching and taking counsel from everything around him. Not the kind of face you usually see on television: that mask of glamour that commands adoration and holds those who adore it at bay. That's what we think beauty is. The beauty of this man's face, its rapt concentration, filled me with grief and longing, and suddenly, with hope.

"I'd like to sleep with that orchestra," I heard myself saying.

A most inconvenient insight, but the minute I had it, I felt a revolution start, in every single cell. I went to the door of the bedroom and was almost surprised to see Lee asleep there. If my thoughts had the power they ought to have, she would already have evaporated. I could hear her small—righteously small—voice, cautioning me not to swim out so far, and suddenly I wanted to swim the ocean, swim all around the world. Fascination was anathema to her. I'd fallen in love with her stolidity. And she had given me what I'd needed: someone to rebel against.

It's a great night for a drive, I said to myself, with mutinous joy, and I snapped the car keys from their hook and took the steps downstairs as lightly as a kid. Outside, a man stood at the cemetery's edge, but it was four in the morning, too late even for prostitutes. I waved to him and he pretended not to see me. No doubt he thought he was just looking for sex. If only something so simple could be true.

I'd forgotten what it was like to drive. To steer, with a touch, a silent, powerful beast along the street, while the world moved past as if on a conveyor belt, to see the dark city lay its avenues open before me—should I turn left, through the college gates, or right, toward the wealthy suburbs where the people who could bring themselves to grapple with the world in daylight were dreaming now in their downy beds? It didn't matter—what would have been impossible in the daytime traffic was effortless now and I crossed the city like a child skipping through an empty house, turning down Main Street under the banners proclaiming, "Hartford Swings" in honor of the Big Band Festival, up Asylum Avenue through the insurance sprawl, and down Park Street past the library. Mr. Klipsch was asleep in the doorway and I felt as fond, seeing him, as if he was my brother. The light was on in the back window of the bakery—Mrs. Arruda would be at work there. It amazed me, but I was coming to know people, to be a part of this place.

Ahead, on the horizon, I saw a thin, rosy line, and heard Ma's portentous: "Red sky at morning, sailors take warning," her voice taking the drama of nature for her own. Who knew, who could guess where I was headed, what would happen? Behind me a state trooper turned out of his roadside lair, and my heart jumped, but he passed me and a moment later I saw him sweep smoothly in beside a disabled newspaper truck, blue lights flashing a silent message: even here on the highway in the last hour of the night, you are not alone. Dawn bled upward until the sky was tinted as pale as old petals. So I was driving east. Of course. Stetson's place was east, just across the river. I was going to see Stetson; it was the most natural thing in the world.

Nine

————

"D ID I wake you up?"

"Well, it's, like . . . five-thirty?" He was standing in the doorway of an apartment so small I could see all of it over his shoulder: a convertible love seat that, pulled out, took up the whole living space, and behind it, a tiny kitchen, a bathroom door. No one would ever guess that its resident was obsessed with folded sweaters: there was a pile of dirty clothes in the corner and one of dirty dishes in the sink.

"What is it? What's the matter?" Stetson asked, beckoning me in, and sitting down on the end of his bed, still half asleep, his hair sticking up every which way

"To answer that, I think I'd have to write a book," I said. How *could* I explain it? Say that I'd decided to move to Middlemarch? That my father had been mauled by a tigress and when my own stripes started to show, I'd had to take drastic action? Or, my mother dreamed of getting out of debt by writing a sex novel, but sex was a mystery to her, so I had to figure it out? Or, the Israeli Philharmonic seemed to need a woman and Grace Jones said she needed a man?

I couldn't say the word "man," though, because Stetson was sitting there in his shorts, all too palpably representing that gender, with golden stubble glinting over his face. His shoulders, his knees, were so big and square, his chest hairless, defenseless, to my surprise. (So, all this time I'd had some image of his body in my heart. Another surprise.) And, his tattoo: what I'd thought was a dagger was the tail of a snake, whose body was wrapped and rewrapped around Stetson's chest and over his shoulders, its head menacing me from the crook of his left arm.

"What?" he asked, seeing me stare. Then: "Oh, that." He looked down at himself and shook his head. "You see why I need to get married. I can't spent my life explaining this guy to strange women. Look." He showed me how the creature's venomous eye was right over a vein. "When it started to pulse, it was time for the needle," he said. "He looks like my father, actually, from a certain angle."

What I noticed was how fully the snake was holding him.

"The thing about a tattoo is, it's permanent," he said. "Nothing else really is."

"I've figured it out—what the letters stand for," I said. I almost reached out to touch them and had to remind myself I had no right.

"You have?" He grabbed a T-shirt from his pile and pulled it over his head. "How?"

"Well, I mean I can guess. 'Don't tread on me.' I mean, more or less. Right?"

He laughed a little, and looked at me with surprise, as if he thought it strange I'd puzzle over this. "In a way," he said. "How was the march?"

Oh, the march. "It was fine, fine. Lee got a little nervous, but otherwise, fine."

"So, then you thought you'd come over and decipher my tattoo?"

"I got in the car and started driving, and I didn't know where I was going, and somehow I got here."

"How do you know my address?"

"I must have seen it at the store, because as soon as I saw the sign for Tilden Street, the number 333 popped into my mind. It's just been kind of a weird night."

He smiled, so fondly.

"Stet, I think I came here to tell you not to get married . . ." I said, as if I were a fortune teller who was only just seeing the clouds of prophecy resolve.

"You got in the car in the middle of the night and drove aimlessly until you happened to pass my apartment, and came up to tell me . . . something . . . which you now realize is that I shouldn't get married?"

"Yes," I said, with some amazement, because it was the first thing I'd felt sure of in a very long time. "That's what I'm saying."

"And," he said, edging discreetly away from me, to fish for a pair of pants, "*why* shouldn't I get married?"

"Because . . ."

"Yes?" He held my eyes with a laughing challenge, and suddenly I knew why, and the minute I knew it, we stopped being able to look at each other. So, with my hands over my face, I pulled all my courage together and told myself to be honest with the man who had been so honest with me.

"Because it would be better—I mean, I'd like it better—if you—married—me."

I stood fixed to my spot, appalled to hear myself. "I don't mean marry," I explained quickly. "I mean—" I stamped my foot on the worn floorboard. "I have an idiotic crush on you." I'd meant to be done with crushes, and a crush on a *man!* Pat had been *right* about me, how infuriating.

"And—" he took a breath, preconfession, "—you've noticed that I have an idiotic crush on you," he said.

I didn't dare hear this, but I felt his arms around me.

"But," he said softly, his head bent over mine, "you were the one who spoke it. You were the braver one."

If tulips had sprouted out of my head right then, I wouldn't have been surprised, because his words fell on me like the first warm rain. It's true, I thought, I *am* brave, no matter how I quaver and tremble and flee—I'd been brave since that first stupid day when I went off to school in my little plaid jumper, with my mother ready to smash a champagne bottle on my bow.

"Stetson," I said, into his collarbone.

I couldn't fit my arms all the way around him, and his smell was so heady that I could only think to say, "Stetson, you're a god!" Two seconds of heterosexuality and I'd turned into Barbie.

His T-shirt read ONE DAY AT A TIME, and I kissed the Y. Then I lifted his arm and kissed the snake's oft-pierced eye. I was going to kiss everywhere anything had ever pricked him, to breathe him into myself; we were going to get to know each other the way most people only dream about.

He took my arms and held me away.

"But you *have* somebody," he said. "And so do I."

As I hadn't realized I was going to throw myself at him, I was ill-prepared to argue this point. Apparently his family didn't follow their hearts so doggedly as mine.

"In ten minutes," he said, "the phone is going to ring and it's going to be Tracy, giving me my wake-up call."

"Why isn't she here?" I asked. This was better than shrieking, "You said you didn't love her!" like the banshee I was bound to become now. (Isn't that what happens to women who fall in love with men? They dash themselves against the cliff face of the masculine heart's refusal, and go mad.)

"She doesn't come here," he said. "See this?" He plucked at the cloth that was thrown over the back of couch, khaki polyester splattered with paint. "It was my bedspread in the halfway house." My heart throbbed the way it always did when he was confessing.

"Most nights I go to her place. She's good at folding," he said, making light of it, but I saw how he intended to live with her in a safe, neat world, keep this dark place a secret of his own. Tracy was beautiful, in a warm, inviting way, and she'd gotten to know Stetson because she loved to shop at LaLouche—I'd seen her through the window there, closing out the cash register one evening, so certain in her movements, as if she had no question that she was where she ought to be. Probably her customers would buy capes and unitards and whatever just in hopes of becoming like her. But I knew Stetson's qualms about her, and from his voice, his hands, his slightest gestures, I knew he loved me. I kissed him, just at the corner of his mouth, and ran out the door, before anything could happen to shatter my perfect vision.

LEE WAS at work already when I got home, and I didn't have to be at the library until ten, so I made myself a cup of coffee and called Philippa.

"So there, you've found the perfect solution!" she said tartly. "How many cars did you say he's wrecked?"

"Well, six, but that was before he got sober," I said.

"He's just like your father, one day maybe he'll crash a plane."

"We can only hope, Philippa," I said, giddy. I had Stetson, and so, I could have Philippa back. She was all ears, ready for my new adventures.

"Well," she said, "I guess a junkie will make for a nice mix with your sister's beau."

"He's not a junkie," I said righteously, but I was thinking that he'd damn well better be a junkie, because that was part of why I loved him—for the raw intensity of his need, his willingness to lie and cheat and court death and disaster to assuage it. *I* was going to be Stetson's drug now.

"I stand in support of a woman's right to choose her own catastrophe," Philippa answered, as staunch as Emma Goldman. "And if this is the only way you can escape from that, that *woman*—"

"Philippa, I can't leave her. What are they all going to say about me? And they'll be right, too. I've been such a—a bull in a china shop, here. Lee moved into the city because of me, and now I'm going to leave her here alone? I promised her I'd stay forever."

"Are you twenty-two yet?" she asked.

"How old was Dorothea Brooke?"

"Oh, oh, Dorothea Brooke? So what, she's a character in a novel. A novel whose author threw herself out a window on her wedding night! Nobody, Beatrice—not you, not George Eliot, but *least of all* the members of the Hartford Lesbian Support Group—is ever going to solve the problem of love."

"Oh, Philippa, I do love you."

I heard one of those little fluttering sounds she made when she was nervous and added: "But, not that way, not that way!" In fact, it suddenly occurred to me that I ought to introduce her to Reenie.

"Marry the junkie, by all means. *Mazel tov.* And may you marry often!"

THEN, LEE. I told her a bit of the truth: that I'd been upset about all the family troubles and just felt so restless I had to go out. She'd said she understood, that we'd talk when she got home, but that right now she'd better call the police and tell them to stop looking for the car.

"You called *the police?*"

"The car was gone," she said. "You have to make a report or the insurance doesn't cover it."

Of course, it came down to insurance. It wasn't that she despised me, even though she had every reason to; she was simply following protocol. She would follow protocol until she was fitted into a regulation-sized box and lowered into the appropriate hole. *How womanly*, I thought, with a raging frustration. How complacent, how determined to be good. And as we lived in an age when good girls were frowned on, she, and the rest of them (I included Dolly and Sylvie and my mother in this category, as I crossed my clenched fists at my chest, to keep myself from putting one through the wall) were looking for culprits: *men*, bad men, who discouraged their ambitions, who kept them down. Well, I was going to hop into Stetson's sidecar and drive right through the picture window of convention into the world of truth.

"Hello," Lee said to me in the Aetna parking lot, when I went to pick her up after work. She didn't look at me, didn't want to see my face.

"Hi," I said. "I'm sorry, Lee, but I . . ." I took a deep breath and was filled with doubt.

"You shouldn't go out at night in that neighborhood," she said. She was angry and she was going to make it a matter of my welfare, because it wouldn't do to be angry on her own behalf. "You're going to get killed."

I waited for her to say she shouldn't have called the police, but she didn't. I was glad—I was chalking up sins against her, waiting until I had enough so I could leave. From that time on, every little sentence she spoke added a new brush stroke to the awful portrait I was painting, in preparation for the great moment when I would turn it on her in accusation. I didn't say anything more about that night, just went back to our life as it was laid out. In another era, Lee would have been married and would have thought herself happy, but for a vague dissatisfaction and a few embarrassing dreams. Really, so little had changed.

That weekend we went shopping for a salad spinner, and tried about twenty models.

"This works just right," Lee said at home. "Look, the leaves are dry and crisp and perfectly fresh." I tried one and pronounced the thing an extremely intelligent choice, thinking—*I came to transgress and instead I bought a salad spinner.*

Everything was just as it had been, except that I couldn't stop singing. All that time, I'd known it made Lee uncomfortable for some reason, so I'd keep it down to a tiny hum if she was around. But now, old Gershwin songs, hymns, Gilbert and Sullivan, Donna Summer . . . rushed through me all day. As long as I was singing I felt Stetson was beside me, doing his job, living his life, quiet and steady and on the way up. And Lee was tense as if she guessed this, though she said it was just that she liked the quiet. On I went, absentmindedly, singing as I folded the laundry or lugged the garbage down the back steps, singing with no thought for anything but the memory of Stetson whispering in my hair.

Ten

I DON'T necessarily think a stint in prison would be the worst thing for Butch," my father said, sounding grandly reasonable. "It's only fourteen months, and really, it may be just the structure he needs."

He faded into a philosophical musing on the subject of youth and age, which I didn't like to disturb by reminding him that we were discussing the future of his grandson, whose father was going back to prison for violating his parole.

"And you've got to consider the possibility that this is for the best," he said, rousing himself to the subject. "Sylvie feels badly now, but that life was hard on her. She's strong, she can do just about anything, and she's got her whole life ahead. Some time apart, it might do them both some good."

"Like the way parents used to send their daughters on a Grand Tour for a year, to take their minds off their beaux."

"Exactly," he said, unaware I was mocking him.

"How's Dolly?" I asked.

"She's taking a nap."

"She's home from school?"

"She hasn't been to school since the accident."

"She's still in pain?"

"I don't think so," he said. "It's just that she doesn't see the point, anymore."

"But . . ."

"She forgets things," he said. "She stares off. And these schools out here, they don't have a lot to offer. We get public TV on the satellite, we watched *Macbeth* last night, she's getting a fine education right here."

"Why does she forget things? Does electric shock make you forget things?"

"I guess so," he said.

"Could you ask the doctor?"

"Sweetie, it's obvious, isn't it? She wasn't forgetful before the lightning. Now she is."

"It sounds like that, but I don't know, and suppose she had a stroke, from the shock, or something. You know there are things they can do so people can regain their abilities."

"Very interesting, if true," he said wearily.

"A doctor would know," I persisted.

"They don't know everything, sweetie."

"No, but they know more than we do about medicine!" I said, feeling like I was about to have a stroke myself. I could hear his ancient, stubborn insistence—*Just because your mother thinks you're so smart*, etc. And I thought how hard I'd tried to agree with him, to show him he was right so he'd love me. Indeed I am a fool.

"Pop, she can't just drop out of school," I said.

"She will be fine," he said. "She's going to stay here with me. She's my daughter." He said this with peculiar emphasis, as if I wasn't. "And I'm sworn to care for her, for the rest of my life." His tone had a swell of patriotic goodness in it, which I mistrusted entirely.

"But, she wants to grow up and go to college and get married."

"Bea, she's deaf, she's so dizzy she can barely stand up, she can't remember anything and she's lost the use of her arm!" he said. Really, that he had to put up with such imbecility!

"She needs physical therapy!"

"Oh, sweetie, we'll get some of that, it'll make her a little more comfortable, but . . . it's hardly going to cure her."

"Why is that?"

"They don't *know* very much about this," he explained sadly. "They can't say with certainty what will happen."

"Exactly."

His patience was thinning. "You're not here, honey, you haven't seen it."

He was right, of course. I changed my tack. "Pop," I said, "People manage with all kinds of handicaps. People in wheelchairs, people with Seeing Eye dogs, people who have to hold their pen in their teeth."

"Well, I guess some people accept their lot with more grace than others," he said, overruling me. "Dolly has everything she needs, right here. She has a father who loves her and will take care of her even if she can't *realize all her dreams*."

His voice twisted bitterly at this reference to my grandiose ideas, such as the one in which I might succeed where he'd failed. And a chill ran over me. I'd certainly failed Dolly. She was his.

"You're two thousand miles away from this, honey," he said. "Leave the problem to me."

"SHE CAME into the world stubborn," said Ma. She'd called Dolly when she knew Pop was out and found her strangely without affect.

"When she was four months old she pushed my breast away as if the milk was sour. It's just the way she was. So I say to myself, if

I failed, I failed. One out of the four of you isn't so bad. You know, maybe my mother didn't love me, maybe Dolly doesn't love me, but I did the best I could."

And her voice, which had been sweetly pleading, as if she were an inspirational speaker looking out at herself from The Great Television on High, snapped back into comic focus: "I mean," she asked, "how bright can a person who chooses to live with your father really be?"

"NO," STETSON said again. "I can't. I can't really even talk on the phone right now." It was the third time I'd called him, and with each one, I felt more foolish. He'd drop his voice and make one excuse after another—no one who heard him would have guessed how he'd spoken to me, less than a week ago.

"Okay," I said, "I get it. There isn't anything to say anyway. 'Bye, Stet, and I'm sorry about all this."

"No, no, wait! No, you're right, we should talk," he said then. "We shouldn't leave it this way."

So we met down by the river because nobody but derelicts ever went there, so we wouldn't run into Tracy or anyone she knew. And when he saw me, he reached out reflexively, just enough space between his arms for me to walk into them and stay there forever.

"Hi, Stet," I breathed, feeling like the last little piece was fitting into some perfect universe and now all the keys would turn and all the locks fly open and sunlight would flood from the sky. "Oh, hi."

He held me tight for one second, then motioned for me to sit down—on a cracked vinyl boat seat that had washed up there on the bank.

"The reason I'm not . . . not going to . . ." Stetson said, "is, because of my recovery."

"Your recovery?"

"Before I left rehab," he said, "I asked how I was going to know if I was getting off track, going wrong. And they told me, 'You know right from wrong, you'll know when you're doing something you shouldn't be.' "

"But, Stet," I said. "It's real feeling, between us. Isn't it?"

"Yeah," he said, a teenaged mumble, so far from the arch fashion talk he'd used when I met him that I had to smile.

"So."

"Just because it's real doesn't make it right. Tracy's planning our wedding, she's counting on me."

"But you're not in love with her!"

"I'm not even sure I know what being 'in love' means," he said. "But I have a good sense with her. I'm not crawling with needs and jealousies. It's peaceful. Arranged marriages are supposed to work very well."

"It might be peaceful with us too," I said. Like all lovers, I was lying, offering whatever I thought might win me his heart.

"Tracey's dad's in AA. She gets the whole thing," he said. "I may have to sell the shop, I don't know yet. I've got to give Duane's widow the money I owe him, she's broke, and Tracy wants to go back to Missouri where her parents live."

"What would you do there?"

"Get a job."

"That shop means everything to you! It's your own creation, and your diligence has made it work!" I was furious with him suddenly, feeling him back away from me, maybe from everything. "I'd help you do what *you* want," I said. "Help you find your way . . ."

"*You* barely know your own gender," he said, so sweetly I just laughed.

"So, we'd be lost together!"

"I don't want to be lost anymore," he said, with a flash of real anger. "Listen," he apologized, "what I mean to say is that actions have consequences. I owe money, I have to pay it. I've asked Tracy to marry me. I gave my word."

He was already looking at me in a kind of puzzlement that might at any minute slip into censure. Was I really so unscrupulous as to betray all these promises, for sex? Because what could it be, except sex? I, Princess Margaret, wasn't going to risk my whole life on a desperate drug addict, was I? That would be as crazy as trying to live on a hundred dollars a week. It made him mistrust me. The saddest thing, sadder than thinking I'd never feel him inside me, was knowing that, if I'd never gone over there, never told him how I felt, he'd have kept coming to visit me, to tell me every little thing. The great, deep pleasure of my life was—had been—trying to put true things into words so I could tell Stetson, and now I'd ruined it all.

"I'll go," I said, and stood up, and he jumped up.

"No!" he said.

For the first time that night we looked in each other's eyes— and everything we'd said fell away. He kissed me, his cheek so smooth I knew he'd shaved especially for me. He tasted as clear and pure as the water from the spring at home.

"I want to touch you," he said—the last, the worst of his confessions.

I spread my arms as if he'd said he wanted to frisk me, and he held his hands half an inch from my body and followed the curves down as if he thought really touching me would send him straight to hell.

Then he closed his eyes and said, "Now, we have to go home."

We walked up the bank holding hands, and he waited with me at the Park Street bus stop. "We'll be friends," he said. "Deep, true friends." As I stepped up onto the bus, though, he pulled me back and kissed me so deeply I felt we must be falling out of Hartford, into another dimension. But no. The late bus riders glanced at me with what I assumed must be envy.

HE LOVED me. It was the most amazing thing I could know. The only thing I needed to know—I trusted it, against everything else in the world. The physical joy of it had already changed me. When I went to the supermarket I felt like falling on my knees in the produce aisle: the eggplants were so smooth and lustrous, it seemed a miracle. I turned my key in the library lock every morning with a light heart: I knew the feel of that lock, knew that if it stuck, I could just slip the key out a little and it would go smoothly. I was a competent member of bourgeois society, doing part of the day's work of the world. I had made a little difference on Park Street, and somewhere ahead of me was the gorgeous life Stetson and I would have together. (I imagined us living inside a rose.)

I was getting the laundry together to lug to the basement, singing "Copacabana," and I stopped for a minute to cha-cha through the little drum section before dropping as far as I could into the bass: "Don't fall in love." Louis Armstrong couldn't have done better.

But I felt a wave of disapproval and turned to see Lee behind me, looking as if she'd seen a specter.

"Listen, couldn't you just get earplugs? I realize I'm not Edith Piaf, but I like singing and if I don't do it here I'm entirely likely to let loose in the library, and we don't want that, do we?"

"Everyone can hear you."

"And?"

"I can't hear myself think," she said, and I heard that pinched Levittown thing in her voice, as if I were disturbing the peace. A wisp of my mother seemed to waft through the room—my holy conflagration of a mother who would surely have burned away to ash by now if not for her plentiful tears. Lee was her very opposite. Except in one way: she didn't want me to stray outside the boundaries of our alliance. She'd have liked to know I was always asleep there in her bed, a sort of footwarmer. She could manage to seeing me swim into deep water, but the singing was just too much.

And as there was perfectly good reason for her to feel this, it sent me into a rage. "Oh, were you trying to think?" I asked satirically, and she burst into tears. "Lee," I said, "Lee." She was crying as if something was thawing in her, breaking apart, floating away.

"They told me," she said, "they all said you wouldn't, you wouldn't—"

"Wouldn't what, honey?" I held her tight, I rocked her back and forth—she was soft and helpless as a child.

"Wouldn't stay with *me*," she said in disgust—at me, at herself?

"Who is 'they'?" I asked her. "What is this big 'they,' and what do you care what they think?"

She sighed and rested against me for a minute, trying to let me convince her.

"I'm right here, honey," I said, and laughed to prove what a silly idea she'd had. "Sorting the laundry and singing. How much more domestic can a person be?"

"You're singing a song I don't know," she said, and I heard in her querulous voice how she was shrinking—the less I loved her, the more fearfully she clung to me and the narrower the compass of her life became. And it was worse than if I'd only fallen out of love—the stream of my life had never even flowed through this apartment. It went from my family, to Philippa, and now somehow to Stetson, and I had to follow it on. What was I doing here, where did I really belong?

I've come out of the wrong closet, I thought. I'd wanted so badly to smash down a door; I'd just taken the first one I saw. I sat Lee down, but I barely needed to speak: there was a confidence in my movements now that I wasn't acting a part anymore, and she knew what it meant. She didn't seem to be crying so much as breaking apart in my hands. I remembered how Sid had seemed to draw power from his lack of love for me, but I couldn't imagine how this had worked. All I felt now was sick at the sight of the mess I'd made. I held Lee tight so I wouldn't have to face her, and stared over her shoulder at her conch shell on the table, the shell in which a young, silly person may hear her own blood rushing and mistake it for the sound of the sea.

Eleven

POP WAXED sentimental over his life with Dolly. "We're not the kind of people who are constantly trying to move up in the world," he told me. "We like this place, we like the people here, they're the kind of folks who know how to be friendly without intruding, who let you go about your daily life without asking a lot of prying questions. But then they're right there for you in a crisis. You know, after the accident we lived for a week on casseroles from the neighbors. No, we're putting our roots down here. We're going to stay."

"Which is great," I said, "but Dolly's growing up. It seems like the life there is too small for her. She needs friends, challenges."

"Bea, something's wrong in her mind," he said, "and it's not just the accident, she was always this way. It's not that she's crazy, she just doesn't understand things." His voice dropped. "You wouldn't believe the things she says, honey. She thinks we're going to *buy a plane. I can't afford a plane!*" he said, incredulous at her deranged ideas. "No, honey, she needs a father who can love her and take care of her, a safe place to live, and that she does have, here with me. Here we are, in big-sky country together."

And before I knew what was happening he was rhapsodizing, naming the tribes: Arapaho, Arikare, Bannock, Blackfoot, Cheyenne, Crow, Gros Ventre, Kiowa, Nez Perce, Sheep Eater, Sioux, Shoshone. He set the scene for me, the braves riding through the violet shadow of Grand Teton—all of it. There was so much in him, such interest, hope, and curiosity, pleasure in the pure sounds of these words, and a willingness to love what he had, what was right there in hand. Who knew what he might have made of these qualities, if only . . .

If only I could go back and change that first instant of his failure, the first small shame—I saw those praying mantises, how if they'd hatched a week later, he'd have made money, and gotten confidence, and the next thing would have been easier, he wouldn't have been so afraid. Instead, it had created an island in his mind, a shadow mass that he tacked around, time and again, as it grew into a continent whose circumnavigation would take a lifetime—if he even dared to try. Instead, he kept in the sunny shallows, extolling the beauties of his little bay with rapt vitality. He was there with Dolly, alone under the big sky.

"BEATRICE, IT'S Stet."

"Hi," I said—a "hi" so swollen with feeling that it embarrassed me and I said again with dry dignity, "I mean, hi."

"Beatrice, I have to water some plants tonight, and I was wondering if you—"

"I *love* to water plants," I said. "Oh, Stetson, I've missed you so much. It's terrible, how much I think about you." I was in the library, and there was someone waiting for me, but I could have talked to him forever. I was dying to discuss this unheard-of phenomenon: requited love.

"I know," he said. "I'm thinking about it half—" He caught himself being less than truthful. "Well, more than half the time."

"Is this the reference?" the woman who'd been waiting asked, as soon as I was off the phone. She had set two heavy sacks down on the other side of the desk. They looked like they contained all her belongings. Yes, I said, this was the reference. I was the clerk, the janitor, the reference librarian, the bouncer. Cyril had seen that I could manage and he rarely came in to work anymore.

"Is it true," this lady asked me, "that, if a guy's been in a car crash, it can . . . you know . . . make his . . . make *it* crooked?" She was fat and she moved as slowly as if she were underwater, so that her face, with its expression of shame and determination, seemed to take minutes as it turned up toward mine. "Because my boyfriend, ever since he smashed up the Firebird, he doesn't want to . . . you know . . . he says it hurts."

I told her he ought to speak a doctor, and gave her a flier from the community health center, but she went doggedly on: "It's like there's something hard poking out, right here . . ." she said, lifting her shirt to point to a spot near her belly button. "I mean, that's what he says."

Troubles of heart, mind, flesh, and no one to look to but me. So then, I would have to help her. I lifted the *Merck Manual* down and opened it to "Genitourinary disorders" and she stood peering into it a long time before she could bring herself to ask me to read it aloud. After I covered kidney stones and a couple of common prostate troubles, she shook her head.

"This is the reference?" she asked dubiously, looking around, then shouldered her parcels again and started off even slower and sadder than before.

"Stop," I said. "Come back here, and sit down."

This was the great thing about that library. I was not the most badly lost person there. And no one there expected me to save them. They wanted only a scrap of information, a heated room, a smile. That much, I could provide. I sat down in the chair opposite her, wondering who had sat with Stetson when his life came apart, who had taken his hand and helped him through. Could someone help Dolly, as I hadn't been able to?

"Tell me some more," I said. "Let's see what we can do."

And just at that moment, something amazing happened—a panel truck pulled up in front and a man jumped out with a book in his hand.

"Interlibrary loan?" he asked.

It was *Gone With the Wind*. I'd sent out the form like a message in a bottle, and here it came, bobbing back to me. Mrs. Arruda's bakery telephone was busy, and I felt like running into the street and calling her with a megaphone—here it is, here it is, I've done something, I've made something happen!

Twelve

STETSON AND I stood together, high over the city of Hartford, backs to the dark river and the highway streaming with lights and the satiny gold of the historic capitol dome. We were contemplating something much more compelling than this, something with such amazing power that any right-thinking civilization ought to quake at the sight of one—for all they promise, all the havoc they've wreaked.

"A bed," I said.

"I know," he said apologetically, and I somehow found the equanimity to laugh a little.

"I thought there'd probably be one."

"Yeah, they're kind of hard to avoid."

We turned away with one unified movement—we were, as usual, in sync. And there it was, Hartford, glittering like a real city.

"What a view, huh?" he said. "You should see the sunsets." He spoke like a man showing off his lands to his betrothed. The place belonged to one of his customers, who traveled on business a lot, so Stetson would go by and water her plants for her.

"They must be beautiful. Even the river looks pretty from up here."

"It's a step up from my place," he admitted, with a shudder, as if his apartment, with the old rehab bedspread, was the physical manifestation of shame. He had nothing to offer me, except love, and that—well, my parents had tried that. It was the torment of love—needing it, longing for it, fearing its loss—that had made the needle sparkle so. Stetson and I had to plant our feet on something more solid.

"We can't," he said, looking away over Route 84 east, back toward Lewiston. I myself never looked east without being aware I was looking away from my family and the farm in their dream.

"I know," I said. All the way there, walking across the park and coming up in the elevator, I'd been steeling myself against this moment because I was afraid if he hurt me, it would set me reeling so I'd never get my balance back. I could hardly speak now, from fear, and I thought how it used to seem impossible to say anything wrong to Stetson. He'd wanted to know all my depths; he didn't pass judgment but tried to understand. One damned kiss and now we could barely face each other.

"Can we sit down for a minute?"

"Okay," he said, nervous, and willing, always willing. If I'd said, "Make love to me," he would have, and then . . . we'd have been doomed to each other. That was the thing the seventies didn't understand—how hard it is to separate yourself from someone you've made honest love to, in all its animal intimacy, its will to reach through the body for the soul. What makes sex electrifying is that desire, and the knowledge of the great harm love can do. We sat down on the end of the bed as if it was a tippy canoe.

"Here," I said. I took his hand, and he sighed in relief.

"That's better," he said. "I thought I was going to have to say you couldn't touch me at all."

"Why?"

"Because we'd . . ."

". . . never stop."

"Right," he said, looking down with an expression I'd only seen once before, the day we kissed each other. His glow—his will to transcend and blaze forward in life—was gone, and he looked young and full of pain. Because of me.

His hand was so big, I held it in both of mine. But though his other hand moved to join the embrace, he kept it back. This infinitesimal slight hurt me like a cigarette burn. That was the terrible thing—that I'd come to trust him so, to let him know me. He was more dangerous to me than anyone else on earth, and my mouth went as dry as if I were facing a torturer.

"Okay," I said, clipped as a busy receptionist. "So we know. We've decided."

He flinched. "Right," he said. Then he laughed. "Because, you know, I haven't been this anxious since I went into rehab. This morning Tracy was doing the books and she asked me to translate something in your handwriting, and I kept telling her I couldn't read it. I felt like if I admitted that I could, she'd be able to see right into my heart."

"Yeah, I know."

"Yeah. So we'll just make a clean break . . ."

I heard myself speaking with interest and surprise, as my heart was shrieking in opposition. But I was too frightened to say anything honest. I thought with fury of Lee's telling me I always said the right thing. It had been easy to say the right thing to Lee—she had no power to hurt me. We'd been lovers without getting on intimate terms. To Stetson I always said unbelievably stupid things now. When I was near him, all I could think about was how to keep him from going away. And he—he'd come to count me with alcohol and drugs, the snares he might get trapped in, out of his own need. Maybe he was right—I hadn't done Lee any good. But this, I thought in furious defiance—this was love.

It was nothing more than a series of tiny, vivid shocks of recognition and understanding that seemed to prove a kind of supernatural bond between us—a bond that gave us new strength and hope.

"All day I thought about us, here," he said, looking sheepishly back at the bed.

"Did we have a good time?" I asked grimly, and he shook his head and refused to meet my eyes.

"It's wrong," he said, with dull insistence.

"We'd make rotten adulterers," I said, to comfort him. There was a wild luxury in the word *we*. And it was something to be proud of, our innocence, our inability to lie.

"I *used* to be good at deceit," Stetson said. "Real good."

"I'm sure you were, angel."

"But I can't, now." He shook his head firmly and I felt him steel himself, the immense block of muscle life—work, that is—had made of him, against me, and what he called my rationalizations. A lot easier to call it sex, make it a craving like the others, not to be given in to by such a strong man. I felt a pulse of pain deep inside, where we ought to have fit together. If things had been different, if we didn't both live on thin ice, couldn't we have found a way across to each other?

"So, if I just hold you and say 'I love you, I love you,' that's okay then?" I said, daring to trace the vein that ran down from his neck over his shoulder and along his arm, thinking how much of a man is visible—his bones and sinews, his erection—while a woman is a smooth vessel, a shape to be filled with dreams. "I love you," I said, my voice failing me, because I was saying it for real.

"You have to go home," he replied.

To another night of Lee's silent misery—comforting her, or pretending not to see, while we waited for the month to run down. I wished I could pass a hand over her face and make her forget me, return her to her crush on Reenie. They'd have been content with each other, content to the point of love.

Stetson and Tracy might be content, if I got out of the way. I hoped to be content someday myself. First, though, I had to repair the rift between my parents (not between the people, but between their voices in my mind). I turned Stetson's hand over and traced his lifeline across his palm—it was broken early, then ran straight and deep for a while until it diffused and trailed away. We could try to unite ourselves, make a true family—the hardest thing to do—but the combined troubles of our lives were so heavy, they'd sink the most buoyant love.

"I see your future, Stet. It's clear sailing from here," I lied, and lifted his hand to kiss the truth away.

He laughed, or tried to, and stood up, with obvious relief. He needed to move, I needed to cry: it comes to the same thing. We were going to grieve for each other according to gender, the way we did everything else.

"You won't forget me—"

He laughed, looking skyward. Then he hugged me, reflexively, and I felt him kiss my neck, while I tried to get my arms around him one more time. I wanted to feel it all, there in his arms, but if I let myself, I'd never walk away. And suppose I did let my guard down, and he didn't?

So I put my lips to his with one little chaste kiss, walked out into the very nicely appointed hall of Riverview Heights, and pushed the elevator button, down.

"Beatrice!" he called, his voice raw, and I wheeled around.

"Don't push first floor, push lobby," he said, laughing a little at my eagerness.

"Oh, okay."

"First floor is really second floor," he said. "That's the French way."

"Thanks, Stet." As soon as the door closed I put my cheek against it, for the cool, and thought: there, I've escaped a person who in a huge emotional moment starts talking about elevator buttons. Then I remembered how he'd said he never knew anything like real love, and thought how we'd made the beginning of a real love together, like children planting a radish seed in a garden, expecting something magnificent to grow. I thought that when I was old and dying and had forgotten everything else, I'd still remember the feeling in our kisses. In the lobby, I was crying, and I walked down Main Street crying in defiance, thinking everyone who saw me ought to envy me for having lost him, and for knowing what a loss it was.

$\mathscr{T}hirteen$

I T'S OUT of the ordinary, that's for sure," I said, with what I thought was great generosity.

"What do you mean?" Ma said. "It's a June wedding. They're common as grass."

Sylvie was getting married. I alone remembered how she'd brushed marriage off, saying she'd never get herself stuck that way. Now that Butch was in prison, though, things were different, and no one could believe I was so callous as to suggest Sylvie refuse his proposal.

"He *needs* me, Beatrice," she said, with eyes flashing.

"It's a happy ending," Ma said. "That's what *I* like about it. You three will all be together, and that's what matters in the end. I don't believe anything should stand in the way of love. Now, let's see. The dress is new, and this will do the rest for you."

It was a gold pin in the shape of a lizard, with two sapphire eyes, and she fixed it to Sylvie's collar with fond ceremony: it had been her grandmother's.

"Something old and borrowed and blue!" she crowed.

We were standing in the parking lot of the Brimfield County Prison, where Butch was to be held for one more night before he went to serve out his sentence in the state penitentiary, which Ma and Sylvie kept referring to as "the pen," much as, had he been off to Harvard, they'd have spoken of "the yard." They wanted to belong somewhere, to speak the local patois, and if that meant using little pet names for various crimes and their punishments, so it would have to be. Sylvie was chain-smoking but still nervous; she jiggled baby Jesse in such frantic rhythm. I expected him to cry, but he slept peacefully in the crook of her arm, dressed in an elaborate christening gown and looking round and fresh as a scoop of ice cream.

"It's the dress," Sylvie said. "I wish I could have gotten something more—" She tugged at it. It was thin polyester, pale green with white tendrils printed on, an elastic waistband that kept twisting and pulling up, and an enormous lace collar. No one at Sweetriver would have been caught dead in it. And Sylvie was so thin, from labor, anxiousness, smoking, that any dress would have looked like a costume on her.

"More traditional, I guess," she said. "Jesse looks more bridal than me," she said sadly. She looked at once too young and too knowing to be a bride. The wind blew her hair across her face and she kept pulling it back so it wouldn't catch the cigarette and burn. Finally, she took a last long draw and flicked the butt away— it bounced a couple of times, sparking on the cement, and when it landed in a puddle she said:

"Okay, here we go," rather grimly and led us in. Butch was to be permitted fifteen minutes for the service, the vows, and a kiss.

A bailiff motioned us through a metal detector and took us into the prison wing. When the heavy door locked behind us, an instinctive terror swept through me, but Sylvie and Ma laughed happily, leaving me out of the joke, as usual. In the visiting area a justice of the peace, a severe woman with tight gray curls and a palisade of dentures, was already sitting at a table; in a moment, an inner door opened, and then another, and there was Butch in prisoner's orange, looking down, and moving as if he took every step under protest. Afraid and lonely, he'd begged Sylvie to marry him, but now he felt we'd come to witness his humiliation, to laugh at the sight—tough Butchy brought so low, he was willing to submit to love.

"Hi, Butch." Sylvie sounded as shy as if he were still a boy she had a crush on.

She stood in front of him and touched her toe to his. Both he and the bailiff tensed, so Sylvie clutched the baby tighter and stepped back.

"Okay, on with it," she said. "Where do we stand?"

The justice of the peace opened her book and they turned to face her. The ceremony took all of a minute, during which I thought only of Stet and Tracy.

Jesse awakened and began to fuss. Sylvie dipped her hand into the dress and lifted her breast out, holding it there for an extra instant, a defiant smile brewing on her face, before she popped the nipple into the baby's mouth—against a milk-swollen breast, there's very little anyone can do. If Sylvie was laughing in the face of the law, well, that's how nature goes.

"You may kiss the bride," the justice said, but Butch was reticent.

"Go ahead, you dope," Sylvie said with a laugh. "It's fourteen months till the next one."

Once he did finally embrace her, he looked like he might be trying to climb into her body, to hide himself there.

"Time's up," the bailiff said sharply, and Butch retreated into sullenness and the guard returned and ushered him away.

"Wait," Sylvie said, but the doors closed, one by one, regardless . . . "I wanted him to hold Jesse," she said. "Your son," she called, but Jesse kept sucking and the doors kept closing and my mother was handing the justice of the peace an envelope, as we filed out into the green corridor again.

"I'd always hoped one of my daughters would have a June wedding," said Ma, stopping just short, I thought, of sticking her tongue out at me. "The nicest wedding I've ever been to, I think."

"Really?" Sylvie asked. I looked over to see the answer.

"Yes, really," Ma said, sounding perfectly genuine, and a little shocked that we might question her. "And the most beautiful bride too."

Sylvie basked and cradled the baby. "I'm so happy," she confided.

A June wedding, a cold, brilliant day with lilacs bursting; the first time I'd smelled fresh cut grass that year.

"I'm so proud of you, for following your heart," Ma said.

"You're proud of her for flashing her boob in a prison waiting room," I said.

"*And* for following her heart," Ma insisted. A terrible thought occurred to me: suppose Sylvie was just trying to entertain us, keep our minds off our own troubles by manufacturing such a troublesome life of her own? There was that sense, between us, that the one who died with the best story would win.

"It's just fourteen months, and he'll be home," she said. "Now he knows he has a wife who *believes in him*," she said. "Someone who'll really go the distance for him. He never had that before."

She was a radiant bride, my sister, and she had gone the distance—all the way to the commissioner's office, to petition for this wedding—for someone, something she believed in: Butch Savione.

"What are you going to do now," I asked Sylvie. "For a job?" She gave several possibilities, the best of which seemed to be taking over for Butch at the Nubestos plant.

"Do you still think you'd like to be a midwife?" I asked.

"Oh, gosh," she said, with a little laugh like a cough, "you've got to have college for that." She was living among people who never dreamed of going to college, and she'd forgotten such a thing was possible. But she'd gone straight to the commissioner's office; that hadn't daunted her.

"It's strange," she said then, "to be having my wedding without . . . without everyone around." She didn't mean Butch, of course, but Pop and Dolly. In all those dreams of love and weddings, she'd seen Pop walking her through the garden, Dolly and me, our arms full of daisies, Ma streaming with happy tears—the groom had been immaterial. In fact, when you thought about it, prison was just the place for Butch—there he could do nothing to disturb our notions. And disturbed though our notions were, we continued in them, like citizens of a small and embattled country who can no longer remember how their customs developed or what purpose they serve, but still have only those customs to rely on.

We squeezed into Butchie's little pickup, and after an hour on the gas line—it was an odd-numbered day—we were back at Sylvie's, where white crepe paper was looped wildly over the trailer awning, and around the fence where she kept the donkey.

"Sylvie!" I said. "This is some garden!" Just planted of course, but it took up the whole lot around the trailer, all fresh, dark, deeply spaded earth, with whorls of pale new lettuce and snow peas putting their fine tendrils out to each other. At the back, a little clump of primroses marked Springtime's grave.

"You like it?" she asked. "I worked my butt off digging it, I will say. And all those tomatoes had to be cuffed against cutworms. The whole back half is corn, though; I'm going to have a stand."

"Sylvie," I said. "It's a . . ."

"Farm," she finished for me, pursing her lips in a dry, laughing submission to fate. "Yeah, it's a farm." The ball field was just mowed, and the green smell in the cold air, the new wet maple leaves shaking out above, inspired me . . . just the way my parents had meant me to be inspired, when they moved to the country all those years ago.

"It worked, Ma," I said, and though she couldn't have known what I meant, really, she gave me a quick, prideful glance.

"I told you it would," she said. "I got a job, by the way."

"No kidding!" I said.

"Well, it's thanks to you," she said. "Without the letter you wrote, they'd never have hired me."

Why this compliment settled with the weight of an anvil I can't exactly say. "You mean, sympathy for lost boys is an ideal quality in a car salesman?" I asked.

"Well, I'm sure the red suit helped," she said. She was going to work selling Mercedes. "Do you know what the commission is, on a Mercedes?" she asked. I shook my head. I wondered how often a Mercedes got sold in rural Connecticut. "Diesel, that's the future," she said.

Inside, Sylvie popped Jesse into his high chair, and bounced a ping-pong ball (red, white, and blue, our biggest seller) on the tray to fascinate him. There was a sheet cake, a baked ham, a pitcher full of lilacs, and five bottles of champagne.

"To marriage!" Ma said, and we drank. I wondered if she remembered at all how she'd felt the day she was married, how fragile and full of hope.

"To family," said Sylvie, with dreamy pleasure, gazing into Jesse's eyes as if he were a crystal ball. The phone rang and she went into the kitchen to pick it up.

"To the criminal justice system," I said, and Ma laughed. Laughter was her saving strength.

"A husband in prison is worth two in the bush," she said. She wiped the smile right off though when Sylvie came back to say it was Larry on the phone. "You can tell him I'm not here," she said, with a grand hauteur.

"Ma," Sylvie said.

"All right," Ma said, "don't tell him anything. I'll just hang it up." As she strode over to it, Sylvie put a hand out.

"Don't, Ma, he didn't mean any harm." And Ma looked for a second as if she'd been struck.

"I'm not going to let him," she said. "No, my father can reject me and your father can reject me and Dolly can reject me, but that is enough and I'm *not* going to take it from him too."

"Ma," Sylvie lowered her voice and clamped her hand over the receiver. "Ma, he stood you up, that's all. He didn't abandon you."

"There comes a time," my mother said magnificently.

Sylvie turned abruptly away from her. "She can't talk now, Larry," she said. "She'll call you tomorrow, okay?" Then she thanked him—he must have congratulated her on the wedding, and then she said, yes, she'd love it if he dropped by the trailer sometime, it could get really lonely when you were home all alone with a baby. She was saying, "Don't worry, I'll take care of you," and Ma's face receded into darkness as if she had glimpsed something over Sylvie's shoulder that had plunged her back into the world of fear and headache, the world she'd once thought my father would free her from, and then hoped he'd take with him when he left.

That world, where we all used to live with her—in which the man you loved so tenderly might secretly be a torturer—descended from a long line, a nation, even, of torturers, so your children may have torturer's genes. Ma's intuition told her there was a danger out there, that there was a pernicious thread to be pulled out of even the simplest, happy scene. But just as the worst of this registered on her face, a flashbulb went off.

420 · *Heidi Jon Schmidt*

"Gotcha!" Teddy said, and turned the camera on each of us in turn. "Like paparazzi!" he crowed. "Get together there, who knows when you'll all be together again?" he asked. "Maybe a funeral. Maybe Pop's funeral."

Ma laughed enormously. "Next week, let's hope," she said. And she'd loved my father once, so intensely, it seemed love was a magic power—a power to heal him, make him the whole strong man of her dreams.

"Back to Nubestos tomorrow," Sylvie said. "God, it's dusty work. But you can't argue with all that money, under the table."

"You'll get hurt," I said, and I saw a quick smile flick over her face at my innocence—yes, indeed, how protected I had been, that I saw some chance that she might not get hurt.

"That's what they say, the experts," she said, with an ironic little laugh, a new laugh for her. What could we know or guess of the world she lived in? But it was her own world, and real.

"Maybe you could go to school at night," I tried. Where was she ever going to learn about the gun hanging over the mantelpiece and how it goes off in the end?

"Maybe," she said, without interest. "You know," she said then, "things are great with me, Beatrice. Jesse's so healthy and strong. I love my little trailer. I love my husband, and I'll finish this Nubestos thing and then get another job—it's not a problem. Fourteen months, that'll go by in no time, and then we'll be together, we'll go from there."

Leave me alone, she was saying. She was proud of her abilities—who'd have guessed, a year ago, that she could do so many things: mother a child, fix the plumbing, grow her garden, and go straight to the commissioner to get permission for the wedding she'd used to insist she'd never have? This was her life, and if its possibilities were shrunken, her future smaller—small as a trailer or a linen closet—there was nothing I could do. I felt that I was waving to her from a ship—that we'd grow more and more distant now until we couldn't see each other at all, until no one would guess anymore that we were sisters.

The champagne popped, the camera flashed, there were cries of excitement, mock fear, more hugging, and Ma waltzed little Jesse around the room. His bright eyes took in everything as they whirled; he was the centrifugal force around which something of our family might hold firm. Even in the worst of Ma's madness, Sylvie and I had known her love, and out of it, we'd begun to weave our own lives. I ought, in return, to "save" her, but I couldn't, though I might possibly keep my own balance if I stopped trying to carry them all on my great, manly shoulders.

And this thought, like most of my thoughts, led me back to Stetson. When you love someone, you think of them so intently, you might as well be praying. Dolly's fury kept Ma always in her mind, her infirmity would make sure Pop was never completely abandoned. Stetson—or Josip, the real part of Stetson—might be thinking of me now.

Which made me feel it was urgent, essential, that I speak to him right away. I had to tell him I loved him, in case he didn't know, in case he was lonely, uncertain, or sad. All the books I'd read in my life were boiling together into a great speech in which I'd tell him that it would be a crime against our own lives not to take the chance on each other, that I wouldn't give him up until I'd had a full tour of his life and knew what he murmured in his sleep and had gotten deeper under his skin than any needle could ever go. I thought how he'd looked in my eyes, how he stood with his arms just wide enough for me to walk into them . . . and how it seemed that when I did, I'd be walking back into the old house on that day we'd picked blackberries, with the jam bubbling in the pot and Ma blowing a wisp of hair out of her face, leaning back and laughing, as if every day from then on would be just that way.

I shut my eyes and made myself think of Lee and how I'd harmed her, trying to live out some notion of love from my dreams. Not again—at least not yet. The future was in my pocket, in the form of a key to the Oxford Branch Library. Like Sylvie's backyard farm, my work might give body to my parents' dream— so they'd have left a real legacy after all.

And that's it, that's all there ever is—the strands of the people you love, the way they weave through you. I thought of Stetson's spontaneous pirouette, Philippa's: "Beatrice, it's a beginning." This was my substance, my wealth. And whatever I'd learn tomorrow; I had that too.

$\mathcal{A}$cknowledgments

Frances Coady has been a brilliant reader, kind friend, and staunch ally. Without her uncanny insight, this book would not be.

Jennifer Carlson's generosity of time, interest, and enthusiasm have been wonderful things for me. I'd like to thank Reagan Arthur for her excellent taste, among other great qualities. Blessings on my friends who are ceaselessly supportive, especially Margaret Carroll and Tom Lindsay who read draft after draft; and on my husband Roger and daughter Marisa, who have been so patient and forbearing. For the unfailing grace and love of my own parents, sisters, and brothers, I am very, very grateful. And particularly I'd like to thank my mother for teaching me when to laugh: always.